The Demons We See

THE DARK ABYSS OF OUR SINS • BOOK ONE

The Demons We See

The Dark Abyss of Our Sins • Book One

KRISTA D. BALL

DEDICATION

This book would not have been possible without the unwavering faith and support of Merc Fenn Wolfmoor.

STATUS QUO

Lady Acardi's Summer Residence
Southern Cartossa

HE LISTENED HELPLESSLY as the royal guards stormed into the great foyer of the estate. Crammed into a hidden corridor with six other mages, he couldn't help their protector if any of them were found. So they all waited, listened, and hoped.

Lady Acardi spoke first. "General, why have you barged into my home uninvited?"

General Bonacieux's voice was loud and unyielding. "By the authority of Queen Portia and the Holy Cathedral, you are accused of being an elemental witch."

One of the mages behind him gasped. Walter kicked her in the shin. The mage made another muffled sound of protest before she settled down. If the Butcher of Fort Bonnet even thought he heard voices in the walls, he'd burn the ancient estate to the ground before risking a mage run free.

Lady Acardi laughed, a mocking sound. "Starve in the abyss, you upstart pissant. How dare you come in here and accuse me, a woman of the blood, to be an elemental! You have no proof."

"I have the authority of the Queen and I require no proof, witch bitch." He paused to regain his composure. "Property to be forfeit and all assets seized, pending investigation."

"You swine! I'll never see a trial and we both know it. You'll have all of my money spent before I'm crushed to death in a mine explosion."

"You can choose to kill yourself now and save us the expense of a trial."

Even through the walls, it was clear Lady Acardi had spat in the General's face. He couldn't help but grin silently at her brass courage. His smile quickly faded, however, as he knew what would come next. It was the same thing over and over.

The General's voice turned enraged. "Guards! Arrest everyone in the house. If she won't show herself the witch we know she is, then we'll send the entire household to the prison mines."

"You bastard," Lady Acardi snarled, even as she grunted and gasped. They must have attacked her. "There are children in this house!"

"Then tell the truth, bitch, or they will all meet the same fate!"

Don't do it. Don't do it. He didn't dare speak the words aloud, but he prayed them as hard as he could, as if the Almighty would condescend, just this once, to intercede on a mage's behalf. As ever, Almighty took the side of oppressors and murderers.

Lady Acardi had spent a lifetime successfully hiding her talent from the world, so it didn't surprise him what came next.

The floor beneath their feet shook as Lady Acardi screamed, "Demons take you!"

He was thrown against the wall as the house shook. Once he found his feet, he pushed his compatriots. "Go!" he whispered. "We have minutes before they discover the panel."

Lady Acardi's screams died abruptly. He closed his eyes and asked the Almighty to accept her into His arms, for she had been good to mages. She had given her life in the fight for freedom.

Almighty, if you care at all, protect us now.

"The only good witch is a dead witch," the General shouted. "Arrest everyone in the house for harboring an elemental mage."

"Run," he said, as they rushed through the underground tunnels of the ancient stone house.

"Where are we going to go, Walter?"

He kept running, heart pounding, knowing that every step might be his last if the soldiers found the loose panel in the foyer. They'd be looking for it, too. They always looked for the secret doors and passageways.

Finally, he said, "Just keep running."

CHAPTER ONE

Orsini Cathedral
Papal Residence

HIS RADIANCE FRANCOIS III, *Holy Father of the Beloved*
  My dearest friend,

   May the Grace of the Lord God Almighty find you in good health. News of the failed assembly reached me this morning. I am once against saddened to discover our lands continue toward conflict.

   I turn my gaze upon your leadership in this matter and realize, with much regret, that I have no understanding about your choices. Have the pressures of your station given you dementia? Another opportunity for peace lost because you refuse to appoint someone who understands the plight of the mage slaves. Appointing a slave owner, of all people, as Arbiter in this growing rebellion is like asking a demon over for tea and biscuits. Surely, you cannot be surprised when the demon destroys the party and kills all of your guests.

   Indeed, I hear that you have expressed astonishment that the former appointment of Lord Castigara as Arbiter made things worse. Castigara owns over a thousand slaves, nearly all of them mages, who he brutally forces to make endless magical trinkets for his personal army. Did you forget that this personal army has been accused by Viscount Perry as having been responsible for no fewer than eight acts of violence against his territories? Tell me, does political news reach the Cathedral or have you forgotten the people who pledge themselves to the faith under your leadership?

The people need a strong Arbiter, trusted and respected by all sides. The mages—I refuse to use that vulgar word "witch" to describe my own kind— are rebelling against their masters, as is their right under the Holy Word of our Lady Tasmin, who wrote Tomas 11:45 that, "All men's lives are their own, to worship the Almighty and to praise his name."

Yet, by appointing notorious brutes to mediate this crisis, you are saying that the Cathedral does not follow the word of Tasmin. And, wasn't that the direct cause of the last full-scale war that sent our entire civilization backwards by five hundred years? Is this your brilliant plan?

I offer my services as both one of the blood, as well as a mage. While I live in retirement, I am very eager to assist you in any way you see fit. Perhaps you could forward your list of potential candidates for the job and I shall curate them appropriately.

I eagerly await your response.

Allegra Vittoria Beatrice, Contessa of Marsina
Borro Abbey

Captain Stanton Rainier smirked at the Contessa's letter to the Holy Father. High rank had its privileges and he couldn't fault her for using hers to say what was on the minds of many people, including his own. "Her wit is sharper than my sword."

"Don't mistake sarcasm for wit," the Holy Father said sourly.

The two men sat in the priest's personal chambers. Personally, Stanton liked the sitting room, though His Holiness found it stuffy and overblown. Stanton disagreed: it *was* the seat of power for the most powerful man in all of Serna. Stuffy and overblown was a requirement in Stanton's opinion. "When did you receive the letter?"

"Earlier in the week," the Holy Father said as he sipped at his glass of wine. "I need your help, Rainier."

Stanton chuckled. "Surely you're not going to make me write the lady?"

Francois threw his head back and laughed. "Gracious blessings, no. I have a better task for you. Travel to Borro Abbey and retrieve her." Francois's smile turned vulpine. "Allegra thinks she can deal with this mess better than I, so I shall let her try."

"Your Holiness?" Stanton blinked at the older man. "What did the cardinals say?"

Francois sighed heavily. The priest had aged a lot in the last two years. New lines seemed to daily etch themselves into Francois's dark, blue-hued features. "Nothing. The inner council is…weary. They are willing to try anything once."

"You think this sarcastic noblewoman is the answer?"

"Allegra is the highest woman of rank that is also a witch." Francois rolled his eyes. "Mage. Whatever they call themselves these days. She is a notorious unbeliever, too, and lives permanently at Borro Abbey. She doesn't own any slaves and her family are all supporters for witch slave rights. Mage slave…Blessings, why can't people stick with the same word everyone else uses?" Francois sipped his wine. "Perhaps she can do better than the rest of us suffering the early symptoms of dementia."

Stanton smiled again at the Holy Father's bitter words. "How is she going to make things better between the rebelling slaves and the nobles?"

"The Contessa is well respected, even if she doesn't appear at anyone's Court anymore." Francois swirled his red wine around in his crystal goblet. "She's intelligent, resourceful, and is not afraid to speak her mind. She was properly educated, too, in not just the fine arts. She speaks and writes four languages, she is skilled in diplomacy, rhetoric, philosophy, and economics."

"She sounds more qualified than most kings," Stanton said dryly.

His Holiness laughed. "Yes, she is."

"Can she stop the rebellion?"

Francois put his goblet down on the table. He considered his words carefully before speaking. "That's the heart of it all, isn't it? Is there anyone who can stop this damnable rebellion before it escalates into full-scale warfare and slaughter? I do not want to live to see the great nations of Serna crumble under that."

Stanton didn't have a reply, for the question was far greater than any one man could answer: could they be turned from the path they were now on? For two years now, enslaved and indentured witches rebelled against the yoke their masters wrapped around their necks. Whenever the masters tightened the leash, the slaves yanked harder at their own end. Runaway witches risked their lives to free their compatriots. Sympathizers risked their property and titles to hide the runaway slaves. And as nations and city-states cracked down on any pockets of resistance, word spread and ten more pockets cropped up in defiance.

The ecclesiastic edicts for calm and peace were unheeded, but Stanton knew the lily-watered sermons carried no weight with the three most powerful nations in Serna. Queen Portia of Cartossa, for example, was a mere sixteen-year-old girl in charge of the largest and most technologically advanced army. She followed her late father's advisors and dedicated her policies to the complete enslavement of all magical practitioners.

Queen Portia's advisors would never tell her to heed anything but papal law. Directives, opinions, and desires were for everyone else. The Council of Cardinals would never excommunicate Queen Portia specially nor Cartossa generally. The cold fact was Cartossa brought in too many golden sovereigns in taxes, tithes, and papal donations for the Cathedral to ever turn its back on them and their heavy purse.

"You don't approve of my plan?"

Stanton smiled at the Holy Father. Even with the pressures of his position, Pope Francois remained a vibrant, energetic man. Still well in his prime of life, Francois was decades younger than any of his nearest cardinal rivals. His election to the papal chair still remained a shock to the establishment, and Stanton did enjoy how Francois held his power like a shard of obsidian. Francois could be a glossy, mesmerizing stone that, when stuck, morphed into a deceptively sharp edge that could—and did—slice through his enemies.

Stanton had known Francois a long time, since before he was the Holy Father. So he knew better than to disagree with the Almighty's messenger. "Actually, I was thinking you have more gray in your beard than last I saw you."

Francois laughed in his rich, basso voice. He stroked his graying chin whiskers. "Yes, well, age catches up to all of us. It will soon find you, my friend."

"I'm more worried about baldness than the gray," Stanton said.

That made the priest laugh. "Not all of us were blessed with hair that stayed past our fortieth birthday. Now, be honest, tell me what you think of my plan, knowing that I'm not going to change my mind regardless of your reply."

Stanton grinned. "Well, you haven't tried appointing a witch. There are worse plans. The Contessa of Marsina. That's quite a title. Is it hers or by marriage?"

"Oh, it's hers," Francois said. "She's unmarried, and likely to remain so. Her brother, the Viscount of Rence, maintains the day-to-day management of her seat of power, but she is an active enough landlord, even if she lives in retirement. She is the richest woman in Amadore and among the richest in all of Serna outside of royal families. Well, actually, including several royal families. She basically owns most of northern Amadore."

Stanton considered the point. "So she is a wealthy, privileged, titled woman of the blood. She's also a witch. She lives in an abbey, but isn't overly religious."

Francois snorted. "She's practically blasphemous."

"I hate to say, Father, but she might be perfect. All of the viscounts and princes from the city-states will love her. The witches might actually send representatives this time from the various factions because one of their own will be leading the discussion."

"When can you leave to retrieve her?"

"I'll leave with a few Consorts in the morning. The roads aren't safe for unaccompanied carriages and I'm sure she won't want to ride horseback all the way here."

Francois scoffed. "She might surprise you."

The double doors opened and both men turned to see the new arrival. In strolled a lean man with smile lines around his narrow, hooded eyes. His straight, silver-streaked black hair was, as ever, pulled back and tied at the nape of his neck before breaking off into two braids. When he saw Stanton, his expression brightened.

"Captain! I didn't know you were in here. Am I interrupting?"

Stanton waved to Francois's husband. "Come on in, Pero. I was preparing to leave, in any case." Turning to Francois, he asked, "Does Pero know her?"

Pero strolled into the parlor and took a seat at their table. "Ah, Rupert has told you his master plan of making the Contessa of Marsina the Arbiter of Justice?" "I still remember the first time I met her. It was…bracing."

Stanton smiled at the Holy Father's husband, one of the very few people who ever called him by his given name in front of others. The privilege of spouses, he supposed. Perhaps one day, he would have his own spouse to breach etiquette rules, too.

"I know nothing about her. What's she like?"

"In a word, opinionated," Pero said, grinning. "In two words, very opinionated. In three words, stunningly very opinionated."

Stanton laughed at that and sipped at his own glass of wine. He only sipped, not liking wine first thing in the morning. However, he didn't wish to be rude and not take at least some of the drink. "What *did* the cardinals say when you told them your plan?"

"Their responses were typical," Francois said.

Pero rolled his eyes. "Here we go."

"Don't be like that," Francois said, his voice laced with annoyance. "We're all frustrated, and quite worried. If violence escalates, this rebellion could destabilize the entire area. We could have civil war! We could even devolve into full-scale warfare, with states attacking each other *and* themselves. Over what? Witch rights? That's hardly worth dying over."

"That's the only good reason for a war, Rupert!" Pero exclaimed, throwing his hands up in disgust. "What else says *faithful* than the willingness to get your hands dirty?"

"We are not talking about a little mud. We are talking blood."

"Blood that our Guardians shed to seal the demon gates! Yes, we should shed that blood now!"

Stanton knew better than to get in the middle of the Holy Father's domestic dispute, so he let the two argue it out without his input. As he listened to the long-time married couple, Stanton was filled with the opposing feelings of loneliness that he had no one to share such arguments…and the relief that there was no such person in his life.

"Pero, we've been over this. There is no freedom in starvation."

"Yes, yes, yes! I've heard the saying before and it is meaningless. The desire for freedom, however fleeting, is a potent one. Denying that basic existence to people who are slightly different than ourselves is an offense against the Lord Almighty." Pero glanced at Stanton and offered a bashful grin. "But, I shall save the remainder of the abolition lecture for suppertime."

"Please don't."

Pero gave his husband a side-eye glance. "Why not?"

"Cardinal Vittorio and his wife are coming to dinner. He's returned from his pilgrimage to Basina."

Pero made a disgusted sound. "What kind of sick man goes to a horror site for his spiritual development? Captain, do you have plans this evening?"

"I'm heading to Borro Abbey. Why? I don't know Cardinal Vittorio personally. Is he horrible?"

Pero gave his husband a disdainful glance. "Anyone who goes to Basina without burning the place to the ground is horrible in my opinion."

Francois smiled. "I find Cardinal Vittorio quite passionate."

Another disgusted sound escaped Pero. "That's not passion, my love. That's senility and cruelty."

Stanton smiled politely at Pero before asking, "Any advice before I depart?"

Francois nibbled on a piece of butter cake. "Allegra is suspicious of most parish priests, most bishops, and all of the cardinals. And she's convinced anyone who comes from Orsini is a moron."

"Just tell her Pero says hi, and she'll be easy," Pero grabbed his husband's wine goblet and finished off the rest of the wine. "Oh, and tell her that the cardinals are wrong about her. That'll help."

"Opinionated and paranoid," Stanton said. "Wonderful combination."

Pope Francois gave Stanton a disapproving glance. "Come now. Look at the world from her perspective. She is a witch—"

"Mage," Pero corrected automatically.

"*Mage*," Francois said, giving his husband an annoyed look. "Her rank has been the only thing that's sheltered her from servitude and slavery. It was only because she is of the blood that she avoided being marked and tagged."

Pero snorted. At his husband's annoyed glance, Pero raised his hands. "Fine. I'll keep my opinions to myself."

"That would be a first. But, yes, she's very political and writes letters, yet she does little more than garden, cook, and attend an annual party or two. She's become a touch fragile, I think. Be gentle to her."

"Oh, please," Pero said, sarcasm lacing his words. "The Grand Duchess thinks she's fragile." He turned to Stanton and said, "Grand Duchess Katherine believes Allegra is a fragile, delicate flower that must be kept from the harsh glare of the sun. The Contessa is a strong woman and knew to get out of court politics before she made enemies."

Stanton grimaced at the Grand Duchess's name. They were well acquainted with each other, as she was once the ambassador to Orsini. In the early days, Stanton was assigned to her personal guard whenever she visited Orsini, until Francois promoted Stanton to his personal staff to create the Consorts.

"Ah, yes," Francois said. "You know the Grand Duchess."

"Didn't you used to work for her?" Pero asked, now munching on a tiny pastry he'd stolen from Francois's plate. "This is stale."

"Yes. The Grand Duchess and I are acquainted." Stanton stood and bowed to both men. "Gentlemen, if there is nothing further, I will take my leave. I shall depart this afternoon to retrieve this delicate lady and ensure she doesn't wilt in the sun."

"Almighty be with you."

"Good luck," Pero murmured.

Stanton gave both men a final nod before turning on his heel to walk back to the barracks. He was not fond of the idea of traipsing about the countryside escorting some rich, old lady, but there were worse assignments, he'd supposed. Latrine digging was near the top.

He weaved his way around the various mothers and fathers of the lower clerical orders who bustled about the outer sanctums of the palace proper. The guards along the main entrances acknowledged him and he gave them all a quick nod. His men weren't going to be pleased with this trip, either. He chuckled to himself, knowing that some of them would be missing tonight's dancers at one of the back alley brothels that the Cathedral guards allowed to stay open *provided* the noise wasn't excessive and the faithful pilgrims never gained admittance inside.

A lean youth slipped into step next to Stanton and said, "Good morning, Captain."

"Good morning, Lex. Your boots are filthy."

"It's your fault." Lex didn't bother to hide his annoyance.

Stanton eyed him. His normally pale, pink face was smeared liberally with dusty sweat and there was a cobweb hanging off one lock of hair that served as a sideburn. "Where in the abyss have you been?"

In a sing-song voice, forced full of cheer, Lex said, "Why, I've been in the stables looking for your missing button, sir. Don't you remember?"

"Did you find it?"

"No, sir."

Stanton grunted. "Maybe it fell off in my bedchamber."

"You didn't think to look there first, sir?"

Stanton stifled a grin. "No, I didn't."

"What is the punishment for hitting a superior officer, sir?"

"Looking for my button in horse shit."

"I've already done that," Lex grumbled.

The two headed up the staircase to the main barracks and Stanton filled his second-in-command in about the Holy Father's plan.

CHAPTER TWO

LIEUTENANT LEX SAT on the long wooden bench and leaned their elbows against their knees. Shit-encrusted boot in one hand, brush in the other, Lex brushed their only good set of boots as the Captain described the details of the new mission. The others were still eating luncheon in the dining hall, so Rainier was taking the opportunity to fill Lex in now.

It also gave Lex the opportunity to clean their disgusting boots. Fucking cow shit. Fucking Rainier for the order to search the fucking cow shit.

Rainier went on about some prissy noble they'd have to pick up from Borro Abbey and then drag back to the palace. Rainier didn't seem overly pleased about the mission, but in his usual form didn't add much personal commentary. Lex both liked that about Rainier and found it vastly irritating, depending upon the situation. But after seven years of working with the Captain, Lex was used to him.

"So do you know anything about this fop we'll be fetching?" Lex asked. Flecks of debris flew in the air and landed on the Captain's shiny boots. Lex gave him an apologetic smile. "Like, what do you know about her?"

Rainier returned the smile with a dirty look. "She's the Contessa of Marsina. I don't know much about her, to be honest."

This time, some of the dried shit hit Rainier in the face.

He scowled. "Could you not do that right now?"

Lex looked up at Captain Rainier and gave the boot two aggressive brushes before offering up a wide grin of apology. "Sorry, m'lord. Happy to stop, m'lord. Anything for you, m'lord."

Rainier crossed his broad arms across his chest. In a stern voice, he said, "Lex, no one likes a smart mouth, and you're not as funny as you think you are."

"Everyone thinks I'm funny, sir," Lex said with a grin. However, they put the boot down on the wooden floorboards and dropped the brush next to it. "But who is she? I've never heard of her."

Rainier shrugged. He crossed the floor and grabbed one of the wooden chairs from the card table. He dragged it over near Lex and sat down. "I've told you everything I know. She's some recluse witch who lives out in Borro Abbey. We're to escort her to the palace. One assumes we'll be escorting her back once her business is concluded."

Lex considered that. They also looked down and considered the state of their boot laces. Lex really had to go into the market soon, or risk having to tie up the boots with a belt. "Is she an older woman then? Is that why we're escorting her?"

The door flung open before Rainier could answer them. The loud, vulgar new arrivals were some of the Consorts, the Cathedral's elite branch of guards. Well, in theory that's what they were. That was the deal Lex had been sold when they came to work for Rainier. However, as the years went on, Lex came to realize that they weren't a part of the *real* papal guards posted at the Cathedral. Instead, they were Francois's personal soldiers, to dispense as he saw fit. It made sense, considering Rainier's military career.

Lex wasn't overly religious or anything, though they believed in the Almighty and the Guardians and the stories of the martyrdoms. Lex didn't *actually* believe the Guardians died sealing an *actual* tear in reality between the demon abyss and this world, but they believed the core of the story that selfless people did great acts to protect others.

So Lex didn't mind working for the papal robes. And Rainier was a good captain, and an honest-to-Almighty war hero. Rainier didn't care who or what Lex was. He didn't care why they were at

Orsini, or who Lex's parents were. Rainier wanted a strong arm and a stronger brain, and Lex could offer both.

"Hey, Lex! You missed it, man. They had creamed celery," Dodd shouted. He glanced at Rainier and said, "Hey, Captain. Creamed celery. You missed out, sir."

Dodd was shorter than most men, but not by much. Lex had a couple of inches on him, a point the two old friends often bantered back and forth about. Dodd's uniform was in need of laundering, the dark green of his jacket now a dingy gray-green. There was a line of mud splatter up the ass of his dark trousers and up the spine of his jacket. He was missing two of the round buttons, meaning he'd lost two of the magical defenses that were woven into the garment by mothers of the faith.

Well, Lex knew one thing. Dodd could shift through the shit for his own buttons. Lex was finished.

"Why do you two look so serious? Oh, good! Laundry came." He hauled off his jacket and tossed it on his bunk. He did the same with his white tunic.

Lex winced. "Dodd, I can smell you from here."

Stanton waved a hand in the air, making a big show of coughing and gagging.

"The maid lost all my shirts, so I've been wearing the same damn one for four days now." Bare-chested, he turned to the communal basin on a dresser between the two bunked beds. He poured in water and began to splash water on himself. "I was tempted to start wearing lavender oil."

"Lavender oil can't work miracles," Lex said. "So, everyone, we got new orders. Some of us will be riding out this afternoon."

The new arrivals who'd entered with Dodd all groaned and protested their disappointment, but they shuffled over to the wooden bench and collapsed alongside Lex.

Dodd spoke first, as he was Lex's equal in terms of rank and seniority. "What dark abyss are we being sent into this time?"

"Borro Abbey," Captain Rainier supplied.

"*Shiiiiiiiiiiiiit*," Dodd said, dragging the word out. He scrubbed his face with his wet towel. "Why are we going there? Oh! Are we invading it?"

"The roads still aren't safe and we have to bring back an important contessa. I got the impression she was an older woman. His Holiness believes she can help with the rebellion, so off we go to fetch her." A corner of Rainier's mouth quirked up. "In two hours."

Dodd groaned. "How am I supposed to get the mud out of my jacket in two hours?"

"Let Lex handle that," Rainier said. "He's very good at cleaning today."

Lex made a rude gesture.

"So, is the whole gang going?" Dodd asked, now scrubbing his armpits with the towel. Dodd didn't have a chiseled physique, but his broad shoulders flexed well-formed muscles as he scrubbed. When Dodd caught Lex looking, Lex wrinkled their nose. "What?"

"You better be planning to burn that towel when you're done," Lex said, eyeing the communal towel. "To answer your question, no. Maybe me, Dodd, Rainier…Martin? Rahna? You two wanna come? Anyone else?"

"Rahna, you should come for sure. Get more experience," Dodd said to their newest recruit.

Rainier and Lex both nodded in agreement. The Consorts didn't have many women—three, counting Rahna—and she hadn't had much experience outside of running errands around Orsini's countryside.

Rainier said, "I think that's a good idea. Martin, you should come, too. Give Rahna some tips."

"Of course," Rahna said. She barely came up to Lex's shoulders, but she was as solid as Dodd. Her skin was almost as pale as Dodd's, with high, round cheeks that were always a touch rosy. She could also kick the consciousness out of a man twice her size in ten seconds flat.

"Sure," Martin said. Martin had joined the Consorts only a year after Rainier had formed them and had grown up working for the Cathedral guards as a runner when he was a kid.

Lex nodded. "Good. All right then, everyone get your shit together. Kingsley, you're in charge of the group while the adults are away."

Kingsley, a handsome, muscular man with a goofy smile, said, "You can count on me, Lieutenant Lex."

Lex rolled their eyes. "Suck ass."

"Always," Kingsley said.

With that, Rainier nodded and headed into his office, which was connected to the main hall where the guard spent their free time. At one point, it had been some cardinal's bedchamber, built back when people had receiving rooms attached to their bedrooms. Now the room was in the administration wing of the palace, where the secretaries, stewards, and housekeepers all busied themselves with the important task of running the palace, while the cardinals all sat in the glitzy new addition to worship the Almighty.

Lex had never been through the entire palace, nor had they visited the Holy Father's residence. They wondered how pompously gilded it would be.

While Lex pondered the expensive nature of the palace, Dodd mimed putting his head into a noose and hanging himself.

Lex picked up the brush and went back to brushing their boot. "What's your problem?"

"Some of the boys and I were going into town to play cards tonight," he whined.

"Why didn't you invite me? What, I'm not good enough for you anymore?"

"First, the last time we played cards I had to wash your clothes for a week."

"That was lovely, wasn't it?" Lex said dreamingly. Looking down at the disgusting boot in their hand, Lex said, "We could play cards right now for boot cleaning."

Dodd rolled his eyes. "If you must know, I didn't invite you because they have those dancers you hate."

Lex groaned. "Figures. Dodd, what in the abyss happened to your hair?"

Dodd grabbed a particularly greasy section of his dark blond hair and pulled it out in front of his face. He studied in suspiciously before looking over at the others. "Beatrix?"

Beatrix Galindo grinned even as her pale skin glowed with a rising blush. "I'm sorry, sir. The others put me up to it last night, when you were..." She coughed. "Passed out."

Lex laughed and leaned over to sniff Dodd's head. "What did you use? Lard?"

"Hey!" Dodd protested, pushing Lex away. "Personal space, man!"

Lex ignored him and continued sniffing until Dodd puckered up his pale, pink lips. It was Lex's turn to push. "Ugh, I know where that mouth has been. Get it away from me."

"I'm glad someone knows where it's been because I sure don't," Dodd said, and the group laughed heartily.

Lex rolled their eyes and tried bringing the conversation back on course. "Anyone here know about this Contessa of Marsina? Martin, aren't you from around there?"

Martin nodded. He was a short, thin man, with black hair that made his light skin seem paler somehow. Martin seemed like a poor choice for the guard when Rainier brought him on board, but soon proved Lex's preconceptions wrong. What Martin lacked in size, he made up for in speed and agility. The man could run for days and not get winded.

"Yeah, I was born up Amadore way. I got a cousin who still lives there. He's a tenant farmer for her estate and he's never said a bad word against the family. They don't have slaves and don't hire them for seasonal work, either. They just pay the locals to come and do it." Martin snorted. "My cousin keeps trying to get me to move back to work on the farm."

"You can leave us," Lex said.

Eyeing Lex's books, Martin said, "There might be less cow shit up there."

"So, she's an abolitionist?" Dodd asked.

Martin shrugged. "I don't know that, but not using slaves is a big statement, isn't it?"

"Rainier says she's a mage. Interesting that they think she can help with the peace," Lex said, but then answered their own unspoken question. "Well, maybe this is the cardinals' way of appeasing the factions, right? Bring in some high and mighty noble who is an abolitionist, but isn't going to make any real changes."

Dodd looked down at Lex's boots. "Seriously, dude, where in the abyss did you go to get so dirty?"

"Cow shed," Lex said, wrinkling their nose.

"Why in the world were you there?"

"Rainier's fault," Lex replied. "Borro Abbey? Where *is* that?"

"Four day's ride from here," Dodd answered. "It's up in the hills, near the base of the Borro Mountains."

"Up there? What in Almighty's name is she doing there?" Martin asked. "Isn't the season happening in Cartossa's capital right now? Shouldn't she be dancing with the Queen or doing something useless like that?"

"Don't women give up dancing after they hit a certain age? My mother did," Lex said.

"Those are the boring women," Dodd said.

Lex eyed him. "Are you saying my mother is boring?"

Dodd winked by way of a reply.

Lex went back to boot scrubbing. Contessas were the worst, even worse than duchesses. At least a duchess knew their place in society; just below that of the royal family. A grand duchess was a member of the royal family. A contessa was a woman of rank, used to rubbing elbows with royalty, but never quite able to get any further. Lex could imagine the attitude this one would have, if she was important enough to be personally known to the papal throne.

"Why do we always get the shit assignments?" Lex complained.

"Could be worse," Dodd said. "We could be going to Vurray."

"Thank the Almighty for small mercies," Lex mumbled.

"I know it's too late, but why weren't you coming tonight, Lex?" Rahna asked.

Lex held out the boot for inspection. Satisfied, they put the boot down and picked up the other one and began the tedious job all over again. "I hate the dancers."

"No," Dodd said, exaggerating the word, "you hate one *specific* dancer."

Lex rolled their eyes.

"Why? What happened?" Rahna asked.

Lex made a disgusted sound and ignored the conversation. Dodd always told the story better anyway. Lex lacked Dodd's flair.

"I'll tell the story, since I tell it better anyway," Dodd said. He tipped his head at Lex. "Lex was so drunk that night I'm surprised he even remembers."

"He was drunk?" Martin asked incredulously. "This I have to hear."

"You don't know the story?" Dodd asked.

"No," Martin protested. "He would never tell me."

A small smile creeped across Lex's face as a wave of contentment washed over them. *He*. Lex had spent so much of their life struggling to fit into the mold. Her this. Her that. Girl. Girl. Girl. Lex was never a *girl*. Lex didn't think they were exactly a boy, either, though they leaned in that direction more often than not. So to be called *he* by their peers filled Lex with a quiet joy and comfort.

There was no word for what Lex was, as far as they knew. Dodd once said that Lex was Lex, and that was the only word anyone needed. Of course, Dodd had been Lex's childhood friend, all the way back to when the pair took cello lessons together. Dodd was even the one who came up with the crazy adventure of trying to get jobs in the Cathedral guards at fourteen, as opposed to joining Southumberland's army. These days, Dodd called Lex "he" by Lex's request. Everyone else followed suit. That gave Lex the luxury to let their own identity flux back and forth on the stream in private, the way Lex wanted it.

"Then she breaks a vase over Lex's head!" Dodd shouted.

That, along with Martin's laughter, pulled Lex back into the present. "The surgeon had to stitch my head up. I still got a bald patch on the back of my skull."

Dodd nodded. "It's true! His hair is too shaggy now…Lord's mercy, Lex, you need to cut your hair. You're looking like one of the sniffer dogs."

"Better a dog than a pig," Lex said with the sweetest smile they could make.

Dodd rolled his eyes, and the conversation devolved into the usual bickering about travelling on the road, sore asses, and how it had better not rain.

Lex chuckled. Life was good these days.

CHAPTER THREE

Borro Abbey

ALLEGRA SCOWLED AT the letter in front of her. For the last year, Allegra had invested over one hundred gold sovereigns into a girls' school just outside of Orsini's palace walls. It was a bold proposal, and one of the bishops had recommended the school contact her, as opposed to the clergy, for investors. They wanted to address the lack of education amongst Orsini's laboring poor, and Allegra had a well-established reputation for being a patron.

In fact, Allegra was the patron of nine such schools catering to the education and upbringing of very poor girls. Outsiders saw it as just another way a rich woman spread a little charity around. Those who knew Allegra understood her motives were far more personal.

Too many so-called witches were the children of poor mothers, ragged from twelve or more births, and pregnant again because their drunkard husbands wouldn't leave them alone. Unable to feed the mouths already born, these desperate women would report one or more of their eldest daughters to a local magistrate. Young sons had an easier time finding grunt work, so daughters were more likely to be handed over. The mother would be given a bounty of a silver crown—easily two months' salary for a laborer—and she could tell herself that the child would be "properly cared for" and given "appropriate training" and all the usual platitudes and comforts.

Allegra knew that was not the reality of things. What faced most of them was slavery of one form or another. Girls with actual magical talent would be sold to merchants and factories to make magical trinkets, all eventually laced with a touch of despair. Many would be defective, and some would bring the users harm if the girls were filled with rage and vengeance. To be discovered creating "defective" items would bring on the beatings, and much worse. If that didn't kill them, they'd be sold to the mines to die horrific deaths underground.

The girls who were just normal and without any magical talent could expect to be sold off as domestics or farm help. Scrubbing floors, digging carrots, working various cottage industries—it didn't matter provided they worked hard. Those with "attitudes" unbecoming of proper young girls would be shipped off to the handful of factories they were cropping up if they were lucky, and mines if they weren't. The prettier ones were eventually sold to brothels to be "taught a lesson" as a priest had once told her.

Allegra hated that priest, and she openly despised the system. It was ungodly, and she didn't even believe in any such being. There was no evidence such a being as the great Almighty even existed and, if he did, he was probably long gone by now. And, if he did truly once exist, she didn't respect him enough to give him her loyalty and devotion. After all, this was all his fault.

Because of the Lord Almighty, so lofty they didn't even bother giving him a name, common people believed mages gained their power from sexual rituals with beasts from the abyss. That ill-gotten power could then lay dormant in a family for generations before it mysteriously cropped up. The Almighty's followers excelled at punishing children for their fathers' crimes.

So here Allegra was, reading yet another letter shutting down her program because the uneducated or the devout, or both, believed her schools went against nature and the will of a non-existent Almighty.

She crumpled the letter up and threw it across her small drawing room. The program would have stemmed some of the abuse Orsini's poor children endured. Allegra would have paid the entrance fees for any impoverished child who wanted to attend the school. She was rich without vices; charity was the only thing she could spend money on these days! It could have worked so perfectly. The school would have quietly identified true mages and Allegra's purse strings would have seen those children moved to a special boarding school to be properly trained.

They'd still be tattooed, but at least they'd most likely avoid subjugation. The others would learn handicrafts and a trade. They'd find work, and be able to support themselves and their families once they finished school at fourteen.

And now it was over before it barely begun!

My dearest Contessa the letter had begun. How dare a man she'd never met address her with such intimacy? He was nothing but a washed up bishop. His family name made him too important to ship to the backwoods, but his incompetence meant he'd never climb the ranks of the Cathedral.

He had canceled her program. He had stomped on the dreams of dozens of innocents for nothing more than his hope of impressing the Holy Father. Well, she had been childhood friends with the Holy Father and he would *not* take kindly to knowing this had happened in *his* name.

You will be no doubt pleased to find that I have diverted your investment toward the purchase of furnishings, linens, oil, candles, as well as ten copies of Archbishop Alistair Sheppard's excellent, and uplifting, publication, Hymns for the Faithful. *I am certain you will be pleased with knowing your kind and generous gift has been used to spread the word of the Lord Almighty to the poor.*

Thief! He knew she wouldn't have approved if he'd asked, so he did it behind her back. He had no intention of doing anything beyond lining his own purse. Linens? What did a school for the poor need with linens? She knew the students were returning home at night to sleep. The only people living at the school were the teachers and the servants, and she'd already paid for their supplies.

She glared at the crumpled paper on the floor. She had sworn to herself not to play the game of politics. She loved retirement at the abbey, where they left her to live in peace and obscurity, doing her good works to atone for her inherently sinful mage heart. But right now, all Allegra wanted to do was mount a horse and ride into Orsini Palace and demand to be treated as the woman of rank she was.

Instead, she opted to pour herself a glass of wine. A very *full* glass of Orsini special vintage, a gift from her brother that accompanied his steward who'd visited her a month ago to update her on her estates' account books.

She leaned back in her chair and imagined stealing all of the bishop's new linens and furnishings and giving them to the poor. Picturing his befuddled and outraged protestations amused her. Those daydreams kept her content through another very full glass of wine.

A knock interrupted her thoughts, and just as well. She was enjoying her daydream so much that the journey was becoming tempting. Her maidservant entered her drawing room and gave a quick curtsy. Nadira was a short, sturdy matron who worked directly for Allegra, unlike the rest of the servants at Borro Abbey who attended her. Allegra didn't force Nadira to wear livery or a uniform, so she sported a simple blue dress with a beige apron, white sleeve protectors, and a gray scarf about her neck to ward against the evening mountain chill. She'd taken to wearing her graying black coils in thick braids tight against her head these days, all ending as soon as they escaped past the nape of her neck. Nadira said she was too old to bother with long hair.

"Pardon the interruption, Your Ladyship, but you have visitors."

"At this hour?" She glanced out her window; the sun was already setting. "Tell them I'm not at home. They can come back tomorrow at a civilized time."

"They come from Orsini Palace, Your Ladyship, on business directly from the Holy Father."

Allegra stared down at her writing desk with a frown, but opted to leave her letters out. Doubtful this company would be here long. She tugged off the billowy white sleeves protecting her dress and stuffed them inside her writing desk's storage. She nodded to Nadira, then stood to smooth down her dress.

Nadira curtsied again and left, entering a few moments later with three dusty men in tow. "Your Ladyship, may I present Captain Rainier, and Lieutenants Lex and Dodd, of the Holy Father's Own Consorts."

The oldest of the three was a tall, broad-chested man, and rather handsome. The insignia sewn into his sleeves identified him as the rank of Captain. He had several days' growth on his face that was longer than the hair on his head. He was darker complexioned than herself, with a firm, chiseled jaw, and very easy on the eyes. Allegra's mouth quirked in spite of her annoyance over the interruption.

Captain Rainier spoke first. "Your Ladyship, thank you for seeing us at such a late hour."

Allegra motioned at the sofa before seating herself on a nearby chair. She kept a tight guard on her tongue. She had no idea why these three were here, but she was certain it wasn't for good.

The two younger companions moved to sit, but stopped when Captain Rainier spoke. "We don't wish to dirty your furniture, Your Ladyship."

"I insist," she said, and the three men sat down across from her.

Allegra suppressed the urge to both cough and put her hand to her nose. They had definitely just arrived. "Would any of you like some broth? I don't like to eat this late in the evening, so I usually take hot broth instead. I believe this one was made with mostly salt beef, so it's quite delicious."

"Only if it isn't a bother for the servant," Captain Rainier said. "Otherwise, we can wait until the morning."

The sad, pathetic expressions of Rainier's companions said their young stomachs could not wait until the morrow. She stood back up, and took a mug down from the rack on the wall. She dipped the mug into the pot near the fireplace, and then wiped it down with a cloth that hung nearby. She placed the mug on a saucer and handed it to the Captain. She repeated the action twice more for the other two, who gaped at her. They had not expected this fine lady to know how to dip a cup into a pot.

Normally, Allegra would have made an innocent quip, but she knew to keep a stern exterior. She didn't trust anyone from Orsini, and she certainly wasn't in the mood for clerical politics today. She could, and would, be polite for politeness' sake, but it wouldn't extend further than the basic hospitality she'd show anyone.

Mugs now safely handed over, she retook her seat, folded her hands on her lap. She let her guests take their first tentative sips. "Now, how may I help you?"

"His Radiance sent us to deliver a letter. Lex?" Captain Rainier nodded at the lean, young man seated next to him.

Lieutenant Lex balanced his cup and saucer in one hand while digging in a side satchel with the other.

Allegra waited for the letter's imminent arrival, giving her an opportunity to take stock of Captain Rainier's companions. Lieutenant Lex was quite lean, with narrow shoulders and long, thin fingers that would have made him a perfect pianoforte player, assuming he'd ever learnt. He was pale, but had enough of a tan from the southern Orsini sun to not look pallid and sickly. He had no facial hair at all, not even a shadow, so he must have been younger than his eyes made him out to be.

The other man, therefore, must have been Lieutenant Dodd. Dodd was the color of cooked lobster. Allegra winced; that was obviously a painful sunburn.

Dodd caught her staring and said, "I lost my hat two days ago, Your Ladyship."

Allegra winced again. "I will have my maid bring you a healing cream."

"That would be *very* appreciated."

"A man of your skin should not be without a hat," Allegra said idly when she spied several blisters on his ears.

Lex found the letter finally and handed it to Rainier. In turn, Rainier stood to hand it to her. "Your Ladyship."

Something about the Captain's name tugged at her memory. The accent suggested he was from the north, perhaps Cumberland or Northumberland. Maybe Southumberland? Summerland, maybe? One of the *–lands*.

Rainier…Rainier…

That name sound familiar, but why. Captain Rainier of Cumberland? No, it didn't mean anything to her, but yet she was sure she should know this man. Damn, it was going to bug her all night now.

Rainier handed over the sealed envelope. "His Holiness said you should read it immediately."

"How lovely," Allegra said before her brain caught the snide remark from slipping aloud. She didn't bother looking up, to save her guests the trouble of attempting to hide their smirks.

She tore through the seal and read the sprawling, educated handwriting inside:

To the Gracious and Humble Allegra, Contessa of Marsina

The Lord God Almighty's greetings upon Your Ladyship. Thank you for your last correspondence. How fortunate I am to have been blessed with such a friend in these trying times. For you to offer your assistance and guidance is indeed a blessing from the Lord God Almighty himself.

I have mediated on this situation. I even fasted in hopes that the Almighty would show me which of the roads before me I should choose. Your letter came as I labored and struggled to comprehend the direction He would wish me to take.

As ever, I should have turned my thoughts to the word of Tasmin, who said "The prideful will fall upon my sword." You must have been inspired by her remembrance in your selfless act.

Therefore, I have dispatched Captain Rainier and his guard to personally escort you to Orsini Palace to begin your new role as Arbiter of Justice for the Cathedral during these most trying times for your kind. I am certain, once you pray upon this, you will know this is the right course of action for all of us. Thank you for volunteering to take on this nigh-impossible task.

May the Lord Almighty smile down upon you.

His Radiance, Holy Father Francois

"I am going to murder Rupert," Allegra muttered.

"Who's Rupert?" Dodd asked. A beat later, he lowered his voice and said, "What? What did I say?"

Rupert was Allegra's childhood friend, rival, potential suitor, and partner in crime. He was more commonly now known as Holy Father Francois, His Radiance, The Annoying One, and so on. He knew exactly what he was doing when he wrote that letter, and most likely was grinning while he penned each word.

Through gritted teeth, she asked, "Captain, are you aware of the contents of this letter?"

Rainier cleared his throat as way of reply.

"I will assume that is a yes."

"We are your escort back to the Cathedral," Captain Rainier said.

STANTON STARED AT the Contessa in wonderment. He knew he was staring. He knew he needed to stop. *And* he knew he was still staring at her. She was nothing at all like what he'd expected. For one thing, she couldn't have been much more than thirty, and while true that wasn't young enough in many aristocratic men's eyes, she was not the decrepit, feeble *old* woman he'd imagined.

She wasn't *pretty,* either, which was a point in her favor. She wasn't all ribbons and silks. No, that wouldn't have suited. The Contessa wore a stylish, but practical dress. She lacked adornments and was without rouge or stencils marring her flawless, golden-brown skin.

There was a hint of arrogant superiority that lingered in her posture, but it never crept into her voice. Her body posture announced her high breeding and station, but that haughtiness was tempered by the haphazard tail of wavy, black hair that cascaded over one of her shoulders.

She was handsome, beautiful, elegant, poised, and confident.
Damn.

She stood up quickly, and the others struggled to their feet to match her movement. She thrust her chin out and said, "I'm sorry for your long journey, but I don't wish to leave the abbey. Please let Francois know I said no. Good evening."

Stanton ignored Lex's elbow digging into him, as Lex tugged Dodd upright. When they got back to Orsini, Stanton was putting Dodd through another round of etiquette classes, and would continue to put him through them until that damned kid decided to act in the manner appropriate to his birthright.

Stanton inclined his head slightly and said, "Your Ladyship, I am under strict instructions from the Holy Father himself to convince you to accompany me back to Orsini, to meet personally with him at the Palace."

"I don't care in the slightest," she said.

Lex made a choking sound. Stanton glared at his second-in-command and made a mental note that Lex would be attending classes soon, too, if he kept this up.

"Sorry. Swallowed the wrong way," Lex wheezed.

The break in conversation did allow Stanton enough of a pause to choose his words carefully. "The Holy Father believes you are the best candidate to broker a…"

"Captain, you have disrupted my quiet evening at home, so give me the courtesy of not lying to me in my own drawing room. He's doing this because I embarrassed him. This is his way of getting his revenge. I will not fall for his tricks. We are not children anymore, and I will not have him treating me as one."

Despite knowing better, a smile tugged on one side of Stanton's mouth.

Fury flashed in her eyes. "Are you laughing at me, Captain?"

"Not at all. Pero warned me that you were a firebrand. Francois said you were frail. I see now which of them knows you best."

The Contessa's dark eyes sparkled and a wicked grin cracked her stern disguise. "Frail? Oh, am I not what you were expecting, Captain?"

"Not even remotely."

Her anger dissipated in a flash and she barked out an undignified laugh. "Did the Holy Father give you the impression I was some frail old woman? Oh! Did he say I was low in spirits?" Stanton's mouth twitched, which was all the affirmation she needed. She laughed more. "He's turned into such a mother hen since his elevation to the papal chair. I am not to be trifled with, and he knows that."

"Indeed he does." Stanton reached down to place the mug and saucer he was still holding on the small table next to the sofa. "I apologize for disrupting your evening, Your Ladyship. We are staying in the stables tonight if you should happen to change your mind. Good evening."

Stanton knew enough from his mother and sisters not to argue with a woman of rank when she'd dug in to make her stand. He bowed and turned on his heel. He would speak to her again in the morning.

Courtesy demanded she'd speak with him first, ensuring she had not offended him, so he had every expectation she'd send for him. Then, after her assurances that she'd meant no offense, his duty would be to insist he had been the offender. They would banter back and forth until, finally, he would guilt-trip her into coming to the Cathedral to salvage his duty and honor.

That was Francois's plan.

"I'm sorry, Captain. I've lost my manners this evening." He turned around to face her; she was still standing. "Please sit and let us discuss this like adults."

DAMN FRANCOIS TO the pit, and his letter with him. And damn that idiot bishop's letter arriving and throwing her off. She was angrier than all of the demons in the abyss, and it was a hair's width tie of which problem topped the list.

How dare Francois send these three here to kidnap her. He knew she never left Borro Abbey these days, and he knew why. Least of all Cathedral politics! Which was why she resorted to only letter writing and charitable donations. She could remain an active part of the world without having to step into it.

But she'd also been rude to her guests, who'd done nothing more than fulfill their duty and assignments. "It's been a long day and I apologize for being rude. Captain, would you mind having your companions step outside?"

"Certainly, Your Ladyship," Lex said.

Dodd nodded sharply to Allegra and said, "Your Ladyship." The two left together without a return glance or a whisper.

Once the drawing room door shut behind them, Allegra sat back in her chair. She motioned with her hand at the sofa. "I wish to begin again."

Captain Rainier inclined his head and retook his seat. "As you wish, Your Ladyship."

Allegra smiled. "Gentlemen's manners?"

"Guilty."

She slipped into court language, the tongue of the elite. She could small talk her way into a decent enough mood, and maybe drag some information out of this captain in the process. "Gentlemen's manners from a guard captain. Well, I suppose you do work for the Cathedral, so I shouldn't be too surprised." She made a scene of sizing him up. He was easy on the eyes, so at least that task was enjoyable. "Obviously, a younger son of rank. The military is usually the province of second sons and the clergy that of third. Hmm, I am guessing you are a fourth son, with no property of his own, and achieved his position through the influence of his two older brothers and perhaps an uncle. Am I close, Captain?"

Rainier's mouth formed several silent words before his mouth quirked upwards. "I'm a fifth son."

"Your poor mother."

"Indeed," Rainier said with a snort. "Later in life, I took a position at the Cathedral, escorting cardinals and bishops between their homes and the palace. Eventually, I was raised through the ranks and here I am, escorting beautiful ladies to the palace."

Allegra shot him an unimpressed look, though she knew the mirth in her voice gave her away. "Flattery will get you nowhere."

"I'm relieved, as that was the extent of my skills."

It was Allegra's turn to let out a little snort. She eyed the letter and asked, "Did they really tell you I was a recluse?"

Rainier made a show of hesitation, but then he nodded. The sparkle didn't leave his eye. "His Holiness for certain, as well as several bishops I spoke with while preparing for my journey. I have a few friends amongst the clergy, so I deliver letters or small parcels if it's not out of my way. Even Father Michael, here at the abbey, was very concerned that I not disrupt you, for fear of unsettling your nerves. It was your maidservant that convinced him you were still up and could use the distraction from your..." he glanced at her writing desk, "work."

"I'll have you know, Captain, that I am not fine lacework. I am made of much stronger material."

"I'm discovering that for myself, Your Ladyship." He leaned forward. "They expect you to refuse, claiming some malady or nervous complaint. Then, there is someone to blame if the peace talks fail once more."

She nearly fell for the bait, but she kept her spine straight and said, "I see you also spoke with Pero."

"Yes. It is his opinion that you should take this position to spit on the slave-owning cardinals."

"Pero's a fop."

Rainier shrugged. "He can still be right."

Captain Rainier was too good at this game, and Allegra was out of practice. He was obviously more than simply a Cathedral guard captain, and it irked her he was getting the better of her. He knew just what words to say to spur her underlying ambitions that hid safely out of view. How did he even know they were there?

Pero, of course. If Pero had his way, Allegra would be holding Elemental Mage Rights rallies while flaunting the law until it caught up to her. Then, upon arrest and a showy trial that would go down in the annals of judicial history, she would be sentenced to the mines. She would burst out into her elemental form, burning through her oppressors and go on the run. Support would gather for her, and soon the people would stand up against injustice and the laws would be changed.

Pero was a dangerously idealistic fop.

"Captain, I have no interest in politics, let alone being the Arbiter. Doing nothing but listening to prattling nobles and merchant upstarts whine about how religious law impedes their pursuits, I...I would lose my mind and my temper."

"Think of the influence you'd have."

She made a dismissive sound. "I am one of the richest nobles in all of Serna. I'm wealthier than some princes. I need no more influence."

"Then do it to spite them all."

Oh, Pero had prepared him well. It had been a long time since Allegra had been at Orsini's palace or the Cathedral. Most of them back at the Cathedral had no idea she kept up on politics, or that she was active in her letter writing, protests, and funding of various peaceful organizations. And, perhaps, a couple of less-than-peaceful organizations who were smuggling elemental mages to safety. But no one needed to know that, especially not a magistrate who would attempt to arrest her.

"I do not want the position."

"Then don't take it," Rainier said. "I'm here to escort you, not to force you into a career."

The very act of her showing up at the Cathedral could cause beautiful trouble. She could visit the Bishop of Orsini himself and give him a very large, very angry piece of her mind; she could even demand to see what her money had purchased. She could make loud protestations about the clergy's treatment of mages, get a feel for the number of abolitionist hardliners in the Cathedral's ranks, and begin a renewed campaign for mage rights.

This was the perfect reason to get her out of Borro Abbey for a few weeks and to cause trouble elsewhere. She didn't have to take the position.

Allegra looked up at Rainier and smiled. "We'll take my carriage."

CHAPTER FOUR

Borro County, Amadore

THE MORNING SKY was obscured by thick fog when Allegra accepted Captain Rainier's hand of assistance getting into her carriage. She was wearing her second-best travelling outfit, which was to say completely inappropriate for travelling. The beige cotton satin dress was tightly-fitted across the shoulders and back, snug armholes and sleeves, and skirts that skimmed the mud. Over one arm, she carried a silk satin brown-striped jacket, one that would hold snug against her torso before flaring out to follow the flare of her skirts.

Allegra wished to travel in trousers and a greatcoat, but Nadira patiently reminded her that a woman of rank travelling with a handful of His Holiness's Consorts must look her best. When Allegra jokingly asked why she was wearing the second-best dress, Nadira pointed out that the Contessa would want to arrive at the palace wearing a dress that didn't smell like she'd just worn it for four days in the heat near horses.

Captain Rainier stepped inside the carriage after her, taking the seat across from her. He held his sheathed sword, and placed it on the seat next to him. He shifted down enough so that he could stretch his long legs across the floor without touching Allegra's more primly crossed ankles. Rainier was wearing his dark green uniform again, which was suspiciously cleaner than it had been the previous evening.

"Did the laundry maids stay up all night scrubbing your uniform?" Allegra asked. "I hope you tipped them well, especially since I had you moved from the stables to one of the guest rooms."

"Good morning to you, too, Your Ladyship. I did ask my chambermaid to have water and a small scrub brush sent up, but beyond that, I assure you *I* was the one up all night scrubbing my uniform."

Allegra gave him an apologetic smile. "You did an excellent job, Captain. Although, you missed one of the buttons."

He looked down at the brass buttons that decorated the front of his jacket, connected by gold braiding. He fingered the button that was dull compared to the others. "I've never managed to get this one as clean as the others."

Allegra nodded in understanding. That button was either enchanted, or all of the others were and that one had lost its enchantment over time, either through use or poor magic. If her nephews were all clothed in magical linens and wool trousers, carefully sewn and enchanted by her, surely a captain in the Holy Father's service would be cloaked in magical protections. Some of them might even work as originally intended, unlike many that flooded the markets made by slave hands.

He was wearing a greatcoat over his shoulders, clasped at the throat by an adjustable cord of dark green rope. He hadn't bothered to put his arms into the garment, knowing that the heat would rise in a couple of hours.

"What are you smiling about?"

She smiled more, though felt a touch of heat rise on her cheeks. "I was thinking about the cardinals if I showed up at the palace wearing a greatcoat and trousers."

"I suspect many would collapse from a shock-induced apoplexy."

"I wonder if there is time to change."

One of the abbey's footmen pulled up the carriage steps and slammed the door shut. He latched the door into place and then bowed to her. He gave Captain Rainier a shallower bow. A moment later, the horses lurched and the small caravan was off.

"Not a supporter of the cardinals, Your Ladyship?"

"I believe the only sure thing the cardinals and I share is a mutual distaste for one another's company."

That made Rainier laugh. "If you united the cardinals on anything, including their distaste of you, you are truly the greatest woman alive. You must become the Arbiter of Justice." Allegra rolled her eyes, eliciting more laughter from the captain. He held his hands up and said, "I surrender, Your Ladyship."

"One volley from me and already you're surrendering. Captain, you are not a military genius, are you?"

"Not even close," Rainier said solemnly. Something flashed across his eyes that Allegra couldn't identify, but it was gone before she could ask about it. The smile returned and he said, "I did promise the Holy Father that I would try to...*encourage* you to his way of thinking, but I also promised Pero that I wouldn't annoy you."

"I'm not certain you can honor both promises." Allegra gave him a friendly smile. She ran her hand along the blue satin interior. The satin had faded from both use and the sun, and the seams along the wall padding were frayed in places. The stuffing in her seat was lumpier than she'd remembered. "It seems Father Michael and his friends have been hard on my carriage. I let them use it, since the lower clergy are often visiting the poor in the abbey's more modest carriage. I'll need to reupholster it over the winter. It's looking a touch shabby, isn't it?"

"You own your own carriage, Your Ladyship. You are already further than most."

"I am well aware of my own good fortune, Captain. I do not require a younger son to lecture me on economics."

Her volley hit its mark. Rainier cleared his throat. "My apologies, Your Ladyship. I didn't mean to lecture you. I was simply trying to..." He cleared his throat again. "I apologize."

"Good. I don't take kindly to being chided nor lectured."

"I am overwhelmed with shock."

Whatever stern visage masking her true feelings she'd managed to maintain cracked at the dry, emotionless words. She threw her head back and laughed. "We are going to have so much fun together."

"That is one word for it, yes, Your Ladyship." His words were dry, but there was a twinkle in his eye that gave away his true amusement.

"Now that we have that out of our way, please call me Contessa. Everyone does, except the servants, of course."

"Then please call me Rainier. Everyone does, including the servants."

Allegra made a show of sizing him up. Captain Rainier wore the standard officer's uniform of the Consorts and other specialized groups within the umbrella of the Cathedral's guard. The green jackets, as they were affectionately called on occasion, were a stylish bunch and Rainier was no exception. The brass buttons on his tunic were all polished, except for one, with gold braiding dancing across his chest. Even the metal buckle about his waist had been polished. He'd put a lot of work into cleaning himself up for today, though she worried he might have been rubbing off the spells that were no doubt laid into his items.

Idly, she wondered if it was truly possible to imbue a polishing kit with transferable magic. She had never tried it, and it wasn't polite to speak of magical technique in public. Allegra always found that odd, considering that most of her circle had various mage-created items. Even her family, who received frequent gifts from her, never talked about the art behind it. It just *wasn't done.*

The black embroidery on his cuffs was worn, but still clearly showed his captaincy. His black leather boots were polished, not to perfection, but well enough. The black slash normally worn to show off one's military honors was suspiciously missing. The decorative red slash around his hips was not. Allegra never understood the sash's purpose, other than to make young women stare at a soldier's lower regions, especially if the tassel ends were strategically placed.

Younger son or not, he wore that uniform well.

"Rainier is a good, strong name, but *Captain* has a romantic vigor to it. I think I'll stick with that title. Surely the title enchants all ladies, does it not?"

Rainier laughed. It was a genuine, unguarded sound. "Contessa, I have been called many things in my life, but this the first time the word romantic has ever been used in any sentence referring to me. I'm not sure if I should be grateful or wary."

Allegra scoffed and waved a hand at him. "Please. Everyone is a romantic, Captain." She leaned forward until her corset threatened to break her ribs. Her words came out breathless when she said, "Even me."

The confused expression that crossed Rainier's face announced she was playing the tease too hard. She was out of practice when it came to courtly behavior and the flirting game; Rainier didn't seem all that practiced, either. She slumped back in her seat, lest she arrive in Orsini with no information to prepare for her visit and a very unfortunate marriage proposal from a lesser son from a nobody landowner in the north.

A wicked grin spread across Rainier's mouth. "I'm not sure everyone is a romantic, but all fine ladies certainly are."

Allegra made a mocking sound. "Tell me you aren't one of those deluded fools who believe rich women are fine ladies waiting to be swept off their feet by a charming man. And, when I say charming, I do mean in his own mind, not in the lady's opinion."

Rainier crossed his boots at the ankles, then followed it up by making a show of crossing his arms across his chest. He leaned back into his seat and eyed her. "Even if I felt that way, I would promptly adjust my thinking now that I've met the likes of you, *Contessa.*"

Allegra beamed at him. "Captain, I believe we're about to have a fabulous journey."

"Provided we don't kill each other?"

"That's why it's going to be fabulous." She grinned. "The thrill."

"I pity the Holy Father."

"So do I."

On their journey went, banter over the rumble of the carriage wheels on dirt road. Allegra was impressed by the road, and commented on it several times. There had been no proper road when she'd first moved to Borro Abbey. Both Borro County and its neighbor, Cherese, had the right attitude during the famine a decade before. They feared unrest, so opened their coffers for labor-intensive construction projects. Most of the work was building roads, but a few wharves were built, too, and the meagre wages paid were enough to keep the people from rioting when the price of bread exploded.

It had all been a knee-jerk reaction, designed solely for the purpose to help the poor afford the oppressive import taxes on grain during two successive crop failures. There was no long-term planning, beyond stopping mass rioting, but there had been long lasting and unforeseen consequences.

Surrounding counties immediately began expanding their roads, and lobbied King Matteo, monarch of Amadore, for more funds. The king, eager to prevent anything that remotely smelled of "peasant revolt," happily gave additional funds. The roads expanded. Technology was developed to improve them. And then more trade arrived. More trade meant more money. More money meant more spending. More, more, more.

The more far-flung nations and city-states were still working on their own segments of Cathedral's Way, as the long highway was soon dubbed, but it was a marvel of engineering excellence and progressive, enlightened thinking by the rulers.

"I wonder if the roads are going north yet," Allegra asked.

"There are several projects," Rainier said. "Cumberland, Northumberland, and Southumberland are building their own network of roads that will eventually connect and continue south to the Cathedral."

"Will it be called the Umberland Highway?"

"Maybe," Rainier said, taking no offense.

Allegra continued to stare out of the carriage window, watching the farm workers picking up the bundles of dried crops. Some were hay, she knew, while others would have been an assortment of the heartier cereal crops that could grow in the shadow of the Borro mountain range before they tapered off into the warm and fertile lowlands.

While at Orsini, she had to remember to send Nadira shopping for the various nalbinding, knitting, and weaving projects Allegra would undertake during the winter months, when snow blanketed Borro Abbey. Borro Village often had a difficult time getting in supplies, for the obvious reasons of knee-deep snow, so she should get as much as she could now and bring it back with her. Weave a little magic into each of the projects and each was a special gift to whoever she gave it to.

She wondered what magic she'd weave for the Captain. There was only so much control most mages had over the magic they enchanted; so much was left to unconscious chance. Allegra had some of the best education money could buy and even she struggled with control. Allegra was very careful to only weave with the lightest touch for people she didn't care about all that much, after the disastrous mittens she'd made her brother's wife upon their marriage. At least the blisters didn't leave any lasting marks and, in time, she'd forgiven Allegra.

Perhaps her magic would weave a whimsical array of protections for the heroic Captain. Something to clot blood in case of grievous injuries, something to keep his feet warm in winter, and perhaps something that glowed bright pink in the darkness of a hidden moon. She looked out the window so that he wouldn't see her smirk.

A little while later, he interrupted her silent revelry. "Pero mentioned you and the Holy Father were friends, but I admit I thought he meant he was a friend of your family, not of yours specifically. You must have grown up together."

"We were the very best of friends. We got into so much trouble. Everyone was convinced we were destined to be together, which terrified my father."

When it was clear Rainier was waiting for more of an answer, Allegra said, "Rupert is the third son of a baron. My father was the Conte of Marsina. I was his eldest child and was to inherit everything. Rupert was hardly what my father envisioned as his future heir's husband."

"Isn't the Holy Father older than you?"

"Only by seven years. He's only forty-two."

"You do not look thirty-five," Rainier said.

Allegra replied with a roll of the eyes.

"Your father must have been relieved when Francois turned out to like men."

"He was furious, actually. My poor father was convinced this was a personal slight against my honor as a woman. Ha! My father went to his grave cursing Rupert, I'm sure. It's just as well he didn't live to see him become the Holy Father. He would have never forgiven the Almighty for that one."

"I'm sorry for the loss of your father, Contessa."

"Oh, it was a long time ago." She smiled at him. "No doubt, he is proud of me in his own way, if the dead can even see us."

"Wouldn't he be upset you never married?"

"Please! No man was ever good enough in my father's eyes. No, when I die, my brother will inherit the estate and the title. And, if I outlive him, he has several sturdy girls and boys to continue on our family line." Allegra let out a contented sigh. "I'm safe, secure, and significantly richer than he was. I'd like to think Father would have approved of some of my life, at least."

She grew quiet for a moment, wondering as she often did if her father would have actually been proud of her. She looked up and saw Rainier's confused expression. So, she drew in a deep breath and said, "I was so proud of Rupert when the Council voted for him. I never expected it. He's about ninety years too young for the position."

Rainier smiled. "Some of those old cardinals do look older than the abyss itself, don't they?"

Silence settled between them again for a few minutes before Rainier broke it once more. "Contessa, why won't you take the position of Arbiter?"

Allegra frowned and went back to looking out the window. There was just enough of a breeze to make the open windows enjoyable without an excessive amount of bugs ending up inside the carriage. She rarely left the confines of the Borro region, and it was nice to see how the countryside was changing—and staying exactly the same.

"It's a waste of time," Allegra finally said, knowing she had to say something. "No one is actually interested in stopping a slave revolt, nor are they interested in changing the laws that are making the possibility of a revolt a reality. This is all for show, as evident by the last several Arbiters. Particularly the last one, who was able to make things worse without having war declared. Impressive, if horrific."

"Something has to be done," Rainier said. "There could be civil war in a year or two, if we're not careful. You would be respected and considered a neutral party, working only for the Almighty. You could help stop the war."

"Perhaps war is what we deserve."

Rainier snorted and looked away. "How typical."

"Ah, yes. I'm merely a pampered peer wanting war. Someone who's never picked up a sword in her life, nor would be impacted in any way by bloodshed in the streets." Allegra didn't bother to hide the sarcasm in her voice. "I might even make a tidy sum from a war, and line my pockets with the sovereigns stolen from the dead."

"That is not what I meant," Rainier said coolly. "I believe you know that."

"What I know is that you were sent here to escort me. And, since I know the Holy Father, I know you were also sent to butter me up." She leaned forwarded and said, "I am not a biscuit served at breakfast."

"And there she is," Rainier said.

"What do you mean?"

"The true woman behind all of the courtly nonsense you've been pushing at me for the last three hours. I was wondering when you'd actually make an appearance."

Allegra scoffed and looked back out the window. Chattingston, her estate in Marsina, wasn't as mountainous as Borro; it was more rolling countryside and green, wide pasture. There, her tenants raised animals, cereal crops, and vegetables. There was even a farmer who had a small orchard in one section of his acre and the apples and plums were a welcome treat that always fetched a tidy sum for him, and the estate, at market.

She hadn't been back there in three years, and that was only to say good-bye to a beloved aunt on her deathbed.

It wasn't that she loved Borro more than home. Borro was different. It was all craggy mountains and grass-covered valleys. Here, they only grew a few types of grains. There were plenty of sheep, though. And cows. Various berries loved the cool air and snowy winters, so at least everyone's teeth were never threatened by scurvy. She hated the cold when she first arrived, but soon grew acclimatized to the crisp air untainted by heat, humidity, and human waste.

And it was quiet. No one expected anything of her. Oh, yes, she entertained the visiting nobles along with Father Michael, and many of her family and friends made pilgrimages to the Cathedral, and detoured to Borro for a couple of weeks to visit with her. The abbey enjoyed the additional revenue, and Allegra didn't have to leave her tiny cottage.

There, she was safe and isolated from the world. She could hide away. Maybe Rupert and the Grand Duchess were right about her all long; perhaps she was as fragile as they seemed to think. Maybe she was of low spirits after all, and shouldn't be travelling about…

Allegra laughed inwardly. What rot. She had no patience for the stupidity of politics, and Orsini Palace, along with the Cathedral, was the heart of politics. She would have to step very carefully there, for a host of reasons. Rupert understood that; he, of all people, knew the risks Allegra took every time she stepped into the middle of the courtly dais. And, yet, he would try this tactic on her now.

"I apologize for taking my frustrations out on you," Allegra said finally. "I hate the Cathedral. I hate the politics of the place. And I *hate* how they stare at me."

"Because you're a witch? I mean, a mage?"

She didn't scowl at him for the slip. At least he knew she preferred to be called a mage, and not a witch. A childhood of *witch bitch* was more than enough to make her loathe the term. "Many of them believe I should have been tattooed. Cousin to Grand Duchess Katherine, the cousin of the King of Amadore, aunt of the Queen of Cartossa. *Me.* Branded like a convict. And they stare at me, and needle me, and do everything they can to see if they can make me snap."

"You should catch someone's hair on fire. That would show them," Rainier said, and a hint of a smile tugged the edges of his mouth.

Allegra laughed in spite of herself. She knew he was referring to elemental magic. She knew it was supposed to be a joke. She didn't feel the joke, but she let it be. "I doubt they'd let me get so close with a match to do the job."

His smile said that he understood the gentle rebuke. "I'd have to arrest you for arson. It would be messy."

She forced a smile, but knew it came across more exhausted than happy. "I loathe Cathedral politics."

"Then you are the right person for the job. If nothing else, you'll provide endless entertainment. I'd vote for you on that principle alone, if I were a Cardinal."

"Yes, as Arbiter, I shall end these rebellions by cuffing the ears of everyone involved and sending them to bed without their supper. Oh, and I would liberate the slaves, make poor mages equal citizens, and stop branding people in the streets."

"It's good to know you wouldn't propose anything radical," Rainier said. "Why *did* Francois ask to see you?"

"If I were to guess, this is his way of inviting me over for dinner."

DARKNESS HAD BLANKETED the sky by the time they pulled into their evening accommodations. They'd changed horses various times throughout the day, but rarely rested more than a few moments to stretch or use an outhouse. They did stop once for half an hour to partake of an inn's hot supper on offer. It was a gray-hued potage of assorted, unidentifiable bits, but at least it was warm and salty. The bread was well-baked, however, with higher quality wheat than Allegra expected to find at a waystation inn.

Allegra's joints and muscles ached, and her intestines loudly protested both the potage and her staunch refusal to relieve herself in the bushes along the trek. Rainier had asked her a few times if she needed the carriage to stop when her guts began their gurgling chorus, but she'd refused. One childhood encounter with poison oak on her nether regions was more than enough for a lifetime.

When the carriage finally stopped, Allegra used only the most basic of manners before stumbling down the carriage's three steps to beg the attending servant for the outhouse's location. For a terrifying moment, she feared Rainier was going to follow her right up to the wooden structure's front door. Thankfully, he only followed enough for discreet protection and kept back enough to allow her as much privacy as one could expect while suffering intestinal complaints in a public outhouse.

Several moments passed before she emerged from the building, feeling both lighter, from the obvious, and dizzy, from the pit's desperate need of being backfilled and relocated.

Rainier was still standing in the same location. A little slip of a boy was holding a lantern on a tall stick near Rainier, cutting through the darkness. A stableboy was rushing over to the carriages with another lantern as Lex shouted into the darkness.

"Dammit all to the demons, I can't see. Boy! Boy!"

"Here, sir!" Came a young voice just as the lantern light flashed on Lex's face.

"Don't shine it in my fucking eyes!"

"Sorry, sir."

Allegra glanced back to her carriage. Lex was balanced on top of the luggage that had been tied to the roof. Lex shouted in the dusk, "Your Ladyship?"

Allegra stepped next to Rainier and the light. "Yes, Lex?"

"Ah! There you are. Which of your bags did you want?"

"Just the black bag on top, thanks."

"They all look black, your ladyship," Lex complained.

Rainier failed to stifle his chuckle. Allegra shouted back, not bothering to hide the mirth in her voice, "It has a gold buckle on the front."

"Found it!" Lex shouted. "Dodd! Catch!"

Lex dropped the bag down to Dodd, who caught it easily. He walked over and Rainier offered to take it. Dodd handed the bag over and said, "Sir, you need us to pull down anything for you?"

"My green carpet bag," Rainier said. Dodd shouted over his shoulder, "Captain's green carpet bag, Lex!"

"Fucking green looks fucking black," Lex complained.

"Watch your tongue, Lex. We have a contessa in our midst," Rainier shouted.

"Yes, Captain. Sorry, Your Ladyship."

"It's fine, Lieutenant." She grinned at Rainier. "Just get those bags down."

"Yes, Your Ladyship," Lex grumbled. "Dodd! Dodd, stop laughing or I swear to the Almighty I will beat your ass."

"Ignore Lex," Rainier said. "He gets angry when he's hungry. Is there a word for that?"

"There should be," Allegra said solemnly, even though her grin hadn't faded.

"He'll settle down once he has an ale and a loaf in his hands."

Allegra smiled and then looked around her approvingly. They were in the back alley, near the stables. There were servants rushing around, along with coachmen in their long greatcoats laughing and slapping each other. The stable boys were unhitching horses or hitching horses back up. Horses snorted and whinnied as they were led here and there, depending upon if they were done working or just getting started.

This was one of the staging inns along Cathedral Way. Horses could be dropped off from other stages and fresh ones picked up; all of the stables had agreements with one another. The first inn they changed horses at would send Allegra's personal horses back to the Abbey with a servant. The rest of the horses were shared between the inns.

"I've stayed here a few times over the years. It's always been quite a respectable establishment." She looked about. "It's grown since the last time I was here. It looks less shabby, too."

Rainier put his hand on the back of his neck as he stretched. "Pero recommended we time our journey to arrive here. He said you'd find it cleaner than most of the other options."

Allegra smiled as Lieutenant Lex walked by carrying a small trunk. "Captain, want me to get us set up inside?"

"Please," Rainier said.

"I'll see if they have anything decent to eat. I'm starving," Dodd said, walking past them and also carrying a small trunk up on one shoulder.

"Leave some for the rest of us," Rainier ordered, but the other two had already turned their backs to walk inside. Lex did raise a hand, waving that he'd recognized the order, though did nothing to acknowledge the order was going to be followed.

"Martin? First watch?" Rainier shouted.

Martin waved to the stable boy and jogged over to them. Martin was short in height, and in his late teenage years or early twenties. Allegra thought he was fair-skinned, though it was difficult to tell through all of the dirt on his face and hands. "Rahna and I will look after things out there. Stableboys said there's servants up at all hours, but we're going to sleep with the Contessa's carriage. Just to make sure and all, Captain."

"Good job. I'll have the servants bring you out something."

"Dodd's handling it," Martin said. He gave Allegra a tight nod and said, "Your Ladyship."

When Martin disappeared back into the shadows of the stable, Allegra said, "You get along well with your men."

Rainier motioned for her to join him and together they walked toward the inn's door. "We've worked together a number of years now. Lex and Dodd, especially. When Francois asked me to form his personal guard, those two were the first names out of my mouth. I couldn't ask for better." A hint of a smile tugged his mouth when he amended, "Well, most days."

The inn was of solid quality, which was no surprise considering the clientele that frequented the place. No back alley bawdy house was this. No, this was where respectable men brought their respectable wives; drunkards, gamblers, and whoremongers need not inquire within. The Prancing Alehouse was just around the corner for them.

Lex and Dodd were busy making arrangements when Allegra walked inside. Allegra was to get one of the best rooms, once the title "Contessa" had been dropped in lowered whispers. Offers of a bath were made, but declined. She was too tired to wait for servants to carry the water up for her. Besides, the last time she'd ordered a bath here, the water was straight out of the well—in the middle of winter.

Rainier was given an adjoining room to hers, with Lex and Dodd doubled up in a lower floor room. Additional rooms were taken for servants and the coachmen, all of lesser quality, of course, on the lower level.

"Your Ladyship, would you like supper brought to your room?" Dodd asked.

"Please," she said, and Dodd turned back to the innkeeper. Allegra turned to Rainier and asked, "Would you like to take supper with me, Captain?"

He accepted and all departed up the stairs to their rooms. Dodd chattered on about the food he'd ordered.

"She's out of hot food for the evening, but she's sending up a plate of cold meats, bread, and the like. Oh, and she's going to send up some spiced wine and tea, to make up for not having hot food. Not bad, huh?"

"Did she have any meat pies, did she say?" Lex asked. "I could murder for a meat pie."

In unison, Lex and Dodd said, "Gammon pie."

Rainier leaned in and whispered, "Whatever you do, do not ask about the gammon pie."

"Why not?" she whispered back.

"Trust me."

This only made Allegra more curious about this mysterious pie story, but they reached Lex and Dodd's room before she could stir the fires. She and Rainier also parted ways on the next floor, with promises to eat together once the food arrived.

Allegra's room was typical of a side road inn. A tiny window with a cracked frame: the perfect home for bugs and spiders. The bed's hay was lumpy and there was no hint of dried lavender or mint when she sniffed the air. At least the ropes were pulled tight and didn't feel as though they were going to snap or sag when she sat down on the bed's edge.

There was a pitcher of water in front of the fire, and a wash basin on the modest dresser across from the bed; she'd take advantage of them in a moment. For now, she unbuttoned her pelisse and pulled off her lace scarf and rejoiced in the air flow against her dusty, sweaty skin.

Allegra eventually peeled out of her various layers meant to signify her station in life and enjoyed bustling about her room in just her linen shift and corset. Nadira wasn't arriving until later into the night; she and some of the other servants were held up by Father Michael wanting to send additional *whatevers* to Orsini. And deciding at the last moment, as ever.

The quick wash in the fire-warmed water did her morale a world of good. A stray thought suggested she could ask one of her travelling companions to help her out of her corset for a more thorough wash. Perhaps Rainier would enjoy the job. Allegra laughed aloud at that. Clearly, she'd been without male company in her bed for far too long. Maybe she could invite all three up to help remove her corset. Why shouldn't a lady have a little orgy in a back alley inn?

She laughed heartily at her thoughts, and the various images of coordinating such an undertaking, and tugged herself into the dress she'd packed for the evenings. It was a stripped pink and brown dress, better at hiding the stains of travel. It was thin linen, however, and it was a cool evening, so she tugged her pelisse back on over it. After shaking out her travelling clothes, she draped them over her bed to air out.

Soon enough, the expected knock sounded. A serving girl, perhaps eight or nine, stood at the door, carrying a wooden tray of food. She curtsied awkwardly.

"Come in," Allegra said, opening the door wide enough for the girl to enter. She noticed the two brands on the side of the girl's neck instantly. One stating she was a mage; the other that she was free. "How old are you?"

"Eleven, Your Ladyship," the girl said in a meek voice. "I'm tiny for my age."

"That you are. You're a free mage?"

"Aye," she said.

Allegra stared at the brand and wondered if it was a real one. "Where did you go to school?"

"Grayson Magical Theory Institute for the Poor in Cumberland," she said instantly in a well-practiced voice.

Allegra smirked. Cumberland was far enough away that no one would bother checking up on this girl. But, Cumberland was also close enough that, in theory, this girl could have travelled here with her family.

"You should work on your Cumberland accent, my dear, to be more convincing," Allegra said. "Some might question your free status."

The girl turned ashen. Her eyes narrowed, though, and she didn't have a hot defense on her tongue. This wasn't her first encounter with prying eyes.

"Don't worry. Your secret is safe with me." Allegra pulled out several pennies from her purse and handed them to the girl. "Do you have to show your tips?"

She nodded.

"Then the pennies are for them to see." Allegra pulled out a quarter-crown coin. "And this is for you to hide in your shoe."

The little girl finally brightened. She shoved the shiny coin into her slouched stocking and wiggled her foot until it was in a safe and comfortable location. Then she pocketed the pennies and said, "Thanks, Your Ladyship." She attempted, and failed, to curtsy properly.

When the girl left, Allegra wondered how she got the brands. There was no faking them. How did a girl in her position get a mage brand, but escape slavery? Either she really did attend the Cumberland school, or someone rescued that little girl. Maybe it was a scheme to extort money from lily-livered contessas with too much money and pity to spare. Probably that one.

A rap at the door interrupted her considerations. "Contessa?"

She smiled and opened the door. Captain Rainier was there, looking refreshed and buttoned down without his green uniform jacket. His white sleeves billowed around him, but were kept from causing too much trouble by the tight cuffs at his wrists. He was carrying his own serving tray of food and drink.

"Good evening, Contessa," he said with a wide smile.

"Good evening, Captain. Look at you, out of uniform. Not even a cravat or necktie. You look practically undressed. How scandalous. What will the people say?"

He snorted and put the tray down on the small table in the corner of her room. "I suspect they'll say nothing, since no one actually cares about me enough to gossip."

"Or perhaps they'll say look at him, finally settling down." Allegra laughed merrily. "We should dine together whenever possible at the Cathedral. Give the old gossips something to write about."

"Letters keep empires afloat," the Captain said in agreement. "The postage taxes alone."

Allegra took her seat and motioned for him to join her. The chair legs were uneven and rocked a few times before she found the right position. "Did you get the same as me?"

Rainier lifted the wooden cover over his plate. "Hmm. Cold ham. That's goose pie, I think." He took a bite. "Duck? This one…meat pie some kind. Beef, maybe?" He took another bite. "Definitely beef. Lex will be happy with that, at least."

Allegra scraped the crusted old food from her fork with her nail before taking a bite from the stew-like center of the pie. "A bit dry, but well-seasoned. So Lex will be pleased with this, will he?"

"Ha! Those two, Lex and Dodd, would eat the Cathedral out of house and home if they were allowed. I don't know how they do it, especially Lex. Skinny as a bannister's railing, that one."

"Dodd, at least, is broad enough that he has room to hide extra dessert."

Rainier laughed and idle chat soon settled between them about their travel plans for the morning, time they'd be leaving, and the arrival of Allegra's servants. Allegra tried to keep up the courtly manner of speech, but her heart wasn't in it. She was tired from the long journey, and tired just thinking that this was only the first night. She has days, if not weeks, of courtly manners ahead of her.

Captain Rainier didn't seem to mind. He teased her about being changeable, and she defended herself by saying she was simply out of practice.

"Manners are an easy skill to forget when you're used to speaking your mind," she'd said.

"On the contrary, I don't think you rude at all. Passionate, opinionated, *wrong*, but never rude."

"Wrong! How am I wrong?"

"I'll tell you tomorrow in the carriage."

"Why wait?" she challenged, though she was smiling when she said it. She had eaten all of her food, plus one of Rainier's slices of pound cake. He offered her the final piece and she took it. "I love pound cake. I don't let Nadira serve it to me whenever I take my meals in my room."

"Why not?"

"The summer my mother died, the servants did everything they could think of to cheer me up. I ate a lot of pound cake that summer."

"Did it help?"

Allegra snorted. "It helped make me too big to fit into any of my dresses, that's about it. But I always think of that summer, and…I suppose in its own way, the cake helped. Although, it most likely wasn't good for me, eating only that and not much else."

"Maybe not," Rainier said. "Even I have to be careful now with the cake I eat. I'm not as young as I used to be."

"Perhaps you need more practice rescuing princesses from dragons."

Rainier scoffed. "Those damned princesses in stories should have been taught how to hold a sword, then they'd never have needed the princes to rescue them."

"Tut," she said. "How dare you deny young women their passions? Even I, as a young girl, dreamt of being kidnapped by a mythical beast and rescued by the man of my dreams."

"I suspect any dragon who kidnapped you would return you with a gold apology."

Allegra slumped back in her chair and sighed dreamily. "Too bad dragons aren't real, then. I could always use the funds to free more slaves."

"Speaking of, did you notice that little serving girl was a free witch?" Rainier asked between bites.

"Mage," Allegra corrected him. There wasn't any heat in her voice; it was nearly automatic these days. She did flash him a quick smile to say she wasn't angry at his verbal slip. At least, he'd tried on other occasions.

"Mage, right. But did you notice her?"

"Of course I noticed her. I gave her a tip for the inn, and a tip to go in her shoe."

"Oh, that was good of you."

Allegra gave him a steady look. "Tell me you gave her coins, at least, so she could divide them up." He cleared his throat. "Oh, Captain! You know better than that, surely."

"I am out of small coins!" he protested. "All I had was a gold crown."

"You gave her a *gold* crown and nothing else?"

"Do you want me to give her a gold sovereign? Because all I have on me is gold coins, not even silver."

"This is why men should never be allowed to control their money."

"You sound like my mother."

"You mother sounds like a wise woman that I could learn much from."

"She'd likely adopt you," Rainier complained. "Or marry you herself."

Allegra smiled at the idea of Rainier's mother adopting her. She missed her own mother sometimes, but there were benefits to being an orphan on occasion. Still, it would be nice to have an older woman to write who wasn't there to patronize her like the Grand Duchess.

Still, there was a question to answer and anything was better than thinking about her dead mother. "To answer your question, yes, I did notice her. Poor thing."

"Why do you say that?"

"Most likely, she was sold off to some government official because her mother couldn't afford her. Then ran away, paid for her free brand with I don't even wish to consider, and now she's here, serving food. I suppose there are worse fates out there, so…" Allegra shrugged. "As long as they treat her well."

Rainier frowned. "You don't actually believe that happens often."

"Which part?" Allegra asked, confused.

"All of it. Any of it."

Allegra pulled an embroidered cloth from the hidden pocket within her voluminous skirts to wipe her fingers. "Of course it happens. A poor mother with too many mouths to feed and a husband who won't keep his hands off her is common enough. She can barely feed the ones she has, and even the little ones are off earning a penny or two a day to keep the family solvent."

"I…"

"She's not had her cycle in months because she's starving, and then realizes too late she's actually quickened with a new child. So now she can't even cease her pregnancy because all options will most likely kill her at this stage. So, what does she do, Captain?"

"I…"

"I'll tell you what she does. She takes the youngest one who could conceivably be tainted with magic abilities to a local magistrate. Says the babe caught the curtains on fire the previous night. Hands her over. A silver crown graces the mother's palm for bringing such a dangerous case to their attention. Well, that silver coin will pay for her birthing, and the early days when she will be too weak to work. Her husband might not even notice he's missing a daughter. Females all look the same to men, do we not, Captain?"

"What foolishness. I don't think that way about women. I doubt anyone of sense does."

"Then you're an idiot with his head buried in the trees because that is how the world sees poor women."

Rainier produced his own handkerchief to wipe the grease off his fingers. "You can't actually believe any of that. Very few parents willingly give up their children."

"You were born into wealth and privilege. How would you know?"

"I could say the same for you, *Contessa* of Marsina, perhaps the richest woman in all of Serna who isn't a member of a royal family!"

"What rot!" Allegra said, throwing her handkerchief on the table. "I have made it my life's business to learn about how the other side lives. Surely you could have done the same!"

It was his turn to throw down his handkerchief. "Of course! Yours is the only interpretation of events! For your next lecture, shall you teach us how we are all fools to believe in the teachings of the Cathedral?"

She threw up her hands. "Well, you are a fool if you believe the nonsense about the origins of mages!"

"Then I am a fool because I believe the teachings."

Shouting from beyond the room interrupted their argument. Rainier stood just as someone pounded on the door. He opened it to find the servant girl they'd been arguing about.

"Captain Rainier?"

"What's going on?"

"You need to come, sir. There's men down below trying to arrest a witch and...just come and help, sir. Please."

CHAPTER FIVE

"STAY HERE," STANTON order the Contessa, and hoped she'd actually obey the instruction. He followed the young servant down the narrow, wooden stairs to the tavern below. "What happened?"

"Magistrate's men," she said in a quavering voice. Even in the dim candlelight of the stairwell, she was visibly trembling.

"This happen often?"

"More these days," she said. They rounded the turn in the stairs and she pointed down at the scene. "They're after her."

Her was a frightened-looking woman of about forty. She wore tan trousers and black boots, along with an embroidered white tunic and a gray greatcoat. Her narrow, close-set eyes darted their gaze back and forth about the room, though she didn't move from her position pinned up against the wall behind a vacated table.

In front of the woman stood Lex with his sword drawn in one hand and a bottle in the other. Lex's jacket was flung over a nearby chair, but it was still obvious he was a part of the Cathedral's military to anyone with a clue.

Flanking Lex was Dodd, sword also drawn. He held a wooden serving platter in his other hand as a shield. He was still wearing his jacket, clearing showing his rank.

Stanton wasn't wearing his jacket that identified his rank or position within the Cathedral's military, but Dodd and Lex's were on display. He hoped that would be enough to stop further escalation.

In a quiet voice, Stanton said, "Girl, go back to my room and get my sword belt. It's on the bed."

"Yes, sir."

Stanton didn't like charging into a fight with no uniform, no weapon, and nothing but good trousers and boots to identify him as a gentlemen. Stanton squared his shoulders and thudded more heavily than was strictly necessary down the stairs and bellowed, "What is the problem here?"

The beaked-nosed fellow didn't turn to look at Stanton. "None of your business, sir. Back to your room. We're dealing with this."

Dodd merely stretched his sword out just a touch more. "Back away and no one gets hurt."

"Not until you give us the witch," snarled one of the attackers. The attacker was average. Average height, average age, average weight. His hair was light brown, as was his skin, though it was from sun exposure and not nature. He was holding a sword on Dodd, and was backed up by six thugs.

"She's not going anywhere," Lex said in a low growl.

Stanton hit the last step. "You're pointing weapons at two of my men. So, no, I don't believe you are dealing with the situation. Lower your weapons immediately and I will not need to report this to the Chief Justice of Borro, who happens to be a personal friend."

The fellow sneered. "You ain't in Borro County anymore. Nat's Crest is Queen Portia's town." He bared his teeth. "Now, get lost, *sir*."

Stanton didn't move. He had lost track of his surroundings travelling in the carriage and had forgotten Nat's Crest was divided between two nations; they must have been on Cartossa's side. Ruled by the teenaged Queen Portia, Cartossa was heavily under the influence of General Bonacieux. A man whose hatred and fear of witches made Cartossa the epicenter of brutality against mages, even free ones. Most of the Cathedral believed General Bonacieux would be the spark that would start the war everyone was trying to avoid.

"Queen Portia is still under Cathedral law," Stanton said. "You will tell me what is going on here or I will report you to Chief Justice Andrewson, who I will *make* a personal friend of mine."

"Report?" one of the thugs in the rear said. "We're on important business for the magistrate, sir. You've got no say in this."

"Shut up, Jenkins," the beak-nosed man said. "Go back to your room, sir. This doesn't concern you. I won't tell you again."

Lex tightened his grip on his weapons. "They're saying she's an illegal mage."

Stanton took a couple more steps forward. He noticed the servant on the stairs with his sword, but he gave her a small signal to stay put for now.

"She got the tattoos and papers to say she's free," Dodd added. "But they won't leave her be."

"Witches aren't free in Cartossa," the head ruffian said.

"The law disagrees!" Lex snapped back.

Stanton's heart pumped hard in his chest, but he kept his voice calm and stern. By his estimation, there were forty people total in this room. A brawl in tight quarters such as this could result in several unintentional deaths. He had no wish for innocents to be harmed, and that included the witch.

"If she has her papers, by Cathedral law you cannot arrest her," Stanton said. "Are you working for a magistrate who is ordering you to break Cathedral law? Or are you lying and simply think you can harass an innocent woman without repercussions?"

"Witches are never innocent!" the beak-nose man said. "A noble's house was burned to the ground two weeks ago by witch bitches like her."

"I wasn't even in Cartossa two weeks ago, you filthy bastard!" the woman shrieked. "Just let me go!"

"You'll be going to a silver mine drugged out of your mind," the Jenkins fellow said. "Nowhere else for a witch bitch killer."

"Is there any evidence she has anything to do with these attacks?" Stanton took another step, veering toward a vacated tables where cards and bottles rested. "Arresting free mages is expressly against Cathedral law."

In fact, it was one of the edicts the Council of Cardinals put forward almost a year ago in hopes of stemming the harassment of free mages. It had always been an unspoken law, but now it was official. These men were breaking a Holy Writ; they weren't just breaking a law, they were breaking the laws of the Lord Almighty.

This was why an active Arbiter of Justice was so necessary, Stanton thought bitterly. If the Contessa would simply accept the role she'd been offered, she could step into this situation, render her decision, and all parties would have to honor it.

"What is your name?" Stanton asked the accused mage, taking two steps closer to her.

It had been a long time since Stanton had been in a tavern brawl. Lex and Dodd had the advantage on him if the situation escalated further. Stanton carefully raised his hands out to his sides to show he had no weapons or tricks up his blousy sleeves. In doing so, he was able to turn closer to the table littered with abandoned mugs, plates, and a large metal pitcher. The table's former occupants were most likely among the men and women pressed up against the far wall under the stairs.

"Not any further," the man said in a deadly voice. He didn't move his sword from Dodd, but he extended his free arm to point at Stanton. "Who in the abyss do you think you are?"

He looked at the witch when he spoke. "I'm Captain Stanton Rainier, of the Holy Father's Own Consorts. These are my men, Lieutenants Dodd and Lex. I am escorting a very important individual to Orsini Palace to meet with the Holy Father. I am keenly aware of your rights as a...mage." She gave him a very slight acknowledgment. He looked at the man he supposed led the merry band of idiots. "Name?"

"Matthews. I work for Sir Bertrand, the magistrate for Montfort County. Which is where we are, since we're all in Cartossa right now and not on the bleeding heart side of Amadore." He pointed at the woman. "I'm not leaving until I arrest her."

"I've done nothing wrong!" she shouted at them.

"You're not in a mine," Matthews said. "That's crime enough."

"You're not taking her," Lex growled.

"You'll be coming through us first," Dodd said. "And good luck with that, Sparky."

Stanton cautiously lowered his hand until he touched the back of a chair. He curled his fingers between the framing. "Let us discuss this like…"

Stanton was going to say gentlemen, but the man standing next to Jenkins threw a bottle at Dodd. He blocked it with his serving platter, shattering the neck. Glass shards sprayed the air in an arc. The bottle hit the floor and cracked more.

Blood trickled down Dodd's face where several slivers hit him. "Bastard!"

Dodd lunged at Matthews, just as Matthews came in with a high slash. Dodd managed to parry in time, and then the real fight began.

Stanton looked over at the stairs, but the serving girl was gone. As was his sword she was carrying. He muttered darkly under his breath and picked up the chair he'd been holding. He smashed it over a sword-wielding woman's back. She was taller than he was, and he wasn't ever going to be considered a petite man. The chair didn't break, but the woman let out a groan and fell to the tavern floor.

"Stay down!" Lex shouted at the witch over the fighting. The man working the meat spit in front of the fireplace grabbed the woman by the arm and pulled her back next to him. He picked up the iron poker and stood firm behind Lex.

Dodd was hacking away at Matthews, spinning, pivoting, and turning as needed. Dodd might have been built like an ale barrel, but he was a gentleman's son. He knew how to use a sword.

Stanton couldn't help, however, since he had his own troubles. Jenkins rushed him with a club, and Stanton only had a chair. Skilled swordsmen and experienced field soldier he was; tavern brawler he was not.

"Let me piss on those boots!" Jenkins taunted.

Jenkins' swing was weak, and Stanton deflected the blow easily with the chair. Jenkins grabbed one of the legs, all the while swinging at Stanton's head. For a little guy, Jerkins had a good reach on him, but Stanton was able to lean back enough to avoid being whacked repeatedly in the head. He jerked the chair. Jerkins stumbled, and Lex helpfully tried to break a bottle over his head. The bottle remained intact, but Jenkins hit the floor with a surprised exhalation. He didn't get back up. Lex turned back to fighting off anyone who got too close to the mage.

Stanton rushed Matthews, who was holding his own against Dodd still, and hit him square in the ribs with the chair legs. There was a crack, and Stanton assumed it was ribs and not the chair as Matthews crumpled to the floor holding his torso.

Lex and one of the older male servants who'd jumped over the bar were fighting off three men with various weapons. Stanton raised his chair to strike the closest to him when a firm, clear feminine voice cut through the air.

"Enough!"

Chair still raised above his head, Stanton snapped his head around to see the Contessa walking down the stairs. She carried his sword belt clenched in one hand, but it was clear she was only carrying it and not intending to use it.

"Put your weapons down," she ordered.

Her voice was merciless. Gone was the woman he'd been arguing with earlier, or the laughing woman he'd shared a carriage with. This was the Contessa of Marsina, a woman of power and authority, and when she spoke, she expected the world would listen.

Stanton eyed the mercenaries. They hadn't put away their weapons, but they had lowered them. They stared at her with a combination of fear and awe. Even if they didn't know who she was, it was obvious she was important and angering her would bring down no end of trouble upon their heads—sanctioned arrest or not.

She ignored him and walked down the last few steps. She stepped over Jenkins' moaning form, not even bothering to look down to ensure she was clearing his limbs, and the dazed man yanked his hand back inches before her heeled boot slammed down on fragile bones.

She glanced at Stanton and gave him an emotionless once-over that made him feel rather self-conscious. He was, after all, sweating, panting, and holding a chair at chest-level, ready to use it as a battering ram. The Contessa handed him his sword and then walked to the back of the tavern where the witch hid behind Lex.

Stanton shouted, "Everyone, weapons away! This is…"

"I can speak for myself, Captain."

ALLEGRA HAD WATCHED the scene unfold from the upper stairs with increased anger. How dare they violate Cathedral law by arresting an innocent mage? How dare they come into this public place and start a brawl, all in the name of justice? This is why there was already a mage rebellion happening, even if no one wanted to admit it. *This* right here was why. *This* right here was why peace was impossible now.

As a noble, she'd heard the horrible tales of her peers being attacked. Their fields burned. Animals slaughtered in their barns. Estates burgled and priceless artifacts destroyed or stolen. She never cared about those the way she cared about this stranger. For when her peers were attacked, she always asked herself: *and how many slaves did he own?* Too often, they deserved whatever the rebelling mages did to them. And likely even more.

Allegra swept through the tavern barely saying a word. Her hands were shaking, though it wasn't all from the fear of walking into a swordfight. The elemental magic within her blood, her innate desire to create fire, swelled and boiled. She pulled on her earliest secret lessons to control herself, and pushed the fire deep into her soul.

While the magic itself was forbidden, she knew how to harness its raw power in other ways. She used it as fuel for the authority in her voice and the hatred in her eyes.

"Are you well?" Allegra asked the mage.

The woman's cheeks were streaked with tears, and she could only give the barest of nods.

Allegra turned back to the mercenaries. "I am Allegra, Contessa of Marsina. Who is in charge? You?"

Matthews nodded, wincing with each breath. "Your Ladyship, we're here to collect the bounty on this witch's head, as is my right—"

"Stop speaking," Allegra said coldly.

"She's a witch," he spat out the word.

Lex sidled up next to Allegra, sword extended. "The Contessa said to stop speaking."

"What crime has this woman committed, beyond an accident of birth?" When he didn't answer immediately, she said, "You will answer my question."

"Fucking around with demons isn't no accident, *Your Ladyship*," he said sourly.

Allegra's heart pounded at the slur. How often she'd heard that cursed justification for the persecution of mages throughout her life. She wanted to slap the man for every single slight ever said against her, but instead she intertwined her fingers tightly in front of her.

"I am a mage, and I can assure you I have not *fucked* around with any demons." She thrust as much venom into the vulgarity as she could.

Matthews twitched, but had the good sense to remain silent. Even Dodd glanced at her, eyes wide in surprise. No one ever expected a lady of rank to utter vulgarities.

"Since mages are apparently not allowed to be free in Cartossa, contrary to Cathedral law, are you going to arrest me?" She took another step forward. "Shall I, too, be shackled? Which of you will claim me as your prize? The great Contessa of Marsina was captured by your mighty hand. Surely that would garner you a substantial reward. What? No one has anything to say? No one wants to step forward and slap ropes upon my wrists?"

"The magistrate is offering a silver crown for every witch," Matthews wheezed. "We're just doing our jobs."

She held her hands out, palms up. "Then, by all means, do your job."

Captain Rainier, Dodd, and Lex stepped in front of Allegra, swords all drawn. Rainier, in a low, dangerous voice, said, "Touch her and die."

It took Allegra a moment to regain her voice after Rainier's warning. She'd not expected any of them to defend her so willingly. In any other circumstance, she might have smiled.

"You see," Allegra said, eyeing the three men protecting her, "we, all of us, know this is illegal. You've gotten away with it until now because you harass anonymous women travelling alone at night, but we both know I'm not just some woman. I am a contessa, childhood friend to His Radiance the Holy Father himself. I am travelling with an armed guard. There's more outside, with the baggage. Did you realize that? You see, no one bothered to call for the rest of my help since these three were more than capable of handling a bunch of back alley rats looking for a quick meal on the back of an innocent woman." Allegra's voice turned to a growl when she said, "I will not permit it."

Matthews glared at Allegra, but remained silent.

"This is Montfort County, isn't it? My cousin is the Duke of Montfort's mistress. I believe I shall write her a letter, detailing the abominable treatment I've received at the hands of thugs hired by a nothing magistrate, who suggested I consorted with demons from the abyss." Allegra returned his glare. "Would you like me to do that?"

Matthews shook his head. "That's not needed, Your Ladyship."

"Good." Allegra straightened. "Go back to your little master and tell him I will report him to the authorities as soon as I arrive at Orsini Palace. Pray he escapes their long reach. Now leave my sight."

The man looked like he was about to protest, but Dodd's protective sword and Lex's firm stance shielding the mage was enough to announce there was no negotiating out of this situation. There were a few "you'll pay for this" and "she's going to regret that" but they were empty words. The thugs tossed their chairs down, kicked tables, and smashed bottles on the floor before leaving, but they left.

Allegra released her breath only when the door slammed behind them. She had never, in her entire life, ever behaved with such reckless abandon to her personal safety. There were blades out everywhere. Those men could have arrested her and she'd be dead in a gutter before the dawn sun rose. They could have killed Rainier, or Lex, or Dodd, and then she'd be alone. The other guards outside? Maybe they were at the brothel. Maybe they were dead. She didn't know and she'd put herself in danger.

She pressed a hand against her corseted torso and took even, steady breaths to calm herself. She could have lost control of herself. Then what? Then she would have been arrested lawfully. What was she thinking? Was she even thinking?

"Contessa?" Rainier asked very gently. He didn't touch her. Just stood close, sword still in hand. "Are you well?"

Allegra ignored his question for fear she'd start crying in the middle of the tavern. She turned to the woman at the center of all this and asked in a whisper, "Where are you headed?"

"Jennings, Your Ladyship."

Allegra wished to ask more, but her courage was failing. As she gathered herself to finish the conversation, Rainier stepped in to help.

"Are you alone?" he asked.

"My maidservant is asleep upstairs and my two footmen are with the carriage."

"What is your name?" Dodd asked.

"Mrs. Patricia Ansley, sir. Thank you so much for your heroic assistance. I am..." She began to weep. "Thank you."

Lex awkwardly patted her shoulder. "There, there."

Allegra drew in a deep breath and said, "I extend our protection for the remainder of your journey. We are travelling to Orsini, so we can escort you back across the border in the morning."

"Thank you," she whispered through her sobs.

Allegra's vision blurred and she struggled to breathe past the lump in her throat. Beads of sweat formed along the length of her spine. The fear and the anxiety had finally caught up.

"Your Ladyship, are you all right?" Lex asked, concern lacing his voice.

Allegra gasped for air. She had never been this afraid in her life. What if they had arrested her? She could never have allowed them to take her, and then she'd have to show her magic. Allegra had fine control over her abilities, but she had never used them against anyone in her life. Would she accidentally kill them? If she had, she would have been a murderer.

"Contessa?"

Allegra looked up at Rainier and wondered how the Captain would have reacted. Would he have arrested her immediately? Would his sword now be covered in her blood?

He reached out to touch her arm gently, but she flinched away. She managed to squeak out, "Please ensure Mrs. Ansley's safety. Excuse me."

Allegra had made more graceful exits, but she prided herself for not having rushed up the stairs in a flurry of petticoats and screams. She reached her bedchamber and shut the door behind her. She flipped the latch lock and leaned against the door, panting from the relief of being alone.

Her hand shook, and she curled a tight fist in hopes to contain the tremors. Instead, her palm grew warm to the touch. She had not meant to get into a standoff with armed thugs. She had not mentally prepared herself for the aftershocks. She was now paying for those choices.

She gritted her teeth, pushing down the after rush that always came with being mentally unprepared. Damn them all into the abyss! This was why she hid in her obscure country abbey away from court politics. This was why she rarely left the abbey. All of the education and wealth in the world could not protect her if she did not protect herself.

And there she was, unprotected, in the middle of a damned room full of people.

But what was she supposed to do? Hide? Let others get hurt, even possibly killed, because she refused to use her power and consequence? Why else be born into wealth and privilege if not to help?

She stared at her hand and knew her title could only protect her so far. She'd pushed herself to the limits of what she could manage, and she had nearly exposed herself. If she did, she couldn't help anyone.

Damn them into the abyss; they were harassing an innocent mage. Little made her blood boil more than seeing one of her own kind tortured for no other reason than existing.

Yet, what would they do if they discovered what kind of mage she actually was? No weaving simple spells into embroidery. No basic spells of protection or speeding healing. She could create fire and, if the world knew, she'd be drugged and beaten before being dragged off in shackles and chains, off to languish in a mine with the rest of her kind.

Would Lieutenant Dodd still protect her with his life? Would Lieutenant Lex stand at her side, or would he use the opportunity to tackle her to the floor? What would Captain Rainier do? Would he have asked her gently to stand down, as a woman of rank, or would he have treated her like a drunken horse thief in a back alley?

"Lord God Almighty, I am thankful you do not exist," Allegra snarled, cupping her burning hand against her stomach. "Because if you did, I would despise you for this life!"

Unable to hold back the magic inside her, Allegra thrust her hand at the fireplace. She sent all of her fears and anger out past her fingertips. Fire erupted and the controlled blast hit the wood in the fireplace. It blazed to life, the heat so intense her eyes watered in response.

With the release, the flame on her hand died away. Allegra sagged against the bedpost, exhausted. She stared at her hand. It tingled, as it always did, but there was no other damage. She hadn't caught her clothes on fire since she was a teenager. She knew her limits, and knew when she needed to relieve the tension.

She focused on the fire she'd created. The wood in the fireplace cracked and popped, and blue flame flickered in the dark. She had been under undo stress from the journey, she told herself. Moments before the fight had broken out, she had been arguing with Captain Rainier. That had been a mistake. She should have not done that. She should have kept her mouth shut and…

"Contessa?" It was the Captain, knocking gently at her door. "May I come in?"

She didn't answer. He had been the reason she'd lost her temper in the first place. She needed to calm herself just a moment longer and…

"Contessa, please. Are you well?"

Of course she wasn't well! She had never been in the midst of a brawl before, and there were swords drawn. Actual swords! She wiped her sleeve across her forehead, mopping up the sweat. Her sleeve came back covered in soot.

His voice was gentler. "Please, simply tell me you are well."

Her heart sank from guilt. He sounded genuinely worried. She was, after all, his charge and he was probably worried sick that she'd charged in the midst of a sword fight and was now hiding in her bedchamber like a frightened little girl.

How she had humiliated herself. Allegra prided herself in being strong and fierce in the face of all adversity. She chided herself for having buckled under the pressure. There was no possible way she could become an arbiter of anything, least of all justice. She would have to shut herself away to survive that posting, more so than she already did.

"Just…hold on," she gasped out the words as she desperately searched for something to scrub her face with.

In the end, she used the inside of her pelisse. She splashed water on her face and the silk lining of her coat was a relief against her flushed skin. She flipped the garment over on her bed, so that the stain would be unnoticeable. Allegra sucked in a couple of deep breaths before marching over to the door and unlocking it.

"Hello, Captain," she said, braving a smile.

"The commotion is over, and the witch…the mage. I keep forgetting, I'm sorry. She's in her room. Lex and the lady's maid are sleeping in her room. Dodd and one of the servants from the tavern are sleeping just outside her door. The stable boy moved her carriage closer to ours, so that her footmen can guard the corridor. She'll be safe tonight." He smiled. "So, now I'm here to check on my charge."

Allegra's smile was shaky, but she forced it out all the same. "Rattled, but well."

"May I come in? We still have an argument to finish."

"Oh. I'd forgotten." Allegra glanced around, ensuring there was no evidence of losing her temper. The fireplace and her pelisse where the only things she could see. She shouldn't let him in. She should tell him she was tired or her nerves were vexed, and leave it be.

Allegra couldn't force the refusal out, however, for she wanted him to join her. She wanted to resume normality as soon as possible. And, though she was loathed to admit it, she didn't want to be alone, no matter how much she should be.

"Ah, I am intruding. I apologize. I will leave you to your privacy."

"Wait," Allegra said, not running the reply by her brain first. She sighed. "Company would do me good."

"I promise to be on my best gentlemanly behavior."

He walked into the room and she closed the door behind him. "If you don't mind, what I need more than that is…simple conversation. No mages, no politics. Just the simple things."

"I can do that." Rainier sat down in his chair. He glanced at the fire and asked, "Are you cold?"

Allegra was fortunate to have been facing away when he asked the question. Her face didn't betray her. She sucked in a deep breath and said, "I'm a fine lady, Captain. Servants think I'm always cold, even during the tail end of summer in the lowlands." She faced him and smiled. "Rank comes with so many oppressions."

"Indeed it does," he said. "Will you sit?"

She nodded and they sat once more to drink their ales. Gone was the heat and passion for justice from before, however. Allegra was too exhausted. There was no way she could accept Francois's offer. He'd not offered it seriously, in any case, and while her contrary nature ached to accept it out of spite, tonight was an indicator that she was not ready for the center dais of attention. Most likely, she would never be ready for it, and that was fine by her.

"What is your favorite fruit pie?" the Captain asked.

Allegra chuckled at his transparent attempt at non-controversial topics. "Blueberry and apple. And yours?"

"I don't know what it's called in the south, but back home it's called Duchess Anne's pie. I think it's apples, pears, raisins. Maybe figs? Then they add all of these spices to it and put in a buttery pastry, and bake it. It's really quite good."

"I should ask the Abbey's cook to make it for me sometime."

"You should," Captain Rainier said with a gentle smile.

She hated running scared. It irked her to hide, but her pride and reputation were small things to sacrifice in the face of the reality of a shortened life in the mines. Her hands were better used writing letters than channeling elemental powers to blast through rock for another man's profit. So she would let this pass to another's lot, and pray it was someone who was as capable as she knew she actually was.

Still, better hiding under a blanket than crushed to death under iron ore.

CHAPTER SIX

THE QUIET EVENING with Captain Rainier, a full stomach, and a roaring fire stealing away the dampness of the room turned out to be just what the apothecary would have ordered. Allegra slept soundly, and woke with a renewed sense of vigor when Nadira knocked on the door, announcing it was time to rise.

Allegra padded over to the locked door on her tip-toe, avoiding any splinters from the rough wooden floorboards. She opened the door and was greeted by a curt nod from her servant. Nadira thrust a steaming mug of tea at Allegra, who accepted it gratefully. The brown tea with cream and honey surprised her taste buds. She hadn't expected that in a simple inn.

As Allegra sipped, Nadira placed a small plate of cold ham, kippers, bread, and preserves down on the small table.

Once the hot drink woke her up, it was set aside while Allegra tended to her bladder. Then, she tackled the kippers while Nadira checked over the other layers of Allegra's outfits. Nadira shook out her mistress's dress from the previous day, inspecting it for any mending requirements. She returned the chamberpot to its spot in the corner, draping the cloth back over it. When Nadira nodded she was ready, Allegra put down her mug and kippers and the women got to work.

A quick wash in cold water was surprisingly refreshing after the heat of the previous night. Allegra used a clean, linen cloth to rub her maid's "secret" mixture of salt-mint-cloves into her gums. Nadira then handed her a small bottle and Allegra rinsed her mouth with the vinegar mixture with bits of mint and fennel floating in it. She spit out the mixture into her dirty wash water.

Once hygiene was taken care of, Allegra peeled out of the shift from the previous day—she'd also slept in it—and Nadira pulled a clean one over her head. Allegra held the bedpost as Nadira laced her into the corset. High fashion these days took on an odd chest-flattening cut, which just displaced one's breasts elsewhere. Some of the larger women in the new fashions appeared to be unable to bend over, lest they smother in their own cleavage. Allegra was happy for her own more modest chest whenever Nadira strapped her into the new style of corset.

Petticoat was next, then the panniers on either side of her hips to flare out her dress. These weren't the outrageous ones for balls; just simple ones to give her outfit slightly exaggerated curves.

Nadira asked, "Do you wish the pockets today, Your Ladyship?"

"Please."

Nadira tied the long straps around Allegra's waist, the large cloth pockets hanging on either side, accessible through the invisible slits in the seams of Allegra's dresses. Thought they were unseen by the world, Allegra had stitched strawberries on each pocket and had weaved a spot of magic into them against holes and thieves.

The dress came next. The dress from the previous day was still clean, and Nadira helped pin and button it into place.

"How do you want your hair today, Your Ladyship?"

"Just in a side braid. I can do that myself."

Nadira nodded and picked up the pelisse that was draped over one of the chairs. She gasped when she saw the soot stain.

"One of those grubby girls must have touched it. This will take an hour to scrub out. Oh, and it's on the silk embroidery, too. Thoughtless little scum." Nadira glared at it. "Has it ruined the spells you think? What if you become chilled in the evenings now?"

Allegra felt very wise in keeping her confession to herself. "I doubt it, but I will add a little extra work to it once we return to the Abbey."

Allegra sat at the tiny dressing table in the far corner of the room. She untied the sleeping braid in her hair and ran her fingers through her thick, wavy hair as best as she could before retying it into a thick braid that hung over one shoulder. She opted not to wear her hat and instead would carry it.

She didn't finish her meal, so Nadira packed up the ham and the bread into a clean handkerchief for Allegra to eat later. She did, however, finish her tea and it quenched the parched sensation in her throat.

"Have the rest of the kippers if you are hungry," Allegra said.

"Thank you, Your Ladyship. Is there anything else?" Allegra shook her head. "Then I shall pack your luggage. Would you like to wait downstairs?"

Allegra did, and she took her hat with her. All the while, Allegra kept her focus on the day at hand and not the lingering self-doubts from the previous evening.

Allegra covered the costs of damages to the inn's tavern. The owners said they could redress the costs through the magistrate, but Allegra insisted. She slipped them three silver sovereigns, which would adequately cover the furniture repairs and the several bottles of poor quality gin that had been spilled in the brawl. Though, losing that foul soup was probably a blessing upon society.

She strolled about the grounds, watching the stable boys leading horses this way and that. Maids were busy rushing about from the water pump back inside, and the chickens were busy eating pebbles and bugs.

She made a final trip to the outhouse, once more avoiding having to face the threat of poison oak in some random, roadside woods. She stepped out of the outhouse and smoothed down her dress. Her carriage had been pulled out, so she headed toward it.

Lex waved at her and said, "Good morning, Your Ladyship! Good weather today."

Allegra gave him a polite nod. "Very much so."

"Dodd will be down with Mrs. Ansley in a bit, if you wanted to talk with her."

"I'm sure Mrs. Ansley has plenty on her mind without me interfering."

"As you say, Your Ladyship," Lex said, smiling as he inclined his head. He went back to bossing around stable boys and other junior members of her guard, who she hadn't been introduced to yet.

Allegra stepped into her carriage and decided to give Captain Rainier the prized forward-facing seat. He had given her the forward facing seat yesterday, as any man of rank would do. Allegra decided to test out her theory that he had more than mere country estate gentility in his bloodline.

It was a harmless prank and Allegra needed something fun to keep her mind off the previous day's events. They'd hopefully chuckle and squabble and it would keep her mind active, and needling the good captain seemed like an excellent diversion. Plus, she knew she could talk about rank and privilege, of mages and slavery, until she was blue in the face and never lose her magical temper. More than anything, that was what she needed today.

She was already regretting the journey to the Cathedral and wished she'd just outright refused Rupert's invitation. But he hadn't invited her as a friend; he'd invited her as His Radiance, Holy Father Francois. Perhaps she could extort some assistance from him for having dragged her all this way.

Allegra watched the servants rush around loading their luggage back on to the carriages. The others were all up now, and even Mrs. Ansley walked by, though she didn't notice Allegra. That was fine; she didn't want to converse with the woman. She wanted to offer her protection, yes, but in case Mrs. Ansley was really an elemental, Allegra didn't want to risk raising anyone's suspicions about herself. It was paranoid, and normally she wouldn't have minded meeting another mage, but not this morning.

Mrs. Ansley's carriage was obviously not as fine as Allegra's, but it was clearly a new purchase. Likewise, her dress and pelisse were of lesser quality, but still new and in fashion. Mrs. Ansley clearly wasn't poor. Allegra wondered why they went after a woman who could afford her own carriage and traveling servants. The little servant girl would have been a better target.

Allegra frowned. The little girl *was* the best target. Who would have stood up for a girl of dubious origins with an even more dubious status? She was prime for the taking and easy money at that for the guards. Maybe she really did need to speak with Mrs. Ansley.

Captain Rainier interrupted Allegra's thoughts. The carriage rocked when he hauled himself up. He stopped in time not to swing himself in and sit on her, but he pivoted so hard that his knee wobbled. He managed not to fall, but it was close.

She smiled demurely at him and motioned at the prized seat. "For you, Captain." He glared at her, and she struggled to maintain her serene expression. "As repayment for your kindness last evening."

He eyed her, still balancing with one hand on the doorway. "Contessa, I cannot take the forward seat."

"I had it yesterday. You can have it today."

"It's not gentlemanly to sit forward when a lady is stuck travelling backwards." He quirked a smile. "A lady must always travel forward."

Allegra snorted. "Sit yourself down before I make the footman push you in."

"He can try," Rainier said, but he took the forward seat. He wore his sword belt today and made no attempt to remove it for comfort. "You'll be pleased to know Mrs. Ansley has joined our procession."

Allegra forced a smile. "I am glad, and thank you for humoring my request."

"I would have offered myself, if you'd given me the opportunity," he said with an easy smile. The carriage lurched as they began their second day of travel. "Did you know Mrs. Ansley runs a lacemaking cooperative?"

"I thought most lacemakers worked at home," Allegra said idly. She pulled at a wayward thread in the carriage's padding. She really had to arrange new upholstery. This was simply shabby.

"She owns small shops where lacemakers work for her. She hires a girl to look after the little ones, and she has all of the supplies on site. Then, she pays the women for their work, and sells the lace herself. Buying wholesale like she does keeps her costs down, so she's able to make a tidy profit and pay better wages than the women can make individually."

"What's she doing here then?"

"Apparently, she owns several shops and came to sell all of her interests in Cartossa. Her workers here in Montfort were being harassed and the magistrate was doing nothing to help. She said she's going to concentrate on her cooperatives on the Amadore side of the border where her people aren't being harassed nearly as much. Shame, really. It's an interesting idea, don't you think?"

The carriage pulled away from the small lane where the inn was located and headed towards Cathedral Way.

"It is very interesting, and it's barbaric that a legitimate business cannot operate."

She considered this history. Would the lacemaking have caused her to be targeted? Why wouldn't they have done it while she was in her shop, as opposed to in a roadside tavern? She mentally shook her head. There was a reason Mrs. Ansley was targeted. Of that, she was certain.

Her heart began pounding hard at the memory of the previous night. Wanting to avoid reliving her experiences, she gave Rainier a little smirk. "Shall we resume our argument from last night? Sadly, you will not have a brawl to save you this time."

He snorted, but stayed silent.

"Nothing from the good Captain?" Allegra chuckled. "Perhaps it's just as well. Still, I am disappointed. Harassing anyone for being a mage goes against Cathedral law."

"Their actions, though wrong, are…" He cleared his throat. "Reflections of people's faith."

"What complete and utter gutter rot," Allegra blurted without thinking. She caught herself and snickered. "You said that on purpose, didn't you?"

"Of course I did, but I do believe some of it."

"Some of what?"

"I do believe mages, as you call them, are dangerous. Yes, we all take advantage of the benefits of magic. I myself wear a protection amulet." He pointed at the decorative brooch on his sash. "All of my buttons are enchanted with healing, enough to keep me alive until a surgeon can stitch me back up. The braids on the jacket are embroidered with warmth, to help protect me from the cold." He sighed. "But you and I are educated. We understand how magic can assist our lives. Mrs. Ansley is a mage, and is running very successful businesses, and she does that in spite of her magic. However, it's only natural that people would fear her."

She regretted the topic now. She didn't think anyone should fear her for being a mage. Fear her power and influence, but not her ability to weave magic. As long as she didn't hurt people, what harm was she doing by existing?

Still, Rainier was only spouting what was said in the pulpit. She tried not to reduce her opinion of him. She failed a little in that endeavor. "What is your solution then?"

"Continue to educate mages, just as the Cathedral is doing. Improving their lot will improve people's general opinion of them."

Allegra thought back to the priest's letter. "A commoner's ability to scrawl their name on a piece of paper is hardly an education. I have tried, Captain, to improve education and have had my money repeatedly diverted to furnishings for gluttonous priests."

"Surely the Cathedral-run schools offer a decent education," Rainier said.

"Some do," Allegra admitted. "Some are ran by people who genuinely care about education, who are intelligent enough to grasp that a girl who can do her sums can be hired in a shop, thereby earning a bit more money than scrubbing attic floors." She mumbled, "Not to mention protect her health." In a stronger voice she said, "But there are other children who are passed from school to school, as funding is never consistent, and too many end up in schools ran by those who cannot even read or write themselves."

Rainier frowned. "We do need to do more to stem that abuse."

Allegra nodded. "Yes, we do. If the child has magic, it's possible they will end up in a country estate working on embroidery and knitting, helping create small items of protection and comfort for their masters. Those that do not have talent...well, the lucky ones also end up at those country estates where the food is decent and the water is clean. The worst end up with the elementals in a mine, where the elementals can just kill themselves in a fit of desperation. A normal would have less opportunity." Allegra ran her hand over the satin covering on her carriage's wall. "So that the rest of us can live like queens."

He was silent for a moment before saying, "I believe there are lay sisters and brothers who make my talismans and whatnot. As far as I know, we don't purchase from unknowns in the market."

Allegra didn't look at him. She was too busy looking at her carriage interior. Where did all of her threads come from? What about her fabrics? Were they made by slaves? Were the people who worked on her carriages freemen? She never knowingly hired slave labor, but she also didn't ask that many questions when she needed work done. Just drop the coins and go about her day.

"Did I say something offensive?"

She looked back at him and forced another smile. "Just thinking on your words. The spells in your uniform need to be weaved by someone who wants you safe and who believes in your mission. Otherwise…well…I wouldn't want to stand in front of an arrow if I were you."

Rainier laughed. "I don't plan to stand in front of any arrows wearing this."

"I wonder what you look like in plate."

"Uncomfortable," Rainier said with bark of laughter. "There's a painting of me at the palace. If you have time, I can show it to you."

"Why on earth is there a painting of you?"

"Pero's idea."

Comfortable silence settled between them, though Allegra did wonder why this particular captain deserved his own painting at the palace. Her desire for quiet won over her curiosity, and she enjoyed watching the scenery go by.

It was a cloudy morning still, so the field workers had a reprieve from the sun's punishment. They were out in full force, harvesting the grain. Then they would have to prepare the fields for the over-winter crop. Hopefully, it wouldn't rain anytime soon. She knew none of these workers owned their land; her own tenant farmers didn't own the land they toiled on for generations. She did wonder how many were treated fairly, however.

How she could change this landscape if she were Arbiter. She could bring the princes and viscounts into line, as well as the parliaments and the empresses. All of them she could force to sit at a table until they saw reason. History would remember her in a way she had only ever dreamed. The mage who ended the slave rebellions and who freed her kind.

Allegra knew what a dangerous path those thoughts could lead her on, but they were deliciously tempting. Rupert knew too well what he was about. Never in her life had she been offered such an opportunity to bring mages into safety and freedom.

True freedom and not the patronizing half-life they were actually granted. Some cities huddled free mages into impoverished camps outside of their wealthy walls, where they had to receive permission from the camp guards to leave. And, if caught at the "proper" village without verification of their approved travel, they faced imprisonment.

She'd fix that. She'd make it all illegal. She'd do everything within her power to extend the reach of religious rule and influence to force progress. She would use and abuse the Almighty's name to get everything she...

Rupert knew her too well.

Desperate for a conversation beyond the temptations of her flattered ego, she asked, "Tell me, do you have an enchanted sword?"

Rainier placed a hand on the sheathed weapon. "Yes. It was a gift."

"You are very lucky. What does it do?"

It was his turn to look out the window. "Kill people."

His solemn tone sent shivers throughout her body. She regretted asking him the idle question, as it clearly hit upon some secret pain.

"May I ask you a personal question, Contessa?"

"You are welcome to ask, though there is never a guarantee I will answer." She smiled to let him know she was teasing.

"Why do you hate the faith? There are many versions and interpretations, so if you don't like the popular one, there are other ways to express your beliefs."

Allegra considered not answering the question, but she felt the sting of his earlier comments. Perhaps he wanted to move away from his thoughts, too, just as she wished to not be alone with hers.

"Setting aside that I don't believe in the Almighty, the fundamental reason why I could never belong to the faith is that they do nothing to stop slavery. The ownership of human beings disgusts me. We have conveniently glossed over the passages about the freedom of all under the Almighty's watchful eye, and instead justify all manner of cruelty by saying mages were created by relations with a demon," Allegra snarled. "One line by one Guardian and suddenly all is justified under a sentence that, I'm convinced, is taken out of context."

"What about demons?"

"The only demon in this world a ten-year-old has ever faced is the beast who forces themselves on the innocent, not some mythological creature from the abyss that doesn't even exist." She drew in a breath. "I assume you believe."

Rainier cleared his throat. "I do believe in demons, though I admit I've never believed the theory that current mages have made a deal with them."

"How comforting," Allegra said tonelessly. "I'm glad you don't think I tumbled around in a grassy field with a beast from the pit to gain my talents."

Rainier's jaw clenched, but that was the only reaction he gave. His voice remained steady and assured, not taking her bait. "I won't apologize for my beliefs."

"I didn't ask you to. You're not the first man to think I mate with the creatures from the beyond."

Rainier shifted in his seat. "I do believe magic in all of its forms come from the abyss, but I'm sure these children aren't sitting around cutting themselves and…well, doing unmentionable acts."

"Like fucking in the grass?" Allegra asked sweetly.

Rainier burst into peals of laughter. "Yes, like that. Almighty protect me, I can't believe you said that."

"Are you blushing?" She watched as his cheeks and nose turned darker. The more her smile broadened, the more his cheeks darkened. "You are absolutely blushing. Don't deny it. It's plain as day."

Rainier snickered, an embarrassed tinge to the sound. "That tongue of yours is wicked."

Allegra beamed at him. "I need to talk to Francois about how he's describing me to strangers."

"Absolutely! I thought he was planning to appoint a woman of a *certain* age to this position to write a few letters over the winter and nothing else." Rainier's voice turned husky. "I wasn't expecting a young, beautiful woman." Then, with a smirk, he added, "And one with a filthy, wicked mouth."

"Only when least expected, my dear Captain. A lady must always know when to attack."

"Maybe that's why Francois thinks you could bring a resolution to this growing conflict."

Allegra made a scene of musing on the statement. "Would my solution be peace or a full-scale war?"

"Either would be progress." Rainier shrugged.

"That's cynical."

"Blame it on being a fifth son. Peace means we can all stop fearing the worst. War would mean we could finally stop waiting for the worst to arrive."

Allegra smiled politely and became silent. And this was why she couldn't indulge her ambition nor her ego. It was bad enough that she was a mage, though her rank afforded her endless privileges. One misstep, one accident, and she would be stripped of all her protection. She would be as friendless and helpless as Mrs. Ansley or the serving girl from the inn.

It scared her more than anything, and she couldn't tell him that. Almost no one truly understood the fear mages had. The very few who did and weren't mages were the abolitionists active in the cause, and Captain Rainier was neither mage nor abolitionist.

They filled the emptiness with picking at the leftover food from breakfast. Allegra's heart grew weary. She kept thinking about the previous evening, about how scared she was. Rainier had been kind and his conversation had been a comfort. When she wasn't talking to him, she kept thinking about what happened if she ever lost control. She had always tried to keep that out of her mind, but it was times like these that brought it all storming back.

"You're from Cumberland, aren't you?" Allegra blurted, desperate to talk about anything other than what was floating in her mind.

Rainier's jaw clenched when he answered, "Yes."

"Rainier from Cumberland," she said. "Rainier…I feel like I should recognize the name. Markus has a cousin named Rainier. Are you related to the Earl of Trenholm?"

"No," he said.

"Are you certain we've never met before at a ball? I attended a few as a young girl in Cumberland."

"What were you doing in Cumberland? That's a long way from Marsina."

"I was on tour with my cousin, and you are not going to change the subject," Allegra said, grinning. "Now, will you tell me who you really are, or shall I continue to guess?"

He sighed. "Do you really want to know?"

"I know that we have two more days in this carriage together, so we either find something to talk about or we invite Dodd and Lex in here for company."

"Almighty spare us that fate," he said. He let out a long, suffering sigh, and said, "You'll find out when we reach the Cathedral. Some people know me as the Duke of Barrington."

Allegra's internal temperature soared and her palms instantly became clammy. She squared her shoulders and adjusted her tone to befit speaking to a war hero and a man of *superior* rank. "Your Grace."

"Captain Rainier is fine."

"Your Grace, I had no idea," Allegra continued, ignoring Rainier completely. She had been picking petty fights with one of the most heroic and beloved soldiers in all of Serna. She was going to repeatedly smack Rupert with her fan. She knew her old friend well enough that he would have asked the Duke to hide his identity from her, and she'd fallen for it.

Damn them all to the abyss to languish!

IT WAS MOMENTS like these that Stanton wished there had been a polite way to reject the King of Cumberland's gift of a title and lands. It had been nothing but trouble, and here was yet another fine example.

For all of her faults—for she had many, though he was certain she'd never admit them—the Contessa was someone he enjoyed talking with during this journey, and he thought that, just maybe, they could one day become friends of a sort. She was passionate and entertaining, and he enjoyed having her think he was only her guard. Because, in her eyes, he was only her guard and not a peer from court. And he wanted it to stay that way.

When he couldn't take any more of her rebuking glare, he said, "You seem angry."

"I feel tricked."

"That was never my purpose." He considered his words carefully. "I choose to live as Captain Rainier. I'm happy this way."

She wasn't listening to him. He could see the cogs behind her dark, expressive eyes churning. "Captain Rainier…Rainier…Of course! We all know the name Captain *Stanton* Rainier! Oh, it makes sense now. You choose to go by your last name and not your given. Your Grace, you wound me with this deception."

He already knew her well enough to know that her last sentence was to rankle him. She had a talent for that.

"Contessa, what does it even matter? You are only one rank below me, and you were born into your rank." He snorted, and it was a bitter sound even to his own ears. "I had to be given mine."

She was still staring at him with that stunned expression that he'd seen on so many other faces. Only, hers did not show the potential for expanded wealth if she could convince him of a particular type of alliance, as most people did whenever they discovered the truth. Hers was of embarrassment and humiliation. And, in her voice, there was a touch of self-reproof that he didn't like hearing.

"You earned your rank, Your Grace. You saved the previous Holy Father, and Rupert, and the King of Cumberland! You! In singlehanded combat. You are a true hero and a true gentleman."

"That is a gross fabrication," Stanton swiftly corrected.

Her mouth quirked. "Which part?"

Instead of answering her question, he asked his own, in hopes of irking her. "You aren't used to being told no, are you?"

If she was at all annoyed, she didn't show it. In fact, Stanton guessed she enjoyed being teased. "I was born the eldest daughter of a comte. I have never been told no in my life. Now, you can answer my question or I shall spend the next two days making wild accusations that will make your skin boil until you have to answer me."

He sighed. She really was vying for the title of the most frustrating woman created by the Almighty. He'd thought His Holiness was mad to offer the appointment to this backwater hermit, and he wasn't too proud to admit how laughably wrong his assessment had been of the woman.

The Contessa was not afraid of anything or anyone. He liked her all the more for it. That last thought crossed his mind as his eyes drifted down to the ruffled lace along her dress's low neckline. He blinked and made a show of picking off invisible lint from his trousers.

"Most of what you've heard is most likely a fabrication, or at least an exaggeration," he said, covering up for the fact that he'd been staring at her décolletage.

A terrifying thought crossed his mind. Perhaps Dodd was right and he really did need to get out to the taverns more. What a horrific thought.

If she had noticed him staring, she made no attempt to let him know. "Hmm. Let's see if I remember the story. Grand Duchess Katherine told me all about it."

Stanton groaned at the mention of the Contessa's cousin and his arch nemesis, if a thirty-five-year-old man could have an arch nemesis. His discomfort only brought back the twinkle in her eye, and he smiled in spite of himself. The previous night's brawl had obviously shaken her, and taken much out of her spirits. Though he'd never admit it to her, it did his heart good to see her true smile return. He could let her tease him for a bit if it meant helping her recover.

This was a part of his mission. Butter her up enough to return her to Father Francois with a smile on her face and a spring in her step. Whatever the Holy Father planned for her, her being in a good mood would most likely assist.

"Stanton Rainier, the fifth son of the Marquis of York, from Cumberland. Am I correct so far?"

"Yes," Stanton said through gritted teeth.

"You accepted a minor position at Orsini Cathedral."

"I was Guard Lieutenant with the Cathedral guard," Stanton said. "My job was to escort cardinals and the like travelling around the area."

The Contessa nodded. "Yes, I remember now. Your first ever assignment was to escort Cardinal Rupert, as he was known then, plus the current Holy Father at the time, Father Otto. And who you thought were two cardinals."

Stanton said nothing. He hated this story so much, and he hated even more how they'd exaggerated it over the years. He was not the hero they wanted him to be. If they only knew the humiliating truth of it all: that he had been so scared throughout it all. That he'd pissed himself when the second charge came. That the nightmares never completely faded. There was no healing talisman nor apothecary ointment that could make the inner turmoil go away. He grimaced and waited for her to continue.

"Bandits attacked the caravan and you were the only guard to survive."

"Three others did," Stanton insisted.

"They died. You did not," she said, and her voice was surprisingly gentle. "You managed to hide the priests for two weeks and protected them against repeated attempts to find you."

Stanton rolled his eyes. "Four days. We were in the hills for four days. We found a village and sent for help. It was another week before we were all back at Orsini."

"Seven plus four is, oh...*eleven* days, so let's compromise and say a week and a half."

"It was only four days that I was in any real danger," Stanton insisted.

"Was the village attacked by the bandits while you were there?"

He stared at her for a beat before looking away. He didn't say anything. So many villagers lost their lives when the bandits followed them there. He tried to organize them, help protect them, but...

"Ah," she said, all playfulness gone from her voice. "I suppose the memories are not as pleasant for you to remember as it is for the rest of us to recite. I will stop."

He didn't want it to end on a sour note, so he said, "You haven't gotten to the best part of the story yet, so keep going."

"All right. You eventually arrived back at the Cathedral and discovered, no doubt to your horror, that you'd been escorting the King of Cumberland all that time. He had been travelling to Sutherland to secretly negotiate a peace treaty, which is why your caravan was attacked. The bandits were in fact assassins sent to murder the king."

He'd yelled at the king several times during their flight. At one point, Stanton had screamed at the man to keep his head down and not say a word or he'd leave him behind. He thought he was dealing with a cardinal who'd never picked up a sword in his life. He had no idea he had an actual king, a member of royalty, with him dressed in robes and a fancy hat.

"Horror really is the appropriate word when I found out. You can also add in liquid bowels and sour stomach."

Allegra pressed a hand against her corseted torso and gasped for air, all the while laughter continued to spill from her. "I can only imagine. That's when the Cathedral awarded you their highest honor: the Sword of Tasmin. Oh, that is why you don't wear your honors on your uniform! I wondered where your medals had gone."

"I only wear them at functions and balls," he said flatly. "But go on, keep going. You're not done yet."

"Are you certain? All right. The King of Cumberland was so grateful for your life, and that the act of saving his life allowed peace to be negotiated, he created a new title just for you for the length of your lifetime."

Stanton rolled his eyes once more. "The title is actually hereditary."

"Is it indeed? How lucky for your descendants! And how much land did you get with the appointment?"

Stanton grimaced. "I got Barrington House and its nine thousand acres of land."

"Modest by many measures, but I'm sure you're making due," the Contessa said, grinning.

"Not all of us can own most of Marsina county."

"Tut, this isn't about me."

Stanton leaned forward. "Let's make it about you. Tell me, Contessa, why does one woman have so much land?"

"Because I am very good at business," she said.

"And was business made easier by who you are?"

"Absolutely. You have to spend money to make money. It's significantly easier to do so when you were born rich. So, why did you lie to me?"

"I didn't lie," he said quickly. Damn, she was better at this than he was. "I left off the truth."

"A lie of omission is still a lie in the eyes of the Almighty, is it not?"

He gave her a hard glare. "I'd like to think the Almighty understands."

"But even your name is a lie! We should call you Captain Stanton, but you use Rainier because everyone knows the name Lieutenant Stanton who saved the Holy Father, and if I were to meet a Cathedral guard named Captain Stanton…" A soft chuckle escaped her throat. "You are a hero in the eyes of everyone. Even in my eyes, and I'm not easily impressed."

He let out a heavy sigh. "Do you have any idea what that is like for me? Whenever I enter a room to give advice, it's no longer about security measures and military matters. It is about a young, foolish boy who dragged four injured men through the woods. It is how I carried on my back the King of Cumberland, thinking he was a Cardinal, who'd taken an arrow in the calf. It is all about that, and nothing else." Stanton drew in a breath. "And getting ideas about matching their unwed children to me…or starting an illicit affair."

"Ah. You saw that I was around your age, unwed, and assumed I would also be like that."

"Yes," he said honestly, without any shame in his voice.

"I am not like that," she said.

"I know. *Now.*"

She grinned at him. "We have finally found common ground, Captain. Being embarrassingly wealthy, titled, and unwed at my age, well, you can only imagine how many potential suitors are thrown at me at every turn. Father Michael has to practically beat away mothers and their younger sons whenever they come to the abbey. I once had a mother trip her son so that he'd fall and grab my breasts. However, his fingernails weren't trimmed, so he scratched me and I had tiny droplets of blood all over my lace for the rest of the evening."

"I was at a ball where a woman tripped me so that I would fall at her sister's feet. I learned that evening that some ladies do not wear undergarments under their gowns."

Laughter burst out from Allegra. "Oh, Captain."

"I was young and inexperienced." He looked up at her, waiting for the barb.

It didn't come. She smirked, so he knew she had an inappropriate comment on her tongue, but she swallowed it down. Instead, she said, "Do you read books, Captain?"

"Books?"

"Yes, books. Do you know of them?"

"A few minutes ago, I introduced myself as the Duke of Barrington, and now you're asking if I know what a book is. Contrary to what you lowlanders think, we northerners are quite sophisticated and literate." He was happy she wanted to change the subject, and was eager to discuss just about any topic with her that was not his supposedly heroics. "You mentioned you were in Cumberland once. Why?"

ALLEGRA'S SMILE TWITCHED before it faded. She considered not telling Rainier about her trip, but he'd told her his identity. She decided a filtered version of her adventures in Cumberland would satisfy the trade of stories, and she could leave off the parts where she was irretrievably traumatized and put on her current path of solitude.

"I was there on tour with my second cousin, Katerina. She was a bit older than me, so it was a chance to get me out into the world. My father had escorted us and the plan was we ladies were going to stay for four months with a distant relation of Katerina's future husband, the Prince of Almsburg."

"How did you enjoy my homeland?"

Allegra's smile twitched again, but she mustered up a false visage of contentment. "What I saw of it was very nice. I didn't travel much while there."

"Well, what did you see, outside of a ballroom, of course."

"My father took me for a tour of an elemental mining island."

Rainier raised his dark eyebrows. "He took you to Basina Island?"

Allegra nodded weakly.

"How old were you?"

"Twelve."

"That must have been hard on you, being a mage."

"My magic hadn't come in fully, and I was still in denial, thinking the odd events around me were accidents. The trip, though. That…I didn't tell anyone about my magic until I was fourteen because of that damned trip."

"I've heard Basina is horrible on elemental witches." He cleared his throat. "Mages."

Allegra looked out of her window. Horrible was an understatement. There were no words in any of the languages she knew that could detail the atrocities she'd witnessed. When she realized she was an elemental, she knew she could trust no one in her family with that secret. As much as she loved her parents, she was relieved when they died, for she was safe from them. When the mantel of power passed to her, with the rank and wealth of her title, she added extra layers of protection. As long as she didn't reveal herself to others.

"Basina Island should be an abomination in the eyes of the Almighty," Allegra said coldly. "Instead, the halls of the Cathedral are decorated in its gold filigree."

"Why do you care? I mean, you're not an elemental."

Allegra lied about being an elemental so much that she could sometimes even forget she was one. She certainly didn't flinch at these kinds of questions. Instead, she channeled all of her disgust into her voice, a natural consequence of her true emotions needing some release.

"How very humane of society to allow me to escape the iron and the ink. It wouldn't matter if I was an elemental or even just a plain everyday person. One accusation is all that was needed and I could have ended up there. A little girl, ripped from her family." Allegra looked up at him. "So, after that delightful and very informative visit, I saw little else of Cumberland. I was too terrified to leave my bedroom."

She looked out of the carriage window. She'd seen a few of the brandings while she was at Basina. She'd seen so much more than that; she had no words for what she witnessed until she was much older. Dehumanizing didn't even begin to describe it. Neither did cruel. Unspeakable didn't even approach the horrors.

Mages had to be registered with an approved school to be allowed to live free and unshackled. There were limited provisions to purchase one's own freedom once enslaved, for a mage was dangerous. The free were tattooed to show they were free, wearing the stamp of their school's name or other identifiers. Slaves, however...

Memories from Basina cropped up in her mind. A hunk of wood. Screaming boys and girls. A branding iron in the blacksmith's fire. Shaved heads. Bare necks. Hands everywhere. Futile struggles.

She closed her eyes and gulped. All of those children were dead by now. Even if she became Arbiter, she could not rescue them. She doubted she could rescue the ones who lived there now. No one would allow her to release these supposed elementals. Considering their lack of training and the horrific mistreatments they've all suffered under, perhaps they were now too dangerous to be in the world no matter who or what they were. Lord Almighty knew the world deserved whatever wrath those poor people would rain down upon their enemies if freed.

Rainier cleared his throat and said, "This is obviously a sensitive subject for you. I apologize for bringing it up."

"The Viscount of Stromly and the rest will be far more invasive and offensive if I were to take the position. Your queries only remind me why I should not accept the job." Allegra turned her cold stare to him. "So, please, don't hold back."

"You still plan to turn him down?"

"I dislike the public eye," Allegra said, matter-of-factly. It was not a lie.

"You would honestly decline His Holiness's request for you to act on behalf of the Cathedral?"

Allegra scoffed. "I'm not even religious. Why would I care to act for the faithful?"

"I don't know how anyone can be a disbeliever."

"Not everyone believes in the Almighty, Captain."

"I realize that. Some people will believe in their own gods and beliefs, but they still *believe*. I think the Almighty doesn't care so much what path a person follows, so long as they live good lives and honor their own gods."

"Then what is the problem?"

"You have no beliefs."

"That is quite a statement," Allegra said.

"How am I supposed to know that you have any moral code?"

"Captain, I have met enough people in my life to know that any artificial moral code handed down from a pulpit can easily be justified away for the smallest reasons. Likewise, can justify the most horrific transgressions."

"Contessa, are you planning to argue with me this entire trip?"

"Maybe. I hope you have the stamina for such an encounter. I can be a very eager debater. I do hope you can *rise* to the challenge."

Rainier choked back a laugh. "I think you will find I am immune to most of your charms."

"Oh," Allegra said. After a moment, she said, "I have a friend who is bishop at the Cathedral. Perhaps you'd like to meet him. He has many of the same beliefs as you seem to possess. He's quite handsome."

"What? Why would I...Oh! Um, no, I mean, no thank you. I appreciate the offer, but it isn't necessary." At Allegra's silence, he said, "I was only attempting to...Lord give me strength...what I'm trying to say is that I enjoy wom—I mean, I like women."

"That was quite a lot of hesitation there. Would you like to discuss your feelings further? Are you sure you like women?"

"I'm sure," Rainier said flatly. When she couldn't contain her giggles anymore, he said accusingly, "You did all that on purpose."

"It was my own way to see if you were interested in women."

"Women, yes. You, increasingly not," he said, though he said it with a smile.

Allegra's laughter only died away when an arrow embedded itself into the side of the carriage and she began to scream.

CHAPTER SEVEN

ONE MOMENT, LEX was laughing at Dodd's exaggerated and animated retelling of the tavern fight to Mrs. Ansley's footman; a retelling made all the more impressive because Dodd was on horseback. The next, heavily-armed soldiers approached them from the west and north. Three warning arrows were released into the air even as Lex drew their sword.

One of the arrows embedded itself into the Contessa's carriage. Her screams were deafening. Her coachman snapped the reins on her coach and four. The beasts' hooves thundered down Cathedral's Way. Lex kicked their horse and galloped to keep pace with the Contessa's carriage.

Dodd shouted at the footman, "Protect Mrs. Ansley!"

Lex did a mental calculation, all the while keeping their head as low as possible, trusting the horse. There were only six members of the Consorts with the carriage on horseback, and two were inexperienced. In addition, Mrs. Ansley had two footmen: one on top of the carriage and the other seated with her coachman. Lex had no knowledge of their experience level.

The footman perched on top of her carriage fumbled with a canister strapped to the rooftop of the moving carriage. Lex assumed it was a bow, or perhaps a small, magical device to strengthen the horses or protect the carriage. Whatever it was, the footman's efforts were in vain. The horses charged at full-speed; it was all any of them could do but hold on for dear life.

Security and protections had all been prearranged that morning, just in case of trouble. Nevertheless, Lex's heart pounded painfully at the unfolding situation. Lex and Martin were to back up Rainier as he protected the Contessa. Dodd, and the remaining guards, along with the footmen, were to stay with Mrs. Ansley.

Lex instinctively ducked as more warning shots whizzed overhead. Lex channeled all of their training into keeping nerves in check and to stay on mission. There was no need to look back, for the pounding hooves and shouting of men was more than enough detail for the situation. If Captain Rainier didn't tell Lex to stop, then they weren't stopping.

"Mrs. Ansley, get down on the floor!" Dodd was shouting in the midst of issuing commands to Mrs. Ansley's coachman and the other guard. "Lex, who are these assholes?"

"No idea," Lex shouted back over the pound of hooves.

Lex's horse was frothing and snorting from the exertion, and the coach horses were thundering down the road as fast as their lungs and legs could make them go. They couldn't keep up this pace for long.

Cavalry came out from the woods along the roadside. Heavy-armored, dangerous, and all wearing tabards with Queen's Portia's heraldry. Was the local militia attacking them? They were Cathedral guards; no military would dare touch them.

Lex tightened their grip on the reins until their knuckles went white. Lex had lived through the Orsini Riots a year ago, and had taken a few lives defending the city from rioters. They could do it again.

Lex concentrated on those experiences and drew strength from the knowledge they'd been in tight spots before. Lex glanced once more at the horsemen riding through the trees and across the fields back into the small clumps of wooded areas. Lex had never fought in a real battle before. Lex's heart pounded faster at that, but they shook off their thoughts. Right now, the only important thing was to...

"Oh shit!" Lex shouted and pulled the reins hard to slow the horse's gallop. Lex's horse protested and reared up, throwing them off. Lex landed on the ground with a hard thud, knocking the wind out of them. Lex rolled out of the way as quickly as possible to avoid any wheels or hooves.

"Lex!" Dodd exclaimed.

"I'm fine!" Lex called out.

The coachmen pulled on the reins hard, and was cursing loudly. The horses slowed their charge eventually, but it was a close call. Mrs. Ansley's coach had to veer off into the ditch to slow the horses, the short brush slowing them. One of the wheels became stuck in the ditch, and the horses finally got the hint to stop galloping.

At the road bend further ahead, where the Cathedral Highway dipped once again into Amadore, was a blockade formed by a company of the militia. Sunlight gleamed off armor and steel. They weren't here to be decorative; they were here for a fight.

Lex struggled to stand, gasping and coughing for air, but they managed to get on their feet. Their horse had finally come to a stop in the ditch and was happily munching on whatever green grew there.

Rainier jumped out of the Contessa's carriage. He drew his sword. Lex mirrored his gesture, and the others all did the same. Lex gave Dodd a firm nod. Dodd returned it. Dodd gestured at Mrs. Ansley's carriage and his detail surrounded it. Likewise, Lex stepped alongside the Contessa's carriage.

If Rainier couldn't talk these people out of whatever was going on, Lex was about to find out if all of the magical talismans on their uniforms were worth their weight in gold after all.

STANTON SQUARED HIS shoulders when he stepped out of the carriage. Normally that would not be a tactically sound move, but they were outnumbered and the way before them blocked. They were not bandits; the livery and uniforms declared them local militia, if he recalled the colors correctly. Either way, they had orders, not greed, motivating them. Negotiation and discussion were valid tactics at this juncture.

Stanton walked toward the carts that blocked Cathedral's Way. "Who's in charge there? You? Explain this madness."

As a Cathedral captain, Stanton had significant powers over local militias and policing establishments, but it was not unlimited. Further, the little display last night in the tavern made Stanton worry that Queen Portia was thinking herself well beyond the Cathedral's rules.

This is why they needed a damned Arbiter! To bring the nations all under the heel of the Cathedral and ensure the Almighty's law was being followed equally throughout all of His lands.

"Well? Which of you are in charge here? Speak."

A young man almost as tall as Stanton stepped out in front of the carts. He motioned to the men behind him before approaching Stanton. His hand rested nervously on his sword's hilt, and though he was pale-skinned, his face was rapidly becoming bright pink.

"I am Corporal Jeeno of Her Imperial Majesty's Home Guard. I've been assigned to Sir Bertrand's service, the magistrate for Montfort County."

Stanton waited, expecting an actual answer to his question. When none came, he said, "And?"

"Sir?"

"I asked you to explain yourself. All you've done is introduce yourself."

"I am charged with arresting Mrs. Patrice Ansley for the illegal use of elemental witchcraft and for being an elemental mage."

"I'm not an elemental!" Mrs. Ansley shouted from her carriage window.

"Harness that mouth of yours, witch bitch," the corporal shouted back.

"Eat horse shit," Mrs. Ansley said in return.

The corporal bristled. "As you can see, sir, she is feral. We need to arrest her immediately or risk her wrath coming down upon us."

"Her wrath?" Stanton sneered. "Mrs. Ansley is no elemental, as you well know. She is a free mage and it is illegal to arrest her. You know this."

"I'm sorry, sir. You have been deceived." He offered a letter to Stanton.

Stanton snatched it from the man's hand and read it. The letter appeared genuine, as did the green and white uniforms the soldiers wore. As did the seal on the bottom of the letter. Faking any one of those was a hanging offense. There would be no reason to go through the trouble of faking all of it to arrest a nobody mage.

Stanton looked up at the guard and frowned. "Your magistrate has proof she is an elemental?"

"I assume so, sir."

"What is this proof?"

He shrugged. "I'm sure it'll come up at her trial."

"There won't be a trial and you know it," Mrs. Ansley shouted. "Captain, please."

Stanton gulped. He had a duty and had taken vows to uphold the laws of the Cathedral. One of them was not to interfere with local laws unless they contravened those of the cardinals. He could stand up for Mrs. Ansley when they were trying to arrest her as a free mage. Standing in the way of an accused elemental, no matter how suspicious the accusation, was an entirely different matter.

The Contessa might never forgive him for what he knew his duty required him to do.

"This is outrageous," the Contessa said from her carriage window.

"This does not concern you, ma'am," the corporal said. "Back inside where you belong."

"Starve in the abyss," the Contessa snarled and swung open the carriage door. She smacked one of the guards in the chest with the door and jumped down the distance with a huff of breath. She stormed up to the guard and snatched the paper from Stanton. She read it, her expression turning dark. "Heathens. This is...this is lies. Surely everyone can see that. What did you do to this magistrate?"

"Nothing!" Mrs. Ansley exclaimed. "I don't even know him. I came here only to sell my factory. Nothing else."

"Who did you meet with?"

Stanton frowned at the Contessa's question, but glared down the guard when he attempted to interrupt her.

"I've only met with my workers to offer them positions in my Jennings factory and offered to pay their transport," Mrs. Ansley said. "Oh, and the lawyers, I suppose."

"You never met the person buying your interest on the Cartossa side of the border?" Allegra asked.

Stanton looked over at Mrs. Ansley, who was still leaning out of her carriage. "No. It was all done through his lawyers."

"If she's arrested as an elemental, all of her property is forfeit in the region, isn't it?" the Contessa asked the guard.

The guard cleared his throat. "I am not certain about…"

"Oh, be a man," Stanton shouted.

"My orders are clear, as is the law. Mrs. Ansley, please come with us."

"You can't let them!" Please!" Mrs. Ansley pleaded.

"Do something!" the Contessa shouted.

Stanton shook his head. "I am not permitted. I'm sorry."

Lex grimaced and looked away as the guards dragged Mrs. Ansley from her carriage. Stanton closed his eyes as her screams and curses filled the air.

"Watch," the Contessa demanded in a cold, harsh voice. "All of you."

So Stanton obeyed and watched as Mrs. Ansley was dragged by her hair across the stony path. He watched with repressed rage as her pelisse and dress snagged and ripped on the stones and bushes. He didn't untwine the fists his hands had formed as Mrs. Ansley's own hands were shoved into iron manacles, nor did he hide the disgust on his face when the servants were equally dragged to kneel next to their mistress.

Stanton glanced at the Contessa, expecting open weeping. What he found was far worse. Unabashed fury.

Do not anger the kind, for their fury will know no limits and their rage no prisoners.

Tasmin's sacred words came to mind as he stared down at the Contessa's face. This might push her over the edge to accept the position. They might all live to regret it, too.

"CONTESSA, PLEASE! I beg you!" Mrs. Ansley wailed. "Do something, please."

Allegra knew she would look back on this moment and know this was the day she picked sides. The rest of her life would now be shaped by this moment, and that realization seeped into her bones along with her barely controlled rage.

"Watch, all of you. Watch and may the Almighty curse your dreams with this. Whenever you are asked why the mages are revolting, think upon this day and know you caused it. Each and every one of you."

"Rot in the abyss!" Mrs. Ansley screamed when one of the guards slapped her maidservant.

Allegra turned to the corporal. "Tell your master I am coming for him."

The corporal took a step forward. "Are you threatening him?"

Rainier and Lex both pivoted to flank Allegra, but she held her hand out. She stepped forward and stared down the corporal. "Tell him the Contessa of Marsina will not rest until she sees him stripped of power. If anything happens to that woman over there, or any of her servants, I will see there is nothing left of his life but the regret of knowing he'd crossed me."

"I am following my orders."

"How noble. You've rid the world of a dangerous elemental. Consider, corporal. If I were an elemental in her position, I would have used all my supposed magic to char the lot of you all to ash. Or maybe I'd open a pit and let you all fall in. She hasn't, because she can't."

Mrs. Ansley's screams turned to desperate sobs. The guard next to the corporal grimaced and looked away.

"Don't be a coward!" Allegra shouted in his face. "Surely you must be brave in the face of the Lord Almighty's work!"

The guard didn't look up.

"May her screams haunt you for the rest of your life," Allegra snarled.

"Get away from her carriage! Hey!" Dodd shouted out.

"Put that down!" Lex joined into the chorus of protests.

Allegra looked over her shoulder. Two of the militia guards had climbed atop Mrs. Ansley's carriage. They tossed the light bags to their fellow traitors on the ground. The large trunks were merely tossed to the ground, exploding open from the fall.

Dodd marched over and shoved one of the men who'd picked up a blush pink corset. "Put that down."

"Stand down, Lieutenant Dodd," Allegra said bleakly.

"You can't be serious!" Dodd demanded. "This is banditry!"

"Captain? We have to stop this," Lex said.

Rainier sighed and said, "She's been accused of being an elemental. They get to confiscate everything, from her servants to her corsets."

"They've only accused her," Lex said. "They can't just...she's only been accused."

"That's all they need, Lex," Allegra said. "Isn't it, Captain?"

Rainier nodded his head. "The servants aided in hiding her identity as an elemental. It is now for a court to decide if they did it willingly."

"That's bullshit, sir, and you know it," Lex said.

"This is fucking bullshit," Dodd shouted. "This can't be legal."

"This is a fucking mess," Lex said.

"It is," Allegra said coolly. "Welcome to why there is a rebellion."

She could not stand here any longer. If they rode through the night, they could be at the Cathedral by tomorrow evening or early the next morning. She could accept the position and order Cathedral troops back. Four days. Mrs. Ansley had to survive four days.

"Mrs. Ansley, I am coming back for you. Do everything you need to do to survive, do you understand me?"

Mrs. Ansley was too busy sobbing to answer.

She turned to the guard on the path and said, "Move. Now."

"Yes, of course. Thank you for..."

"Move!" Allegra screamed in the corporal's face. Spittle sprayed him. He blinked, not expecting her to act in such an unladylike manner. "Move your men out of the way or I swear to the Almighty I will strike you."

While the blockade moved, Allegra marched back to the carriage. Dodd, Lex, and Rainier were all shouting for the guards to show Mrs. Ansley and her people respect, but their pleas went unheard. Allegra didn't bother to speak. There was no point unless she was prepared to burn them all alive: something that she was sorely tempted to do.

Instead, she stepped up to her carriage and glared at the soldier she'd hit previously in the chest. He fumbled to pull the stairs out for her. He offered her his hand, and she slapped it away as if he was a leper.

She sat in her carriage and let Mrs. Ansley's sobbing shrieks etch themselves upon her soul. This was her doing. She had done everything possible to avoid this very fate for herself, and her own narcissistic complacency meant an innocent woman would pay the price instead. This was the price of her freedom: the enslavement of others.

Rainier approached the carriage. Allegra latched the door lock. He gave her a quizzical look. She did not want him anywhere near her. She didn't care that he was just following orders. Everyone was just following orders. An innocent woman was suffering b*ecause they were following orders.*

Orders could burn in the abyss for all she cared at that moment.

"Tell the coachman we are riding straight to the Cathedral. No stops except to change horses."

"I don't think…"

"I didn't ask your opinion, Captain." Without waiting for a reply, she snapped the window shut and pulled down the blinds. There, in the privacy of her darkened carriage, she gave herself permission to sob for not just Mrs. Ansley, but also because she knew her own life was never going to be the same now.

CHAPTER EIGHT

Orsini Cathedral
Papal Residence

"WHERE IS HE? Where is the Holy Father?"

Allegra stormed through the corridors of Orsini Palace. They'd ridden for almost two days straight, stopping only long enough to change the horses and to eat. Even then, Allegra had not allowed them more than a quarter hour's rest. She'd not changed her clothes since the ordeal began. She'd not freshened up or tended to the most basic of hygiene. Servants bustled around her, all offering assistance, and she ignored them. She made a promise to Mrs. Ansley and she didn't have a moment to spare.

"Your Ladyship, if you would but wait..."

"We're here to see the Holy Father," Lex said sharply, following just behind her.

The other booted footfalls were Rainier's. "Is Father Francois in his study?"

"His drawing room, Captain," the servant answered, "But..."

Rainier took a hard right turn and Allegra matched his quickening pace. She'd not spoken more than ten words to him in the last two days for fear her anger would boil over. For years she had been ignored whenever she suggested this kind of criminal activity was taking place. No one believed her. Some accused her of hysterics. Others patronized her with comments about how her delicate, retired life meant she couldn't possibly understand the ways of the world. Even Rainier had acted like she was exaggerating. Well, they'd seen a fine example of it with their own eyes and it ran to script like a play.

"Your Ladyship! Please!" one of the servants called out behind her. "You're not decent to see the Holy Father in your current condition!"

"I do not care about the state of my dress. I need the Holy Father right this minute."

"We cannot be delayed," Rainier said.

"But you don't have an appointment!"

"I don't care," Allegra said.

Lex shoulder checked a liveried footman who attempted to block their charge down the corridor. "Out of the way. This is Consort business."

She reached the double doors of the Holy Father's private drawing room. The tall, white doors were guarded by two footmen. One put his hand up. "Do you have an appointment?"

"Is the Holy Father within?" Allegra demanded.

"Do you have an appointment?"

"I shall take that as an affirmative. Open these doors or I shall open them myself."

"And you are?"

"Allegra, Contessa of Marsina."

"You do not have an appointment, Your Ladyship. Captain."

"I don't need one." Allegra pushed past the footmen. She grabbed both door latches and pushed down.

"You cannot enter uninvited!" the footmen exclaimed and grabbed her arm.

Lex slammed his bony shoulder into one of the footmen, knocking him off balance. Rainier shoved the footman who'd grabbed her into the door frame, just as she swung the door open. The joint force of her anger and the footman's momentum pushed the door into a table. Glass decanters shattered on the floor and the aroma of expensive claret filled the air.

"Allegra!" Francois said, stunned. "What...what has happened?"

The four men and two women seated next to Francois were all adored in regal religious attire of the inner circle of cardinals. "Did you mean it?"

"Mean what?" Francois said guardedly.

"Your Holiness, did you mean it? A woman's life and that of her servants are at stake," Rainier said.

"Yes," Francois said. "Yes, the offer was genuine. What is going on?"

"Then I accept. Rainier?"

Rainier turned to speak to Lex, but Lex was already turned to face the Cathedral guards in the corridor. "Dodd's already gone to get the Consorts. You! You! Let's go! Move!"

"Father, what is going on?" Cardinal DeLancey asked. DeLancey was a wrinkled hag of a woman, with piercing blue eyes and liver-spotted pale skin. She gave Allegra a withering glance that would have shrunk her away any other day. "Child, you've forgotten your manners. Kindly fetch them before you return."

Allegra glared at the woman and said, "Out."

Francois glanced at the Cardinal and back at Allegra. "Contessa, perhaps we should..."

"Get. Out. Now." Allegra snarled the words, glaring at Rupert. He met her gaze for a moment before breaking it. He nodded to the others and said, "I'll have my secretary reschedule. I apologize for the interruption."

The cardinals glared and grumbled as they left, and one made a snide comment about backwater mages being put in irons. She ignored the comments.

"You, too, Captain," Allegra said. "I want to speak to him alone."

"I'll be right outside," Rainier said.

The doors closed behind them and Allegra shouted, "How could you, Rupert? How could you do this to me?"

The Holy Father topped up his glass of wine. "You just demanded I make you Arbiter. I have done nothing to you."

"You knew what would happen on the road here. You knew those bastards are out there arresting mages for no damned good reason and you knew it! This was all a ploy to get me to accept your damned offer. Damn you, Rupert! Damn you to the abyss!"

Rupert put down his wine. Puzzlement crossed his faced. "What are you talking about? What is going on?"

Allegra detailed the circumstances around Mrs. Ansley to a sputtering Rupert. "That is what I'm talking about. The subjugation of mages!"

"I'm sorry you had to see that," Rupert said. He sat down and motioned for her to join him. She refused. "Things are deteriorating daily. That little event by the magistrate will incite more unrest and the news will spread. If we're lucky, some of the rebels will get to her before she's shipped off to Almighty knows where. The guards won't make it back in time. She'd already gone."

"That's it, then? That's the recourse we have? Hope that the criminals help out the innocent? You've lost all control!"

"We all have! Do you think it's easy for me, surrounded all day by the faithful who believe all mages should be shunned and exiled? Do you think the world stopped getting worse just because you're off hiding from it?"

Allegra squared her shoulders. "I am not hiding."

"Don't lie to me, Allegra. We're known each other since we were children. Do you honestly think you're safe? All it will take is one letter from that magistrate when you cross back through his territory and you'll be the one in irons."

"Don't you think I know that? You, of all people, know that is what I fear most."

"Then do something about it," Rupert urged.

"And what if I'm found out?"

"My dear, if something doesn't change soon, no one will be safe, least of all you!" He drew in a breath and said, "Shall I assume you will keep serving as Arbiter, or have you already tired of the position?"

"You are such an asshole, Rupert."

"I am nothing if not practical."

"I refuse to work out of Orsini. I will only conduct negotiations at Borro Abbey."

"That doesn't come as any great surprise. Agreed, assuming Father Michael will be fine with his Abbey being used as your headquarters."

"He will," Allegra stated with absolute authority. "He likes me."

Rupert snorted. "Oh, Allegra. How I've missed you."

"I've missed Rupert. This Francois is an ass."

Rupert shrugged, unoffended by the comment. "The Holy Father's mantle is a heavy one, my dear. I always thought the name change was silly, but now I understand its purpose. It's so easy to lose one's self under all of the velvet and rules."

"I want a security team," Allegra stated.

"Of course. Do you want some of the palace guard?"

"I'd prefer Captain Rainier and some of his people."

Rupert made a pleased sound. "Taken a shine to the captain, have you?"

"I want someone I can trust," she said coolly. "I think I can trust him."

"You can," Rupert said seriously. "What else do you need?"

"Your support."

"This was my idea, after all."

"No, I want your full support for ending the rebellion. I want you to agree with every word that comes out of my mouth for the duration of the negotiations."

"You know I can't do that," Rupert said. "I've heard the things that come out of your mouth."

Allegra pushed herself up from the chair. "Tell Pero I send my regards."

"You always ask too much."

Allegra whirled on him. "I don't ask nearly enough. You say you support me, well then support everyone who is like me."

Rupert leaned back in his chair. "You'd press to make elementals legal."

"You're damned right I would. I'd drag every single one of these backward idiots into the modern world. So you can help by agreeing when I say elementals are not caused by demonic influence."

"I can't do that."

"You don't believe it any more than I do!"

"I know, but...I'll support you in everything else, but that's too far. The people would never accept it."

"You're their leader. You are the one who clears the trail for these lunatics to come up with their shameful laws."

"Allegra, if I say that, I could start riots."

"Rupert, there are already riots. The more people like Mrs. Ansley are mistreated, the bigger the riots will be. Choose which side you want history to remember you standing on, because there is only one right side in this."

Rupert looked away. "I'll think about it."

"You'll put it off."

He scowled. "I will openly support everything you say, except on elementals. I'll keep my peace, though. That's the best I can promise."

"Your silence might be seen as a rejection of my proposals."

"Or of quiet acceptance." He shrugged. "I can't promise more than that. The Cardinals won't give you full powers in these matters, and you know it. Plus, Allegra, if I'm not careful, there's going to be a war."

Allegra laughed.

"What's so funny?"

"There's going to be a war regardless. You can't enslave people forever before they use their chains to strangle you." Allegra scowled. "I will try to get enough concessions to ease their immediate concerns, but people chafe, Rupert. They chafe until their skin turns raw. Eventually, they won't care about living or dying because they have already been condemned. Then they will come for us all unless we stop this now."

In a quiet voice, Rupert quoted scripture. "Choose carefully when the kind are enraged, for their wrath can alter the course of history."

Allegra's laugh was mocking. "I am not kind. Make your announcements. I will begin preparations immediately. And Rupert?"

"Hmm?"

"I can act with full authority, correct, to correct any injustice I see?"

Rupert narrowed his eyes. "Like what?"

"Like how I'm going to have the magistrate arrested on my return trip. I want his property confiscated and sold to support...I'll think of something."

"You can't do that," Rupert said.

"Yes, I can. I am the Cathedral's representative, am I not? I speak with the Cathedral's authority. The last Arbiter did whatever he pleased. Surely I can when Cathedral law is violated willfully in the name of greed." Allegra lifted her chin. "That is my price."

Rupert's words were clipped when he said, "I shall have my secretary deliver the necessary seals to you later today."

She inclined her head and turned to walk away.

"What happened to friendship?" Rupert asked.

She didn't turn around. "Friendship is no longer enough when my kind are fighting in the streets for their very lives."

"I will protect you," Rupert said.

Allegra looked over her shoulder and gave her oldest friend in the world a sad smile. "I know you would try, right up until they slapped the iron shackles on my wrists and ankles. Then, no holy edict from you would come and I would die. And that guilt would destroy you. So hope it doesn't come to that."

Then Allegra walked out, knowing her life had just changed forever. And, she silently prayed to an Almighty she didn't believe in, just in case he did exist, that he would watch over her.

CHAPTER NINE

STANTON LEANED AGAINST the open door of Allegra's temporary office and smirked. She was writing, and by the snarl on her face, it was a furiously-toned letter. He could hear the quill tip scratching against the paper even from the doorway.

"I know you're there." She didn't look up from her page. When he didn't answer, she said, "You are welcome to sit, provided you have a sense of adventure."

Stanton strolled across the worn, burgundy carpet and eased himself into one of the chairs across from her oversized desk, and risked toppling over when he shifted his weight.

"What the…"

"One of the legs is wobbly," Allegra said. When Stanton rose to sit in the other chair, she said, "Don't bother. That one is worse."

He lowered himself back down, careful to brace himself this time. "Is this the clerk's way to punish you, or is this your way to punish anyone who visits you?"

She flipped her sheet of paper ninety degrees and continued writing, now across her previous lines. "The head clerk is Rafe Gotto, my third cousin on my mother's side. He proposed marriage when I was seventeen."

"I can imagine your response."

She paused in her frenzied writing, just long enough to flash him a wicked smile. Then she put her head back down and kept writing. "It appears he still harbors some ill will over my youthful reaction."

Stanton shifted to find a comfortable spot. Instead, he found a stray splinter that poked his ass. He winced and stood as carefully as possible, in the desperate hope that he'd not ripped the seat out of his best trousers. "If you won't be insulted, I will stand."

"I considered asking Nadira to burn the chairs."

Stanton walked over to the fireplace and mused, "The garbage heap is too good for them."

She snorted and stopped writing. She put her quill down, folded her hands in front of her, and smiled up at him. "So, what do I owe the pleasure of this visit?"

"Boredom."

Allegra chuckled. She had a rather infectious smile that Stanton loved to see. There was a twinkle in her that signaled the intelligence behind her coy court manners. "I assume no word from Lex and Dodd?"

"No, but that's no surprise. They'll have to find where Mrs. Ansley was taken. I suspect we won't hear for another day." He rested a fist on his hip and look about the room. "Your office is shabbier than I'd expected."

The Contessa heaved a frustrated sigh. "This is only until I can move back to Borro. I've already written to the bishop. I suppose I'll have to give up my little cottage for one of the estate suites."

"You do hold an important position now, Your Ladyship."

"Let's hope that will last."

He examined the room. It really was shabby. What was once a bright yellow papered wall was now a faded, dirty pattern with peeling corners. The rug was threadbare; the barracks had a nicer rug than the one now protecting Allegra's wooden floor. Her desk was too large for her. The Contessa wasn't a tall woman, and she'd been given a chair that fit her frame and a desk that didn't; she looked like a child behind her father's desk as opposed to a great figure of authority.

He was taking dinner with Pero tomorrow; he'd mention this insult to him. While Pero held no official title within the Cathedral, he wasn't without power. After all, he was the Holy Father's husband.

Mindful that he was staring about her room and not speaking, he asked, "When do you speak before the cardinals?"

"Three days from now. The abolitionists delayed voting on my measures until more of their block could arrive from the countryside."

Stanton absently nodded while he ran his fingers across the mantle, leaving paths in the dust. He didn't know what this room had been previously used for, but they hadn't even bothered to send in the maids to clean before moving the Contessa in. He glanced at her and saw her looking at him, a wry smile on her face.

"When are the maids coming to clean?"

She shrugged. "I think they're waiting to see if the cardinals haul me off to the dungeons."

"There are no dungeons in the palace, Your Ladyship."

Allegra snorted, a sound that was oddly feminine on her. "What is Toll Gate Prison?"

"That is above ground," Stanton said with mock outrage. "How dare you suggest an aboveground prison is a dungeon?"

"How could I ever make such a horrendous mistake? Oh, this is why I have big, handsome men around to tell me what to think."

Stanton grew quiet. "Handsome, huh?"

Allegra rolled her eyes in reply. She picked up her teacup, a pretty little rosebud set that he recognized from the Holy Father's private breakfast room. He inwardly grinned at that. She noticed him staring at the cup and said, "Yes, Rupert gave it to me. I think it was his way of letting all of the inner circle of cardinals know I had his support. Of course, now they will just be craftier with their backstabbing."

"Not all of the cardinals are bad."

"The ones who aren't generally are the ones who never say anything in opposition of those who are." She sipped at her tea as she walked over to the floor-to-ceiling window. She didn't push back the sheer fabric that draped from the ceiling for muted privacy. "Do they scream as loud for mage rights as their counterparts do for enslavement? Do they fight for the rights of the poor? Do they offer up their political ambitions to do what is right?"

"If they can remain moderate…"

"Yes, yes. They must remain moderates until in power to affect real change. Only, they are moderates for so long, thinking of their own power for so long, that they cannot see what is right if it threw a tea cup at them. All they see is how to compromise and that will never change with more power."

Stanton walked over to join her, taking a moment to run his hand along the back of his trousers. No holes. "Compromise isn't all bad."

"Compromise is what got Mrs. Ansley arrested."

ALLEGRA SIPPED AT her tea in an attempt to quell her sting of anger. She was in a bad mood today, though she was often foul when at the Cathedral. "The letter I was writing? It was to the wife of the Duke of Montfort, about Mrs. Ansley and the entire mess. I'd already written the Duke, and his patronizing reply arrived this morning."

"I've never met him, but I've heard he is assured of himself."

Allegra barked out a little laugh. "That's diplomatic. His reply was nothing more than a collection of *my dear lady* and *may I comfort you* and all of that court rot. What a…a…" Words and insults failed her.

"Shall I ask Dodd for an appropriate vulgarity?"

"I might require it if he replies to my scolding."

Allegra leaned against the window's frame, as much as the stiff back and her over-tightened corset would allow. "I believe I was a rash fool to accept this position."

"This is the time of fools," Rainier said.

Allegra looked into his dark eyes and sighed. She was not used to making such close friends with a non-mage. Perhaps she was lonely. Perhaps she needed to find herself a nice, young mage who would like to enjoy a more experienced woman's bed for a weekend of nights.

"What are you smiling about?"

"Finding a lover," Allegra said frankly and sipped her tea.

Rainier choked when he gulped. She sipped more tea.

"Well, I do hear there are some junior cardinals who love dark-haired beauties."

"I said lover, not a murder victim."

Rainier laughed and it was a huge sound, all the way from his belly. "You are impossible!"

"You say it like it's a bad thing, my dear Captain."

Allegra let out a long sigh. She was worried. Tomorrow, she would face the cardinals, where they would vote on her proposals. Speaking of compromise.

"I wish I could be there tomorrow. For support."

Allegra looked at him. She believed him. What's more, she wished he could be there, too. "Might we have tea when I'm done?"

"I'd like that. My office or yours?"

"Mine, though I recommend you bring a chair."

ALLEGRA SAT IN the holy chambers across from the innermost circle of the Cathedral cardinals and waited Francois's arrival. His tardiness reduced her to idle chatter with the cardinals and she was running out of topics and fake smiles.

"Did you have a pleasant journey here, Your Ladyship?" Cardinal Devonshire asked. She was a frail, elderly woman with high cheekbones and wide eyes that announced she had been quite the beauty in her youth. She was also a moderate and rumored to be, if not an abolitionist, then a sympathizer to the cause.

Allegra gave the elderly woman the most genuine smile she could muster, forcing all of the sarcasm and anger out of her voice. "It was horrid, Your Grace. I was assaulted, ambushed, and accosted."

Cardinal Vanida made a contemplative sound. He was a withered, arrogant, weasel of a man whom Allegra had hated since childhood. He narrowed his heavily hooded eyes until they were slits and said, "Then perhaps you were too hasty in accepting this vital position. We require an individual with significant experience, mental fortitude, and intelligence to bring a firm hand to this witches' rebellion."

"Mage rebellion," Allegra corrected him. She smeared jam on her slice of cake and took a bite. "The pastries are always excellent here."

"I beg your pardon?" Vanida asked.

"Hmm?" Allegra asked through a mouthful of cake.

"You interrupted me." Vanida didn't hide the contempt in his voice. "Now, as for this witch rebellion—"

"We are called mages, not witches, Your Grace. As for who is needed in this position, perhaps we need someone who doesn't have a vested interest in keeping mages enslaved." She gave the Cardinal another fake smile before turning away. To Cardinal Devonshire, Allegra asked, "More wine, Your Grace?"

"Please, child."

Allegra poured the old lady a glass of deep red wine, and then topped up her own glass. Allegra sipped from her crystal goblet, careful not to gulp down the comfort afforded within the intoxicating liquid.

Cardinal Giso flashed a chastising smirk at Allegra. Giso was a proud, open abolitionist, but he was also a pragmatist to his core. "My dear Contessa, I am sure you will bring your own unique approach to the current situation at hand. Lord Almighty knows you couldn't do worse than some of your predecessors. The rational for why the conclave choice a slave owner to broker a peace treaty will always elude me."

That was when Cardinal Reinhold, silent until now, said in his deep voice, "Politics."

With that one word, the four cardinals at the table began bickering. Allegra stayed out of it, opting very wisely to munch on caraway seed cake. She sat at a table with one anti-mage, one pro-mage, and two who only cared about compromise, politics, and ambition. There were several other members of the inner circle that weren't here for this meeting, but Allegra felt they were a decent representation of what she was about to face within the conclave's chamber walls once she presented her position.

She would have to put forward a compromising set of proposals for the cardinals to approve. She had to impress a majority of the two hundred and thirty-seven cardinals. Not all of them would be present for the voting, which was why it was delayed for days.

The doors flung open as the voices within were becoming heated. Francois entered in a flurry of robes and servants. "Forgive me for my tardiness. Ambassador Alencherry is a talker. I was convinced she would never shut up."

"She does like to prattle," Allegra said absently, the first words out of her mouth in several minutes.

Cardinal Vanida rapped his tea spoon against the table, drawing everyone's attention. "You are speaking of Cumberland's Ambassador to the Cathedral. Mind your tongue, young woman."

Allegra drew her shoulders back. She could see that Rupert was about to correct the Cardinal, but she spoke first. "I do believe you have forgotten your station, Your Grace. I am the Contessa of Marsina and the Cathedral's Arbiter of Justice until I retire or am removed from the position. You will accord me the respect due my rank."

She had played this game with Vanida since she was a child and she was not going to let some upstart butcher's son shame her in public ever again.

"Of course, Your Ladyship," the Cardinal said, sarcasm lacing his words. "Whatever you say, Your Ladyship."

Allegra glared at him for a moment longer before flicking her gaze to Francois. "Shall we get started? I have much work to do."

"Yes, indeed, Your Ladyship," Francois said with a twinkle in his eye. "Whatever your command."

Allegra glared at him. He was enjoying putting her in here with these fools. Allegra did not get along with cardinals. Everyone knew it, including the damned cardinals.

Francois took his seat at the round table. One of the servants poured his wine, while another fussed about bringing additional sweets and nibbles from the sideboard over to the table. Once the nutritional needs of the Holy Father were addressed, the servants bowed and left as wordlessly as they'd entered.

Francois began the meeting when the double doors clicked shut. "Her Ladyship's time with us is short and there are a number of items we must prepare before she leaves for the country. First..."

"I do not agree with her conducting Cathedral affairs at Borro Abbey," Cardinal Vanida said.

Cardinal Reinhold nodded his agreement. "Borro Abbey is far too isolated for the Arbiter to host meaningful negotiations. Her Ladyship should remain here, at the Cathedral. Surely, we can find suitable lodgings for her, as I understand her current ones are subpar for a woman of her position."

"I wish to return to Borro," Allegra said cautiously.

"All previous arbiters have conducted their business here," Giso said.

"All of the previous Arbiters have failed," Allegra stated. "I take this position very seriously, Your Graces. It is my belief that proximity to the Cathedral and, therefore, the seat of religious power, had given many of the nobles a false sense of security and boldness. By forcing them to meet at Borro Abbey, they will be without their blocks of power. Everyone will be on equal footing there."

"Surely you do not think a prince is on even footing with a slave?" Vanida asked.

"They will be when they are seated at my negotiations table," Allegra said.

Vanida's eyes widened. "You don't mean you will have actual witches...at the peace talks?"

Allegra thought it was a joke at first, so she laughed. Her mirth died away when she realized she was the only one laughing. Giso's face was etched with a smirk and Francois kept a cool, neutral demeanor, but the others were scandalized and made no attempt to hide it in their expressions or voices.

"You cannot invite outlaws to the peace talks!" Vanida exclaimed. "I will not support anyone who would consort with those who should be imprisoned."

"Ah, yes, Vanida! Let's lock up all of those pesky mages since they are the cause of all that we complain of," Giso said, his voice dripping with sarcasm.

Devonshire raised a withered hand. "Gentlemen, this is an old argument that will not be solved today."

"It could be," Allegra said. "Do you not all hold the power to end the rebellions today?"

"That is an argument for another day," Francois said.

"Agreed," Devonshire said.

"Then, what exactly is my purpose in this role? Your Graces, forgive me, but what exactly did you think I was planning to do with this position?"

Her words were met with silence, which came as no great surprise to her. She knew what the position of Arbiter of Justice was for: it was the equalizing voice between nations and city states, to ensure all followed the will of the Lord Almighty. No one nation could act out of step against the Cathedral without being severely punished, true, but it also meant there was a neutral party to settle disputes.

Allegra held a different interpretation of the position, one which she guessed Francois had figured out over the last few days. In a cautious voice, he said, "The historical purpose of the Arbiter of Justice is to bring order and ensure lasting peace, so that all of the Almighty's people can live in peace to bring glory to His name."

"Exactly," Allegra said with a wolfish smile.

"Then what is our disagreement?" Giso asked.

"To ensure lasting peace, I must bring together various representative from all of the Almighty's people."

Vanida sneered. "How would giving witches recognition solve anything? They'll conjure demons as soon as we turn our backs."

"Mages," Allegra corrected him coolly. "The correct and preferred term is mages."

Vanida waved her hand. "That doesn't matter. What matters is..."

"Actually, Your Grace, it does matter. It is a small token of respect that those of us in power can show."

Devonshire frowned in Allegra's direction. With a soft voice, she said, "My dear child, it is just a word. What does it matter in the face of these issues?"

"If it is just a word, then you will have no objection to me calling Cardinal Vanida His Horseface at the conclave's assembly tomorrow. After all, it is just a word and what *truly* matters is the rebellion."

The room fell into silence once more. Vanida's face contorted as he formed his venom to spew, so Allegra took the opportunity to continue. "I will be inviting several prominent members of the abolition movement to spend the winter at Borro Abbey. I have already taken the liberty of informing the Bishop of Borro that accommodations will need to be made."

Devonshire tsked. "I remain unconvinced that this is a wise course of action, child."

Giso, however, was laughing. "The anti-block is going to have a stroke tomorrow."

Vanida, as usual, scowled. "Your Ladyship, you would be wise to heed our advice."

"You mean your advice," Giso said with a snort. "Lord Almighty, Vanida, she's a mage! She's never going to listen to a slave owner like you."

"This slave owner follows the word of the Lord Almighty."

"As does this abolitionist," Giso said, pounding his chest with his finger.

Allegra ate two slices of lemon caraway cake and had another glass of wine before the argument finally turned back to her.

"Don't you have anything to add, Your Ladyship?" Vanida demanded.

She finished her wine. "The lemon cake is excellent."

Giso snorted.

"This is not funny!" Vanida shouted.

"Your Grace, check your tone," Francois said. Turning to Allegra, he asked, "Tell me, Contessa, how would you respond to, let's say, Queen Portia calling in her militia to quash a mage riot and dozens of children are killed in the process."

Two years ago, this would have been a useless hypothetical question. Times were changing. "I believe my first action would be to demand the Cathedral issue a firm reprimand and then I would personally travel there to defuse the situation."

"How would you defuse this situation?" Cardinal Devonshire asked. Her question appeared innocent, but Allegra knew she was auditioning for the old cardinal's support.

"Precise action would depend upon the particulars, of course, but I would travel to meet with the Queen and beg her to meet with local mage representatives to come to a compromise to end the bloodshed."

The old woman still had no emotion on her face. "What if you fail at this compromise? Let us suppose this triggers another riot. What would you do then?"

Allegra searched her soul. Six months ago, she would have pulled the covers over her head and closed her heart against the screams of her own kind. She feared risk, yet the time for personal peril had finally arrived.

"Then I would follow in the footsteps of the late Arbiter Paladin. I'd go into the streets with the mob and use my stance to humiliate both her majesty and the Cathedral into action." At their shocked expressions, she continued. "Arbiter Paladin lost his life in a riot over bread for peasants. The situation now is even graver than what he faced. And, if I recall my history lessons, the Holy Father at the time excommunicated the Prince and the forces of the holy invaded."

Francois snorted.

"Your Radiance, this is no laughing matter. This witch—"

Devonshire interrupted Vanida. "Mage."

"What?"

"She wishes to be called a mage, Vanida. Treat her with the respect her position demands."

When Vanida scoffed at the old woman, Francois said in a very casual tone, "I know several remote monasteries in need of a new abbot."

The meeting turned frosty after that. Vanida kept his opinions to mere disapproving grunts, and the others mostly glared at each other. Allegra answered questions politely, if tersely, and basically nothing was solved other than confirming that the cardinals truly did loathe each other as much as rumor implied.

When the meeting ending, Francois lingered to speak to Allegra. "That was invigorating."

Allegra snorted. She collapsed on the chaise longue and put her feet up. "I hate Vanida so much."

Francois took up the chair opposite her. "I thought he was going to bleed from the ears when I told him about your appointment."

"Will he cause trouble for you?"

"Undoubtedly. I look forward to it."

"Power suits you, Rupert."

"It does, doesn't it?" His smile faded. "You are playing a dangerous game inviting mages to the table."

"I plan to invite elementals."

Rupert choked on his wine, spilling some on his white vestments. "Are you insane?"

"You knew full well that I would bring elementals into the discussion. There is no room for peace until we move past this superstitious nonsense and embrace that we have all been created equal."

"Allegra…"

"Am I not equal to you in the eyes of your god?"

"Yes, of course, but…"

"There is no but. Either I am, or I am not."

"It is not that simple."

"Yes, it truly is. We are equal, or we are not."

"You're going to start the war we're all trying to avoid."

"We are already at war. You just can't see it for all of your gold filigree and fine silks."

CHAPTER TEN

YOUR LADYSHIP,

I have investigated the disappearance of Mrs. Ansley, as per your directive. I regret to report there is no record of her transfer to any facility, nor can we find a record of imprisonment or a statement of death. In fact, we have found no trace of her.

There was a report of a woman seen fleeing the area in tattered clothing, but the description and circumstances do not match Mrs. Ansley. Nevertheless, I have sent two Cathedral guards to investigate this other woman in case she requires assistance or knows of Mrs. Ansley.

I regret that our efforts were not more fruitful. We have alerted local constabulary to the situation. However, I do not expect much assistance considering that they are under the shadow of both the Magistrate and the Duke.

I shall make a more detailed, formal report in person when you are out of session with the cardinals. Send a servant to the barracks for myself and Dodd at your convenience.

Lieutenant Lex
Holy Father's Own Consorts

Cold crept through Allegra as she stared down at the letter. Here in her gown, ready to approach the cardinals in all their splendor, and this was when she got this news. If there was indeed an Almighty, he must certainly be laughing at her arrogance now.

She could still stick to the plan. Walk in there, say her piece, and quietly use her authority to find Mrs. Ansley's whereabouts. Asking forgiveness was certainly easier than asking permission in these circumstances.

Pressure pushed on her throat, making it difficult to breathe. She could feel the noose tightening around her throat, even now. It would come. They would hang her in some back alley, string her up as the mage who got away. One day, her luck would run out. They would accuse her. There would be no trial. No chance to dissemble.

No, she would be drugged and stripped down to her underclothes. They would grab her hair and drag her half-naked through the streets. They would assault and violate her dignity, and then they would murder her like the barbarians they truly are in their hearts.

Allegra closed her eyes in a vain hope to push aside the fear that boiled in her gut. It hadn't happened yet. For now, she could take this position and use it to not only protect herself, but protect those who had no such protection. She must think of her own kind first.

"Your Ladyship? It's time."

Allegra looked up at her new maid servant. She was a lean girl, about sixteen years of age. Her olive skin was free of all blemishes, and Allegra found herself smiling about it every time the young thing came into her room. At her age, Allegra was a mass of painfully swollen bumps. Kia had perfectly smooth skin that sixteen-year-old Allegra would have been impossibly jealous over.

"Thank you, Kia," Allegra said, smiling.

Kia gave a bob of her head and curtsied. She turned over her shoulder and said, "Your Ladyship? Good luck."

"Thank you, Kia."

The Chambers of the Holy Court of Orsini lived up to its name. Allegra had never been inside the heavily-guarded room before; now she knew why. She was led down the corridor with its polished marble tiles and priceless artifacts on full display. The walls were covered in various paintings, all depicting the sacrifices of the Guardians.

Tasmin with her sword drawn leading the charge into a massive demon portal, thousands of horsemen behind her, determined to plunge into the abyss and stop the chaos from the other side.

Lonstein with his children screaming for him not to go as he wrestled with a demon, being dragged into the pit to save his children.

Kasta leading the others of his country, a wall against the demons who spilled out of the abyss. An entire generation sacrificing themselves to save the one that came before and after.

The myths and the paintings gave her chills. She didn't believe the stories, but they were powerful parts of the world. The entire notion of duty and honor was a reflection of the Guardians, who gave their lives to stand against evil. When she was a little girl, she wanted to be Tasmin, leading the charge into battle against an implacable foe, giving her life in sacrifice to the greater good.

However, Allegra soon learned she was not that brave. Oh, she could mouth off on occasion, but she was not brave enough to step in front of the elemental mages and shout stop. No, she continued to live her life while her kind suffered and died at the hands of weak, frightened men.

The endless lectures of the previous night replayed over and over in her mind. Pero and Rupert argued over the best approach for her today in the conclave. Pero wanted her to accuse the cardinals of not being true representatives of the faith and that she planned to act in accordance to the truest meaning of the faith.

Rupert said she was best to outline simple measures she wanted to take, ones that were nothing more than mildly controversial, but that could have a temporary effect on the riots and rebellions. That stirring up the cardinals was not in her best interest, that they were far more powerful than she and that her newfound power, no matter how vast, was at their discretion and theirs alone. She worked for the them, and not the other way around.

She'd even asked Captain Rainier his thoughts. He said the cardinals had several voting blocks, but mostly she had to convince the progressives. Many wanted to do the right thing, but were scared to do so for various reasons, not including their desire to move into more powerful positions within the Cathedral. He'd said, in the end, there was no right way to handle them today, for they were all so very different.

She had outlined several speeches before she decided upon her current course of action. She eyed the painting of Tasmin, this time one of her on a rearing horse, as the demons clawed at her. How could she feel affiliation with a woman who never even existed except in myth? Well, either way, she was going to challenge whatever part of her that longed to be Tasmin and stand in front of the waves of demons.

Allegra smoothed down the front of her gown. She'd worn her white dress with the wide skirts and the gold ruffles and embroidery. It was difficult to keep up with fashion trends, but this was demure enough not to offend the very conservative, but would speak of her wealth and power for those who needed such things spelled out for them and put on display.

Her shoes clicked on the floor and echoed around her. She should have worn her flats, as opposed to the heeled satin shoes. These were too noisy. Nevertheless, what was done was done.

She arrived at a double door and the guards nodded to each other before bowing to her. One of the men at the door, a tall man with brown skin and a bald head, bowed deeply to her. "Your Ladyship, the Chamber is ready for you."

Allegra gave him a curt nod of her head. The doors opened and Allegra nearly gasped audibly. Over a hundred cardinals in their rich purple robes and white fur collars stared at her. Each sat upon a gold-plated chair, covered in red velvet. In front of each of them was a small writing desk. The walls were painted frescos, from floor to ceiling. Landscapes, important moments in the Cathedral's history, the Almighty in his faceless light guiding the faithful to stand against the demons. Gold leaf wainscoting divided the various frescos. It covered the ceiling, the baseboards, the desks, the doors. There was enough gold in this room to feed an entire nation for a month.

Allegra gulped as the guard pointed out the podium where she could stand before the cardinals. But, she squared her shoulders and raised her chin, as a woman of the blood would do before standing in front of such an important body of people. For all of her self-doubts and worries, she was a contessa by blood and birthright. She was wealthy, powerful, and deserved to be in this place.

Greeting her was Holy Father Francois. Gone was her old friend. No, this man was not her friend in this place. He stood when she approached the dais where the inner circle sat. He wore his formal robes: purple with a leopard stole over his shoulders, a gold braid about his waist, and a gold crown on his head. She curtsied low to him, her outstretched hands nearly touching the floor.

He motioned for her to rise. "Greetings, Your Ladyship."

She gave him a guarded smile. "Your Radiance."

"Touch the blue crystal on the podium when you are ready to speak."

She nodded and walked to the wooden podium. It was covered in gold leaf, except for the shelves hidden from the main view of the auditorium. Likewise, the surface where the crystal sat, along with a glass of wine, was plain wood, if anything in this room could be deemed plain.

Allegra touched the gem and saw a hundred other blue lights glow throughout the room. How in the name of all that was holy did they get these? She didn't even know it was possible to enchant stones in this way.

Her first speech she'd prepared was an agonizing compromise that said many lofty words and possessed no teeth, no direction, and no true purpose. It was a miserable, soul-destroying speech that said nothing that was truly in her heart.

If she said what she truly wanted to do, they would drag her into the town square and stone her for being a heretic. She licked her lips. She looked down at these people. Too many of them would all happily send her to a mine to be forgotten, if only so that they could dispute everything that ever came out of her mouth.

So what did it matter what she said? They would vote her down in any case. She was appointed to speak and act on their behalf between governments, but she could only act with their blessing.

She opened her speeches, the two she'd prepared. She shuffled the pages and chose her path.

"Thank you, Your Radiance, for this humbling opportunity to stand before this Chamber today. Since accepting the position of

Arbiter, I have been asked by many what my plan will be to bring about an end to the current brewing conflict. How can I, a woman from a quiet, isolated abbey, hope to bring peace and continued posterity at a time when rebelliousness and rioting are increasingly commonplace through all of Serna.

"When I consider the magnitude of the decision before me, a decision that affects not just this Chamber and how the world sees those within it, but how my choices will affect the lives of every single person we touch, from the lowest prisoner rotting in a cell to the grand houses of princes and kings, I am humbled by this responsibility.

"Many of you feel that I am inadequate to this task before me, and I would be lying to you today if I did not say I feel the terrifying reality of that inadequacy. For, today, I know with all certainty that the path we decide upon today will bring about an end. Only the Almighty knows if it will be the end of unrest or the end of the comfortable existence we all know and love."

Allegra drew in a deep breath. She saw many of them nodding now. She had debased herself the appropriate amount that was needed. Now the real words began.

"When I reflect upon the task before me, and the lives that will shortly depend upon my actions and my decisions, my rulings and my judgements, I know now within my heart what I must do.

"I am but one mage, but I now will speak for all mages when I say we live with the constant fear of being labelled an elemental. The poor and the troublemakers, who have no such talents as others, share in this same fear. There is no test to prove someone is or is not a mage. Just an accusation and the palming of a silver coin is often the only proof we require. Local magistrates arrest innocent women that are competing against them in business, and promptly have them killed, without any trial, without any independent investigation. All of those are a contravention of this Chamber's expressed word. But we do nothing.

"Could any of you live your life with that threat hanging upon you? What if I were to say I was an elemental? I would be dragged from this stage while you fought over who confiscated my property. What if I accused the Holy Father of being one? I am his childhood friend, after all. How many of you would be salivating at the idea that you might have the opportunity to climb the final step on the ladder of power?"

The crowd was muttering now. They were shocked by her words. They expected contrite, useless measures. No, not today. Not ever again. If she were to expose herself to these vultures, than she would show them her teeth, too.

"Can you not see the world of paranoia and fear we have created? For some of us, we hide. We remove ourselves from as many people as possible to avoid accusations that would ruin our lives. Others become abolitionists and agitators. They know they risk imprisonment, but they refuse to live in fear. They know they are already hated so much that any of their enemies would declare them heretics, demon worshippers, and elemental mages just for the sheer, perverse joy of watching them be dragged away. How is this godly? It is not godly."

"How dare you speak of godliness? You are a heathen!" a voice shouted from the floor.

Several of the cardinals pounded on their desks in approval. Others booed, though she wasn't completely sure if they were booing her or her detractors.

The man next to Francois stood. "Silence in the Chamber! Cardinal Vanida, you will control your outbursts." After a moment, he said, "Pray, continue, Your Ladyship."

"The comment from the floor is a valid one, even if given out of turn. So I shall answer it, if you wish."

Vanida crossed his arms.

"I do not know, yet, if I believe in the Almighty, but I do know I believe in what the Almighty stands for: peace. For too long, I have feared the Almighty, not because of my own sins, but the sins of others. I fear what might be done in His name against me and those I love. No more. No more.

"As I stand here today, from this day forward, I shall put aside my fears, all of my uncertainties, and I shall represent the Cathedral, and focus all of my power behind the total abolition of the mage slave trade in all of Serna."

The Chamber went wild. The abolitionists, for there were several wearing cardinals robes she knew, jumped to their feet and clapped. They cheered and praised the Almighty. The status quo block, those who did not want to help the people they pretended to represent, jumped to their feet to decry the abolitionists. Still others, stunned by her words, sat in their seats staring. Some were tugging on their compatriots to be seated, or else whispering to those seated next to them.

She did not care. Her course was set.

"Silence in the Chamber! Silence!"

The voices did not die down until the Speaker of the Chamber stepped up to the podium, touched the crystal, and shouted, "Show some restraint!" His voice boomed throughout the room, silencing all of the arguments below on the floor. "You will show the proper decorum in this Chamber." He looked at Allegra and bowed. "I apologize, Your Ladyship."

She gave him a weak smile. She was ready to vomit.

"I know this path is not easy, and I will not exercise beyond the mandate you vote for me today. However, you have a right to know, from my own lips, what my true intentions are. All of us must take upon ourselves a share in the current situation we find ourselves. We are all guilty. If we wear an amulet or wield an enchanted sword, or have a scarf that keeps us warm in winter, or speak into a crystal for all to hear our voice, we are guilty of causing the rebellion outside of our doors.

"We all benefit from magic, from the lowest to the greatest. We cannot exonerate ourselves by casting blame on others. No, Your Graces, we are all complicit, so let us work together to fix the mess we now find ourselves in."

They were back shouting at her now, disgusted that she had told them they were culpable in the mess that was happening in the real world. The Speaker of the Chamber again stood, but Allegra shouted back. "Sit down or I shall request His Grace to treat you like suspected elemental mages and have you locked in the basement pending investigation!"

There was a shocked silence that came over the room. Even the Speaker stared at her, his mouth slack. "I know some of you are conspiring to label me an elemental. I have heard the whispers. I have heard the snide comments. If you continue to disrupt me, I shall name your names."

"That is blackmail!" Cardinal Vanida shouted at her.

Allegra had heard no such rumors. No one in their right minds would ever whisper a hint of it in her presence. Yet, she'd had her suspicions all the same. So, it came as no great surprise that Vanida was the one to shout the loudest at her words.

"Cardinal Vanida, sit down this instant! You will have the opportunity to speak and vote when Her Ladyship is concluded. Your constant interruptions do nothing but prolong this meeting. Your Ladyship, I humbly beg your forgiveness. The Chamber is normally significantly more cordial." He leaned toward the speaking stone, "Especially considering the abolitionists were not this disruptive when Lord Castigara stood here and demanded all mages be dragged from their homes in chains."

The old man stepped back, but did not sit down. Instead, he stood next to her, a body guard for her words. She gave him a small nod and continued.

"First, this Chamber must address the situation of accused elemental mages, be they mage or not. I have been inside a prison mine. It is the most wretched place on earth. The canaries are living, breathing men, women, and children. They live in the depths to blast away the rock and clear the rubble. They explode the gases, and sometimes explode with the gases. They die by the thousands and we do nothing to stop it. This room is coated in the blood of mages. My dress and its gold thread is stained with the blood of mages.

"Many of those accused of being elementals are not even mages. Those who have been sold into slavery either due to poverty or the cruelty of another risk endless abuses. Women risk further illness from repeated childbirth that was not of their own choice. Children are routinely abused. Men are worked until they collapse. How can we draw a veil over this truth and pretend it doesn't exist?

"The blind see better than we have all chosen to see. And, yes, I count myself in this. But no more. No more will I sit in Borro Abbey and be comfortable. No more will I keep my own counsel. Let the consequences damn me if they will. Cart me away to keep me silent if you choose. But I will no longer rest until I see the end to this offensive and sinful practice."

ALLEGRA SAT IN her small room and sipped her bitter tea. She drank it in spite of the taste, the unpleasantness seeping into her soul. She had done it. Lord Almighty, she had ruined her life. Oh, it might not be today, or even a month from now, but her life was ruined.

She surprised herself by caring far less about that fact than she'd always assumed. She had hidden herself away all these years hoping to shield herself from making this very choice. Now that it was here, there was a weight off her shoulders and a fire in her belly.

As long as the fire stayed within and never on a pyre with her screaming for mercy, she could live with her choice. With the mood she was in today, even if the pyre became her end, she could still live with her choice.

"Do you need some company?"

Allegra was already smiling when she looked up to see Captain Rainier standing in her doorway. He was in his every day green jacket uniform, complete with the sword at his hip. His boots were polished within an inch of themselves and were most likely clean enough to eat off, if it wasn't for the fact that blackening polish was poisonous.

His smile was infectious and she found hers growing. "I would love some company."

Rainier walked in and took a seat across from her. He adjusted his sword so that he could sit and then cross one leg over the other. "So, I heard an interesting rumor. Did you really tell the cardinals that you were going to use your position as Arbiter to eliminate slavery?"

She smiled at him while taking a dainty sip of her tea.

"That takes guts, Contessa. I salute you." Noticing her grimace, he asked, "Don't like the tea?"

"It's very bitter."

"Put some sugar in it." She met his eyes and he sucked in a breath. "Tell me you're not joining the sugar boycott, too. I've had to listen to Pero rant about sugar for six months now."

Allegra placed her saucer down on the small table between her and Rainier. Her corset made the gesture difficult, causing Rainier to rescue her by accepting the dishes. She inclined her head by way of thanks. "I don't believe in doing anything by halves. For better or for worse, I am the Arbiter of Justice. I shall openly dedicate myself to the cause of peace, and equality for mages is the only path to those ends."

Rainier glanced at the untouched sugar bowl. "The cardinals won't vote in your favor."

"I know."

"Then why do it?"

That was an excellent question and one she even asked herself while at the podium. Why *did* she do it? Her speech was more radical than Pero's recommendations. What had she been thinking? The answer always came back to the same thing.

"I'm tired of hiding."

"What do you mean?"

"I've been hiding my whole life from what happened to Mrs. Ansley, and for what? She has disappeared, mostly likely among the unaccounted dead."

"We did all that we could. This was not your fault."

Allegra pushed herself up from the chair and walked over to the large window that overlooked the busy courtyard below. Brisk trade was taking place there, with various enterprising merchants selling their wares out of carts and wheelbarrows. This wasn't the courtyard visitors and pilgrims saw. They kept to the clean markets near the popular sites. Back here, in the working parts of Orsini, were the butchers and bakers, tradesmen and women, and uncertified beggars who weren't allowed in the rich courtyard.

The scene was the reality of life, much more than the sanitized brickwork visitors so frequently saw. This part of Orsini was gated off under the guise of *private quarters*, but this place was like her own heart. Oh, she put on a good show for the populace, but she knew what her own heart harbored. Shame, secrets, and a gripping anxiety that one day her life would be laid bare for the world and, in that moment, her life would end.

"You are too hard on yourself," Rainier said. He walked over to join her at the window. He pushed back the curtain to look out with her, and the lace fell behind them. It gave the illusion of privacy, with the sun beaming in through the window.

She looked up at him. He was the epitome of rugged handsomeness, with his well-trimmed beard that had a couple of white flecks in it. His black hair was cut short against his scalp. For a man who had been in one of the most famous fights in all of Serna's recent history, he had no noticeable scars. Just perfect dark skin that shimmered in the sunlight.

"When did the sugar boycott begin?"

"When I stood at the podium today, I made the decision to dedicate my life to ending the mistreatment of mages. Captain, do you know where Cathedral sugar comes from?"

Rainer pointed at the carts outside. "I assume one of them."

"I asked one of the clerks. She said most of our sugar comes from Lasyrium. The last I've heard, they almost exclusively use male mages."

"I did hear that," Rainier admitted.

"So until I know where my sugar comes from, I won't use it. And that goes for my gold, my gems, my silver, my coffee, and my cocoa." She blew out a breath. "If I have to extend it to my cinnamon, my nutmeg, and even my wheat, I shall. I have hidden long enough and I feel the weight of the consequences."

"Isn't this gold thread in your bodice's embroidery?"

There was a terrifying moment where Allegra thought he was going to run the tip of his finger along the decorative edging. Instead, he touched the bell cuff of her sleeve. He hooked it with his finger and held it up for inspection. He smiled like he meant it, and released her cuff.

She began breathing again. "I originally had this dress made for my brother's wedding, five years ago. I have had it remade every year to suit fashion, in case I required a fancy dress. The damage caused by the purchase of that thread is long done, so I will honor the lives that were sacrificed for it by continuing to wear it until it can't be worn anymore. Then I shall have Nadira bring the scraps to the market to sell to an enterprising sort who can turn it into reticules, hair ribbon, and whatever else they can imagine. And I won't have sugar in my tea."

Rainier's facial expression shifted and Allegra realized she'd been staring up at him in what some might misinterpret as…expectation.

She turned away to look back out of the window. She gave Rainier a final side glance, once she was sure he didn't notice. She made it a personal policy to only become emotionally involved with mages, as they were the only men she could truly trust with her life. And Rupert, but he was her friend before she'd discovered her elemental abilities.

Sadness settled over her when the realization of her loneliness hit her. She often didn't notice at the abbey, with the quiet routine of her life. The same people, the same scenery, the same gossip. It was so much easier to repress that part of her humanity when there was no temptation.

She shook off the pang of interest. Captain Stanton Rainier was a stranger and a normal. A handsome stranger, to be sure, but still not a trusted friend. Perhaps one day, but not today.

"How long do you think the conclave will argue my proposals?"

If he was offended by her behavior, he didn't show it. "How many did you put forward?"

"Twelve," Allegra said with a hint of a grin.

"Were any of them, 'free all mages'?"

"Only one," she said defensively. "The rest were more realistic goals."

"Do you think they'll pass any of them?"

She shrugged. "If I could get three of them, I'd be happy. I asked them to make slavery illegal at any Cathedral property, in that all slaves were automatically freed and without compensation to the owners."

"That's never going to pass," Rainier said gently.

"I know, but it's possible they might vote an amendment to it, by offering compensation or that slaves who arrive there with masters couldn't be forced to leave." She sighed. "It's a long shot, but it would make the Cathedral a beacon for amnesty."

"And if they reject it, it shows the Cathedral doesn't care and it will just increase the protests, which will move to targeting parishes."

Allegra's mouth twitched upward. "Oh, what an unforeseen side effect."

Rainier snorted. "You are devious."

"Someone has to be."

"Your Ladyship!" called a voice from further away. "Your Ladyship? Are you here?"

Allegra turned around and pushed the lace curtains away. "Lieutenant Lex!"

Lex was about to speak when Rainier stepped out from behind the curtain. Lex's words died before a smile tickled the corners of his mouth. He gave Rainier a knowing look before he turned back to Allegra. "Your Ladyship, the Chamber has requested you."

"Have they made a decision?" Allegra asked.

Lex nodded. "Sounds like it. Did you really tell the cardinals you would have them all imprisoned as suspected elemental mages if they kept interrupting you?"

Rainier choked. "Contessa!"

"I was making a point," Allegra said defensively. "Lead the way, Lex. I shall face my executioner."

CHAPTER ELEVEN

THE EXECUTIONER WOULD have to wait. Allegra eased herself into her chair and stared at the room around her. She was Arbiter with a mandate to ease the suffering of mages across Serna. They rejected her call to end slavery, but they accepted her proposal to make Cathedral properties sanctuaries of freedom. No slaves were allowed to work at any Cathedral property, and they had granted Allegra, of all people, the authority to grant freedom to individual slaves.

She stared at her dusty walls unsure if she'd heard them all correctly. The formalized writ would be delivered to her in a couple of days, but they read from the temporary one. Fifteen hours. That's how long they debated before giving her unquestionable authority over the lives of mages.

She was also authorized to investigate any rumors about the mistreatment of elementals in the mines. She was authorized to inspect, without announcement, any Cathedral-funded or supported property, be it abbey or mill. If the Cathedral purchased so much as a thimble from an iron works, she was permitted to investigate the plight of mage workers.

They apparently would provide her a generous budget (details to still be worked out) and a staff of five. She did not get to pick her staff, so she would most likely to saddled with youthful exuberance or incompetence. She was also allowed to hire four additional servants to assist in her efforts, and she was given up to half the Consorts as her personal detail under the new head of her personal safety, Captain Stanton Rainier.

What had she gotten herself into? She had expected, at best, a vague mandate to allow meaningless prattle and letters. She had not anticipated such a detailed directive to her proposals.

Terror crept through her as Allegra made the startling realization that she really did now hold the lives of mages in her hands. She now held the scales of justice and the outcome of all of Serna might rest upon her judgement.

Then Mrs. Ansley's terrified face flickered across her memory and Allegra hardened herself.

"Well?"

She looked up to see Rainier darkening her doorway holding a small lantern. "I assume you've heard."

"I heard some of it, but I'm sure it's just gossip."

She invited him to join her and recited what she could remember from the proceedings. "Most of what they said is a blur, to be honest. I can't believe they did all this. How desperate are they?"

"Very," Rainier said. "The Holy Father has already informed me that I am to head your guard detail."

Allegra licked her lips and searched for the right words. "I will understand if you don't wish to move to Borro. I will speak to Francois on your behalf."

"Hush. I offered my services yesterday."

Heat rose in her cheeks. "I didn't know."

"Well," he said, and she could hear his own embarrassment. "I couldn't very well allow you to return to Borro by yourself, now could I? I'm also looking forward to your random inspections. Dodd and Lex are drawing up a list of potential targets. It's mostly of bishops who've been rude to them."

Allegra's chuckle turned into a yawn. She needed to get out of this dress soon. "I don't wish any Consorts to be forced to come. Please, volunteers only. Cardinal Giso assured me that Cathedral guards were available to fill out any numbers, if needed. I don't believe I'll need twenty guards, however. That does seem excessive."

"There will be a very large target on your heart once you free the first noble's mage slave or close the first cotton mill for mistreatment of its workers. You are about to whack a hornet's nest."

A lump formed in Allegra's throat, as so often did when she felt both overwhelmed and physically exhausted. She needed sleep and quiet to process what she was about to do with her newly-appointed powers. "I wasn't expecting most of this. I don't know what my plans are. It might be months before I decide."

Rainier was very gentle when he spoke. "You shamed many of the abolitionists. You put them on the spot and they had to fight for more than they ever would have because you made them look like hypocrites to their critics."

"Many are hypocrites."

"Look what they have given you. For you now speak for the Lord God Almighty."

"I don't even believe in him," Allegra said, very quietly.

"He clearly believes in you."

"What if I start the war I am here to prevent?"

"Would you order the release of a child who is chained to a cotton wheel? Would you let that child stay there, under that machine until he eventually lost a limb or died from the dust in the lungs? Or would you release him, even knowing that a riot would break out which would usher in the next war?"

Allegra drew in a breath. "Lord help me, but I would still release the child."

"That is why they gave you power. We are already on the brink of war. If you do set it off, we will all look back and know it was done with the best intentions. No one can ask more."

"What if I fail?"

Rainier put a hand over hers and said, very gently, "Everyone fails. What's important is that you do your best."

Allegra looked down at his hand and forced a smile past the terrified tears that welled in her eyes.

LEX SHARED A nod with Dodd before they walked into the main barracks of the Consorts. The room was basic, as far as Orsini accommodations ran, but Lex had seen worse. Their furniture and beds were old, but solid. Plus, the room was never too hot nor too cold, which Lex counted as a blessing from the Almighty. They hoped Borro Abbey would be as pleasant.

Lex and Dodd put down their own candles; there were plenty in the barracks that their additional lights weren't needed.

"All right, listen up," Lex said to the guard. "We've all been assigned to the Contessa of Marsina's personal security for the new negotiations."

Various groans and complaints filled the air. Lex held up a hand and said, "Don't bitch at me. I had nothing to do with it."

"Borro Abbey is in the middle of nowhere," Martin complained.

"Then you take a right hand turn," Dodd said in agreement. "But, Lex is right, folks. We've been assigned to the Contessa."

"Now, let's get one thing straight," Lex announced to the room, "Rainier says this is voluntary, but there had better be a damned good reason for choosing to stay behind here than protecting her Ladyship."

"When are we leaving?" Martin asked.

"We'll know more in the morning, but be prepared to move in two days," Lex said.

"But I got me a new girl down in the village," Martin whined.

"I'm sure she'll be fine without you," Lex said deadpan, in a tone that suggested they didn't actually give a care if the young lady waited or not.

"I hate this job," Martin bellyached.

"What about my girl?" Samuel asked. "She's going to be popping soon."

"Dodd and I are meeting with the Captain in the morning and we'll work out all of the details. I suspect those of you who are married or who have kids can stay behind. I'll see if the abbey has extra space for any families who want to come." Lex frowned. "The rest of you, leave your whores and rakes behind."

More grumbling.

"I mean it!" Lex said sternly. "And, so help me, if any of you fiddle around with the locals and cause trouble, I'll castrate you with my bare hands and a spoon."

Dodd snorted. "I'd pay good money to see that."

Lex made a disgusted sound. "You're so gross."

"The ladies like it."

"The ladies are clearly desperate."

"That stings!" Dodd said, a wounded expression on his face. "It isn't my fault the ladies prefer my charms over yours."

"I don't even like women," Lex said. "And, even if I did, I wouldn't like the women who liked you."

"That hurts, Lex. That really, really hurts." He tapped his fist against his chest. "Right here."

"I'm sure an old fashion tit rub will help soothe the pain," Lex said.

Dodd let out a dreamy sigh. "There's nothing like shoving your cock between two giant…"

"Shut up!" Lex exclaimed. "Almighty in the sky, please! Shut the fuck up!"

Dodd started laughing. "You're such a prude, Lex."

"I'm not a prude. I'm not disgusting."

"Same thing," Martin said.

"Shut up, or I'll write to your mother."

"You wouldn't dare."

"Don't tempt me," Lex said. "All right, shitheels, start packing. We have a lot to get done and little time to do it."

They began pulling out trunks and organizing what was theirs and what was to stay at the palace. Lex had a sheet of paper and a pencil out, so that they could all record any supplies they needed for the journey. Dodd's trunk had a rotted bottom, for example, so Lex made note.

Orsini was more than just the pope's palace. There was a huge population of civilians, too, and various shops and tradesmen. The only difference between Orsini and most cities was that it was significantly cleaner, with significantly less crime, and significantly more religious people.

Lex had lived in Orsini for a number of years now and had gotten used to it. They'd made a lot of friends, even if mostly among the guard...or at the local tavern. Lex hadn't found anyone special or anything, but had the occasional affair when the need took. Lex glanced at Dodd and a little smile quirked their mouth. The friendships were what was important, in any case.

ALLEGRA PILED HER letters into a basket held by Kia. She'd burned through two sets of four-hour candles last evening writing all of these letters of introduction to the royalty and peerage of Serna's various city-states and nations. She took extra attention to write all of Cartossa's peers *and* the clergy. She did enlist assistance for the letters to the clergy, however, as parish priests, fathers, and mothers of the cloth were too numerous to count without a ledger of names.

One of her helpers stood next to Kia. Serafina, her newly-appointed secretary, was dressed in livery and her long hair was neatly pulled back into a tail at the nape of her neck. She had alabaster skin and dark brown hair, along with her dark, upturned eyes that had just the hint of crow's feet forming. Tucked up under her delicate ear was a circular mark that she recognized all too well; the symbol of a mage trained at the Cathedral.

"Please bring all of these to the postal clerk in the main hall, not the one downstairs," Allegra instructed Kia. "Tell them two-penny post, too. Don't let them bully you like yesterday."

"Yes, Your Excellency," Kia said, a smirk upon her face.

"Your Ladyship will do, Kia," Allegra said, sighing at her new title.

Kia's smirk didn't fade, but she did cover it up with a curtsy. "Whatever you wish, Your Ladyship. Shall I have the bill sent to Master Rafino or shall I use ready money?"

Allegra glanced at Serafina, as she had no idea. It took the woman a moment to realize the question was being asked of her. "Oh, yes. For now, send the bill to my study and I shall take care of the accounts. I should go to the banker today and arrange some ready money to have on hand for our journey. Your Excellency, we'll need to discuss your budget once we arrive at Borro Abbey."

"Your Ladyship will be fine," Allegra said absently. She was busy reaching for a letter she'd dropped on the floor.

"Of course, Your Excellency," Serafina said. "I mean, Your Ladyship."

"Don't strain yourself," Allegra said through gritted teeth. She snagged the wayward letter before her corset's whalebone snapped under her contortions and handed it to Kia. "Be off with you. I'd like those sent today."

"Yes, Your Excellency. I mean, Your Ladyship," Kia said with a final curtsy and hurried off with her reed basket of sealed letters.

"You grew up here?" she asked, motioning at Serafina's mage mark with her chin.

"Yes, Your Excellency. Bishop Tolana was my mother. The Holy Father at the time allowed me to study and work here. Once I completed my training, I've been working for the Cathedral ever since."

"You've been very lucky, then," Allegra said absently. She was digging in her drawer for a letter she'd stuffed away for safe keeping. She couldn't seem to find it now that she needed it.

"I am, Your Excellency," she said. Then, after a pause, she added, "Though, not as lucky as yourself, of course."

Allegra glanced up at her thoughtfully. She had no mark on her own skin. Her parents had lived long enough to stand before the king and the clergy and argue that a peer's daughter was never to be forced to be marred by ink, brand, or knife.

"Perhaps my luck will help me advance the mage cause," Allegra said. She saw the familiar handwriting and said, "Ah! There is it. The cardinals have yet to send over their official writ, but Cardinal Giso sent this over. It outlines the income associated with my position. That should help you begin your sums, yes?"

Serafina accepted the letter and read it. Her jaw dropped when she hit the figure. "Ten thousand gold sovereigns? You've been granted an annual income of ten thousand gold sovereigns? Gracious Lord Almighty."

"Hmm. I don't believe that figure is for my personal use. If I understand correctly, the Consorts' incomes come out of that, as well as my rent at Borro Abbey, my servants, my carriages, my postal expenses." Allegra frowned at the door where Kia had escaped through moments before. "Post alone might eat up most of that."

"I'm not entirely sure, Your Excellency," Serafina said. "With your permission, I'd like to consult Cardinal Giso on this. If I am reading this correctly, you have personally been granted an income of ten thousand a year specifically to support your role as Arbiter."

Allegra frowned. "I have no need of an income. I have my own."

Serafina stared at Allegra as though she'd sprouted wings. "I…I will speak with Giso."

A thought came to Allegra. "Ask him if it is personal income, am I authorized to spend it however I please."

Serafina was a young woman, but she wasn't stupid. A knowing look cross her face. She bowed and said, "I shall inquire if this income is beyond the Cathedral bookkeeper's eye."

"That would be lovely, thank you," Allegra said. "Oh, when we arrive at Borro, would you look into finding Nadira a local boy? She isn't as young as she used to be, and she could use a little help. Get someone quick and eager to please."

"Of course, Your Excellency."

Allegra didn't bother to correct her secretary this time.

"Is there anything else?"

At that moment, Captain Rainier darkened her door. She smiled up at him, relieved to see a friendly face who'd want nothing from her, and said to Serafina, "That'll be all, thank you."

She curtsied, again, and left the room. She did stop to curtsy at Rainier, and then scurried out of the room. Allegra motioned for Rainier to close the door and he did. He leaned against it for a moment before asking, "Are you using me as an excuse to hide from well-wishers for a few moments?"

"Absolutely!"

Rainier laughed, a deep, rich sound. "You should have sent a servant to fetch me. I would have rescued you hours ago."

Allegra made a dismissive gesture. "There are so many things to arrange before I leave. I might as well get them done."

Rainier eyed her face before asking, "You look tired."

"That is because I didn't find my bed until almost four this morning. I had so many letters to write. Serafina brought over two apprentices and we wrote letters all night. My eyes still ache." She yawned into the back of her hand. "As do the bones in my fingers. I cannot wait to be back at Borro in my riding trousers and out of these clothes."

Rainier walked over and took up the chair across from her desk. "I never understood why keeping up with fashion was so important here. They all wear robes. Why would they care how others dressed? I'm stuck in the uniform regardless, but at least it's comfortable at times."

Allegra eyed him in his officer's uniform for the Holy Father's Own Consort Guard. The green jacket was clean, and the metal decorative buttons on the black braiding were shiny and well maintained. The metal buttons that held the jacket in place, however, were more worn, a result of constant handling. The Captain's rank decorative cuffs were still black, though had faded a touch in the sun.

His red sash with its long tassels was expertly tied at his waist. He wasn't wearing his sword belt, however, and it seemed out of place not to have it resting over top the sash like normal.

His trousers were probably once regulation issue, but were now customized to suit his active commission. The dark green wool trousers matched his jacket, but had brown leather sewn into the inseam to protect against the constant wear from riding. He was sporting his tall riding boots, too, and they were buffed so well she was sure she could apply lip color in the toes if she had to. Not that she ever wore lip coloring, of course. This was her natural color of lips. At least, that's what she told anyone who asked.

"I came to ask if you'd like to meet the Holy Father's Consorts. Everyone's packing, so it's a good time to come meet them all."

Allegra pushed herself up from her chair. "I could use the exercise."

She locked several documents, along with her journal, in her desk drawer before shoving her hand holding the key into one of the slits on the side of her voluminous skirts. She deposited the key into the secret pockets that were tied about her waist.

"Two days on the job and you are already dealing in secrets?" Rainier asked.

"My dear Captain, the entire purpose of this job is to horde secrets until I can wield them like daggers in the night."

Rainier smiled. "If you ever get tired of bossing around nobility, there'll always be a job for you with the Consorts. We could use your skills."

"If I ever run out of money, I'll be sure to speak to you first."

They walked outside and along the cobblestoned road. This part of Orsini was spotless. Every street corner had two children with a bucket, brush, and shovel to clean up dung and garbage. Not a scrap of debris or fleck of dirt was to be found on the stones, lest a cardinal's robes become mired in filth.

The stables were behind the great buildings, out of sight and smell. The poor weren't allowed to beg in this area of the Orsini, except by special permit. There was an actual person somewhere within these great halls who issued seals of permit to beggars of merit, to solicit within the paths between the palace and the Cathedral.

Food also wasn't sold in this area; it had an odor. No, everything had to be perfect here to create the illusion that the Almighty's grace was upon the Cathedral. It was all well and good, but this arrangement caused a slight problem.

"Is there anywhere decent to eat nearby?" Allegra asked.

"What's wrong with the food at the palace?"

"I hate swan. It tastes like...well, I won't say what it tastes like. Is that lady still down by the river dock? You know, the one with the goiters on her neck? She makes that—"

"The salt pork stew in the cabbage leaves? Sorry, she died last winter."

"Oh," Allegra said disappointedly. "From the tumors?"

"Childbirth," Rainier clarified.

"That's a pity. Well, where do you eat?"

"Adwin should still have some pork biscuits left, if we hurry."

"Sounds perfect."

Allegra followed Rainier as they weaved their way through a couple of back alleys that were suspiciously scrubbed clean only as far as street view allowed. They ducked several lines of dripping clothes, and Allegra had to tug up her skirts to keep them out of the mud puddles.

They emerged on to a busy market street, where vendors shouted their wares list to shoppers. The sound was deafening, only matched by the eclectic aroma of the place. Curries competed with roasting meats, while baking breads competed with fish sitting in the sun.

There was every kind of produce here, and in all varieties and sizes. All kinds of cheese, along with grapes, citrus, and various root vegetables. Plenty of garlic and herbs, too, alongside wilting greens in the harsh sunlight.

"Lemon, Captain Rainier?"

They turned around and a young girl with a basket curtsied. Allegra winced. One side of the girl's face was melted away and her skin was a painful hue of pink across part of her forehead, one eye, and across her cheek to her missing ear. She wore a knitted cap of bright colors, which did a passable job at hiding the missing hair on one side of her head.

"Yes, please," Rainier said as he dug in his money purse. "Your Ladyship?"

"Yes, please," Allegra said automatically.

"Halfpenny, please, Captain," she said in a cheerful sing-song tone. He handed over the coin and she curtsied to Allegra, grinned at Rainier, and scampered off to accost other potential customers.

"Adwin is over there. Let's see, oh, looks like he has some buns left. You're in luck," Rainier said as he peeled the top of his lemon.

"What happened to her face?" Allegra asked, looking back over her shoulder.

"Fire," he said. He picked up his pace and waved at the costermonger. "Any pork buns?"

Adwin was a gaunt man who towered over Rainier. His blue-black skin glistened in the bright sunlight. "No pork, Captain, but I got some curry lamb ones."

"I'll take one. Contessa?"

"What other ones do you have?" she asked.

Adwin went through the list of what was left, and Allegra's growling stomach decided upon the last sausage-stuffed bun at the kiosk. Rainier paid for the food before she could pull out her coin purse, and she thanked him.

They headed down through the market, away from the food vendors. This part of the market was full of repair shops and used clothing, and furniture of all kinds. There were trinkets and oddities for sale, alongside the more practical shops selling pots and pans, menders, and repairers. This was where servants bartered on behalf of their masters and mistresses.

"Nadira is here somewhere, no doubt," Allegra said absently. At Rainier's questioning look, she clarified. "I had some jewelry I wanted sold. I've been putting it off, since I'd get a better price here than back in Borro."

"Ah," Rainier said again, still snacking away at his bun.

Allegra was running out of conversation pieces, so decided to follow in silence. They no longer weaved through alleyways, for which Allegra was grateful. There was significantly more muck in this area of the city. They kept to the street-sides and ate their food in silence.

Eventually, they arrived at the barracks. The barracks were inside an older stone building, with simple raised lettering on it quoting from the word of Tasmin.

"Oh, I've been here before. The archives are downstairs," Allegra said. She lifted her skirts to ascend the steep stairs.

"They've been moved over to the old tax collector's building," Rainier said. He wasn't breathing hard at all.

Allegra slowed her steps. She wanted to keep up with him, but with the combination of the corset, her shoes, the precarious steps, and the skirts, she was seconds away from panting, and that was undignified.

Rainier turned around to see her falling behind. "Sorry. Do you need my arm?"

"I'm fine," Allegra said too quickly. She amended and said, "I don't dare let go of my dress."

"That's what you get for following fashion, Contessa."

"Indeed," she agreed.

Rainier chuckled. "Contessa, you never cease to surprise me."

If they were to be working together, and closely, Allegra decided to move past some of the formalities. She needed an ally and a friend. She side-eyed him and said, very quietly, "You are welcome to call me Allegra, Captain."

His grin was wicked. "Only if you call me Stanton."

Allegra bit her lower lip in a failed attempt to hide her smile. "Well, *Your Grace*, I am humbled to have that honor."

Rainier gave her a stern glare, but it faded away in the glow of her beaming grin. "You are trouble."

"Always," she said sweetly. She reached the top of the stairs and exhaled in relief. "Whew. Those were tough."

"Come on. The gang is up another flight of stairs."

"I am coming to hate this building," Allegra said.

They made their way up the narrow stairwell. The stairs opened into a huge room, similar in scope to a ballroom, only more sparsely decorated. There was a worn carpet spread down the length of the room, but it was too narrow for the room and only covered a little more than half of the center of the wood floor.

The walls were sparsely decorated. A couple of religious paintings hung on the walls; the standard depictions of Tasmin smiting demons done in oils. The paintings were clearly old like the carpets, as they were equally dingy and faded from time, light, and dust. The walls were lined with wooden doors. Some were opened, revealing messy beds and boxes.

The main room was full of trunks and boxes, and several people were mock wrestling and laughing. Others were packing. The heat was stifling in the room and many of the men were shirtless.

"Her Ladyship wanted to meet you before we headed to the abbey," Rainier said. He frowned. "I wasn't expecting everyone to be naked."

Dodd laughed. He was bare chested, with his dingy white shirt dangling from his belt. He wasn't tall for a man, but he was broad shouldered. His muscles weren't cut the way some of the thinner men's were, but he looked strong enough to bounce them all off his chest and not even notice. "I'm sure her Ladyship can handle it."

Allegra's eyes fell upon Lex and her smile froze. Lex was in his usual green uniform trousers, but was in bare feet. He had long, narrow feet that matched his long, narrow fingers. And he was wearing a crisp, clean corset. The white garment was different from anything Allegra had ever seen. It only came just under the breasts and had lacing in front and on the sides. It seemed to pull on like a pelisse – arms in, tie at the front.

There was silence in the room and Allegra was acutely aware she'd been staring. Dodd glanced over his shoulder and quickly said, "Oh, Lex. Yeah, see he hurt himself moving trunks and shit, so I gave him my corset. It's good for bad backs, did you know?"

Allegra gave Dodd a look that said she wasn't buying that the lean, muscular Lex could snugly fit into anything from Dodd's clothing trunk.

"It's all right, Dodd," Lex said in a cool voice. "If the Contessa wishes to stare, she can stare."

Allegra blinked, realizing she was being unconscionably rude. "I apologize, Lex. I'm…stunned by your corset. Where did you get such a garment? Where can I have one made?"

"Um…" Lex said.

"It's…mine, Your Ladyship," Dodd said.

Allegra rolled her eyes. "I would give a year of my pin money to have something like that. Does it chafe under your arms?"

"Um…" Lex said.

"Um…" Rainier added helpfully.

Allegra stared at them all and realized they were expecting a very different reaction from her. Yes, she had been momentarily surprised, but she didn't need them to continue some kind of farce to make her comfortable. Though, it did make her smile inwardly knowing that the people who'd be her guard placed protecting their own from an employer, if necessary, high on their priorities.

Allegra decided the best way to defuse the situation the others might think was unfolding. "I asked my mantua-maker back at Borro if she could make a corset that didn't dig into my hips when I rode. She put lacing at the side. Which is fine, I suppose, but it still means I'm in a full corset while on horseback. I simply must speak to her about this design."

"Um, my mother had it made."

"Who is your mother?" Allegra asked.

"The Viscountess of Alvery," Lex said.

"May I write to your mother for the design?"

LEX STARED AT this wealthy, pampered peer and wondered what the fuck was going on. Lex was standing there in a damned corset with their modest breasts snugly bound. Martin had handed Lex his own tunic when the Contessa had walked up the stairs, but Lex hadn't the chance to tug the garment on before she spied them.

Lex had been braced for the inquisition from this fine lady, but it didn't come. Even with Dodd's pathetic help and Rainier's useless support, the Contessa didn't pry. She'd even attempted to deflect the entire awkward situation by discussing the awkward garment openly.

"Um...sure. I'm sure my mother would be...honored? To receive a letter from you, I mean," Lex said, still confused. Was this a trick?

"Excellent. Perhaps she can forward me the construction details. Now, I came up here to meet everyone, since you have been appointed to my guard and personal safety. However, I wish to skip all of that, and I want to know the intricate details of Lieutenant Dodd wearing a corset. Please tell me this is not a fabrication." In a hushed tone, she said, "Please tell me it was in vibrant red velvet."

"Pink, Your Ladyship," Lex said.

"Tell me everything," Allegra said.

And the gang erupted into the tale, each talking over each other. First it was Dodd who very sternly stated he had injured his back wrestling a bear in the defense of several small children.

"You were wrestling me!" Lex exclaimed. "Here, in the barracks!"

"You've hair enough for a bear," Dodd complained bitterly.

Lex looked down on at the blond downy hair on their arm. "If I look like a bear, you look like a matted fur rug."

Martin helpfully pointed out that Lex had put Dodd into a backbreaking hold and Dodd refused to give in, so Lex held the pose until Dodd's back began to spasm.

"That's when I made Lex stop," Rainier clarified. "That fool over there would have let Lex break his back before losing face in front of everyone."

Beatrix chimed in excitedly, "So, like, Dodd was in significant pain, right? So Mother Valincroft was called, right? Cause she was the local priest in charge of, you know, ministering to the poor and all that."

"So she comes in there, tuts and frowns," Rainier said.

"Don't forget lectured!" Martin added.

"Then she insisted that Dodd needed a corset to help his back heal," Lex said.

"But no one here had a corset big enough to fit Dodd," Rainier said. He was smirking.

"Ugh, here we go," Dodd said. He was putting on a good show, but Lex knew he was grinning inwardly. Lex also knew Dodd would happily have this story told if it meant making Lex less uncomfortable. Of course, Lex wasn't bothered by the situation. Lex was Lex. This Contessa could accept the reality or not. Accept it, and she earned their trust and respect. Reject it and well, Lex wasn't going to change who they were just to suit someone, no matter how important they thought they were.

"So one of the older priests leant him one of hers," Martin said.

"And it was pink?" the Contessa asked hopefully.

"White," Dodd said through clenched teeth. "But it smelled like rosewater."

"But Dodd was too proud to wash his own laundry," Rahna said. "He had the nerve to ask me to do it."

"It wasn't because you're a girl," Dodd said contemptuously. And it wasn't. They all knew it. "You were new."

"And a girl," Martin emphasized.

Dodd sighed and gave the Contessa a shrug.

"Oh, Dodd," the Contessa said. "Tell me you didn't let her wash your laundry after that."

"I did," Dodd said.

"He did," everyone else chimed in.

"He certainly did," Rainier added.

"It took two months for his back to completely heal," Lex said. "And the entire time, he was wearing a pale pink corset underneath his manly green jacket."

"Many men wear pink," Dodd said.

"Very true," the Contessa said. "I'm certainly not going to judge. Or, I wasn't until I saw the blush creeping up your cheeks."

Dodd burst into laughter, and soon the entire hall was laughing and joking with this new boss of theirs. Lex tugged on the shirt offered by Martin, all the while watching the Contessa. The Contessa glanced at Lex and offered a small incline of her head. Lex mirrored the gesture.

Perhaps they'd all misjudged her; Lex most of all.

CHAPTER TWELVE

ALLEGRA'S RETURN TO Borro was delayed by a week. There were simply too many fine details to organize. Serafina appointed Nathan as her new apprentice secretary. Nathan was Pero's cousin's son, a nervous, scrawny kid whose voice had only recently fallen and who looked like he was about to faint from starvation.

But for all of his *ums* and *aws*, he already had a solid reputation for thorough and complete work, so Allegra didn't argue with Serafina's request to hire him. He'd worked for the previous two Arbiters in various capacities, so he knew where files, ledgers, and other various archives were located better than anyone else. He was to remain at the Cathedral for several weeks to organize the paperwork before joining Serafina at Borro Abbey.

"Nathan, did you get that list together of abolitionists?"

"Yes, Your Ladyship," he said. He fumbled about in the stack of books, letters, and pages in his arms until he found what he was looking for. "Here it is."

Allegra examined the list, ignoring the sweaty fingerprint stains and a wine ring stain. Most of these people she knew by reputation. Some had approached her in the past for various types of help. She had given money and letters of recommendation when she could, but most had called for her to publicly stand up for mage rights or elemental rights, and she had politely turned them down. There was no doubt she would come to regret those past decisions. She planned to dig deep in her grovelling letters to all of them.

She smiled up at Nathan and said, "Thank you. Has the post arrived yet?"

"Yes," he said and, again struggling, dropped several letters on to her desk from on top of his stack of papers.

"What is all that?" Allegra asked, motioning at the books in his arms.

"Journals and ledgers from previous Arbiter secretaries over the last two decades." He handed over a significantly smaller stack of letters. "These are for you."

"Do you think you'll be able to find anything useful for me in the old notes?" Allegra asked absently as she opened the first letter. From the handwriting, she guessed it was from her sister-in-law. She glanced over it, confirmed that it was, and put it aside for when she needed a pick-me-up.

"Well, Your Excellency, I planned to, um, I could identify which situations have changed or remained unchanged. Then, um, we could prioritize which were in need of your intervention first. For example, erm, there might be easy ones that could quell unrest in localization areas, which would bring immediate, if temporary, secession of hostilities."

She smiled tightly. "I think that's the correct approach. Carry on."

"Yes, Your Excellency. And, um, thank you for this position. It, um, means a lot to me to, um, work with you on such an important, um…thing."

Allegra smiled. "You're welcome."

He stood there.

"Well, I have my letters to read."

"Right. Sorry. I will go now."

"Yes."

It was several more seconds before he finally turned himself about to exit her appointed study.

The first three letters were of the same forced congratulations and general sucking up. The Bishop Samuel of North Wadesboro, a pompous old fool who had less depth than a glass of water, wanted to "continue, nay extend, the friendship between his peaceable little corner of the world and the mighty Cathedral where the Almighty himself looks down upon us all." Of course, Bishop

Samuel was a powerful slave owner who reportedly had his personal militia harass free mages. He enacted local ordinances on Cathedral property that all slaves be chained by the legs so to prevent escape. And the people adored him for it, because he was keeping them safe from the demon-worshipping mages. Bringing the word of the Almighty with leg irons. How predictable.

Allegra stuffed the letter into the journal labeled: *For Future Considerations.* Once settled, she would find some guards to pay the good bishop a visit.

The second was from her cousin, Katherine, the Grandest of Grand Duchesses. Kat's letter passive-aggressively implied Allegra would need to hike up her skirts to get the job done. Ah, that's what older, prettier cousins do, even into their forties. Somehow, the letter cheered up Allegra's flagging spirits. Some things never do change.

Unsurprisingly, the third was from the Bishop of Borro. Father Michael wrote to say he had the servants improving the summer cottages to winterize them for Arbiter business. He did hint, however, that the cost of such upgrades would tax the abbey and "any assistance" the Cathedral could offer would be "greatly accepted and put to good purposes for the glory of the Almighty's work."

"Are you settling in well?" Pero strolled into the room and smiled. "How is my cousin's son? Have you murdered him yet?"

Allegra laughed. "Nathan will be fine. He's just...scatterbrained, I believe, is the right word."

"That's one word. So, how are you doing?"

"Did Rupert send you?"

"Ah, His Holiness is far too busy to something something blah blah blah..." Pero flashed her a grin. "I promised Katherine I'd check in on you."

"Of course she'd send you. How is my emotional stability these days? I'm sure there are various people reporting back."

Pero sat down. "Well, let's be honest between friends. You have used that excuse for the last two decades."

Allegra failed to withhold her grin. "Being a mage is a difficult burden for anyone to carry."

"Are you saying wealth and consequence didn't help ease the struggle?"

"Ah, Pero. You must come to Borro more often." Allegra chuckled. "You and Father Michael could out argue each other."

"Alas, my duties keep me here. What would Francois do if we all abandoned him?"

"I was merely asking you to visit, not run away with me."

"Think of the gossip, though, if we did!"

"The cardinals would get no work done." She smiled. "So, is this really just a social call?"

"No," Pero said, and his smile faded. "I've come with the warning."

Allegra cocked an eyebrow.

"Nothing sinister, I promise. Some of the abolitionists have decided not to assist you without certain assurances."

"Such as?"

"They want guaranteed immunity for their actions. They want elemental rights combined with mage rights. They don't want them discussed separately. They want you to speak, as necessary, as to the role of a mage."

Allegra sucked in a breath. "You know I can't promise any of that."

Pero held out his hands. "Those are their demands."

"Or what? They won't help?"

"They won't help *you*."

"We're all on the same side."

"Are we?" Pero's expression hardened. "What I see across from me is a woman who has refused for her entire life to do anything remotely public to aid mages. You were appointed to your position out of spite, and likewise you accepted out of spite. How can we trust that you won't bury your head in the sand again whenever you are forced to recognize you are a mage?"

"I have never denied being a mage, and I resent your implication that I have done nothing to assist the cause. We both know I have funneled a significant amount of my personal wealth into emancipation."

"No, Allegra. You have funneled your money into financially rewarding slave owners."

Allegra rolled her eyes. "We have been over this before, Pero."

"And we shall go over it again. Buying slaves is not the answer."

"The money also went towards helping get them set up in positions, finding them housing, all that," Allegra said defensively.

"Some things never change," Pero said. "I like you, Allerga. I don't like your politics. They are...cowardly."

"And I like you. And I think your politics are...dangerous."

"So can I tell the abolitionists that you will be supporting their demands?"

"You can tell them that I will not abuse my positon and that I will act in accordance with my conscience." She took a deep breath and said, "You can also tell them that their demands, in my eyes, are no different than the dozens of other demands, requests for favors, and veiled threats I've received this week alone. You know me well enough to know that I will not be cowed in to the corner and I am offended that you hadn't the decency to convince them otherwise. Now, if there is nothing further, I have work to do."

She watched Pero leave and frowned down at her letters.

"Is everything all right?"

Allegra looked up to see Captain Rainier standing in her doorway. "Captain! To what do I owe this pleasure?"

"I heard you and Pero arguing, and I thought I'd look in on you."

Allegra smiled, even though it was a little weary. "Ah, don't mind us. Tomorrow, I'll receive a gift of molasses taffy and flowers, along with a note apologizing for his hot temper. Please, have a seat."

"This argument has happened before, has it?"

"Pero and I have a lot in common, but his actions are governed by his faith, whereas mine by my sense of duty. Our end goals are the same, but we have very different opinions about how to get there. It causes conflict."

"Why should you fight, since you are on the same side?"

"That's a rather simplistic view."

"I'm a simplistic sort of man."

Allegra laughed. "I highly doubt that. Educated at...hmm..."

Rainier raised his chin to strike a pose.

"Oh, clearly Ostarium School for Boys. Then acceptance to Cornwallis University, where you studied religion. The law is too clever for you."

"You wound me, my lady!"

"Am I wrong?"

Rainier made a face. "My brother closest to me in age was studying the law. We weren't getting along at the time."

"Ah, brothers."

"Now, I believe I'm here to discuss your personal security, as opposed to my family history," Stanton said easily. He had a busy day ahead of him, not to mention all of the packing he needed to do. He'd have to arrange for his valet to send his personal items ahead to Borro Abbey, as soon as the Contessa heard back from the Bishop of Borro.

And he needed to find a new valet, since his quit as soon as the words *move to Borro Abbey* were spoken.

She sipped her tea and smiled. "I apologize. I'm using you as a distraction from my duties."

"I see you found some honey." He pointed at the small jar on her serving tray.

"Ah, yes. Kia heard about my boycott and, well, she was very enthusiastic to help. She has a couple of mage friends."

"How are the new servants working out?" He was genuinely curious.

"Kai and Calm Seas are fine. A bit young and chatty, so Nadira loses her temper some days, but overall, they'll be fine together. Sandra and Malcolm hate each other, so that's awkward, and Roosevelt leers at Calm Seas way too much for my liking. I'm leaving him behind to forward packages that come for me. He can read, so…"

"And the new staff?"

Allegra chuckled. "Staff! It's strange, really. My brother looks after the day-to-day running of my estates, so I don't really think of myself as having staff. But it's all coming back to me rather quickly, and perhaps a bit too easily. I find myself having missed the intellectual challenges."

"Watch out, Serna. The Contessa has a taste for power."

Allegra chuckled again. "Just a taste, my dear Captain. Just a taste."

"Will we head directly back to the abbey, or did you want to make a slight detour?"

Allegra's mouth twitched. "I believe we'll be stopping by our dear friend, the Magistrate of Montfort, to investigate. Just as a random check, of course."

"Of course. Should I arrange for extra guards?"

"That might be wise," Allegra said. "Come, join me."

They snacked on slices of tea cake and sipped tea while they went over various other plans. Allegra didn't want to punish those with families, and insisted that coming to Borro was voluntary. She also insisted on bringing the Consorts' immediate families who wished to move and promised to find them housing in the town of Borro. She couldn't guarantee that there would be enough room at the Abbey for even all of the consorts, but she felt a small garrison in the town itself might actually do well to keep ahead of any situation.

"I agree. Would you like me to assign people or did you have any one in mind?"

Allegra shook her head. "I'd prefer if Dodd remained at the Abbey."

"I don't see a problem with that. Do you want Lex in the town, then?"

"Actually, I wanted to speak to you about him."

Stanton squared his shoulders. "Is there a problem?"

"Not at all. Pero and Rupert, and actually a number of cardinals who don't even like me, believe I need a small security detail at all times. I think it's unnecessary, but I've relented. I was wondering if Lex would be good for the job."

"Lex would probably enjoy the challenge."

"Good. I'll work out the details with Lex once we're at the abbey. I might need the Consorts or guards to do occasional tasks for me. Who will I need to clear that with? You?"

"Please. If I'm not available, Dodd or Lex can handle things."

"Good." Allegra looked at him over the rim of her cup, smiling as she drank.

"What?"

"Will you make time for your Arbiter to continue these mid-day visits?"

"I will make the time, *Your Excellency*."

TRANSITIONS

Montfort County
Near the Cartossa-Amadore Border

THE PLAN UNFOLDED flawlessly. The stew and ale had been adequately altered, and those who didn't ingest too much were already snoring off the effects. The hearts of the gluttons had most likely stopped by now. Walter preferred not to leave behind corpses, but it was the fault of the greedy, not his, that they consumed too much ale and stew. They could have left some for the mages or the low servants. Then, no one would have died and the plan would have failed.

With the full moon illuminating their way, the small band of rebels made their way to the camp of dead, dying, and unconscious men. One of them found the keys and unlocked the chains that barred the small coal mine's entrance.

With the door closed behind him, Walter chanced to light the lantern. Most of his men would remain outside, in case any of the guards roused. Walter crept down the ladders, stairs, and walkways, following the faint glow of a lantern down in the bowels of the hand-dug pit.

The light flickered out. Walter took the final lift down, his lantern still flickering. Blank, dirty faces stared back at him. Then, confusion when they realized they did not know him.

"I'm Walter Cram," he whispered. "I'm here to get you out. Come quickly."

"You're that mage," one of the dirty-faced men said.

"I am. Now, hurry before the guards awake."

A woman lay on her side, moaning. "What's wrong with her?"

One of the other women shook her head sadly. "Arrived a few days ago. They'd hurt her bad. Don't know who she is. She's not gotten up since. Not right in the head no more."

"Can she walk?"

"Both legs broken, sir. They threw her down here, waiting for infection to kill her."

"Can medicine or healing help her?"

The woman shook her head. "I think she's well past any help other than the Almighty's."

"All right, leave her. Everyone else, let's go."

"But…"

"If she's going to die anyway, there is no purpose in the rest of us dying to rescue her," Walter said sharply. "If you want your freedom, let's go."

"Cram! Hurry! Some of the guards are waking!" a voice shouted from up above.

"You heard him!" Walter shouted.

Moving back up the mine shaft was tedious work. He waited until the others made it back up. He took one last look at the broken woman on the ground. Another nameless nightmare to haunt him. Another tableau to fuel his hatred, as if he didn't already have more than his fill.

Once he exited the mine himself, an all too common scene was unfolding before his eyes. Some brutally enacted the justice denied to them with stones against skulls. Others ran, no thought to being barefooted and nearly naked. Others stood unmoved, too shocked for their flight instincts to work.

Maybe it would have been kinder to have killed the guards with the drugs, but then these people would never have their vengeance.

Once the bloodlust was sated and the realization of freedom began to dawn upon the terrified, Walter summoned up his will. The earth shook under their feet and then the mine collapsed in on itself.

It was the ninth this month. He'd not even made a dent in Cartossa's evil.

CHAPTER THIRTEEN

Montfort County, Cartossa

THE FIRST ORDER of business was to return to the abbey. With the horses and carriages packed, they began their journey back to Borro. Allegra travelled with a holy writ basically granting her immunity from local laws and proclaiming that she acted with the authority of the Holy Father and the papal office. One of the main reasons she'd waited was because Allegra was convinced she'd be arrested by some petty noble on her journey otherwise.

She also travelled with the authority to arrest and detain anyone committing a various list of crimes that boiled down to anyone contravening the laws of the Cathedral. Since their law was supreme, Allegra had every intention of using religion for her own gains.

She didn't believe in demons, the Guardians who protected them against the demons, or even the Lord God Almighty, but she could set aside her lack of faith to harness the power of religion. For too long, religious belief had terrified her. Now, she planned to use it to the fullest extent of her abilities.

She sat across from Rainier in her carriage. He stretched his long legs across the small space between them, sitting crosswise to give himself the maximum space possible. She, regrettably, was in her best traveling attire and was laced up tighter than a winter roast over the spit.

"Why are you grinning?" Rainier asked her.

"I was thinking about my visit to the Bishop of Orsini this morning." That pompous fool had the nerve to talk down to her. He came to regret it very quickly.

"Be careful with him. He's not as toothless as he seems," Stanton cautioned.

"I know his brother is a cardinal." Allegra snorted. "You should have heard him, Captain. At one point, he interrupted me and said, 'Actually, my good lady, that's not the best way to educate mages. Here's a fun fact for you.' And then went off on this patronizing tangent about mage education and why poor women, in particular, shouldn't have their heads filled with literature and mathematics since it would give them improper views of their futures."

Rainier snickered. "He is a bit of an ass."

"Just a bit? He didn't realize I was a mage! This entire time, and we've corresponded back and forth several times over the last year, and he had no idea. Despite the fact that it was in my very first letter to him, but of course men like him know everything. So I laid into him, right there, in front of everyone. I demanded he reinstitute the poor school. So then he says he had to shut the school down because there were no funds."

"I thought you had offered him one hundred gold sovereigns of your own money?"

"Indeed, I had. So here he was trying to impress this room of bishops and a couple of cardinals, and I destroyed him." Allegra smiled. "I can see now why they say power is addictive."

"I'm pleased you're enjoying your new position."

"The real work hasn't even begun. It won't always be this rewarding, I'm certain."

Allegra knew it wouldn't be. She was preparing for a long winter of delegates bringing their petty differences to her. She wanted to concentrate solely on easing the burden on enslaved mages, as well as instating protections for the free mages, but that was a fantasy.

The reality was going to be significantly more boring. The last several arbiters had done little to mediate the rising conflicts. The role of arbiter was to be an impartial representative who could settle disputes on the national level. Arbiters didn't care about petty magistrates; arbiters cared about the viscounts and princes who pitted their armies against each other and the innocents who were caught in the middle.

She had taken both Francois and Pero's advice to heart and had decided to first deal with all of the small, petty differences. None of the leaders would travel to spend the winter with her in any case – Borro Abbey was in the mountains and that meant snow and cold. Instead, she could spend the winter writing letters, dealing with smaller issues, and bringing stability by inches.

Then, when the spring came, she could invite the leaders for a summer summit – the mountains would be a pleasant break from the heat of the lowlands – and the real work could begin. It was a solid plan, if dull.

Though, Allegra did have a small amount of excitement scheduled.

"Why are we turning here?"

"We're going to a coal mine on the Earl's property, who is the magistrate of Montfort's uncle I might add, and we're going to free all of the mages. Oh, and then we're going to confiscate the Earl's estate, and then we're going to drive over to the magistrate's house and do the same there. And then, we're going to ensure some of that money is redistributed back to the mages who had their property and lives stolen. And we might keep doing that until we find Mrs. Ansley." Allegra smiled sweetly.

Rainier's expression darkened. "You can't be serious."

"I accepted this position for one purpose only: the freedom of mages. Since I cannot do it directly, I shall use every single tool within my legal grasp to bring down this fraudsters."

"It would take us months to deal with an estate confiscation."

"That's why Pero is travelling with us."

"Pero is travelling with us?"

Allegra grinned. "His carriage is an hour or so behind ours."

"Does Francois know?"

Allegra frowned. "I knew I forgot something."

Rainier rubbed the back of his neck. "You're killing me, Allegra."

Their eyes met as he uttered her given name for the first time. She gave him a pleased smile and said, "Isn't this fun, Stanton?"

STANTON WAS SURPRISED by how smoothly the entire process had gone. He did manage to convince Allegra to have guards remain with the mages while the remainder of the guards, including Pero's new arrivals, dealt with the messy business of arresting both the Earl and the magistrate.

The Earl was, to no one's surprise, enraged that his position meant nothing to Allegra. He'd made the mistake of assuming she was some lowly merchant's daughter, who'd gained her position by some circumstance of chance and luck. It was only years of training and practice that kept Stanton from bursting into gleeful chortling when Allegra identified her own title and that she was now the outstretched hand of the highest office of the Cathedral.

The magistrate was busy spilling his guts to Pero, placing all of the blame squarely on the Earl, when Allegra was satisfied enough to continue on her journey.

The mine was small, only able to handle about forty workers. Most were dirt-smeared women and girls, though there were a few men in the mix. She announced their freedom, but asked them to wait for a couple of days while Pero and his men issued them papers of pardon, purchased them clothing, and ensured they had both coin and transportation home.

Mrs. Ansley wasn't there, however. She'd never arrived at the mine. Missing. Disappeared. Gone. There was a tiny coal mine in the neighborhood, but locals said it had collapsed a week ago in the middle of the night. No one made it out alive. Nine mines in as many days had collapsed. Some said mages were involved, but no one knew for certain.

Stanton held on to the hope that Mrs. Ansley was still on the run, or that she was working as a domestic within one of the great houses. Allegra was far more cynical.

"She's likely dead already," Allegra said. Her voice was cold and low.

"You can't be sure," he'd argued, but Allegra wouldn't respond further.

They rode in complete silence for three hours. They changed horses at a small inn and took a half hour break for hot food. Allegra purchased hot tea and a biscuit, nothing else. Stanton had taken the standard fare offered: mutton stew, bread, butter, beer. He'd hoped Allegra would sit with him in the common room, but instead she took her mug into the lady's waiting area and isolated herself there.

"I asked about Mrs. Ansley," Lex said, sitting down across from him.

"Thanks," Stanton said. "Pero did, too. He said Sir Bertrand lost her to the Baron of Mansbridge in a game of cards. He's going to send people to check Mansbridge's property for Mrs. Ansley, but…"

"I wouldn't believe that asshole if he said rain was wet," Dodd mused. "How's the Contessa taking it?"

"Not well," Stanton said with a heavy sigh. "I don't know. I feel responsible somehow."

"How?" Dodd demanded. "Sir, the way I see it is this. We were sent to get the Contessa. We got her. It was chance and nothing else that brought us across Mrs. Ansley's path."

"Do you think the Holy Father would arrange such a kidnapping, to persuade the Contessa?" Lex asked.

It bothered Stanton that he didn't deny the accusation outright. Finally, he said, "No, Francois and Allegra are childhood friends. For all of his politics, even he wouldn't do that to her."

"Allegra, is it?" Lex asked with no trace of sarcasm.

"Allegra, is it?" Dodd parroted in a bad impression of Allegra's accent.

His two most trusted lieutenants had a good chuckle before he asked, "Are you two done with your fun yet?"

"I don't know, sir," Dodd said. "Lex?"

"I still have a bit more in me yet, Sir," Lex added. "I am a romantic at heart, of course."

"Oh, I am, too," Dodd quickly added. "Late summer is the time for love, after all."

"Spring, Dodd," Stanton said. "Spring."

Dodd shrugged. "I don't know, sir. I find love every time I go into a whorehouse."

Lex made a disgusted sound. "I'm surprised your dick hasn't fallen off yet."

"He has a point," Stanton said, motioning to Lex with his crust of bread. "You're going to end up in mercury, Dodd, if you're not careful."

"Lord Almighty be with me. I thought you were both of the world, not celibate monks hiding in the mountains," Dodd said, clearly disgusted. He shoveled more stew into his mouth by way of his bread. "Sheep intestines. Go down to Miranda's and she'll get you all set up, sir. Even puts a nice ribbon on it for you."

Stanton snorted. "I'll pass, but thanks for the tip."

"Just the tip, sir?" Dodd asked. Lex began choking on his bread and Dodd pounded his back helpfully.

Stanton's reply was cut short by feminine shrieks and Allegra's terrified voice calling for help.

ALLEGRA SCREAMED FOR help, even as she was dragged across the women's sitting area of the small inn and coach stop. The brute had her arm gripped tightly and was dragging her across the rough wood floor despite her protests. She didn't have the strength to pull away, so she tried to tangle herself up by any means possible.

Bystanders did nothing to stop the scene. Once the brute called her an escaped elemental mage, everyone backed away as if she carried the plague. Or, perhaps more accurately, as if she was about to burn the building down around them all.

"Help!" Allegra screamed. "Captain! Lex! Dodd! Help!"

"There's no one to help you," the brute sneered. "We've been watching for your carriage. Orders, ya see."

Allegra managed to hook her foot around a table leg and she dumped both table and the food upon it with her. He struck her once in the head and the world faded to a blur.

LEX WAS THE first through the door into the lady's area. They scanned the room, spotted a dazed Allegra bouncing off chair legs. Lex pulled their sword and shouted, "You there! Unhand that woman."

"Fuck off, you little sprat. This doesn't concern you."

"That is the Arbiter of the Cathedral. You are manhandling the very hand of the Holy Father. Get your filthy paws off her now," Lex commanded. They pointed their sword at him. "Or I will run you through."

The asshole dropped the Contessa to the floor. She flopped bonelessly; he must have struck her in the head. He spat on the Contessa's moaning form. "The witch bitch comes with me."

"I don't think so," Lex said.

Rainier stepped into view behind the asshole and then hit him in the back of the head with the pommel of his sword. The blow sent him to the floor as well, joining the sluggish Contessa.

"Where's Dodd?" Lex asked as they both rushed to the Contessa's side.

"Getting the others," Rainier said. He patted the Contessa's face. "Allegra? Allegra, you with us?"

Lex kept their opinion of that particular thing locked away. Rainier rarely used anyone's given name outside of the Consorts. And he *never* used the given name of unmarried women. But the Contessa was around his age. Maybe that made a difference. Yes, because Rainier *always* paid special attention to unwedded women his own age.

"Stanton?" The Contessa groaned. She reached up to touch her head. "Ow."

The asshole was moaning, too, so Lex pulled out the length of thin rope on their sword belt. It was cut the perfect length to tie up a man's hands and feet. Fancy that.

"Want me to take him outside, Sir?" Lex asked.

Rainier nodded and Lex grabbed the tail end of the rope and dragged the asshole out of the inn. He whined and bitched about being dragged across the pebbles, so Lex turned enough to drag him over some broken glass shards. He howled and protested.

"It's not so great when you're the one being dragged, huh?" Lex said. "Remember this the next time you drag a defenseless woman."

"Fuck you."

"Yeah, whatever, asshole."

Lex approached Dodd and the carriages. Four more men were kneeling on the ground, their hands tied behind them in a similar fashion to Lex's new friend. "What do we have here?"

"The Earl's men. Apparently, they were here to arrest the Contessa, accuse her of being an elemental, and ship her off to some mine while the good Earl got back all of his slaves and a huge apology from the Cathedral." Dodd kicked one of them in the kidneys. The captive grunted and slumped over. "But it seems we've messed up the plan."

"She's a fucking mage," Lex's asshole captive said.

"Oh, shut up, or I'll drag you back over the glass."

"Fuck you."

Lex rolled their eyes. "You already said that. Dodd, what's the plan? Local constabulary anywhere?"

"I sent a runner for the local militia. I've asked them to send over a comfortable prison box."

"Good work," Lex said.

Dodd quirked a smile. "Why thank you, Lieutenant."

Lex gave him a playful shove. "Shut your trap."

"How's the Contessa?"

Lex frowned and looked back toward the door. Rainier wasn't in the doorway anymore, so they assumed the Contessa had managed to get to her feet and was seated somewhere. "Disoriented. He slugged her hard."

Dodd snarled.

The first of the militia arrived within the hour. The blue and white uniformed woman jumped from her horse and saluted. "Corporal Antilles of the Ninety-Fifth Swords. We received your message."

"Lieutenant Lex of the Holy Father's Own Consorts. Thank you for coming so quickly," Lex said, offering a hand of greeting. Antilles took it and they slapped grips. "I'll get Captain Rainier for you."

Lex headed inside to look for Rainier. He wasn't in the lady's waiting room, nor was the Contessa. Lex found both of them in the common room. The Contessa was drinking from a mug and was speaking to Rainier in a low voice. Lex cleared their throat and said, "Captain? The militia are here. I'll sit with the Contessa."

Rainier nodded and patted the Contessa's hand. He gave her a comforting smile, then a stiff nod to Lex, and left the room.

"How are you feeling?" Lex asked, slipping into the chair left still warm.

Contessa held up the mug. "Better."

Lex leaned forward. "Beer?"

"Gin," the Contessa said.

"That stuff will kill you," Lex said.

"Speaking from personal experience?"

"Loads," Lex said with a laugh. Then, more seriously, they said, "We'll get you back to Borro safely, I promise."

"The Captain said the same thing," the Contessa said with a sad smile. "I can't believe...I spent my entire life hiding so that I'd never be faced with this. What was I thinking? I will make so many enemies and this is how they will come after me."

Lex was silent. What was there to say? The Contessa was right. She had already made several powerful enemies, and she'd only been on a job a couple of weeks.

"Why did I do this to myself?" The Contessa took another pull from her mug. She coughed. "This tastes like it was made in a rusty wheelbarrow."

"It probably was," Lex said. "Look, Your Ladyship? I don't know you very well, but seems to me you took this job because you knew you could do it better than everyone else. As odd as it seems, the fact that you've angered so many powerful people in such a short time says to me you probably should do the job."

"I can't hold off accusations of being an elemental forever, though," the Contessa said.

There was something in her voice that Lex couldn't quite place. Desperation? Fear? "Is being called an elemental the biggest fear a mage has?"

"It's mine," the Contessa said simply. "You saw how everyone acted. They didn't care about a lady in fine clothes being dragged from a public room. I have guards to protect me, and a writ from the holy father himself that only he can repeal."

Lex frowned. "What would happen to you if the Holy Father was…to die?"

The Contessa's eyes widened. "I have no idea."

Lex nodded slowly. "I'll send Martinez back with Pero. Just in case."

"Thank you," the Contessa said. Tears welled in her eyes. "Rupert, I mean, Francois, is my oldest friend."

Lex offered what they hoped was a supportive smile. "Pero will look after him."

"Will you stay with me? While…while they deal with outside?"

Lex looked over their shoulder. There was a lot of work to deal with still. They were needed. "I'm needed out there." At the Contessa's deflated posture, Lex said, "Come on. Let's get you into the carriage so that we'll all be looking after you."

"I'd like that."

Lex stood and offered the Contessa their arm. She took it, and seemed grateful for the support. Lex led her Ladyship out to her carriage and then got to work.

CHAPTER FOURTEEN

Borro Abbey

THE REMAINDER OF the journey was uneventful, except for the knotted anxiety in the pit of Allegra's guts every time they stopped at a waystation inn. At times, she couldn't muster the courage to go inside, so Serafina or Martin would fetch her a plate of food and Stanton would remain by her side. She refused to use the outhouses without someone standing just beyond the doors, in case of trouble.

It took an entire day before she could even step inside an inn's front door. They'd planned to sleep the night there, but after two hours of gripping the edge of her bed, she woke Nadira and both women slept in the carriage. After that, they didn't stop at any inns to sleep, and merely slept on the road.

When they arrived at Borro, relief spread through Allegra. She was home. She was safe. Whatever she'd endured on the way here, she could recover from. The bruises were healing, the scrapes scabbing over, and, soon, her spirits would recover.

Servants hurried out into the main courtyard of the abbey. Father Michael came a short time later, arms extended in greeting. "My dear Contessa! I am so pleased to see you." He bowed hastily and then kissed her on both cheeks. He gripped her arms and said, "I have been praying for your safe arrival. We received your runner's letter yesterday. Oh, my dear child. I have not slept a wink since. How are you doing? Shall I call for the apothecary? Do you require a healing stone? I'll get you a hot restorative. Gertie! Gertie! Oh, where is that girl gone? There you are. The Contessa is in need of…" He motioned at her to order from the young maid.

"Welcome back, Your Ladyship," Gertie said with a curtsy.

"I believe some hot food and a soft bed will do nicely," Allegra said.

"At once, Your Ladyship," Gertie said. She curtsied again and rushed off in the direction of the lower kitchens.

Allegra smiled back at Father Michael and said, "Thank you for the prayers."

Father Michael beamed at her. "You are always in my prayers, my child."

"I'm glad," Allegra said. She meant it. Though she did not believe, there was comfort in knowing Father Michael *did* believe and he used his private time with the Lord Almighty to think of her.

"Captain Rainier! Hello, Captain! Nice to see you again." Father Michael gave Rainier's hand a firm, enthusiastic shake. "We have the entire east wing set aside for your soldiers tonight. We shall organize the details better once you've all had the benefit of a good meal and some sleep."

"Thank you, Father," Stanton said gravely. He was standing next to her, a protective presence through her ordeal.

"I thought we were going to be put into the cottages?" Allegra asked through a yawn.

"I feared the cottages were too unsecure, especially now with threats upon your person. Plus, I don't believe you should be hiding in some rundown cottage in the corner of the estate. No, no, no! I will not stand for it. So I had everything moved. We will work out the details later."

Allegra blinked the sleep from her eyes. "Father…you moved my things?"

"Your maids did," he said. He clasped her hands and said, "Please don't be angry with me for long. I would never forgive myself if anything happened to you while you were in my care. Please, you must believe I did this for your own safety."

"I'm not angry, but you didn't have to do that."

"Nonsense! Nonsense! We'll assign quarters later. Let the servants get your bags and we'll bring you food. Nadira! Good to see you, my dear! Good to see you!"

Allegra blurrily followed the abbey's housekeeper up the stairs. She'd been assigned one of the ambassador suites; a gorgeous set of rooms meant for working, entertaining, and sleeping. She ignored all of the splendor and collapsed on the bed, removing nothing but her shoes.

It was her bladder which first woke her in the morning. She was still in the same position as she last remembered, sleeping on her stomach with her arms under her pillow. Her clothes were rumpled and pulled, and she had sore spots from a night of seams, wood, and whalebone digging into her flesh.

It was a long moment before the disorientation of waking in a strange room wore off. She pushed herself up off the bed and looked for a chamber pot. The full wooden throne was set up behind a decorative embroidered screen. Once the necessities were cared for, Allegra peeled out of her dusty pelisse and reached inside her dress's tight front to pull out the wooden busk she'd forgotten to remove the night before. No wonder she was stiff and slightly light-headed.

Allegra opened the double wooden doors of her bedchamber into her private drawing room. It was a richly decorated room. From there, there were three more doors. She opened one and discovered a small closet with an altar. The other was clearly designed for letter writing and business. She hated leaving her cottage, but she had to admit this was better suited than her cottage for work.

With a good night's sleep and, judging by the height of the sun, a good morning's sleeping, too, she was more rational to make decisions about accommodations and safety.

Allegra looked around the room for a few minutes before she found the bell for the maid. She pulled it and went back to exploring her new home. There was a personal balcony off the drawing room, with a small table and chairs, and various potted plants. It overlooked the mountain where the abbey was now a proper building as opposed to living rock. It was a safe location.

Allegra's hands shook as she thought about how close she'd come to being dragged off to the dark pits somewhere. It was an acute reminder of how much was personally at stake for her. Allegra tried to remind herself that she was doing this for the mages who couldn't hide behind their rank and wealth, who didn't have strong, capable men and women like the Consorts protecting her.

She could do this.

Soon, there was a knock at her door and maids and footmen bustled into her room. Nadira, bless her heart, bossed them all around as they carried in Allegra's trunks. Nadira knew where everything went better than Allegra did, and she shooed her mistress away to organize the new abode in peace.

Allegra changed into gray riding trousers; the ones with the leather strip sewed into the inseam. She tugged on her long boots and abandoned her corset in favor of a tight button-up shirt. Over that she pulled on a white tunic.

"Nadira, how warm is it outside?" Allegra called from her bedchamber.

Nadira didn't answer. She simply walked into the room, thrust a long coat at Allegra.

Allegra tugged on the brown leather coat. It skimmed the tops of her boots and possessed a long slit in the back. She tugged her hair out of its fashionable up-do and braided it on one side of her head.

"Eat, Your Ladyship," Nadira commanded.

Allegra grabbed a roll from the tray of food set down on the table. "Don't let them throw that out. I'll eat when I'm back from my ride."

"Understood, Your Ladyship," Nadira said.

She sent word ahead, so her gray mare was saddled and ready for her when she arrived at the stables. She thanked the stable boy and swung herself up on the mount. It had been a few weeks since she'd rode, and time at the Cathedral was enough to drive any sane woman into a gibbering mess; she needed fresh air.

So she rode. Further up the mountain's slope was a clearing filled with alpine flowers and small ponds. The ponds were mostly gone this time of the year, and the flowers had faded, but the clearing was still the perfect place to regain her center.

Allegra came out here to mediate a couple times a week. It helped her keep calm and to suppress all of her boiling rage at the injustice around her. Allegra sat down at her favorite rock and let her horse wander. The old mare didn't like to wander anymore, so she didn't have to worry about tying her up.

She'd written several elementals amongst her acquaintance while at the Cathedral. They'd all been open agitators for change. All of them rallied for elemental rights and had been involved in various ways in the abolition movement. They had varied methods and philosophies, but they all shared one common goal: the freedom of mages.

In guarded language, she'd asked them to step forward as representatives of the mage movement. She couldn't risk exposing herself, but she could help protect them while they did. Yes, it was hypocritical, but she was scared. She was so scared. She knew what the mines looked like. She saw drawings of sugar cane farms, of cocoa farms, of fish processing wharves...Was there anything untouched by the forced work of mages or those accused of witchcraft?

She knew what happened there. She knew all too well and she would rather fall upon a sword or jump off a cliff than subject herself to that horror.

Some letters had already arrived, with their polite refusals. They would be happy to write letters and speak about abolition, but some had managed to keep their magical talents hidden from the world. They weren't even ready to expose themselves that far; asking them to publicly declare they were elementals? Well, she knew their answers before even writing, but she had to ask.

So what did that leave her? Princes and empresses and kings who cared only about themselves. The aristocracy cared only about their lands. None of them would stand up for the helpless. Oh, sure, they would give lip service, but they would all stuff every single mage into a pit if it meant keeping their asses warm upon their thrones.

"Contessa?" called out a masculine voice.

Allegra turned to see Stanton walking across the field. She could see his horse was tethered to one of the shorter trees. She waved him over. When he was within speaking distance, she said, "I thought I was alone."

Stanton smiled down at her and said, "Nadira told on you."

"So you've enlisted the servants against me."

Stanton sat next to her on the rock. "Don't be angry. I came to check on you and discovered you'd slipped out already."

"I needed to be alone," she said.

"Next time, tell me." His words were gentle and she couldn't hear even a hint of rebuke in them.

"If I tell you, I won't be alone."

Stanton chuckled. "I'm merely doing my job."

"I know."

Stanton let out a contented sigh. "It's beautiful here."

"You should have seen it a couple months ago. This entire field is nothing but little flowers. All of the snow run off creates ponds all over the place. It's paradise."

"Maybe I'll still be around in the spring to see it."

She smiled at him. "Perhaps."

"Look, if having me around is awkward for you, I can ask Dodd or Lex, or even Martin. Or one of the women. Whatever you want."

"I think Lex would rather be with Dodd than with me."

"Do you have problems with him?"

"No, nothing like that. I mean, I think Lex would much rather be with Dodd than anyone."

"Yeah, they've been friends since they were children. Thick as thieves those two."

"I was thinking more of something else between them," Allegra said, stating what she was convinced was the obvious.

"What? No. Lex and Dodd? No. You're just misunderstanding the friendship."

Allegra shrugged. "I see what I see."

"And you see what you want to see."

"Oh, yes. I forgot. Fine ladies always see romance everywhere their eyes land." She batted her eyelashes at him. "In a week, they'll be talking about us."

"They already are," Stanton said, nudging her with his shoulder.

Allegra groaned. "I knew I gave up court for a reason."

Stanton gave her an appraising look. "Tired of the gowns, I see."

"Almighty save me, yes. If I had to wear one more uncomfortable outfit, I was going to run through the streets stark naked raving like a lunatic."

"I'd like to see that," Stanton said in a low grumble.

Allegra turned to look him in the eye. She debated several remarks, all of which her sense told her would greatly escalate the tension. He was handsome. There was no debating that. But there was a lot more at stake than turning away from an excellent jaw line and warm, dark eyes.

So Allegra looked back down at her boots and said, in a voice a touch too hoarse for her liking, "I should be heading back. I have a lot of work to get started."

Stanton rose and offered Allegra his gloved hand. She took it and ignored the commentary of the lonelier parts of her brain. "Shall we ride out here every morning before breakfast?"

"They don't serve breakfast at the abbey. We still keep the strict country traditions of dinner at eleven sharp, followed by a simple supper of nineteen dishes a course at six in the evening."

Stanton made a disgusted face. "I suspect I'll be rising with the servants starting tomorrow to liberate some morsels from the kitchen."

Allegra laughed heartily, both at the look of feigned horror at the meal schedule and of his earnestness of kitchen raiding. She had come up here to relax, but as she watched Stanton smiling down at her, pleased to have made her laugh, she realized she was going to have to be very careful around him.

CHAPTER FIFTEEN

LEX STRAIGHTENED THEIR jacket before taking long strides across
the Contessa's main reception room to her study, waving at
Serafina and a newly-arrived Nathan who were seated at a small
table and bickering quietly. Lex hadn't been in this part of the
abbey yet, as they were focused first on arranging the personal
security and guard detail for the Contessa.

Lex looked around the richly-appointed room that was divided
into smaller working areas by way of strategic placement of
furniture. Small writing desks were near the windows. The middle
of the room was blocked by a square of sofas and end tables. At
one end of the room, peeking out from behind a vibrant silk
folding screen, was a long dining table. Nearby that, a mahogany
sideboard was the home of several silver-domes, protecting the
snacks and food underneath from both flies and hungry lieutenants
who were still unused to the lack of breakfast in this backwater
abbey.

"You asked to see me, Your Ladyship?" Lex said as they walked
into the room.

"Yes. Please, close the door."

Lex obeyed and stood at attention awaiting orders. Lex felt
things had been awkward since the incident in the barracks. Lex
was disappointed by that, since the Contessa seemed easy with the
situation, once she'd worked out her own confusion and
embarrassment. But she'd been cold to Lex the last handful of
days, and they couldn't help worry that Allegra's time to think had

caused unpleasant feelings to settle where the easy smiles first existed.

The Contessa was well dressed, but then she often was. She wore a blue dress with a gauzy neck wrap for modesty, as all fine ladies were required to wear by the unspoken rules of decorum. Of course, the Contessa's gauze was so thin that her bosom was still quite visible. Lex stifled a snort thinking about how Rainier would appreciate the still visible heavy bosom, but only just.

"Please sit," the Contessa instructed, motioning at one of the embroidered chairs. Once again, Lex obeyed. "I sent for you for two reasons. First, I want to ensure that I have done nothing to offend you."

Lex narrowed their eyes. "I don't understand, Your Excellency."

The Contessa licked her lips. "I am uncertain if I behaved appropriately when I discovered...I mean..." She drew in a breath and collected herself. "If I have done anything incorrect or improper towards you, please let me know so that I can correct the situation."

Lex smiled at that. "Your Excellency..."

"Please, I'm not one for titles. If you will not call me Allegra, at least call me Contessa."

Lex inclined their head. "Contessa, I thought you were the one offended."

"Why? Oh, I've been distracted lately when I've been around you, but that has nothing to do with you. Well, it does, but it's related to a particular task I'd like you to perform for me, if you are up for a challenge." She waved a hand. "But, first, I want to ensure I have done nothing to make you feel uncomfortable."

Lex's lips curled a fraction. "Are we counting this conversation?" The Contessa's eyes widened comically and Lex laughed. "No, you have been fine. I'm not a delicate flower, you know? I can handle a little adversity."

"Perhaps, but why should you have it from me?" The Contessa smiled. "Is 'he' still the appropriate word to use to describe you? Or do you prefer another term? I only used it as that's how you were introduced to me. I ask because I heard Dodd call you 'them' a couple of times, but then 'he' and I was concerned I was not using the correct words. As I harp on people saying mages and not witches, I don't wish to be a hypocrite towards others."

Lex was pleased by the question. "Thank you for asking. 'He' is fine. Dodd's a different case because he's known me since we were kids. I often refer to myself as 'them' or 'they' and so Dodd sometimes uses it. But I've asked the guys and the Captain to introduce me as 'he'."

The Contessa nodded. "Thank you for clarifying."

"Thank you for asking."

It didn't bother Lex being asked. In truth, they preferred people asking than just guessing. Lex's own personal slider moved day to day, and they decided a couple of years ago that 'he' worked better for outsiders. Lex's own thoughts could swing accordingly and in peace, and the outside world could remain consistent.

"Now, I'd like to speak to you about a task."

"What is it?"

"Do you know who Walter Cram is?"

Lex whistled and leaned back in their seat. Chills spread through their body at the name.

"I see you do."

Walter Cram wasn't just a mage; he was an elementalist. He was considered *the* elementalist. He was wanted by every government, city-state, and local magistrate in most of Serna. He went into hiding years ago, occasionally popping up to stir up mage rebellions and even fought in a couple of skirmishes. He had a network of supporters and sympathizers who kept him so well hidden that no torturer nor spy could infiltrate. It was thought he was behind the latest string of collapsed mines along the Cartossa-Amadore border.

"Oh, I know his name." Lex stared up at the Contessa's face and winced. "Tell me you don't want me to find him."

"Indeed, I do." The Contessa picked up a sheet of paper from her desk and handed it to Lex. "If you leave notices at each of these locations along the border, I think his network will get word to him. Now understand, I want him brought here safely. You cannot tell anyone who he is."

"How am I supposed to find him if I can't say I'm looking for him?"

"You are looking for Brother Lancaster Rivers."

"That is the dumbest name I've ever heard," Lex muttered.

The Contessa laughed. "I agree, but that's his real name. Walter is just his cover. Very few people know his real name."

Lex cocked an eyebrow. "How do you know?"

The Contessa grimaced. "There's history between us. We didn't end on very good terms, but I think with the right wording, he'll understand why I'm looking for him. Get him here as safely and anonymously as possible."

"I'll try." Lex stared down at the list. "Should I take Dodd with me?"

"I'll leave that to you and Captain Rainier."

Lex tapped their thumb against the chair. "Is there a monk or someone here we can trust to bring? It would add some validity to us looking for a missing brother, if we have one with us. One of us can dress up, sure, but none of us know the clergy well enough if we get challenged."

"Sister Sanderson knows the mission details, so you can talk freely with her. Enlist Father Michael's help if necessary. He knows Walter."

"How?" Lex asked, not completely sure if they wanted to know the answer.

"He lived here at the abbey for a summer."

"Oh, yeah. I really didn't want to know that after all."

TEN DAYS LATER, Lex found themselves in a seedy Cartossian tavern surrounded by a group of mage-hating morons and no closer to finding the notorious Walter Cram.

"You never take me anywhere nice," Dodd bitched into his mug of skunk water ale.

"You never deserve it," Lex said, drinking their own ale, gagging after every gulp. "This is terrible."

"Would you like me to fetch you a good claret?"

"This place wouldn't know a good claret if it hit them over the heads," Lex complained. "How are we even supposed to find this fellow if we can't actually say we're looking for him."

"Lex, let me tell you something about outlaws."

Lex rolled their eyes.

"They fear anyone in a uniform," Dodd said.

"Well, perhaps we shouldn't be in a uniform," Lex countered.

"But then why would anyone be looking for a clergyman if not the Holy Father's Own Consorts?"

Lex made a face.

"Hey! You!" a drunken fool shouted in their direction.

Lex groaned disinterestedly, but slipped their free hand under the table to their sword. Dodd did the same.

"You're from Orsini, aren't you? They put a mage in charge over there!"

"Oh fuck," Dodd muttered.

They'd split up to spread the word around to the brothels and merchants that they were looking for a missing monk. The plan was to meet back here, but by the looks of the crowd, Lex worried there might not be a tavern left by the end of the evening.

"I'll take the one on the right," Dodd mumbled. "You get the guys on the left."

"There's eight of them on the left."

"Exactly." Dodd flashed Lex a fierce grin and then successfully ducked the flying bottle which signaled yet another tavern fight.

"Fifteen against two," Lex shouted. "How sporting!"

TWENTY MINUTES LATER, hiding in the brothel across the street and licking their wounds, Dodd and Lex grabbed their swords when a knock came at their door.

"Piss off," Dodd shouted. He motioned at the massive bump on his hand and mouthed at Lex, "Ow."

Lex rolled their eyes and pointed at the aching lump that was forming on their temple. "Ow."

The voice from beyond the door said, "I'm looking for the men from the market this afternoon."

Dodd glanced at Lex, who nodded their head. "Might as well see."

Dodd opened the door a crack and peered out. "Yeah?"

He repeated his inquiry. "Was that you in the market earlier, looking for the monk?"

"Who are you?" Dodd asked, ignoring the question. "Cause if you're here to finish off what your drunken little friends just started, well, I'm not in the mood right now."

Lex stood off to the side, out of view of the door, in case he pushed past Dodd. Dodd was solid and significantly heavier than Lex, but there was always someone bigger and stronger. Lex held a defensive stance just in case.

"What does the Contessa look like?" the man asked.

Dodd hesitated, but Lex gave him a quick nod. Dodd described her and restated the phrase they were supposed to say. "The Arbiter of Justice, Allegra, Contessa of Marsina, acting upon the will of Holy Father Francois, is seeking a missing monk, Lancaster Rivers. Both the Holy Father and the Arbiter are very concerned about his disappearance and we are here to find him."

"How does the Contessa know Rivers?"

Lex stepped into view of the man. "Remove your hood."

"Not until you answer my question."

Lex licked their lips and glanced at Dodd before saying, "Rivers spent a summer at Borro Abbey while the Contessa lived there. Hood. Now."

The stranger removed his hood. He had a high forehead and a prominent nose that was dotted with freckles much darker than his light-brown skin. His long, dark hair was pulled into a braid and the uneven patchiness of his beard gave him a shabby appearance.

"Walter Cram," Lex whispered. "I saw you during the Orsini riots."

Cram didn't answer. "Why are you here?"

Dodd opened the door and said, "Get in. There's spies everywhere."

"Not until I know I am safe," Cram said.

Lex said, "Dodd, bring the lantern over here. Rahna? Hand me the letter from the Contessa."

Cram examined the seal before snapping it. He read the letter and nodded. "What are your names?"

"Lex, Dodd, Rahna. We work for the Cathedral and for the Contessa."

Walter looked behind him and whispered into the darkness of the corridor, "Stay out here." He looked at Lex and said, "Shall we talk inside?"

Dodd opened the door enough for Cram to come inside. After accepting an offered glass of cheap wine, Cram asked, "Why does Allegra want me at the peace talks? I'm a wanted man. She understands that I have no intention of being dragged away from the peace talks by guards and then dumped down some mine shaft, right?"

Lex accepted their own glass from Dodd. "She understands. She can't guarantee your safety before you get to the abbey, but once there, she will have a guard patrol placed with you at all times. She's also willing to give you immunity for the duration of the peace talks. If anyone attempts to harm you, they will be in violation of the rules and they will be expelled, not you."

"Why can't she just give it to me now?"

"The terms of her powers only extend so far. Basically, you need to be at the abbey and she can grant you immunity that way." Lex shrugged. "Politics, but she's pushing the rules as far as she can to get you there."

"So what they're saying about her is true?"

"She said elemental rights are mage rights, and she wants you at the forefront."

Cram scoffed at that, a bitter sound laced with anger and resentment to Lex's ears. "She would put me in front of the arrows if she could get away with it. How am I even supposed to get to the abbey?"

"She recommended you come with us," Dodd said.

Cram laughed. "Me? Go with Cathedral guards? You are drunk?"

Dodd gave an unconcerned grunt. "You can find your own way there, if you think you'll be safer that way."

"The Contessa said to tell you she knows she's asking a lot of you, but she also believes it's important to have elementals like yourself involved in the process," Lex said.

"I'll have to think about it," Walter said.

"Understood. We leave at dawn tomorrow," Lex said. "Otherwise, we'll see you if we see you."

"Understood." Then, Cram hesitantly asked, "How is Allegra? Is she well? Are they still coddling her like she's made of fine porcelain?"

Lex's internal voice nagged at them, but they swatted it away. "From what I've heard, yes."

"Their mistake," Cram said. "She's one of the strongest women I've ever known."

CHAPTER SIXTEEN

Borro Abbey

STANTON STEPPED AROUND Allegra's desk to lean over her shoulder. He rested one hand on the back of her elegant chair. She was still wearing her riding clothes —simple tunic and woolen trousers— and she could feel the edge of his hand resting against her back. He leaned forward, other hand on her desk, skimming the letter, ignoring her completely.

She chanced to look at his profile, a stolen look she rarely gave herself permission to take. He was more than merely handsome: he was every measure the heroic figure. She shouldn't have asked for the hero who made her laugh.

"Pardon me saying this, but that is the bitchiest letter I've read in a long time," Stanton said, glancing over at her.

"I'm glad it wasn't just me," she said, but the words came out huskier than she'd planned.

She tore away from his gaze before she did something completely stupid. She cleared her throat and a pathetic sound escaped her that could have been called a chuckle. "I think I'll write to my cousin and enlist her aid."

It took a heartbeat or two, but Stanton got the hint. He straightened and stepped away from her chair. He walked around her large, but practical, desk and stood by the fireplace. Like he did so often at her office in Orsini, he rested one hand against her mantelpiece and another on his hip. Her heart didn't stop pounding and she turned her gaze away from the cutting figure he made by firelight.

"You mean Grand Duchess Katherine?" he asked. "I worked for her once."

"And how was it?" Allegra said, aiming for any conversation to get her mind off Stanton's body pressed against hers.

"She left a lasting impression."

Allegra barked out a laugh, far louder than she'd planned. Her cheeks heated up. "Yes, Kat does that well."

"Well, I should probably go," Stanton said. He motioned at the door. "Unless…"

"Unless?"

"Would you…I mean, would you like to take a late meal with me tonight? I plan to raid the sideboard in the bishop's drawing room at my earliest convenience."

"There's a sideboard?"

"Card night," Stanton explained.

"I'd love to," Allegra blurted.

"Then I'll see you later this evening."

"I'd like that."

Allegra watched Stanton walk out of her office and sighed. She closed her eyes and tried to picture what he looked like underneath all of those layers. When the room's temperature began to rise, Allegra shook herself out of her daydreams and went back to her letter writing.

Grand Duchess Katherine was a powerful figure who had her fingers dipped in various political soup pots. It was once said that no decision was made in Serna without the Grand Duchess's input and that no government ruled without her tacit support.

Katherine was planning to attend the peace talks, as soon as she was done her sport in the country. Almighty forbid if the deer were left alone. Allegra never really liked her cousin; she was a controlling, manipulative person who thought too highly of her own talents and accomplishments. Though, Allegra also begrudgingly had to admit Katherine's support would go a long way to adding credibility to the peace talks. If Katherine agreed, even slightly, with anything Allegra put forward, it would advance mage rights by leaps as opposed to the crawling pace her own influence could create.

Allegra worked away, getting through the niceties and flattery early in the letter. Those were always the easy parts for Allegra; her thorough education included letter writing etiquette and diplomacy alongside mathematics, geography, and languages.

The next part was trickier. How to explain to her cousin that she needed her to handle Queen Portia, but delicately lest she'd make things worse.

A knock at the door interrupted her thoughts. A beat later the door opened. A very dirty Lex entered, followed by an annoyed Stanton, and a man she would recognize anywhere.

Lancaster Rivers, aka Walter Cram, wore the clerical robes well, but he was always a consummate actor when he needed to be. He was of average height and build, a study in averages as he stood next to Lex and Stanton. His beard had more silver in it these days, and still looked as shabby as ever. His dark eyes still sparkled with their usual brightness, though there was a hardness there that didn't exist before. And there were a lot more lines around his eyes now than last she saw him.

"Hello, Walter," Allegra said, and the words came out far more breathless than she'd intended.

Walter Cram gave her one of his half-cocked grins and said, "Same to you, gorgeous."

Allegra laughed, even if it sounded strained and forced to her own ears. "You made it here in one piece. How unexpected."

He bowed with a flourish. "When my lady has made a decision, who am I to deny her will?"

Allegra flinched at his words. While he said them with a smile, she felt the verbal dagger slip between her ribs. "I'm glad to see you've changed your opinion about a lady's will."

"I had an excellent teacher," he said, not bothering to hide the bitterness in his voice now.

Lex glanced at Stanton, who was busy staring between Allegra and Cram. Allegra could only imagine what was going through both of their minds. She tried to swipe that thought away. She needed Walter here for the talks. Without him representing the elementalists, the talks wouldn't be seen as taking mage rights seriously. With someone like Walter Cram at the talks, protected with full immunity, well, that would change the landscape.

She hoped.

"We will need to discuss security arrangements, Contessa," Stanton said finally.

"I should probably bathe," Lex said. "May I make my report later tonight, Your Ladyship?"

"Tomorrow will be fine. Thank you, Lex," Allegra said. She inclined her head slightly, dismissing him. She turned to Stanton and said, "Let's discuss security over dinner with the Bishop, shall we? I'm sure Father Michael will be happy to see Walter again. Would you mind postponing our plans?"

He glanced at Walter. "As you wish. I'll inform the bishop you will be joining him for dinner." "

Stanton said all of it through a clenched jaw. His duty discharged, he gave Allegra a curt bow and left without saying another word. Though, he closed her door rather harder than Allegra thought strictly necessary.

"I think he likes you," Walter said.

Allegra ignored the jibe. She stood up to walk around her desk. She never thought she'd be in the same room with him again and the bittersweet memories tied her stomach into knots. Allegra motioned to the chairs near the fabric screens and said, "Please sit."

Walter did so, though not until she had seated herself. Now close to him, he stank of horse and sweat. It was a bit of a relief, actually. It was in such contrast to her memories that it gave her brain time to separate the memory from the man.

"I assume Lex filled you in?"

"Yes, though I'm still confused why I'm here. It's not like we're friends."

"No, we're not," she said bluntly. "I do need you here, and, if I believe half the rumors coming out of Cartossa about you, you need me even more."

"I used to think that," he said, a bitter laugh escaping him. "But, I was young and foolish."

"You were foolish," Allegra said sharply. "Walter, I didn't ask you here to fight. I need your help."

"Yes, yes, with your precious peace talks. They're an ambitious plan," he said, shaking his robes until a puff of dust and odor escaped the fabric folds. He smiled when Allegra winced. "There wasn't an opportunity to bathe while we fled for our lives."

"You're here now, and that's all that matters. Now, will you help me?"

"With what?"

"The peace talks."

"What could I possibly offer? I'm an outlaw, or did you forget that very fine point?"

"I didn't forget," Allegra said. "Walter, I'm trying to help you here."

"You want to help me? Announce that you are an elementalist, join hands with me on the balcony, and dare them to come after us."

Allegra drew in a sharp breath and frantically looked around the room. There was no one else there, of course; this was the only entrance. Beyond the fabric screens was her private chambers and sitting room, but the servants had to come through the only door. And she was staring at it. Nevertheless, her heart thudded in her chest and her vision blurred.

"Ah, I see the mere mention of it still makes you panic like a frightened horse."

Allegra swallowed back the hot, vulgar reply that came to mind. She steadied her breathing and reminded herself that no one had heard. If they had, the shocked gasps and the crashing of silverware would have been obvious clues to her identity's revelation.

"We are not here to discuss me. Will you help?"

"Why should I?" He crossed his arms. "It's not like you will help your own kind."

"I beg your pardon? I have been working as hard as I can to make these talks successful. It's not enough to end the rebellion. We need to end the subjection of mages. We cannot talk about that without talking about the plight of elementalists. I can't do that. You can."

He grunted, pleased with himself. "It's always hard to tell what's real and what's fake with you."

"You know what, Walter? Go fuck a goat," Allegra snarled. She stood up and spoke as she walked across the room toward the door. "I regret even thinking you were mature enough to put aside our past differences…"

Walter grabbed her by the arm to stop her steps. "You killed my child."

"I did nothing of the kind," Allegra shot back. "You were about to leave on your grand adventure as a rebel. What was I supposed to do? Stay here and raise a child that could be used as leverage against you? No."

"That was my child," Walter snarled, tightening his grip on her arm.

"If you don't let go of my arm right this second, I will scream," Allegra said in a very calm voice. "And once Captain Rainier storms in here and hears that you assaulted me after I extended you safe passage, you will find yourself drugged and in chains being dragged to those mines that you fear so much."

Walter let go of her, pushing her a little in the process. She'd expected it, however, and didn't lose her footing. "I hate you so much."

"I don't care," Allegra said. "Will you help me?"

Walter looked away before saying, "Yes. Damn it all to the abyss, yes, I'll help."

"Good," Allegra said, her voice hard. "Now, get out of my sight. And if you ever touch me again or accuse me of murder, I will make you regret the day you laid in my bed. Have I made myself clear?"

"Like a crystal wine goblet," he said, once more giving her a wild flurry of his hands as he bowed.

DEMONS IN THE DARK

The Woods Near Borro Abbey

WALTER EXAMINED THE black smudge on the tree. He didn't dare get too close. He frantically looked about him, but he was too far into the thick trees to be seen through the forest growth. It was merely him and the demon mark.

The third one this week. The first time, he'd assumed it had been an accident. The second? Clearly one left here from ages ago. This one, newly-appeared along the path he walked every morning, was not a coincidence. Someone was actively attempting the summoning of demons.

Walter had no suspects. The ability to create summoning portals, triggered only by the presence of an elemental mage, was rare knowledge. So rare that not even he held it. He considered himself amongst the rare elementalists for knowing how to close summoning gates and how to handle demons. He'd defeated seven demons, if one could call a creature the size of a man's hand a demon. But, in Walter's opinion, where there were small, so too were there large.

Elemental mages who held firm beliefs in the faith often choose to die over trying to summon up their untrained and untapped abilities for fear of opening a portal into the abyss. It was rubbish taught by ignorant priests, but that teaching brought about countless deaths when a good earth tremor could have saved their lives. Or ended torturous agony swiftly.

Walter wondered at the purpose of these markings. He couldn't imagine any elemental mage with this level of skill and ancient knowledge willing to sacrifice the potential for peace. There was a reason for these symbols to be around Borro Abbey. He'd get to the bottom of it. First, though, he'd get rid of this before some hapless idiot ruined the thin chance they all had at peace.

CHAPTER SEVENTEEN

OVER-WINTERING AT Borro Abbey had always been a quiet affair for Allegra. Those days were long over. At first, the annoyances were minimal, a blur of the same conversation over and over, with only minor variations. Sometimes, Allegra thought she was reading from a play, for surely it was impossible to be this similar.

She'd sit in a room of disputing this or that's. Sometimes, they were brothers. Sometimes, neighbors. Sometimes, both. It didn't matter. She'd urge for calm. They'd argue. She'd urge for calm again. She'd be ignored.

"Gentlemen! We are getting nowhere," she'd say with the last of her patience.

"But he said that!" one would protest

"That was twenty years ago!" the other would defend.

"And I want an apology!" one would demand.

"Never!" the other would insist.

With the last tethers of sanity, Allegra would ask, "Then, gentlemen, why are we here?"

One such time was between three brothers. Each controlled a small city-state smaller than her own property. However, together, all three men held a small territory that was home to four thousand citizens. They owned mostly coal mines, but there were a couple of tiny copper mines, plus their freshwater fishery, their agricultural concerns, and all told the three brothers ran a thriving, if insular, community.

Of course, because they were brothers, the petty arguments that got in the way of progress weighed down any compromise Allegra could offer.

"Just because you were always Father's favorite doesn't mean you'll get your own way here," Godfrey, the eldest son, accused.

Josken, the youngest who excelled at eye rolling, said, "Father's been dead for twenty years."

"And you're still acting like he's alive!" Godfrey said.

Allegra looked at Sabastian, the middle brother, a silent man whose mouth was curled in a perpetual smirk, and asked, "Do you have anything to add?"

"Not at all, Your Excellency. I plan for them to argue themselves into an early grave and then unite the three cities into a small nation."

For three days, the brothers argued as if they were the only concerns on Allegra's mind. Three precious days of work were wasted trying solely at the urging at four different cardinals, including Cardinal Giso, who said in his letter that he was going to invent new laws to have the brothers arrested if she didn't solve their problems.

By the fourth day, Allegra decided Giso was on to something. "Gentlemen, I have listened to your concerns for half a week now. I suggest we discuss the actual issue at hand, which is to find a resolution, even temporary, as your bickering is affecting the mages in your cities."

"They wouldn't be affected if he didn't keep freeing them!" Godfrey said, jabbing an accusatory finger at Josken.

Sabastian nodded.

Josken, for his part, merely shrugged. "I believe in freedom for all of the Lord Almighty's children."

"Horseshit," Godfrey and Sabastian said in unison.

"Your Excellency, my brother here is purposely raiding my mines and stealing my slaves. I am legally allowed to have them. And then he is freeing them, to be hired by him!" Godfrey accused.

"Do you deny any of this?" Allegra asked.

Josken grinned. "On the contrary, I welcome the opportunity to publicly state that there is no slavery in my fare city and that we are able to run our mines and our farms."

"You have two tiny coal mines! That's it!" Godfrey exclaimed.

"I am very happy to do everything in my power to release these individuals from the grips of cruel men."

"Jos, please. You're selling them back to Godfrey when he has a labor shortage!" Sebastian said.

"You misunderstand. I am acting as broker. I find them apprenticeship positions, where they are required to work for a certain number of years. After that, they have a trade and income."

Allegra narrowed her eyes. "Indentured servitude. You are freeing Godfrey's mage slaves to put them into indentured servitude."

"They aren't slaves anymore."

"And your pockets are lined by the finder's fees," Sebastian said.

"Which I use to then liberate more slaves."

"Enough," Allegra said, raising her hands. "Enough."

She sat there and stared at these three heartless men. She didn't know what exactly she was tempted to do, but she suspected it involved having them put into stocks at their own mines. Starvation was rampant throughout all of Amadore's child apprentice programs; nowhere was safe from the abuses that the program dished out. While she didn't want anyone to be a slave, she also didn't want them rescued, only to be dumped into a servitude where there was no guarantee they'd come out alive at the end, let alone with a useful trade.

"This petty bickering is getting us nowhere," Allegra said. When the brothers began to object, she raised a hand. "You want to know why mages are revolting in your land? Well, I'll tell you. It's because you treat them like unthinking creatures. You treat them like property and not people."

"They are my property," Godfrey said.

"What is the life expectancy in one of your mines for an elemental?"

Godfrey looked confused. "I don't know."

"According to your ledgers, it's ten months."

He shrugged. "So?"

"A person is declared an elemental, even if they are not, and then they are sent to live out the rest of their lives in the dark. And, in your mines, it's ten months."

"Mining is dangerous work, Your Ladyship. You cannot possibly understand the—"

"Please explain it to me."

"I beg your pardon?"

"Please explain to me why mines without elementals have a life expectancy of decades, whereas your mages don't even make it a year."

"As I've tried to say, the details are complex..."

"Again, explain them to me."

"What's she's asking for, Godfrey, is for you to admit you don't even let your supposed elementals up in the fresh air. They sleep and work down in the tunnels. Many kill themselves after only a few weeks. Others end up so exhausted they cause accidents. Others do it on purpose. Sometimes, it's just an accident, since mining is dangerous," Sabastian said. "Oh, did you think I didn't know about how your mines were ran?"

"So, are those the work conditions for your elemental slaves?"

He didn't answer.

"Right. And you, Josken? Anything to add."

"This isn't the issue. The issue is..."

"The issue," Allegra said, very firmly, "is that there have been three riots in the last three months in each of your cities. Neighboring militia has had to come help quell the unrest which lasted several days during the last event. Now, tell me, is the standard working conditions helping or hindering your pockets?"

"I don't think you understand..." Godfrey said.

"You aren't here to think. That is my job."

Allegra's resolution was swift. The brothers had to implement basic humane living conditions for the mining slaves. That meant no sleeping underground. They were allowed to come up on a schedule set by the Cathedral Mining Commission, ran by Nathan under Serafina's watching eye.

They were angry, but accepted her ruling. It was her job after all, though she suspected she was the first to actually do the job.

And on it went.

One particular county had seen near-continuous rioting and had sent a representative of the noble whose lands were being affected. The mages sent one of their leaders, but he was ambushed on the journey. The noble had the gall to say to Allegra's face that of course he had the leader killed; he was sure he was saving her the trouble.

Allegra would have arrested him on the spot if there was any possible way she could justify in the eyes of the law having a noble, and the cousin of the prince, arrested. Since he had not murdered the man himself in cold blood, there was nothing she could do.

Except, of course, order him to release all of his slaves over the age of fifty and under twelve. He flew into a rage over that and slapped her across the face. For that she could have him arrested, which she did. The king was so embarrassed that he donated half of his cousin's lands to the office of the Arbiter of Justice, which Serafina appointed agents to auction off what was possible and turn the estate into a monastery and a school. Some of the funds from the auction were used to compensate the released mages, to help them re-establish new lives. The rest of the funds would eventually make their way to the Cathedral Mining Commission. Nathan and Serafina already used over a thousand gold sovereigns of Allegra's personal salary to hire several of their mage friends as mine inspectors, accountants, and managers.

Again, not a great solution, but it had stopped the rioting. Cardinal Vanida's supposed hysterics over this solution were just a bonus.

Word had spread quickly that Allegra would grant individual freedom to any slave who asked her for it. Further, any slave who made it to Borro Abbey would be protected by the Arbiter. Hundreds risked their lives to make the treacherous journey up the mountainside.

The first time it happened, it had been two men. Both were suffering extreme frostbite, and later died from their injuries. But they lived long enough for Allegra to declare them freemen before they succumbed. Twice more this happened within a week.

Alarmed, Allegra asked for word to be spread for none to attempt the journey to Borro until the spring. The mountain slopes were too dangerous for those not accustomed to the trek or lacked appropriate clothing and equipment. Stanton assigned guards at several abbeys within a day's ride, along the highway, in hopes that they would seek refuge there. Those abbeys were all run by abolitionists, or at least friends of abolition, and Allegra trusted them to not be tempted by coin nor threat.

Queen Portia did not look kindly upon this. Cartossa's ruler issued new orders that free mages were to travel with papers at all times or be imprisoned as runaway slaves. Allegra's letters were rarely answered. If they were, they were clearly written by Portia's advisors and not the Queen herself.

All this crackdown did was put pressure on the Amadore side of the border, as free mages escaped Cartossa's militia. Due to standing agreements between the neighboring countries, Cartossa militia was allowed to cross Amadore's border in the pursuit of dangerous elementals and enlist local assistance. Soon, anyone caught leaving Cartossa risked the label of elemental mage. So more risked the journey to Borro to obtain a holy seal.

After the deaths of three free mages who froze during the night trying to reach Allegra, she dispatched Nathan with letters bearing her seal. She granted temporary powers to several local monasteries and abbeys to act on her stead to give sanctuary to anyone who asked, no matter their actual or accused status. She hoped they could make the journey to Borro in the spring when it would not risk their lives. With any luck, she would have gotten through to Queen Portia and the measures reduced.

Risk they did, however. Hundreds of Cartossa's mages crossed the border and dragged themselves through snow storms on their trek through the foothills of the Borro Mountain range. Most of the fleeing mages—be they slave or free—eventually converged on St. Croix Abbey, less than a day's carriage ride in good weather from Borro. Fighting broke out as the taste of freedom mixed with desperation. Several mages were arrested by local authorities, on suspicion of elemental magic. Cathedral guards, led by Martin of the Holy Father's Own Consorts, tried to bring order but they failed in the face of the local militia's hatred of magic coupled with the desperate crowd's pressing needs. A wayward stone stuck the Marquis of St. Croix's wife, killing her before she even hit the ground. There was no stopping what came next.

Mother Ruth, Bishop of St. Croix Abbey, stepped into the fray. Allegra remembered her to be a frail, tiny woman, with steel-gray hair and an imperial nose that always looked too large for her tiny features. Martin's report said she walked out there into the middle of the unfolding riot, head held high like she'd known something the others didn't.

And she did, all right. Mother Ruth stamped one tiny foot to the ground of the snow-covered marketplace and the earth split in half. She repeated the gesture, separating the Cathedral guards from the mob. But her efforts put her with the element of the mob that wanted the damned demon-summoners away from their righteous little town.

Mages, slaves, locals, Cathedral guards, and the militia were all forced to helplessly watch as the mob burned Mother Ruth alive, unable to cross the fissures she'd created. A Cathedral guard, hitherto unknown to be even a mage, blew a gust of wind from his mouth toward Mother Ruth's pyre. Martin and several other witnesses had thought the guard was hoping to put out the flame, but instead he fueled the fire. The blast incinerated Mother Ruth and spread to the crowd. Dozens were burned alive. In the commotion, the guard escaped.

Overnight, Mother Ruth became the symbol of the mage rebellion. They had found their martyr. Allegra had teased Walter that she'd thought he would always ended up on that pyre, and not some unknown backwater bishop, but even she had no mirth in her voice. For, again, they both knew what would come next: reprisals.

Couriers bundled against the mountain winter risked hide and hair to deliver the constant stream of updates, letters, missives, and pleas for assistance. Allegra did all she could from her abbey's warmth, but they were not equipped to drag a military force throughout the lands stopping the slaughter of mages by ignorant villagers, nor the slaughter of aristocrats by enraged mages. All she could do was write letters, her soul dying a little more each time at her choice of staying here as opposed to Orsini, where the lowland climate would have made travel somewhat easier.

But her arrogance had wanted her to be near Cartossa's border. There she'd been so sure the war would break out. Instead, it was breaking out all over and she was powerless to stop it. It was that mounting fear that the violence would spread that caused the first wave of refugees.

Father Michael called them pilgrims because, as he said, the word gave the people more dignity than migrant or refugee, but that is what they were in Allegra's eyes. Twice, small pockets of them came, often arriving half dead from frost. Twice, they'd accepted them, for what else could they do? It had been the folly of her edicts that had caused these people to come. It was four days later, however, that Allegra accepted in her heart that the war had already started and that waiting for an acknowledgment of the words was doing none of them any good.

It was early in the morning, in the midst of the first real blinding blizzard of the winter that the abbey's alarm was raised. Allegra bundled herself in furs and wool and went outside, flanked by six members of the Consorts, and Stanton in front of her, sword drawn. It was snowing so badly that Allegra couldn't see the watchtower except for the lantern that shone inside its small protective structure.

A light slid down what she knew was a ladder and two members of the Cathedral guard rushed for them. "There's hundreds coming."

Fear gripped Allegra's insides. "Hundreds? Hundreds of what?"

"Them," the guard said, pointing.

A woman came into view, dragging a sled behind her, a mound of children under a tattered blanket huddled for comfort. "Are you the Contessa of Marsina?"

Chills that had nothing to do with the howling winds spread through Allegra. "Lord God Almighty. What are you doing in this weather?"

The woman's answer was to collapse into the snow. Her children sobbed, but made no attempt to pull themselves from the make-shift sled.

"Get her inside!" Allegra screamed. "Move! Move! Nadira, where are you?"

"Coming, Your Ladyship!" Nadira came rushing outside in nothing but her indoor shoes, skirts dragging in the snow. "Kia! Calm Seas! Hurry!"

Allegra watched in horror as more and more and Almighty knew how many more dragged themselves forward. Most collapsed when through the gate, once they'd realized their journey was over.

Allegra shouted orders, all the while her heart pounding in her chest. "Get the servants out of bed. I need broth on the boil. Get the brandy out of the cellars. Get the linens out of storage."

"Tell the chambermaids to start lighting the fireplaces in the main ballroom and the chapel. Kia! Move!" Nadira issued forth. "Calm Seas? Get the rugs out of the attics. All of them! We need to put them down on the ballroom floor. Ladies! Let's move!"

"Merciful Lord," Father Michael whispered at the frozen faces who passed by him. "Get them inside."

"How many are you bringing inside?" one of the servants asked.

"All of them!" Father Michael shouted. He looked at Allegra, fierce determination on his face. "We are bringing them all in."

"Get those rugs up off the foyer floor and get them laid down on the ballroom floor," the housekeeper shouted to a footman. "As we bring them in, get the sickest near the fires first. Nathan! Go wake up the footmen and the coachmen. All of them!"

That morning was only the beginning. Over the next three weeks, over five hundred refugees arrived at the abbey. Slave. Free. Elemental. Normal. It didn't matter. All of their lives had been threatened in some way and Borro Abbey had become their refuge. Allegra couldn't turn them away. But the abbey was not designed to hold that many people. Fights broke out, accusations of theft and unfair treatment were leveled, and food stores were running dangerously low. The servants resented being ordered about, and the few wealthy patrons who stayed at the abbey for winter solitude felt put upon and threatened by the swelling numbers of ragged mages.

"Your Ladyship, we cannot continue taking these people in," Father Michael shouted at her, his nerves frayed by the steady stream of humanity. "We are not equipped."

"I cannot leave them to freeze to death!" Allegra yelled back.

"Child, you are the Arbiter of Justice, not of compassion," Father Michael shot back.

"Is there no room for compassion in justice?"

"There isn't when there is no bread left in the abbey! What good will come of us starving alongside these people?"

Allegra had not considered the impact of her edicts. Neither had the Cathedral's cardinals, who wrote furiously for her address the pilgrims, refugees, or runaway slaves – the terminology changing with where the writers' loyalty resided.

"Fine." Allegra grabbed a sheet of paper from the Bishop's desk and began to write. "Serafina, this is a letter of authority for you to charge to my accounts. You are authorized to spend three hundred sovereigns. I need as much grain as you can get your hands on. Take my footmen with you and my winter sleigh. Get the coachmen to take you to the surrounding areas. Let's leave Borro alone, since they're struggling. Get me everything and anything. Barley, wheat, rye, all of it. Take three Consorts with you."

She'd have to write to her brother and request he forward five hundred gold to her personal account held at the Cathedral. It was more pin money than she spent in a year, but she also knew he'd release the funds. After all, they were her funds.

"Nathan, you're in charge of supplies. Take Nadira and some consorts. Find blankets, used clothing, heavy fabric, burlap, and scraps of fabric, all of it. Needles, thread, buttons. I need to put people to work sewing. We're out of blankets and warm clothing." She glanced over at Nathan. "You, too. Find me living supplies. Dried goods, small pots, utensils, linens, that sort of thing. We're going to erect tents and makeshift shelters between here and Borro. We need enough supplies for everyone to be somewhat self-sufficient, or else we're going to end up with another St. Croix here. Captain, I need you to beg the Duke for fifty palace guards. I don't want the useless ones, either. I want the real guards."

"He'll send twenty."

"Then ask for seventy. And ask Queen Portia for the loan of ten of her personal guard. We need additional protection here and she can spare them, since this is her mess we're dealing with. No, wait. Father, you write to Francois and you get him to order Portia to send those guards. If she wants to play politics, then let's play."

So it went throughout the winter. Allegra's staff worked tirelessly to help both Borro Abbey and the town of Borro deal with the burgeoning population. Employment was scarce; few wanted to hire runaway mages. A few times, locals tried to steal back "their" mage slaves, many of which weren't even mages. In the end, the additional guard presence helped keep the peace, even if there were still misunderstandings, fights, and endless petty crimes.

Allegra's own sovereigns disappeared, as did the additional money her brother sent her. Nathan and Serafina charged as much back to the Cathedral as possible, but even still, Allegra knew she could not spend her entire Arbiter's budget in the first three months of the year and not have to answer for it.

So they all made sacrifices. Nadira chopped up eighteen of Allegra's finest gowns to distribute to the seamstresses to make sashes, purses, and the like. That kept many busy in the idle hours of sitting in the cold with nothing but a small fire to keep them warm, and it gave them the hope of some additional income when traffic would again flow along the Cathedral highway.

Stanton put in three hundred gold sovereigns of his own money to help keep food in refugee bellies, even as more flooded in by the day. Lex and Dodd, likewise, wrote to their parents, begging for funds to help with the crisis. Even the abolitionist cardinals sent Allegra ready coin to assist in her humanitarian efforts.

It kept them alive. When the spring thaw came, the small hamlet of Borro was little more than a tent city of over a thousand freemen and mages and a full-fledged crisis. Its former one hundred or so residents were overran, terrified, and resentful. It was only the careful attention of the abbey that kept tempers from flaring.

Some of the people moved on once the roads cleared and were safe to walk without freezing to death. Allegra had no money in her budget to give them all something to live off or a relocation allowance, and she certainly wasn't going to get compensation when slave owners were angrily demanding compensation for loss property.

The worst for Allegra was when the Marquis of Marsden showed at up at the abbey with the first spring thaw. He was a middle-aged man, fit and broad, with chiseled features that announced rakish tendencies in his youth. He was also married to one of Allegra's many second cousins. She'd assumed he was there to visit, as a courtesy family visit and attempt to wring some financial deals out of the arrangement. That was what all of her other cousins were doing by letter the entire winter.

"How dare you steal ten of my best mages?" he'd demanded.

They were alone in her study, as always when meeting any member of the aristocracy. "I didn't steal anything, Colin."

"I passed those ten mages in the courtyard living in the slums you turned this place into. And they have the nerve to tell me they don't have to come back if they don't want to. Because of your say so!"

"As Arbiter, I have been given…"

He spat in her face. "Now, you make them come back with me right now or so help me Lord God Almighty, I will teach you a lesson you won't soon forget."

"Get out, Colin."

He grabbed her by the sleeve and slammed her to the desk. Allegra screamed as Colin knocked over the ink well and he pressed her face into it. He slammed her face down into the ink two more times, demanding his mages back. When Lex charged through the door, Dodd hard on his heels, Colin had a dazed Allegra by the throat in a death grip.

Lex kicked Collin hard in the back of one knee. The crunch of bones splintering was a sound that haunted Allegra for many nights after that. Dodd grabbed the semi-conscious Allegra and wrapped her protectively in his arms, while Lex beat the life out of the Marquis.

Stanton and a servant had to pull the enraged Lex off the Marquis, who was curled into a fetal position to protect himself from Lex's punishing kicks. Stanton grabbed the back of Colin's ornate jacket and hauled him to his feet, all the while Colin screamed about how he was a man of power. Stanton kept his cool, even when Colin punched him in the face. Blood trickled from one nostril, but Stanton hauled Colin down to the local militia who'd been assigned by the local magistrate to assist with the refugees.

THE DEMONS WE SEE

STANTON RUSHED BACK to Allegra's rooms as soon as his duty was discharged. He took the stairs two at a time and rushed into her rooms. Various maids were on their hand and knees scrubbing the ink from the papered walls of her office. Likewise, her polished wooden floor had been splattered and the ink stains came out into the main sitting room. Calm Seas and several of the abbey's chambermaids were on their hands and knees scrubbing before the ink set and ruined the floorboards. Allegra was seated on a chair close to her balcony doors, well-wrapped in a blanket and flanked by Lex and Dodd. All were stained with ink and blood.

Nadira leaned over her mistress, scrubbing her face with a paste of salt, soap, and butter, and the silent tears that trickled down her cheeks. Most of the stain was gone now from her golden brown flesh, leaving behind temporary red rawness.

"May I speak with the Contessa alone, please?"

Kia, who'd been scrubbing the paper with a fine brush, said, "Of course, Your Grace. Your Ladyship? I'll have the footmen replace your stained rugs. Would you like me to find you a new desk?"

Allegra's red-rimmed eyes were dull. Gone was the sparkle that Stanton had come to love. Not in a romantic way, he corrected his thoughts. Just in that cheerful way her eyes always made his feet feel just a touch lighter whenever she looked at him.

"I would love a new desk, please."

"That's all I can do for your face anyway," Nadira said. "The rest will fade away in the next day or two." She frowned. "I hope you don't bruise too badly."

"Thank you," Allegra said, and her voice was small. She didn't look over her shoulder.

Lex flashed Stanton a worried look before saying, "Contessa, we'll discuss new security arrangements when you are feeling up to it. I promise you'll never be left alone with a madman ever again."

"No one's getting through if you don't want them here," Dodd said, patting her awkwardly on the shoulder.

Stanton waited for the door to close behind the trail of servants and helpers before he sat down next to her. "How are you?"

Instead of answering his question, she asked, "Was all of this a mistake?"

He wanted so badly to wrap his arms around her, to protect her and promise to always keep her safe. He berated himself for letting this happen. Rank had blinded him. All of the precautions against the mages for what? A gentleman to dance his way into their midst to brutalize her.

"It was never your decision. It was theirs." When she didn't respond, he kept going. "You've become a symbol for them. You're a mage and you are tasked with the Lord's justice."

"Justice. All I've done this winter is mediate petty disputes, write letters to pompous fools begging their assistance, and for what? Hmm? To lose the respect of the people I'm trying to change." Allegra scoffed. "How many people died trying to get here only to starve and freeze?"

"I'm sorry he hurt you," Stanton said into the silence.

Allegra's jaw trembled. Most of her face was still a deep, angry red where Nadira has scrubbed the ink from her skin. Her neck was bare and the tops of her breasts heaved with each breath under the strain of her tightened corset. The usual white linen that decorated her neck was draped over a desk's edge. Her red and yellow striped satin dress was stained.

"Will you be able to save the dress?"

Allegra snorted, a half sob-half gasp sound. "It's ruined. Nadira is hoping the laundry can salvage the skirt, but I doubt it. This was my favorite dress, too." She cupped her face into her hand and began to cry. "Crying over a dress when people are starving outside of our doors."

She twisted until it was obvious she wanted him to hold her, and he did. He wrapped tight arms around her and let her cry out her fears and hurt.

CHAPTER EIGHTEEN

ALLEGRA WAS ON the hunt for blankets and candles. She could have called for a servant, but her heart refused to calm its frantic pace while sitting in the very room the Marquis had attacked her in. She determined it would do her good to go search for herself. Nadira and Kia had left for the village to find soothing tea for Allegra. Both had women insisted and, with the two of them so rarely agreed on anything, Allegra felt it was best to let them be.

There were a couple of mage women living in the tents who made restorative blends. Father Michael swore by one particular astringent blend that purported to whisk away his morning aches and pains. Nadira herself had been caught sipping such a blend on occasion when the weather was particularly damp. With Allegra's luck, however, her faithful servant would return with a blend containing enough valerian and lemon balm to knock out a draft horse.

Allegra instructed Rahna, the Consort guard outside of her room, to remain there. She wanted to wander the abbey in peace. Rahna agreed and said she'd not allow anyone to enter her rooms beyond the servants. Allegra thanked her and went about her hunt for supplies.

Eventually, Allegra found herself on the lower level of the abbey, a place she'd only been once before on an ill-advised kitchen raid attempt. This part of the abbey was suspiciously empty. The noise and bustle of upstairs didn't reach this dank part of the building, though the scents of the kitchens still seeped down the corridors.

Cold crept up her arms and she shivered. It wasn't the kind of cold that came from the dampness, however. She had no words for it, other than *wrong*.

She looked around the narrow corridor, but there was no one in sight. Not even the flicker of a small candle to signal another's presence.

Allegra shook off her concerns as nothing more than the exaggerations of an overactive and tired mind. She pressed on, looking for the damned storage room. Why didn't they keep the candles in the closets on every floor, along with the linens? They used wax candles upstairs where the quality guests graced the gilded hallways. They could store the wax upstairs without issue.

This was the unlivable part of the abbey. No chimneys, no warmth. Just the damp coldness of stone and crates upon crates of storage. The priceless items were stored in the attic, where the square brick chimneys helped chase away the moisture. Down here, however, were the things that could handle a little mildew without much complaint.

Like candles.

Allegra tried a door, but it was locked. This was turning into a bad idea. She'd never been to this part of the abbey before, where the walls wept from the dampness of being inside the mountain's face.

She was about to turn back when light caught her eye ahead. She took the dozen or so steps and around the corner. She didn't recognize the symbols on the wall, and couldn't even determine if it was merely decorative or some form of writing. None were bigger than her thumbnail, but there were several of them.

She put her own small candle down on the floor to then brush a hand across the wall in an attempt to clear away an errant strand of spider's web. Her hand erupted in flame. Allegra screamed until she realized it was her magic, and not an uncontrolled flame, that had engulfed her. She shook her hand several times, terrified, looking around in case a servant had seen. She smacked her hand against her dress without thinking, and the fabric caught ablaze.

Allegra shrieked. She dropped to the damp floor and rolled around on the cold stone, smothering out the flames on her dress. Her engulfed hand also extinguished, but the job had been done. The wall glowed not with symbols now, but with the blackened image of a small, but monstrous, creature. Similar in shape to a bat, only with one, long arm ending in talons.

Allegra gasped. She knew what that image was. She grabbed the candle lantern which was still flickering away on the floor and hauled herself to her feet. She had to get out of here. *Now.* Even being seen near this image would be enough justification for some to lock her away for the rest of her life.

Screeching filled the air. Allegra looked back at the wall. The sound grew closer and, with horror, Allegra realized the dark image was not an image at all, but a hole…a portal…

Allegra ran down the corridor. She lost her shoes in the process and kept sprinting in her stocking feet. She screamed as the creature's screeching grew louder, and all the while ran faster. She didn't want to think about what was coming behind her. She shut off all reasoning parts of her brain and listened only to the delirious, terrified parts that told her to run for her life.

The screeching reached a crescendo and she knew she wouldn't clear the dark corridors in time. Allegra whirled in time to see the demon from the wall etching flying at her, its misshaped clawed hand stretched out ahead of it.

Allegra pushed all of her fear and terror into her right hand and a blast of red-hot flame hit the demon square in its misshapen face. It tumbled backwards as Allegra fell to one knee from the exertion. She searched her memory for the words to say, the famous quote from the holy writs.

"Back to the abyss with thee, foul reflection of mine sins," shouted a deep voice behind her.

The demon-creature squawked and flapped its wings, rushing back to the markings on the wall. The words had caused it to burst into flame and it screamed louder as it rushed the portal opening. It dove back through the wall.

Walter ran behind it, shouting the incantation over and over, and the flames flickered brighter with each sentence. He slammed his hand against the wall opening once the demon was through and the stone cracked. The glow disappeared.

"Ally!" Walter shouted, rushing back to her side. He slid down to his knees, at her side. "Are you hurt?"

"Markings on the wall," she said. It was hard to keep breathing. She wanted to wail. "There were markings. Was that…was that a…"

"Yes, that was a demon. One of the small little bastards. They're easy to frighten away. Are you hurt?"

"I…demons? I…"

The growing pain behind her eyes overtook her and she passed into quiet blackness.

"I CAN'T BELIEVE that bastard choked her," Dodd was saying. Neither he nor Lex had changed their clothes yet. They'd been taking statements from witnesses all day. They'd send those notes off to the local magistrate who, Lex felt, would be very keen to both put away a nobleman who attacked an unarmed woman and score some Cathedral political points.

"I've had guards posted at the top of the stairs, but that's just to stop the riffraff from wandering up there and stealing the silverware," Lex said. They sighed heavily. "I never considered that one of our own kind would hurt her. I should have, though."

Dodd clapped them on the shoulder. "Ah, it's not your fault. Shit happens, right? We'll have to come up with a better plan now, though."

Lex nodded, grateful for Dodd's support. "I think we'll keep the guard near her chambers all of the time now. I'll get Rainier to talk to her about it."

A servant rushed by with a covered silver platter. Dodd tried to get his attention. "Pssst!"

The young man, thin and pale, stopped and asked, "Yes, Lieutenant Dodd? I'm late for Father Michael's afternoon tea."

Dodd picked up the cover, despite the servant's protests. He snagged two pieces of cake, passed one to Lex, and said, "A growing man needs to eat."

Lex snorted, but took a bite of the cake. Pound cake with caraway. "The only way you're growing, Dodd, is out."

"That hurts, Lex."

What was to be their friendly banter over Dodd's expanding waistline was interrupted by the floor shaking. The servant held steady, but Dodd and Lex both dropped their cakes to the floor.

"What was that?" Dodd demanded.

"Did the mountain just move?" Lex asked, eyes wide, surveying the room.

"Earth tremors. They happen all of the time. Nothing to worry about," the servant said.

"Nothing to worry about, he says," Dodd said, trying to mock the boy's voice.

The servant rushed off, needing to get his cakes to the obviously starving bishop and his friends. Lex bent down and picked up both cakes. Dodd accepted his with thanks and popped the remainder into his mouth. Lex's had broken in two pieces, so they blew the dirt off both pieces and ate them one at a time.

"Was that an earth tremor?" another servant asked, arms full of blankets.

"Apparently," Lex said.

The servant complained about how she'd need to find some of the under-footmen to hunt through the lower corridors to ensure nothing had caved in "this time." Lex did *not* like the sound of that.

"This time?" Dodd asked through a mouthful of cake.

"Yes, sir. Didn't you know? There was rock slides further up the slope before the snow came. On the side that normally never happens. Now, since that happened, it's nothing but avalanches."

"I'd just assumed mountains, snow, avalanches," Dodd said, still chewing his cake. That's what he got for shoving it all in his mouth like an animal.

"No, sir. It's just the Almighty telling us he doesn't want anyone living in the west cottages anymore. Just as well. They were getting shabby."

"Good of the Almighty to care about the abbey's housing needs," Dodd quipped after finally swallowing his cake.

"I better be off, sirs. I have some lazy footmen to find."

Lex turned back to Dodd and they both chatted about plans to improve security around the Contessa. Dodd still liked the plan of security at the stairs, and suggested that they speak to Father Michael about moving some of the servants on the fourth floor attic back down to the lower level, near the kitchens, so that there would be less foot traffic up and down the elite wing.

Lex also suggested, if that didn't work, that they could divide the abbey into more established wings. The abbey already boasted several wings; surely they could move some people around to make it easier to secure residents and visiting dignitaries.

A muffled cry caught Lex's attention. "Did you hear that?"

"Hear what...wait, I hear it, too. Is that someone calling for help?"

"Hello?" Lex called out.

"Help!" A man's voice, strong and closer now. Lex spun around to the door for the lower levels. Walter Cram was on his hands and knees, covered in dirt and blood, dragging himself up the stairs.

"Ally," he gasped. "Help her."

Servants rushed from various parts around the main lobby who'd been cleaning and scrubbing during all of this. Dodd reached an arm under the collapsed Cram and said, "What happened to you, man?"

Lex looked down the dark staircase. "Who's Ally? Where is she?"

"Part of the ceiling caved in, down below." Cram wheezed out a cough. "Allegra. Couldn't get her out. Came...for help."

"Dodd! Go!" Lex ordered, and Dodd grabbed a lit candle from the wall and rushed down the stairs, careful to protect the flame and its shield with his cupped hand.

Servants dropped what they were doing, all to rush downstairs. Lex called out to one by name and said, "Get Captain Rainier. Get all of the Consorts. Move! Get me a physician! Now! Move! You! Get me healing stones! Now!"

Lex pulled off their jacket and wrapped it around Cram's head. He winced as the brass buttons pushed into his scalp, but Lex hushed him to stop fussing. "I have four healing buttons on my jacket. Stay still and let them stop the bleeding before you ruin the carpets."

Cram's mouth twitched. Blood seeped through the cracks. Lex winced. "Tasmin's holy sword, Cram! What were you both doing down there?"

"Arguing. We were arguing about..." Cram seemed to search his memory. "Candles. She was looking for candles. I followed her, and then some of the stone from the ceiling fell. I couldn't haul her out, so I..." He broke off coughing.

"Nadira is going to murder you when she finds out," Lex said with a weary sigh.

A pained sound that was almost a laugh escaped Cram. "She probably will."

"Sir, I got him," one of the servants said, almost pushing Lex out of the way. "You go. I'll send Captain Rainier down as soon as he comes."

Lex snapped off a couple more orders to snooping servants before the housekeeper arrived. The old battle axe clapped her hands, shouted for people to either get to work or get out of the way, and took immediate charge of the situation. Lex eased up, gave Cram a tight smile, and joined the trail of footman heading down the stairs with candles, blankets, shovels, and buckets.

Wall sconces were being lit, a flickering spotlight down the corridors. They all followed the trail of servants, with Lex weaving and pushing to the front of the queue. It was slow going, as the servants were pulling out digging supplies from various storage rooms along the way. Lex was surprised by their calm efficiency; they'd been through this before. It wasn't that they didn't care that the Contessa was trapped. It was just that they knew how best to get her out.

When Lex finally pushed their way to the cave in, their heart sank. The Contessa was in the midst of several shattered masonry stones, as well as the rock face that this part of the building was comprised of.

The servants were forming a queue. The tall, older man at the front carefully pulled a stone out from the slide and carefully handed it down. The rock passed back the line out of the way.

"Contessa! Can you hear me?" Lex shouted and was rewarded with a groan from the woman. "Hurry!"

"Can't hurry, sir," the older gentlemen said. "Go too fast and we'll bring this entire area down on our heads. Then we'll all need a rescuing. Join the line and we'll all get her out."

Lex gritted their teeth, but joined the line. Several painstaking minutes passed until the hole was big enough to allow Lex to scrabble through. There were days Lex complained about their lean stature. However, when it was necessary to crawl into tight spaces to get out of tighter situations, Lex was always grateful for their size. And now, that size meant the Contessa could get help sooner.

Lex crawled over the wall, taking great care not to disturb any of the rocks and cause them to hit the Contessa. Once more, Lex leaned back to accept a lantern. The Contessa was dirty and part of her dress was burnt away. That was a little strange, but not something Lex wished to concern themselves with.

The Contessa blinked her eyes and asked, "Lex?"

Lex laughed and shouted back, "The Contessa is awake!" Back to her, Lex said, "Are you hurt badly?"

"Why are you here?"

"Don't you remember? There was a cave in."

"Lex! Lex!" Rainier bellowed. "How is she?"

"She's all right, Captain!" one of the servants shouted back.

"Is that Stanton?" Allegra asked, her words slurred. She tried to sit up, but Lex held a firm hand against her shoulder. "Easy now. We still need to clear more of a hole before we can get you out. Can you sit up?"

The Contessa nodded and, with Lex's help, pushed herself up. "But what happened...there were...there was a...I saw..."

"Cram is fine. He told us about the cave in. He's a bit beaten up, but he'll be fine."

"Walter? Right, Walter was here. Why was he here?"

"He said the two of you were arguing and you came here for candles, so he followed to continue to argument."

"I was arguing with him?" Allegra asked.

Lex chuckled. "Your Ladyship, you hit your head."

"I did?" She touched the back of her skull and her fingers came back bloody. "Oh, I did."

Servants pushed blankets through the hole and Lex accepted them gratefully. They wrapped the Contessa up in them and also accepted the mug of hot broth for her to drink, most likely laced with expensive healing fortifications reserved for the most important clientele of the abbey.

Lex and the servants, and even several of the brawnier members of the clergy, labored to carefully widen the hole. Rainier stripped down to just his trousers; sweat poured off them all in the stuffy, confined corridor. Servants passed a bucket of water with a ladle up and down the line. Father Michael pulled himself out of his own clerical robes and worked in everyday trousers and a linen shirt. Nathan and Serafina both helped in their own way; Serafina taking orders of whatever was needed and Nathan either fetching those items himself or finding someone to do it.

"There, Contessa, you see? Everyone is helping get you out."

"My head doesn't hurt as much," she said.

"That's because I wrapped you in Rainier's jacket. He has healing buttons sewn into his uniform that help stop bleeding. They're doing their job until we can get you out of here."

"Lex, help with this rock," Rainier called out.

"I'll be right back," Lex said, easing the Contessa back down. Lex stabilized the stone on their side while Rainier and two servants shoved iron bars under it and slowly rocked it loose. Lex pushed as Rainier and a big, burly man grunted and groaned to get the damned thing positioned to do a controlled roll. Once it was out of their way, there was enough room for Rainier to crawl through.

"All right, I'm going in. Stand ready to help her out," Rainier said.

Rainier climbed into Lex's little patch of corridor. He whispered to the Contessa, hushed words Lex couldn't understand. Not that they wanted to eavesdrop. She must be rather special for him to change his mind about making friends with his charges.

Rainier picked the Contessa up and, together, they eased her through the hole and into the corridor of waiting hands. Once she was through, Rainier eased himself through the hole. Then, he reached back his hand and helped Lex through.

Lex slapped the captain on the back and said, "Go on, sir. You stay with her. I'll stay down here with Dodd and help the servants. There might be someone else further back. You never know, right?"

"Are you sure?" Rainier looked around. "You could use another strong   back."

"There's plenty of strong backs here," Dodd said.

"And you're too big to be crawling through the tunnels we're making, Your Grace," one of the servants said.

Lex smirked at Rainier's grimace, but it did the trick. He gave them all a stiff nod before following the men who carried the Contessa from the basement. Lex turned to Dodd and said, "All right. I'm going back in and seeing if there's another cave in and if there's anyone else down here."

They all worked through the night making sure there was no one else caught in the rubble. They found the bodies four punishing hours later.

CHAPTER NINETEEN

IT TOOK A full day for Allegra's hands to stop shaking and her head to stop ringing, but both finally gave her relief. The physician had recommended nothing but broth, but Allegra vetoed that quickly. She had a few bumps and bruises, and a pounding headache, but beyond that she was fine. The fastest way, in her opinion, to recover was to eat a big meal now that her stomach had stopped dancing about.

Allegra was wrapped in her heavy dressing gown and shift, as the physician had banned all visitors beyond himself, Father Michael, and her two servants. Not even Serafina or Stanton were allowed to visit her. The quiet had done her good, but as Allegra looked down at the eight porcelain chafing dishes in front of her, she wished for company.

A full pigeon pie was too much for her to eat alone, let alone the addition of boiled chicken in sauce, sweetmeats, creamed celery, rice pudding, boiled salted beef with vegetables, and a gammon pie. She regretted her insistence for a heavy meal right up until she served herself some of the boiled chicken.

The spiced wine sauce warmed her belly and helped chase away some of her aches. With a day's reflection, she wondered if she'd really seen the demon that her memories kept insisting she'd had. She hadn't had an argument with Walter over candles. She was sure she'd have remembered that. She remembered him fighting the demon. She remembered him slamming his hand on the mark and screaming for her to run. She remembered the floor and walls shaking. She remembered Walter trying to go back to get her. She remembered falling.

Had it all been a dream? No, it couldn't have been real. It was all a twisted nightmare. So why was her hand shaking again?

A knock interrupted her reflection and, a beat later, Rahna stepped inside, carefully closing the door behind her. "Your Excellency, Walter Cram is insisting that you see him."

Allegra put her fork down. "Of course."

"I told him that the physician said…"

"Rahna, it's fine."

"Would you like me to stay in the room with you?"

Allegra should have smiled at the offer of protection, but it just made her sad. "No, I'll be fine with him."

Rahna inclined her head. "We're right outside if you need anything. Sir? She'll see you."

Walter had several superficial scrapes and cuts on his face and hands, and a massive bruise that covered most of one side of his face. He walked with a limp and a slight grimace.

"I see you have an appetite. That must be a good sign."

Allegra gave him a weak smile and motioned for him to join her. She passed him her small dessert plate and a dessert fork. "Help yourself."

"So," he said as he helped himself to some of the boiled beef.

"So," she echoed.

"What do you remember?"

"A cave in," Allegra said, licking her lips.

"Nothing else?"

"I remember you in the corridor shouting scripture," Allegra said. Walter met her steady gaze. Her heart pounded in her chest. "Was what I remember just a dream?"

"Is that what you want?"

The question weighed down on her. If it was all real, if she indeed remembered it the way it replayed in her mind, then her world just became a new, strange land. She was a woman of sense, not spirituality. Demons would mean everything they said about mages could be true. It would force her to reconsider everything she'd ever believed. She'd have to work so much harder to dispel the lies.

"Tell me."

So he did. He told her about the demon symbols appearing in the woods around the abbey since the autumn months. How they occasionally appeared in the depths of the abbey. How more were appearing closer to the tent homes of the refugees.

"Demons are real," Allegra whispered. "Walter…"

"I told you years ago that they were real. You elected not to believe me."

"I thought you were talking belief and faith, not actual bat creatures with creepy feet who fly at you in dark corridors shrieking! You're saying demons are real, and I was attacked by one? Is that really what you are saying? You're lying. You know I hit my head and you're lying to be cruel. You're doing this on purpose. This is some kind of game to you, isn't it?"

"Then how do I know you came across symbols on the wall? When you brushed your hand along them or got too near, they would have ignited your innate abilities; in your case, fire. That's how your dress was burnt. By exposing the symbols to your elemental power, you triggered the spell to complete, and the portal was ripped open. The symbols called a specific type of demon, in this case, a bat-type thing, and it attacked you. And you blasted it with fire, which slowed it down. Then I came along, and I got it out of our realm. And then you fainted because you don't know how to handle your magic still. Almighty be damned, Ally, how many times have I told you to go find yourself a cave and learn some fine control?"

"You don't get to call me Ally," Allegra snapped. She took a deep breath and tried to sort through her thoughts. Everything he said was exactly how she remembered it. "Demons are…real?"

"Yes, Allegra. They are real. That's really not the point I was trying to make right now."

"I'm sorry, but…they're real? Like, everything the Cathedral has said is true?"

"Lord Almighty, no. But, yes, they are real. And, yes, elementals are the only ones who can call them through to our world."

Allegra swallowed hard. "Did I summon a demon?"

"Yes, but it wasn't your fault."

"But I summoned one…"

Allegra's heart sank. She had never even believed the monsters in the abyss existed, let alone that she would summon one. "So...demons really are the manifestation of our sins?"

Walter made a dismissive hand. "I don't know. I think it's mostly superstitious rot, but I'm no expert on demons. As far as I can tell, demons are just...they just are. The same way we just are. They exist elsewhere, but they can invade this world if we aren't careful."

"And I wasn't careful?" Allegra asked. "I would never summon a demon. Until today, I didn't even believe they existed."

"I think it's a trap," Walter said. "I've been finding more of these markings around the abbey for the past few weeks, but I can't find who is making them. I've sent for a few people I trust, to come help search – quietly, of course. I was already in the basement when I heard you screaming."

"But why? I don't understand why anyone would be putting these symbols up. If they know it can summon these horrors, why do that?"

"Maybe to test how many elementals are in the abbey? Maybe to see how powerful we are? For all I know, it's designed to trap me." Walter made a bitter sound. "It's not like I've kept my elemental status a secret, though I don't think anyone knows what I can do. Beyond you."

"The cave in," Allegra whispered.

Walter leaned forward. "You have to believe me. It was an accident. There was an entire wall covered with those markings near the portal. In trying to close the one, I triggered them all and accidently caused the cave in."

"Three children died," Allegra whispered.

"I know," Walter said, very gently. "I had to close those forming gates or we would have been overrun with something well beyond my abilities. As far as I know, I am the only other elemental living inside the abbey, beyond you and whoever is making these portals. It's not as easy to move about the abbey as it used to be."

Allegra ran a hand through her hair. "It's real."

"Yes, Allegra," Walter said with a harsh edge to his voice. "The demons are real. Can you please focus on the real danger, which is that someone is trying to purposely have demons summoned during your little jamboree you got going on here?"

"I am trying to avert a war, you son of the bitch," Allegra snarled.

"Someone else is trying to ensure you start one," Walter snapped.

"Fine. Tell me everything you know."

"That's going to take more than one evening."

"Then take however long it takes."

CHAPTER TWENTY

STANTON STOOD TALL and proud against the wall and brooded. He knew he was brooding, and yet he could not turn it off. So he continued to stand there, guarding and brooding.

The long table next to him held all of the usual dinner offerings. Allegra was off to the side, laughing and talking like nothing had happened to her. His feelings were mixed on that score. Part of him understand and celebrated the need to carry on; Almighty knew he'd done before. Yet, another part of him was raw and sullen that she'd taken to trusting Cram with her secrets and not him.

He watched her with Cram, as she introduced him to this and that visitor who were arriving steadily now that the Abbey's roads were safe. He wanted to pretend he was jealous, but he watched her. He knew she had no feelings for Cram. She didn't look at Cram the way she looked at him. Even now, while she was avoiding him, she still looked at him differently.

Stanton shook off his melancholy. Hadn't Allegra told him repeatedly that she only ever trusted mages? Had she not said that with both her words and her actions? Why couldn't she trust him? Why did she have to trust that outlaw?

A goblet half-filled with brandy obstructed his view. "Have a drink, sir."

Stanton accepted the glass from Lex. "Why are you here?"

"The Contessa asked me to keep an eye on our good friend Cram over there, now that we have visitors. There's something about that asshole that I don't like."

"Him being an asshole is probably the thing you don't like," Stanton said. He took a sip of his brandy. It was rich and smooth, and burned pleasantly going down.

Allegra glanced in his direction and she gave him a rictus twitch of her mouth before she turned back to the abolitionists and anti-abolitionists who were gathered around her arguing with Cram.

"It takes a special kind of man to bring both sides of this dispute together in their hatred of him," Stanton mused.

Lex's snort was muffled by the large glass he was drinking from. "Exactly how many of these little parties are there going to be?"

"Hundreds," Stanton said with disgust.

"Save me from the abyss, Lord God Almighty," Lex mumbled. "I need some food."

Stanton motioned at the side table spread with assorted meats, cold pies, cakes, preserves, candied fruits, and cheeses. "Help yourself."

How could she bring an outlaw elementalist here? Cram openly defied the laws of the land and of the Almighty by his public admissions of his supposed powers. No one had ever seen his amazing talent, of course, but everyone had heard the stories. Seeing him now, however, Stanton was a little disappointed. Cram did not measure seven feet tall, nor did he crush his enemies with a mere glare of the eye. He was just a man.

Stanton frowned at that. Was that why he didn't like Cram? That he was just a man, and not the legend? He didn't like how that gnawed at the back of his thoughts.

Lex wandered back a bit later with a mountainous plate of food. Stanton stared at the pile before saying, "How can someone so small eat so much?"

"Dodd keeps eating off my plate. So, what's up with you and the Contessa?"

"Nothing."

Lex made a *hmm* sound. "Are you sure? You've not been by to see her since the accident."

"She hasn't asked to see me," Stanton said.

Lex gave him a disapproving look. "You're the captain of her personal guard. I'm pretty sure you're allowed to visit her whenever you get the urge."

Unfortunately, that was when Dodd ambled over and greeted them. "Hey, you two. You're both looking glum. Oh, nice. Ham."

As Dodd ate off Lex's plate, Lex gave Stanton a look that conveyed very clearly, *See what I mean.*

"The captain here is concerned about our new guest."

"Our new guest is a raving lunatic," Dodd said. "But harmless."

"Harmless?" Stanton said. "He is an elemental."

"So?" Dodd grabbed the last of Lex's ham off his plate.

"Hey!"

"What? I'm hungry."

"Get your own plate."

"Yours is right here, though. Thing is, sir, I've met a few elementals in my life. You don't give them any trouble, they don't give you trouble."

"And if you give them trouble?" Stanton asked bitterly.

Dodd shrugged. "You probably deserved to be turned into the soot stain on the floor."

"Comforting." Stanton frowned when a disturbing thought came over him. "Dodd, if you knew someone was an elemental, you'd report it, right?"

Dodd pointed at Cram. "Sir, that man over there is an elemental mage. Told me so himself, he did."

Stanton sighed. He'd deserved that.

"Sir, listen, we're going to have a lot more than him by the time this is over."

"I don't like it," Stanton said.

"You don't have to," Lex said. "I can't stand Cram, but we still have to protect him."

"Heretic!"

Stanton whipped around to see Brother Malcolm, one of the clergymen from Borro Village, take a swing at Cram. The inexperienced gesture gave Father Michael enough time to push the brother out of the way.

Stanton grabbed Malcolm by the waist, but he was a slippery thing. In his thrashing to get free from Stanton's tight grip, he grabbed a serving knife and amateurishly waved it in the air.

"Heretic! You shall meet the Lord God Almighty's wrath!"

"Calm down!" Stanton shouted. He didn't want to hit a man of the faith, but Almighty be with him, he'd have to if he couldn't get the man settled down.

Lex grabbed a wooden board that was under a hot dish to protect the delicate abbey furniture. He wielded it as a shield against the flailing brother.

"Brother Malcolm, you're going to hurt someone with that knife," Lex said in a calm voice you usually use for scared dogs.

"That man is an affront in the eyes of the Almighty!"

Stanton rolled his eyes at Lex and made a *do something* gesture. Brother Malcolm kicked Stanton in the shin. It hurt. A lot. He shouted in the priest's ear, "Stop kicking me!"

The shock of Stanton's voice suddenly in his ear froze Malcolm. Lex seized the opportunity and slapped away the knife with the board.

Dodd and Lex grabbed Malcolm by the arms and hauled him off. Father Michael shook his head and said, "Malcolm's been into the liquor. Mr. Cram, I apologize for this. I'll…" Father Michael threw his hands up. "Can I just go one day in this place without something happening?" And then Father Michael stormed out of the room.

"You all right there, Cram?" Stanton asked after a moment, though he was mostly staring at a very silent Allegra.

Cram made a show of patting himself down and said in a jolly voice that somehow felt forced, "I've been through worse just getting to the abbey! But thank you, Captain. I am relieved that you and all of the good Consorts are here to protect my demon-loving self."

Stanton stared at Cram until the air grew uncomfortable. Cram turned away and chatted amiably with one of the anti-abolitionists, as if nothing had just happened and he was chatting with his best friend.

Allegra approached Stanton a few moments later and said, "I'm returning to my room."

She gave him a weak smile and walked off, Beatrix and Martin hurrying off behind her, both carrying plates of food.

ALLEGRA SAT AT her pianoforte and quietly sang along to the folksong she played. She closed her eyes and focused on the words. *Come be with me and be my love.* She let her fingers dance across the ivory keys by memory alone, letting her concentration turn to the song. *Come marry me and be my love.*

As a child, Allegra hated playing. *A lady must have many accomplishments to get the best men,* her mother would say. She was the eldest of peers. Both of her parents had been titled. She had been educated by the finest tutors. All with the plan that she would unite in marriage the Marsina line with the property and lineage of another great house. Her mother had eyes on the Duke of Larwick from Southumberland. A man forty years Allegra's senior would mean she'd not have long to put up with the marriage bed and then could enjoy the added elevation in rank. Her mother was nothing if not practical.

A smile tugged across Allegra's face. Her mother almost got away with her plans, too, but Allegra's magic had come in. Gone were the language and geography tutors, in favor of magical tutors. That was where Allegra had found true learning, for she'd not simply been taught how to weave a supporting spell of water protection into a pair of socks, but she learned rhetoric, the mathematics of accounts and ledgers, science, the law, medicine, and politics.

The reasoning was two-fold. First, the tutors needed to challenge the mage's abilities to find where her skills could best be used. Secondly, and more practically, the school's matron knew all too well that a female mage, no matter how rich, would struggle to find a husband. So, the women were educated on the same level as the men.

Now look at her. *Come tell me what you want, my love, my only love.* Would her mother have approved of her now? The Arbiter of Justice. One of the richest women in all of Serna. Unmarried with no prospects. Filled with a fear and dread that the world was falling apart all around her. Avoiding her friends for fear that they would know the heavy burden of her secrets.

Come to me and I will give you all you desire, my love, my only love.

Allegra had come to appreciate the music as an adult, freed from the marital expectations of her mother. The music became another way for her to quiet the stirrings within. When she wanted to scream at the world, she could sit down to the instrument and sing along with whatever she wanted to play. No great compositions for her now. Nothing by the masters. Just the quiet folk songs that common women sang in taverns and in the fields.

"I didn't know you sang."

Allegra hit the keys hard in surprise. Stanton leaned against the doorframe of her drawing room. He was still in uniform, though was looking more rumpled than when she'd seen him earlier that day. He wasn't smiling.

They'd not spoken in private since the cave in. She'd spent nearly all of her free time the last few days with Walter, learning everything he knew about the use of elemental magic and demon portals. Actual portals! They were real. This remained an ongoing struggle for her mind to comprehend, and so she'd taken leave of Stanton's company in the hope that she wouldn't spill her turmoil to him in a weak moment.

Instead, he'd also become distant. He did his duty, certainly, but there was a confused coldness between them now.

"Did anyone else try to stab Walter?" she asked, forcing a smile upon her face.

He stepped inside and closed the door behind him. He crossed the floor to join her. He didn't accept her offer to sit, however. Instead, he stood behind a wooden chair decorated with floral needlework cushions. He gripped the back of the chair as he spoke.

"I considered it."

This time, her smile was genuine, if tired. "Walter brings that out in most people."

"Good to know. I was wondering if you would speak to Cram about a certain matter. I would but…he doesn't seem to like me."

Allegra stood up from the bench and poured herself a cup of tea from the silver tea service off to one side. She motioned if he wanted a cup, but Stanton shook his head. "Walter is like that with all non-magical people. Don't take it personally. What did you need me to say? Did he do something wrong? More than the usual, I mean."

"Cram has apparently been introducing himself as Walter Cram, outlaw elementalist mage and demon whore."

Allegra buried her face in one hand and sighed. "I'll have a word with him. I didn't have the opportunity to speak with you earlier, but thank you for protecting him."

"It's my duty," Stanton said stiffly.

"I know, but I've not made your job easy, and for that I apologize. Things have been very difficult for me the last few weeks and..." Allegra stared down at her mug. She gulped back the lump in her throat. "I'm sorry I've been cold to you. I needed some time to lose myself in my work."

"This is just the beginning."

Allegra closed her eyes and whispered, "I know."

"Then why keep him here? Why parade him out whenever important guests arrive? If he wants to help, send him down into the village and have him train the damned elementals you've granted amnesty to before they blow us all into specks of dust."

Allegra slammed her cup and saucer down hard on the end table, porcelain clattering in protest. "Is that what you think? That those people down there who risked their very lives to get here want to hurt us? All they've ever wanted was to live their lives the way the rest of us do!"

"You could be next," Stanton said in a quiet, dangerous voice. "Have you considered your own life might be forfeited in this?"

"Do you think me such a simpleton that I cannot see what might be in front of me? I will not be frightened away from doing what is right. No more, Stanton! This is where I have drawn my line. This is where I take my stand. I will not back down."

Allegra was overcome with the urge to shake Stanton until he saw reason. She got the impression that he, too, was feeling that same impulse. She was standing there with her dark eyes narrowed and stern, ready to take on the entire world with nothing more than sheer defiance. He was there, dark eyes narrowed, too, ready to stand between her and the world.

And, for the briefest of moments, Allegra wanted to know if his lips felt as good as they looked right now in the tight, firm line he'd pressed them into.

"Contessa…"

"Allegra. My name is Allegra," she said with heat. "If you are going to speak to me as a friend, then call me by my name."

"Allegra," he said, giving her the slightest incline of his head, "I am worried for your safety."

"No one would dare take down the Arbiter appointed by the Cathedral."

He took her hand into his. "A day ago, I would have said no one would dare an assassination in the bishop's parlor, either."

Allegra looked down at her hand, still covered by his. She didn't pull away. "If I am called upon to die for the freedom of mages, then I shall give my life."

The words came out of her laced with fear and anxiety, and yet, once they tumbled out of her mouth, her expression hardened. She didn't want to give up anything, but she would.

He trailed his index finger along her soft skin, not moving his hand from hers. "For your own safety, we should keep the mages and elementals elsewhere."

"No," she snapped and pulled her hand away. "I'm a mage, Stanton."

"That isn't what I meant."

"I know exactly what you meant. Get out."

"But, I only meant…" Stanton cleared his throat and said, "Of course. I meant no offense."

She turned away from him, dismissing him from her sight. "You most certainly did."

She heard his booted feet pound against her floor before the steps stopped. "One of these days, you'll have to trust someone."

Mocking laughter escaped her. She whirled on him. "Trust? You think I've never trusted? My entire existence is about trust. I have to trust that my friends do not betray me to some petty magistrate and call me an elementalist. I have to trust that my position as a woman of the blood means I won't be forced to have tattoos and brands burned in my skin. I have to trust that people don't run screaming from the room whenever I walk into it, for fear that I shall summon demons to destroy them all. All I ever do is trust!"

Stanton had no reply for that.

"Now get out, before I say something I might regret in the morning's light."

CHAPTER TWENTY-ONE

"STANTON SENT YOU, didn't he?" Allegra finally accused Lex.

He'd been sitting in her parlor for twenty minutes now without really saying much of anything. He fidgeted, and hummed, and hawed, but at no point did he saw anything of substance.

Lex let out a sigh. That was answer enough for Allegra.

"I see."

"Don't be angry with him," Lex said. "Look, he thinks I'm here to discuss security arrangements for Queen Portia's visit next month. That's all."

"I'm not angry at him. Not really. He just got under my skin and wouldn't let go."

Lex let out a little laugh. "He can do that. Listen, he has a point. Having people like Cram around is risky."

Allegra slouched in her chair, shoulders resting against the firm cushion of her arm chair. "I know it's risky, but I need agitators like Walter and the others."

"Why?"

The truth was that Allegra feared outing herself. Walter and his compatriots were already out in the public view. It would surprise no one if Walter opened a crater in the abbey's courtyard out of sheer boredom.

More and more, Allegra struggled to sleep. The nightmares varied, but they all ended on the same thing. A demon manifested in the dining hall. She lost her temper in the midst of a meeting. She was accused of being an elemental. It didn't matter the situation. They all ended with her using her fire magic and being shackled.

That wasn't an answer she could provide, however. So, instead she said, "I cannot do all of the work myself. I need to appear somewhat neutral."

"Contessa, I like you. I really do. So, as your friend, I'd like to share a little secret about you that you might not realize that the rest of us know."

Allegra knew Lex had no idea she was an elemental, and yet her stomach muscles clenched in fearful anticipation. She covered it up well with a laugh. "I've already heard about me and Captain Rainier."

Lex made a dismissive sound. "That's been going on since the Cathedral. No, I mean that there are over a thousand runaway mage slaves or free mages or just plain ol' poor folks out in the abbey's front yard."

"Yes, I believe I've seen some of them. What's your point?"

"Well, let's just say no one neutral would have them littering up our garden."

Allegra failed to hold back her chortle. "Fair point, Lex. A very fair point."

"So, listen, when the Captain comes to visit you today about Queen Portia's plans…"

"I will apologize to him, yes," Allegra said. She blew out a breath. "I was planning on it anyway. I'm simply exhausted and he set me off last night."

"Well, I wasn't going to suggest it was all your fault." Lex grinned. "I've known him a lot longer. Trust me when I say at least three-quarters was his fault."

She rolled her head over her shoulder, never moving her head off the back of the chair, and asked, "What have I gotten myself into?"

"A whole lot of trouble."

"Thanks, Lex."

"Anytime, Your Excellency. Dodd says my helpfulness is my best feature."

Allegra sat back up, prime and proper again. She poured herself more wine. "You and Dodd are close, aren't you?"

"The closest. Dodd and I go way back. I've never had a closer friend."

"Friend?" Allegra asked, putting significant emphasis on the word.

Lex rolled his eyes. "You sound just like my mother. Yes, we're just friends. No, there's nothing going on between us. Yes, I'm never going to get married. Yes, I feel the disappointment I am giving my mother on a regular basis."

"I sometimes wonder if my mother is somewhere beyond the grave watching me bumble my way through life, shaking her head in disgust." Allegra glanced at Lex. "At least my mother can't write to me anymore."

"I told my mother she should just adopt Dodd. She's always adored him."

"And does Dodd…adore you?" Allegra asked, trying to give her voice as matronly a tone as possible.

"Dodd adores buxom widows of a certain age trying to relive their youth," Lex said with a grimace. "Besides, he's my friend. Like, eww."

"What would be eww, Lex?"

"Captain!" Lex exclaimed, swivelling around to grin. "Sleeping with Dodd."

"You're sleeping with Dodd?" Stanton blurted.

"Lord save us all from the abyss, no!"

"Good," Stanton said. Then he eyed them. "So, you're both just sitting here, talking about sleeping with Dodd? Your Ladyship, is there something I should know?"

Allegra smiled sweetly. "A lady never tells." And she took a bite of her cake.

"Except to me, of course. No one can say no to this face."

"It's the cheekbones," Allegra said in agreement. "I just had to tell him everything."

Stanton made a growling sound. "It's that baby face of yours. Lord Almighty, are you ever going to look your age, Lex?"

Lex shrugged. "I can't help how the Almighty made me, sir. Well, I should be going. Let me know if there's anything else I can do for you, Contessa. Oh, I'll let Dodd know your door is open tonight."

Allegra beamed. "Oh, please do."

Lex laughed and closed the door behind him. When he was gone, Allegra said, "I like him a lot."

Stanton rolled his eyes and grabbed a piece of pound cake from the tray on her table. "Are you going to sleep with the entire guard?"

"If I do, I'll start at the top."

Stanton choked on his cake. "Um…"

Allegra smiled.

"Um… thank you?"

Allegra laughed. "You should see the look of terror on your face. Good lord. Tell me you've been with a woman before."

"A gentlemen never tells."

Allegra smile. "Captain, what are you doing for the next hour or so? Would you join me on the balcony? I have some thoughts about Queen Portia's visit and I'd like your opinion. That is, if you'd like my opinion."

"I always want to hear your opinion," Stanton said. "I am very sorry that I angered you with mine."

Allegra put down her tea cup and stood. She faced Stanton and said, "I was tired and took it out on you. I am sorry. Shall we be friends again?"

"We never stopped."

What should have been an hour stretched into four leisurely hours about security, mages, the horrid state of the abbey's bread supply, and the odd taste most of the cheese had developed since the cave in.

Allegra sat on her modest balcony, wrapped in a heavy blanket to ward against the early spring chill. From here, she could see the vast expanse of the fields that surrounded the abbey. Further away began the patchwork system of houses and taverns, outdoor markets and indoor crafters, formed a dark blight in the midst of the green and yellow of the fields.

She looked over at Stanton, who sipped at his glass of brandy. Stanton smiled at her. His legs were stretched out in front of him, crossed at the ankles. When he used to visit her, he would stand as straight as a board. Now, he reclined on her little wicker chair, munching on nuts, cheeses, and fruits like they were an old married couple. Allegra looked away so that he wouldn't see her grimace.

"Have you heard about Sanchez?" she asked. When he shook his head, she said, "I received a letter this morning. Some rebels burned down three estates. They all owned slaves, and rumor is none of them were even actual mages. Just children who were born poor. Anyway, the families were burned in their beds."

Stanton blew out a breath. "Did they catch them?"

"Some. A couple of the fools got drunk and bragged about it at a brothel in the next town over. The hen in charge there sent for the militia." Allegra licked her lips. "The bastards were dragged to the town square, tied up, and whipped, right there. No trial or anything. One of them tried to catch his ropes on fire, but it appears he had no control over his magic and..."

"He caught himself on fire?" Stanton guessed.

"More like a good part of the town square. No one was killed beyond the obvious, but..." Allegra sighed, an attempt to gather her emotions. "This can't go on."

"No, it can't."

"This is so much bigger than one person with a fancy title. I was a fool to think otherwise."

Stanton shook his head. "You always knew it was an impossible task. But think of the good you've done with the post. You have saved lives and you have made a difference."

"It won't be enough," she said quietly.

"Maybe not, but you'll always be able to lift your head high knowing you'd tried."

She pushed herself up from her chair and leaned against the railing. "Stanton, I'm so terrified. Everyone expects me to fail. What if I am the frail creature they all think I am? What if I make it worse?"

A moment later and he was next to her. He took her hand into his. Just a brush of skin against skin, but the fine hairs on her neck stood on edge anyway. "They are all fools."

Allegra closed her eyes and fought off the urges that stirred inside her. With Stanton, it would end in more than just tears. It would end in soot and fire and smoke. There would be nothing left to her but a crumpled, burnt form on the ground.

"What is it?" he asked. He released her hand, only to torture her further by cupping her elbow in his hand. "You can tell me anything."

Oh, she really couldn't. She wished it were true, but it wasn't. Yet, she wanted to tell him. She wanted to feel his body pressed against hers. And even the image of the soot stain on white marble floors was not dissuading her.

She had to act, or this illusion of intimacy was going to ruin everything she'd worked her entire life to hold on to.

Allegra turned to face Stanton. She grabbed the front of his vest and pulled him down. She reached up and brushed her lips against his. She had only meant it to be a light touch, but when his mouth met hers, they lost themselves in the kiss.

Allegra pulled away, her breath thick in her throat. Even as she shook her head, she knew that this was both a mistake and something she had to do. She kissed him again, harder this time. Stanton pressed a strong hand against the small of her back, saving the other hand to grasp a handful of the hair at the nape of her neck.

Stanton's moan drowned out the petrified voice inside her that screamed she needed to regain control of the situation. Allegra knew she was desperately close to falling in love with him and this kiss threatened to push her over the edge. And yet, she did not pull away. Stanton's strong hand travelled up her back until it brushed the top of the lacing. He trailed a finger back down the binding, as if asking her permission to pull the laces free.

Allegra found her inner strength and pulled away from the kiss. Her heart thudded in her chest. Her body shouted for her to stop listening to reason and to let Stanton take her right there against the railing.

She smiled up at him, knowing her sadness and disappointment were showing. But she forced the smile. "I'm sorry."

"Don't be," he whispered, his voice low and husky. "That was—"

Tears welled in her eyes and she looked away. "I simply cannot…this cannot happen, Stanton. Not now."

"Then why did you kiss me?"

She flinched at his tone, but not because it was harsh. It was full of earnest kindness. They both knew why she'd kissed him. They both knew why they'd been fighting lately like schoolchildren. It was easier to manufacture petty divisiveness than it was to address the undercurrent that delighted whenever they looked at each other.

Allegra let her tears flow. He didn't understand because he couldn't. If he knew what she was, everything she had worked for, everything she had sacrificed would end. At his hands, no less. There was more at stake than her cold bed. Thousands of mages depended upon her. She could not, *would not*, let them down.

But she couldn't lie, either. "I kissed you because I wanted to."

He touched her cheek. A sad smile spread across his face. "I understand. We should get some sleep. Tomorrow promises to be a rather big day."

CHAPTER TWENTY-TWO

ALLEGRA WORE HER bluebell blue brocade dress as she stood in the main foyer of the abbey and awaited the first of their esteemed visitors of the day. This dress had survived the winter culling because two days of Nadira's handiwork had updated the dress to be consistent with current styles; there was no way she was going to get rid of it now. The embroidered woolen dress was gathered about her false hips and rump roll in the back. A gauzy neckerchief embroidered with bluebells was stuffed into the plunging neckline of her altered dress, protecting both her exposed skin and her dignity.

Her hair was a tumble of curls; she'd slept with her hair in rags and then Kia and Nadira applied hot iron rods to her hair to achieve the Cartossian style. She applied her usual carmine-tinted lanolin lip soother she preferred and delicate silver sword earrings her brother had given her two years ago. Beyond that, she opted to forego the usual Cartossian style of artificial blemishes and rouge.

Serafina hurried down the stairs, the skirts of her practical dress gathered up in her fists to make the rushing safer. She skidded to a halt at Allegra's side and failed to quell her panting.

"You going to live, Serafina?" Allegra asked.

"Sorry, Your Excellency. I was unable to decide which dress to wear."

Allegra eyed the young woman's dress, striped with wide bands of brown and pink. "It looks fine to meet a few assistant diplomats."

"Then why are you in your best dress?" Serafina asked innocently.

Allegra smiled. "Because I'm the evil mage to these people. You're just the hired help."

"Do not listen to her, my child. She is like this every morning lately."

Allegra looked over her shoulder at Stanton and Father Michael, who arrived together. Dodd and Lex were in tow, too, and both were wearing brown, wide-brimmed hats decorated with an ostrich feather.

"What are the two of you wearing on your heads?" Allegra demanded.

"Do you like it?" Dodd asked, though the question was more a statement. He took off his hat and twirled it on top of his index finger. It teetered to one side and he grabbed it again, plunking it back on his head. "Lex and I won them at cards last night."

"From who?" Serafina asked.

"Oh, just a couple of the militia who thought they could beat us at two partner draw," Lex said smugly. He flicked the brim of his hat. "I so like a jaunty hat."

Allegra smiled and turned back to the carriage that was unloading at the front. Stanton stood next to her. In a low voice, he said, "This is just the advance guard, right?"

She chuckled. "Queen Portia's secretary's letter said we would be expecting her personal priest, a Brother Ambrose, along with one under-secretary, one under-accountant, and two under-assistant diplomats."

"A lot of unders there," Lex muttered, still playing with his hat.

"I'm feeling like we're not important enough for the important people," Dodd said in agreement. He was also fiddling with his hat's placement.

"Dodd," Allegra said in a firm voice.

"What?"

Allegra swatted Dodd's hand away from his hat. She adjusted it so that the feather went front to back. "Stop picking at your hat."

"Yes, Mom," Dodd said darkly.

Allegra faced the front door so that Dodd couldn't see her smirk. "Ah, here they come."

Father Michael and Allegra stepped forward and greeted the middle-aged woman. Father Michael gave the greeting. "On behalf of the Holy Father in Orsini, welcome to our humble abbey. May the grace of the Lord God Almighty shine upon your efforts while you are here."

The woman wearily smiled. "I am Shu Adolo, under-secretary to Queen Portia of Cartossa. This is…"

Allegra's jaw dropped. She knew exactly who she was staring at. "General Bonacieux."

The General was a tall, broad man with ruddy, angular features that announced he would have always been described with words like rugged as opposed to handsome. He had two long scars down one side of his face, skipping over the eye.

And he was the most feared man among mages.

Allegra swallowed her fear and trepidation. She outstretched her hand and said, "General, it is a pleasure to greet you. We met six years ago at Wellington Palace. I am…"

"The mage." He looked her up and down appraisingly, not accepting her outstretched hand. "I didn't believe the news, but it's clear the Holy Father really is a mage lover. No wonder things are falling apart."

Allegra paused long enough to ensure she wore a neutral, emotionless expression and removed all heat from her voice. "I am Allegra, Contessa of Marsina, and I welcome you here to the epicenter of the peace talks."

"I have informed Her Majesty that she cannot attend this little show until I deem it safe and not a total waste of her time." Bonacieux sneered down at her. "So far, the evidence is not encouraging."

Allegra summoned up her will and forced a smile until her cheek muscles ached. "How lucky for the queen to have a military general who cares so much about both her time and her person."

Bonacieux ignored her and turned to Father Michael. "Where will I be billeted? I don't wish to be near any of the rabble that we passed on the journey here. Disgusting creatures."

"Well, General, we were not expecting you, so we are ill-equipped to—"

Allegra interrupted. "You can have my villa."

Bonacieux didn't look at her. "I don't require anything cushy and pampered. I am a soldier, not a puffed-up mage."

Father Michael chuckled. "Excellent. Then the Contessa's old villa will be perfect for you, for you shall find no comforts there."

"Unless, of course, it is too rustic for you," Allegra said. Her smile was still intact. Her face ached.

The general finally turned his attention to her. They both knew he always stayed in the best suites when he visited. In fact, he stayed in the royal suites which Allegra currently occupied. She could imagine his rage when he discovered that after a night or two freezing in her old, little cottage on the outskirts of the abbey.

She had never interacted with Bonacieux during his three previous visits to the Abbey, but she enough about him to know life was about to become unbearable.

"Tell me, girl, is it true you have plans to bring witches into the discussions?"

She stared at him for a moment, wondering if she should correct any of his statements. She decided they were meant to sting her, so she didn't give him the satisfaction of seeing her so stung. "Oh, they are already here, General. Some have been here for months. I believe you even know one of them." At his questioning expression, she said, "Walter Cram."

Bonacieux's jaw clenched. Allegra kept on smiling.

"I shouldn't have expected much better from the likes of you, but really, Father, I'm surprised you would allow this."

"The Almighty does not condition his love, so neither shall I," Father Michael said, a hint of chastisement in his voice.

"No, but we do have a clear picture of who is to be trusted and inherently not, don't we?" the general said. "How will you ensure there are no elementals in the mage delegations, beyond the outlaw?"

"I don't understand your question," Allegra said sweetly.

"How will you determine if spies have infiltrated the mages?" he said, slower, as if she was a dim-witted child.

"I hope to attract several key rebellion leaders and abolitionists. So, to answer your question, I won't care if the mages aren't all exactly who they claim to be."

The general stared at her. "So you will be luring them here to arrest them?"

"No," Allegra said with a tight smile. "I have authorized that elemental mages can attend the peace talks, in safety, with no risk of arrest both upon arrival and departure."

"That is illegal," the general said.

Allegra drew in a breath and forced out a second wave of cheek-aching smiles. "On the contrary, General, I am permitted. Unlike you, Sir, and your policy of trapping people inside buildings until they burn to a crisp because one of them might be an elemental." Her voice turned icy. "But you don't see me asking Captain Rainier here to arrest you, now do you? So if you wish to remain here under the banner of truce, then you shall stay away from the matches."

He took a step toward her, hoping to use his height to intimidate her. He loomed over her, and she'd have to crane her neck if she wanted to look him in the eye. Instead, she turned her back on him. She took several steps before saying, "Are you coming, General? The Father and I would be pleased to escort you to your new rustic home for your visit."

ALLEGRA SAT AT her desk blurry-eyed. She'd spent a goodly part of the previous evening being belittled by General Bonacieux at an impromptu reception for him. He was displeased with the lack of a fish dish, as well as the sorry state of the abbey's supper table. It took several assurances and downright grovelling by Father Michael before Bonacieux was convinced their supper's near "poverty" was due to a late thaw of the snow and nothing more.

Bald-faced lies, of course, but Allegra appreciated any bishop who could lie through his teeth to protect the will of the Almighty.

And the will of the Almighty had been Father Michael asking residents of the abbey to reduce their table for the assistance of the poor.

After the reception supper, Allegra spent several hours responding to letters. Some asked her advice on how best to deal with small pockets of unrest. As ever, Allegra urged compassion, common sense, and the will of the Almighty to be followed. For those with border disputes and large-scale rebellions, Allegra offered to arbitrate between local rebellion leaders and appointed officials. She said the rebels would trust her because she had Walter Cram here as a show of faith.

Just as she was readying for bed, Walter crashed into her suites through the hidden servant entrance in her prayer closet. He'd found more demon markings, three in a row this time. Walter feared that he might open them into one large rift and he'd need assistance defeating what he called a "small" demon. Thankfully, under Walter's instruction, Allegra was skilled enough to close the smaller symbols. It took them under an hour and the danger was resolved.

Still, Allegra wasn't coping well. She'd somewhat accepted there were things in existence beyond what her skepticism wanted to believe. That she was dealing with through nightmares and cold sweats. *That* she could eventually handle. It was the potential risk these demon rifts would cause. Walter feared that the curtain between their world and the demon world would eventually weaken and rip if these portals kept opening.

After that horrible realization, Allegra got little sleep. She'd instructed Walter to find out whoever was doing this. Walter had already written to some trusted friends of his for them to join him at the abbey. He said they could help investigate the demon summonings, as she was risking too much running around in the middle of the night with him. She agreed whole-heartedly and offered safe harbor to Walter's friends.

Allegra was growing tired of mornings like these, where she ran on only a couple hours of bad sleep. She struggled to maintain her focus on her letter, yet another dispute between a factory worker whose mages were purposely, he said, ruining their enchantments and costing him money. So he cracked down, and then they all went on strike. And then the militia were called in. And then things got predictably out of hand.

Footsteps drew her attention to the door and, a moment later, Stanton marched into her office. "We have a problem with Bonacieux."

"Did he freeze to death last night?"

"He moved into the North Wing shortly after you retired for bed."

Allegra put her pencil down and smiled up at the captain. She motioned at the seat across from her and he took it.

"So your problem is Bonacieux survived the night?"

Stanton gave her a wry smile. "I'd best not answer that. I'm not feeling charitable. He has sent several of his men into the village to investigate elemental activity."

"Oh, that does *not* sound good." Allegra leaned back in her chair. "Did you explain to him that we have had no credible magical issues since the refugees arrived?"

"Yes. I won't repeat his reply. He's also posted soldiers in the corridors."

"But the local militia and the Consorts are already providing internal security," Allegra said. "Did Father Michael agree to this?"

"Father Michael is rather upset with Bonacieux right now, as two of his soldiers broke into the bishop's bedroom in the middle of the night."

"Good Lord, why?"

"To see if they could catch him doing magic."

Allegra stared at him in confusion. "Setting aside the fact that Father Michael is *not* a mage, what are they even trying to prove? Hand me some thread and I could embroider a small magical talisman into your cravat right now."

Stanton raised his hands and said, "Exactly."

"What did Father Michael say?"

"He said it was your area of responsibility as he feared he was about to request Bonacieux's excommunication."

"I see. Well, can you have someone fetch the General for me?"

Stanton shifted uncomfortably in his chair. "I already spoke with him. He said if you wished to say anything to him, you could go to his study. He does not take orders from…It's not important what he called you beyond that he does not respect your office. Or, more accurately, you."

Allegra snorted. "I see someone thinks I'm terrified of his scowl."

"Allegra," Stanton said, warning in his voice.

"My dear Captain, are you attempting to chide me?"

"I wouldn't dream of it," he said with a wicked smile. "I simply mean to caution your anger. He is a vile rat, but he knows how to suck the best of us into the sewers. I wouldn't want to see that happen to you."

Allegra smiled at him and said, "Stanton, I have come to appreciate your company and guidance over these last months."

"But?"

Allegra's smile widened. "This isn't my first dance."

"I never thought it was. Try not to step on his toes."

She raised her voice and called out to Serafina, who was busy organizing letters in the main sitting room. When the young woman rushed in, Allegra said, "Have General Bonacieux sent for. If he refuses to come, bring me the men responsible for any harassment of mages, no matter how small. That will get his attention."

CHAPTER TWENTY-THREE

IT TOOK THREE days, but General Bonacieux eventually darkened Allegra's door. Each week began with a small dinner in Allegra's suite, with Father Michael, Lex, Stanton, Dodd, Serafina, Walter, and Nathan, attended by one lone footman. Stanton refused to call the meal *dinner* as he said he was a cultured man from Orsini and this was clearly a late breakfast or an early luncheon.

"Father Michael, it's been months now. Please, for the love of the Almighty, ask the servants to serve breakfast like the rest of the world," Stanton complained good-naturedly as he did at every dinner meeting.

"My dear Captain," Father Michael replied in between sips of his beet soup, "if we had breakfast like you worldly people at Orsini Palace, we would never know the simple joy of old cellar beets turned into soup."

"We could have the soup for luncheon," Stanton protested.

And then the conversation, as ever, devolved into an argument over the old country style of two meals a day and the more fashionable three daily meals. In between friendly banter over mealtime, they also discussed the upcoming concerns for the week, visitors, meetings, ongoing aid necessary to keep Borro going, and so on. So that was when Bonacieux decided to barge in.

He threw open her closed doors, scanned around until his eyes locked on Allegra. "How dare you!"

"Good morning, General," Allegra said. "Should I assume you are here to discuss my dismissal of your men?"

"How dare you dismiss my men from the abbey! On what grounds?"

Allegra had been prepared for this outburst, so she was pleased that she had several witnesses for it. If nothing else, the presence of her friends helped bolster her courage. She dipped her spoon into the cow marrow in broth she'd just been served by the abbey's liveried footman.

"Oh, the marrow is excellent," Allegra said. "As for your men, they were harassing citizens under my protection and, therefore, I've asked them to leave under threat of arrest."

"You have no right!"

"I have every right to do my duty."

"You should have informed me, witch!"

"I prefer the title, Your Ladyship, but I'll accept Your Excellency," Allegra said before dipping her spoon back into her bone marrow. "This is delicious."

Bonacieux slammed his fist down on the corner of the dining table. "I am not to be trifled with, little girl."

Allegra put her spoon down. She made a show of cleaning off her hands in her napkin so that he would not see her tremble. She held the napkin in her hands, giving her fingers a task. "I requested your presence and assistance three days ago. You have refused to work with me. You have refused all civil discourse. Instead, you have abused the hospitality of the abbey and of the Bishop monstrously. You might think yourself above the law everywhere because Queen Portia is too young to put you in your place."

"Outrageous!" he shouted. "I am a loyal subject..."

"You forget yourself, Mathias Bonacieux. I am Allegra, Contessa of Marsina, Arbiter of Justice for the Holy Orsini Cathedral, anointed by the Holy Father himself. You, General, are the son of a butcher."

"The Queen will hear of this."

"I hope so. I wrote to her yesterday detailing the disrespect you've shown me. I've also written to Grand Duchess Katherine. We're cousins, you see, or had you forgotten that small fact while you tried to insult me?"

"I don't take orders from witches," Bonacieux said.

Stanton rose. "No, but you will take orders from the Duke of Barrington, Captain of the Holy Father's Own Consorts. Am I to understand you are threatening the Arbiter?"

Bonacieux clenched his jaw. "No."

"Good. Master Nathan here coordinates the Arbiter's very busy schedule. If you wish to speak to her further about this topic, please speak with him," Stanton said. "I'm sure he can arrange a time that is both convenient for her and the increased personal security she will require for your visit."

Bonacieux narrowed his eyes and said, "This isn't over, witch bitch."

"The bone marrow *is* excellent," Allegra said. She turned to the footman. "Hans, can you see the General out, please? And fetch more marrow. This is simply exceptional."

"Of course, *Your Excellency*."

Maybe it was Allegra's imagination, but she thought Hans put extra emphasis on her title for Bonacieux's education.

ALLEGRA YAWNED INTO the back of her hand. She'd been meeting with Walter and his two elemental friends—who refused to give their names and who wrapped their faces so she couldn't identify them. She'd received an update of the Borro Village situation, and then another two different reports on anti-abolition activity in Cartossa and one for Westumberland's situation over the winter. *Grim* was used a lot.

She was exhausted, and it was a tiredness that sleep alone couldn't conquer. Then again, she couldn't remember the last time she'd slept through the night. Between her nightmares, her racing mind, and her jaunts into the darkness with Walter, she was barely conscious most days.

One more meeting. All she needed was to get through one more meeting.

"I'm pleased to say that Martin and Rahna returned today with the West Cartossa Abolitionist Union representatives," Lex said.

"I've arranged for a reception to be held tomorrow at supper to meet them," Nathan said, consulting his ledger. "That would allow Her Excellency to also meet with Baron Amator and Lady Berard."

"Who are they?" Allegra asked.

"They are who the West Cartossa Unionists are fighting against."

Allegra groaned. "Serafina, you're in charge of smoothing out the feathers before I get there. So help them if I have to explain why 'witch bitch' is offensive one more time."

"I am already prepared, Your Excellency," Serafina said confidently. "I have always spoken with the abolitionists and as soon as the others arrive, I will do the same."

"The abolitionists are never the problem," Allegra said through a yawn.

"We can't be seen taking sides," Serafina said.

Allegra made a grunt that was equal parts derision and agreement. "Have the thefts settled down in the village?"

Dodd made a so-so gesture. "Father Michael's people have been encouraging the local farms to hire some of the younger boys to help keep them out of trouble. Most of the thieves are children ten to fourteen, mostly boys. So we're trying to find positions for them. Father?"

Father Michael nodded. "Many of them are bored and poor, which is a terrible combination. There's so little work in Borro that children are getting into trouble. I've also requested that the Cathedral send us three more lay sisters to assist with basic education. The two sisters and four brothers here are overtaxed with offering basic schooling to the very little children."

Allegra yawned so hard her eyes watered. "What is the response of the farmers?"

"Varied, as you'd expect. Tenant farmers follow the will of their landowners, obviously, so it can be slow going," Dodd said. "However, the good Father here has made some inroads."

"I do the Almighty's work wherever I can."

"What else?"

"Rahna has successfully convinced five more merchants from Orsini to relocate out here. We've also secured significantly more supplies to come from neighboring towns and farms," Lex reported.

"How did Rahna manage that?" Stanton asked.

"One of them is a cousin of hers. So she got her mother involved," Lex said.

"She also assisted me in hiring two local men to travel with a wagon every other day to various farms and towns within a day's return. This is allowing them to stop at several locations to procure goods at a substantially lower rate, even factoring in the cost of horses and salaries," Serafina said. "Rahna has become indispensable to me."

"We should probably assign guards. There's increased banditry along the Cathedral's Way," Allegra said. Her eyes were drooping. She blinked several times in hopes she could force the fog from her mind.

"Captain, let's put Martin and Rahna in charge of that. They could both use the experience and Rahna and Serafina work well together."

"Sure," Stanton said.

"I was thinking...we could use militia for the supply guards," Dodd said. "It might help keep the peace if we are letting the local militia do what they do best. Plus, the magistrate can hire some more, if necessary, and that all comes out of..."

Music from cellos, violins, and various flutes floated in the air. Stanton had his hand on her hip and they danced to the music. Allegra closed her eyes and danced a waltz with him. They twirled about her abandoned sitting room, furniture pushed against the wall... morphing... changing...

They were in the ballroom at Orsini Palace. The room was empty of dancers, though the orchestra continued to play from some hidden nook.

His hand moved and trailed up her back. He kissed her neck, her shoulders, and across her collarbone. He traced a line up to her ear in tender kisses until he gave her ear lobe a tug with his teeth.

She'd wanted this for months now. The feel of Stanton's strong arms around her. This was exactly how she'd imagined it, too. Here, she was safe and protected from the world. They couldn't touch her here. She wasn't a mage. She wasn't Arbiter. She wasn't even a contessa. Just a woman dancing to a waltz.

Stanton pulled her to his mouth and kissed her hard. Tongues lashing, hands roaming. He pulled down the front of her dress and it tore easily, tumbling to the floor in a puddle of expensive silk. He pulled off his own shirt, his boots disappearing. He tugged her down on the bed in the middle of the ballroom.

"ALLEGRA?" RAINIER ASKED for the third time.

"She's out," Lex announced.

The Contessa's head lolled to one side and her eyes moved frantically behind closed lids. Her quill had fallen to the floor, flicking ink on the wooden floorboards.

"Is it just me or is she looking more and more tired?" Dodd asked.

"It's not just you," Rainier said.

"Nadira and Kia both have told me the Contessa isn't sleeping well. Kia has found her some mornings asleep at her desk," Serafina said. "I've been struggling to come up with a way to address the issue with Her Excellency, but each time that I attempt, she says she is too busy for sleep and changes the topic."

"She yelled at me the last time I mentioned it," Nathan grumbled darkly.

"Would you like me to talk to her?" Rainier asked.

Lex gave Dodd a knowing glance, which made Dodd smile. There was a barrack's rumor that those two had been taking private morning snacks on the Contessa's very private balcony.

"I'll get her papers," Lex said. They bent down and picked up the various papers that had fallen to the floor. The Contessa's hand twitched violently as it dangled limply against the side of the chair. Lex intended to move her hand to her lap, so that her movements wouldn't wake her.

However, when Lex touched her hand, they let out a squeak of surprise at the scorching heat. Lex fell back on their buttocks, not having suspected...

Lex stared at her in rising horror. They'd never suspected.

"What's wrong with you?" Dodd asked.

Without thinking, Lex stuffed a finger into their mouth. "Splinter from her chair. Ouch, that hurt."

Lex's mind raced. It explained so much of her behavior. Now that it was in front of them, Lex felt like a fool for having never figured it out. Now that the truth was before them, Lex's memories raced, updating all of her peculiar comments, fears, and behavior with the knowledge that the Contessa was hiding from everything.

"Did you get it out?" Rainier demanded.

It took Lex a beat to know what he was even talking about. Lex inspected the uninjured finger and said, "Looks like it just pierced me, didn't go in. It'll be fine once the stinging stops."

"Have I told you about my friend from school who..."

"Yes," both Rainier and Lex said at the same time.

"I'm sorry for wanting people to know they can lose their hand from a splinter," Dodd said defensively.

"Yes, we all know Dodd," Lex said, with an edge in their voice they didn't mean to come through. But this was bad. If the Contessa was indeed an elemental, she was in real danger here asleep in her chair with her hand as hot as it was.

Besides, it was a crime not to report an elemental mage.

Lex watched the Contessa jerk, and a few gasping breaths escaped her. Lex looked down at her hand. As the Contessa's moans increased, her hand began to cast a light glow.

Again, without thinking, Lex slapped their hand down over the Contessa's. *Hard.*

The Contessa gasped and looked around the room wildly. Her eyes focused on Rainier and she let out a whimpering sound. Then, her face flushed crimson when she realized she was awake.

"Oh, did I fall asleep?" the Contessa said, still gasping.

"You did," Rainier said with a laugh. "Lex lost his balance and woke you."

"Yeah, sorry, Contessa. I bumped into you trying to get back up. I didn't mean to wake you."

The Contessa clenched her fist hard, her eyes widening. She looked at Lex, pleading and anguish filling her eyes. "My hand fell asleep."

"Sorry to have bumped it, then," Lex said. They tried to force the shock from their voice, but that was an impossible task. The Contessa was an elemental.

Almighty above, that was why she and Cram got along so well! That explained why she spent so much time with him, too. She needed someone of her own kind to trust.

Lex's thoughts spun out of control as the Contessa stared at them with widening eyes.

"Nathan, the Contessa needs sleep," Lex blurted. They pushed themselves to their feet and said, "Cancel all of her appointments for tomorrow, too."

"I'm...fine..." the Contessa stammered. She looked close to tears.

"Her Excellency is..."

"So exhausted that she cannot even stay awake during meetings," Lex said firmly. It dawned on them that her exhaustion was probably what had caused this. If she was afraid of being found out, on top of all of the stress of her office, well, it was no wonder that she was falling asleep. But, next time, it might be Rainier and...

Lex didn't want to think about that at all.

"Captain? Some help here."

Rainier shrugged. "Allegra, do you need a rest?"

"I..."

"Contessa, please," Lex pleaded. "You need a break. When was the last time you had an entire day off?"

The Contessa shook her head. "I don't remember."

Rainier finally clued in and said, "Then it's been too long. You should have said something. Nathan, how could you let this happen?"

"I...I..."

"It's not his fault," the Contessa said through a groggy yawn. "I could use a day off."

Lex offered her their hand. "Come on, Contessa. I'll help you to your room."

"I'm fine," the Contessa said, still cradling her hand protectively to her chest. But she followed anyway.

Lex escorted the Contessa to the door of her bedchamber. "Do you want me to call Nadira?"

The Contessa shook her head. When she stepped inside her bedroom, she asked in a whisper, "Did anything happen?"

"No. You didn't even drool." The Contessa didn't look as though she believed Lex, so they added, "Though, you did sound like you were either running from demons or enjoying the best sex of your life. It was hard to tell."

"Oh!" The Contessa chuckled nervously, but Lex clearly saw the tension release from her shoulders. "Let's go with being chased by demons."

"That's probably the best option."

The Contessa crawled on top of her bed and was asleep before Lex could even ask if she wanted the fire stoked.

"Dodd, stir up the fire?"

"I'll do it," Rainier said. Lex frowned at Rainier and back at the Contessa. Rainier should know. It was obvious he was falling for her, assuming he hadn't already. But...Damn. She'd been lying to everyone all of this time.

Lex wanted to be angry at her, but they had nothing but sympathy.

CHAPTER TWENTY-FOUR

PERO,

Are you aware that the Contessa of Marsina's guards have been detaining mages for petty crimes? They've been handed over to the local militia and the magistrates. Do you have any idea what can happen after they've been arrested? Imprisonment. Slavery. Indentured Servitude. Death. Torture. Who knows what will become of them because our traitorous Arbiter has decided to turn a blind eye to the consequences of her actions.

My old friend, I implore you to speak with her. She must be made to see reason. I cannot understand her betrayal of the cause. We supported her because she promised to be a friend to mages. Now look at her! Drunk on power and destroying all of the advances we've made.

For the love of the Almighty, Pero, talk some sense into her before everything we've done is ruined.

Your humble servant,
Cardinal Giso

Allegra looked up from the letter at her dear friend's husband and said, "You came all this way to tell me Giso is having a tantrum."

"This is serious," Pero said. He paced about her office. He was still in his travelling clothes. "I'm sorry, Allegra, but my conscience forces me to advocate for the plight of all mages, including those driven to the depths of depravity and violence."

"Pero, for the love of the Almighty, get off my back!" Allegra shouted. "So I should have just let all of the thieves go? Let them steal to their hearts' content because they *might* be mages. Is that seriously what you're asking of me?"

"Are you listening to yourself? You've become an apologist."

"I most certainly am not," Allegra said. She flicked the letter across her desk and it fluttered to the floor in front of Pero. "I offered protection from slavery, not from their own stupidity!"

"Oh yes, of course! The mighty Arbiter who has never faced hardship in her entire life understands all too well the plight of the ten-year-old orphan who steals a loaf of bread."

"That ten-year-old orphan also attacked the baker he was stealing the loaf of bread from!" Allegra shouted. "What was I supposed to do, Pero? Pat him on the head and send him on his way?"

"You should have shown compassion!"

"I did by opening the doors to people like Little Ferret in the first place!"

"Oh yes! Forgive my ignorance, oh mighty Contessa upon her throne."

"Shut up, Pero. Just stop." Allegra stood and jabbed a finger at Pero. "You've been in Orsini this entire winter. You have no idea how close it was for all of us. There were days that we all went hungry because there was no food. Don't you dare come here and judge me."

"I will judge you. You brought those people here."

"I didn't do anything of the sort! They came here!" Allegra shouted. "This is a monastery, not a jail. I am the Arbiter, not the Chief Justice of this land. I must hand over those who commit crimes."

"Being an elemental is a crime," Pero said. "I don't see anyone arresting Walter Cram."

"That's because I am able to give him sanctuary."

"Then why not give sanctuary to the boy?"

"Because he is a thief."

"You have all of the authority you wish to take, so why not take it for the little boy?" Pero said. "Rupert will stand by you."

"You cannot keep demanding I do things your way, Pero. I am trying my damnedest to stop this war. I need allies, not people pointing out how I'm not going far enough. Your actions would start the war you say you wish to avoid!"

"Don't be hysterical," Pero said.

Allegra walked around her desk to face him. "What did you just say?"

"I believe calm is needed in these trying times and not the whims of a…of an emotional—"

"How dare you treat me like I am a child, too young and foolish to know her own mind! Rupert might be your husband, but he was my friend before you. You do not get the privilege of speaking to me like that."

Pero stepped up to her and said in a whisper, "Yes, because we wouldn't want the dear Captain to know about our dirty little secrets, would we?"

Allegra hadn't registered what she'd done until her hand stung from the slap. Pero closed his eyes for a moment. Rage filled them when he opened his eyes.

"Get out!" Allegra snarled. "Get out before I have Lex throw you out."

Pero spun on his heel and walked out of Allegra's study. Her hands shook, only it was not from the pent up magic. It was from the surge of blood pounding in her ears and the instinct to fight and run and do anything but let him walk away and cause trouble.

Allegra turned her back and looked out the frost-covered window of her study. The servants had sewed delightful cozies for the window sill, to help protect from the drafts, but there was no such thing as complete protection from the cold air. Allegra scraped her name in the frost, the sensation of cold and scratching sending goose bumps up her limbs. Anything to cool the rush of blood in her veins.

"Well," came the voice behind her.

Allegra snorted at Father Michael. "You heard all of that, did you?"

"If it helps, I only heard the slap," he said. His shoes clicked against the floor as he entered her study. A moment later, the doors latched. "Did you wish to speak privately, my child?"

Allegra turned around and smiled. "Father, you have been a great friend throughout all of this, but…what I need is peace and quiet. Not…" she waved her hand vaguely at the door. "Harassment."

Father Michael shoved his hands into his cloak's bilious sleeves. "He does mean well, my child."

"Oh, I know he does, but surely he understands the pressure I am under. His letters all winter were bad enough. Now, he's here and it's already wearing on me." Allegra sat down. "Between him and Walter…it's like they both want the same thing but they both have very different approaches. Yet, neither can understand that I'm allowed to also have my own approach."

"You would be wise to listen to the Lord's message to your heart and not the mere words of these men."

Allegra snorted. "Father…"

He raised a withered hand. "I know, you do not believe. That doesn't change the voice inside your heart. The one that tells you whenever you have been led astray from the path of righteousness. You alone must know the correct path and you must follow it, no matter where it leads you."

"I don't know what to do. I am trying so hard to stop this war. But, I feel it breathing down my neck. Every time I move, or think, it is there like a dark shadow, waiting and watching. It is a living thing, waiting to attack us all." Allegra clenched her fists. "And I cannot stop it. I can only delay it."

"Perhaps delay is all you need," Father Michael said. "Would that not give the world more time to learn kindness and compassion?"

"We've had over a thousand years to find our compassion, Father. I don't see us finding it in the next month or two."

"Maybe not, but I remain faithful." His voice grew somber. "As long as you remain safe, my child."

"As much as any mage can be in this climate. Most days, I expect one of my enemies to storm in there and accuse me of being an elemental and dragging me from my study by my hair. Perhaps I should cut it all off, to make it more difficult for them."

"It would be an affront in the eyes of fashion," Father Michael said with a kind smile on his face. "No, my child, you must prepare yourself. For if this war does happen, and I hope by the grace of the Almighty that it does not, but if does, you must be prepared."

"I know," Allegra said quietly. "I am resolved to fight to the bitter end."

Father Michael lifted his chin. "Spoken like a true leader."

"Hopefully, they won't see my hands shaking as I do it."

"The Almighty does not give us burdens we cannot handle. Always trust his guiding hand is there, helping you along."

"I'd rather he help guide some people along out of my way," Allegra said darkly.

"We have no control over the Almighty's plans. We can only have faith that we are living up to the gifts and talents He has given us."

Allegra frowned at the priest. "What do you mean?"

"I mean that your talents were gifts from the Lord. And it is a grave sin to hide them in a cave from the world."

"I hide my talents, as you call them, so that I do not find myself hiding in those very caves as armed guards chase me, Father, and you know it."

"My child, you will be forced to choose a side." He frowned. "Those who are not like you will not accept you, no matter how hard you try to be like them. You will never be one of them. You will always be an outsider. So it is your choice to stand with your own kind now or later. But, later, neither side will accept you."

"I have a duty and a responsibility to be fair and neutral in this."

"Sin is never fair, nor is it neutral."

"My magic is not a sin!"

"I wasn't talking of the magic, child, but of the hiding." Father Michael shook his head. "By hiding your gifts, you are hiding the will of the Almighty."

"Father, that is the opposite of every sermon I've ever heard."

Father Michael chuckled. "Perhaps I'm mellowing in my old age. I shall not take any more of your time. I had only dropped by to see how you were feeling. You should rest more regularly. Did not Tasmin take two days of rest before she issued the order to plunge into the abyss?"

"I believe her general drugged her to force her to sleep," Allegra said wryly.

"Then beware of your generals might do the same thing," Father Michael said, his eye twinkling. "Or, your captains."

"Thank you, Father. As ever, I appreciate your council and wisdom."

He smiled down at her, very paternalistically, but she found all priests did that. He turned and walked away.

Father Michael was right about one thing: she would have to choose sides. Pero and Walter had been saying the same thing, in their own ways, for months now. Now, the father was saying it, too. She had to choose.

By handing over petty criminals to the local authorities, she'd chosen to side against her own kind. She believed she had no choice in the matter, but it seemed she was alone in that belief. Even now, her own heart betrayed her. She should have done more to reduce the pressure the refugees' arrival had caused. She should have not offered immediate sanctuary until there were more trusted troops to position in the town.

She had no idea so many would brave the journey to Borro in the snow. She had no idea Cartossa would take to blatant enslavement of free mages, causing them to flee. She had no idea how bad things had become in Cartossa. She could have never known any of this.

So why did she feel like she should have known? That she'd failed for not knowing, for not foreseeing these events. In the light of hindsight, they seemed all but certainties. She had not been nearly as smart as she'd thought she was. For all of her fine silks and kid leather gloves, she was still just a silly little girl hiding behind her father's great name.

Allegra stomped on that thought as immediate as it appeared in her mind. It was rubbish, and she knew it. A voice created by the exhaustion and stress of the situation. She reflected and realized she couldn't remember the last time she'd gotten a full night's rest without the use of restoratives or wine. Or had a few hours of peace and quiet to herself. Messengers came at all hours of the day and night. Even with her assistants and servants, there was simply too much work.

"WHAT DO YOU think I should do?" Allegra was asking Walter that evening in front of her fire. She was bundled in a blanket, wrapped tightly around her shoulders, and held a mug of steaming broth.

"Does it matter? I could tell you what to do, but you'd just do whatever you want."

"Fair enough," Allegra said. "Remember when we used to do this?"

Walter smiled. "It seemed simpler back then, didn't it? Two mages against the world."

"I remember two very awkward children learning about life for the first time."

"It wasn't all bad for you, was it?"

Allegra smiled. "No, it wasn't. I was young and scared and…I made a lot of choices that summer, but I don't regret any of them." She looked over at him. "I am sorry that my choices hurt you."

"I believe you," he said quietly. "I still hate you for them, but some of that is because I thought you didn't love me."

"I did love you." Allegra turned back to the fireplace and sipped her broth. "I suppose I loved my privacy and isolation more."

"And I loved you," Walter said. "And I suppose I loved my adventure and my politics more. Now look at us. Old and worn out."

"I'm not old," Allegra said. She sipped more broth. "I just feel it some days. Walter, I have no idea what I'm going to do."

"You should go to Rainier tonight and fuck him until his eyes bleed."

Allegra laughed so hard she spilled the broth on her blanket. She hissed as some of it spilled on her hands and she alternated shaking the burning liquid off them. "Tempting, I admit."

"Then why don't you? I've seen how he looks at you. He'd be willing."

"He is the captain of my guard! And he's…"

"Normal?" Walter said.

"Normal," Allegra agreed sadly.

"Do you love him?"

"I don't know," she lied.

"I don't believe you," Walter said.

"I find it interesting that you, of all people, are encouraging me to sleep with a normal. I remember your bold declarations that you would never let a normal touch you."

Walter shrugged. "The heart wants what it wants."

Allegra rolled her eyes. "I'm too old for trite."

"But never too old for tripe."

"You're impossible." She smiled at him. "Thank you for visiting this evening."

He shrugged. "I've not been as good of a friend to you as I should have been throughout this. I've asked way too much of you."

"That doesn't make you unique from everyone else," Allegra said. "It's like we're standing on a pyre waiting for lightning to hit. We're wagering whose will be struck first. But it doesn't matter because when one of us burns, we will all burn. I see our end and it is not glorious or heroic. It is covered in blood."

Walter was silent for a long moment before he said, very gently, "Whatever happens, always know you tried your best. No one person can stop what is coming. All we can do is reduce the innocents caught in the hurricane's wake."

"Is that even enough anymore?"

Walter didn't answer.

IT HAD BEEN a huge mistake to talk with Walter. They'd talked about the last three years of his life, of running from safe house to safe house. He'd told her about how he'd encountered a swarm of wasp-sized demons and, ever since, had been studying demon banishment. He'd told her that he'd met some who might eventually turn to demon summoning to defend themselves. Others he knew were doing it to entrap elementals in the highest form of hypocrisy: one elemental entrapping others. But they all could feel war in the air, so it came as no surprise that they were running scared and thinking only of themselves.

That didn't help Allegra sleep, however, for she had nightmares of monstrous creatures eating her alive. She tried sleeping with a lit candle, a dangerous prospect, but she'd hoped the light would help. Instead, it highlighted shadows on the walls. The faded world between awake and sleep would seize hold of those flickering shadows and haunt her, trapping her in a waking dream until she screamed and jolted herself out of it.

She finally crawled out of bed and shoved on her warm dressing gown over her chemise and stockings that had fallen around her ankles in folds of embroidered fabric and ribbon. She glanced at the ticking clock on her mantelpiece and sighed. It was the middle of the night.

She faced an insanely long week, with the arrival of Prince Mallencroft and his brother, and rival, Grand Duke Mersey. Not to be forgotten, their half-brother, the Earl of Sandbridge, was also going to drop by because he was an abolitionist and, as Allegra suspected, was doing everything he could to stir up trouble for the brothers' estates. As always, their petty sibling rivalry was ready to rip the powerful family apart, and the mages and servants were caught in the middle.

Helping her would be Empress Ediva's diplomatic envoy, Tipkin, a weasel-faced little man who made her skin crawl. Nevertheless, he was rumored to be exceptional at playing the role of the manipulator and the Empress sent him as a personal gift to Allegra. They'd met once as young girls.

Serafina and Nathan were working on the details for the ball Allegra would be throwing in a month. The invitations had just gone out. Then, assuming it was a success, she'd throw another at the Cathedral during the summer and do it all over again.

But none of that mattered because she couldn't sleep. In fact, she was too terrified to sleep. What if these symbols began showing up on the main walls? What if more hostilities erupted and there was no stopping it? What if they found her out?

She had to conquer her fears, and soon, or else she had to step down from her job. She left her room behind, not even sure where she was headed other than away from her nightmares. She gave her personal guard a nod and promised she'd only wander around her wing and would send for a servant if she wanted anything out of the kitchens. With limited options and the desire for both privacy and not to be alone, she eventually ended up in the barracks.

Lex and Dodd, as well as one of the local militia whose name she didn't know, sat on the floor playing cards. While it looked like they weren't doing their job, they blocked the entrance down the corridor where the militia and Consorts lived. No matter how focused on their game they might have been, an intruder would have to step over their heads to get by them.

Lex glanced up and frowned. While Lex had given her no indication anything had changed between them, Allegra had a nagging feeling something had happened the day she'd fallen asleep in the chair. Her hand was burning, a side effect of exhaustion and the dream. Lex had been standing right there, and Allegra was certain she'd been wakened by someone grabbing that hand.

If Lex knew...

But all Lex did was nod his head and say, "Captain's room is at the end of the hallway."

Allegra hesitated. Was that actually where she wanted to go? What was she going to do when she got there? Maybe she should go back to her room.

"I think he'd like to see you, if that's..." Dodd shrugged.

Lex sighed and elbowed Dodd, giving him a significant look.

"Ow," Dodd complained, all the while Lex kept his gaze straight ahead with a neutral expression plastered across his face.

Allegra turned to head back to her room when Lex said, "He's probably still up. He was playing cards with Father Michael and Pero until an hour ago."

Allegra pulled her robe a little tighter. She nodded to Lex and began to walk back down the corridor. She paused and said, "Um, could you not tell anyone I'm here, if they're looking for me? Except for...what's the name of the hairy guard that's in my wing?"

"Henry, Your Ladyship," Lex said in that professional, neutral tone he so often used. "Don't worry."

"It's no one's business what you do on your time off, Your Ladyship."

Lex glared at Dodd's grinning face and Allegra realized, with great amusement, that Dodd's entire behavior was never to embarrass the other person; it was solely meant to tease Lex.

Allegra smiled at the young people and walked down the short corridor to Stanton's bedroom. She looked back over her shoulder, but the other two were too absorbed with their own bickering to notice her.

She knocked tentatively. "Um, Stanton? Are you awake?"

She heard movement and a moment later, the door cracked open. Stanton winced at the light. "What's happened?"

He was shirtless and, from the way he was leaning away from the door, perhaps pantless as well. Allegra realized this was a very bad idea. Stupid Walter for putting this into her head.

"I shouldn't have bothered you, I'm sorry," Allegra said.

She turned to walk away, but Stanton reached out and touched her arm. "Stay. Give me a minute."

He shut the door for a brief moment and opened it again, wearing a white tunic that was long enough for decency, but barely. He opened his door and said, "Come in."

Allegra didn't let her eyes linger on him, and Stanton didn't turn his back to her. She stepped inside his bedroom, tugging her robe even tighter.

Stanton rubbed the back of his neck, until he realized it tugged the hem of his tunic up to questionable lengths. He stopped and cleared his voice. "Is everything all right?"

Allegra's stoic expression cracked and she began to weep. Stanton didn't speak. He simply stepped up to her and wrapped strong arms around her. She hated feeling frail, and here she was crying in a half-naked man's arms. If this was not the definition of fragility...

He brushed her hair away from her wet cheeks and made shushing sounds.

"I'm sorry I keep picking fights with you lately. I'm so tired."

"Oh, Allegra. Don't worry about that."

Allegra sniffled as she gained control over her tears. After an awkward moment of staring at each other, Allegra said, "I'm sorry I got you out of bed."

He motioned at the small settee near the window. "Have a seat. I will find trousers."

"I don't mind," Allegra said, the words tumbling out of her mouth before she'd even ran them by her brain.

Stanton gave her a startled look, but he laughed and said, "Go sit." He grabbed his trousers from a nearby chair. He turned his back to her and tugged them on. She looked out the window, giving him the dignity she'd want him to show her if their positions were reversed.

She didn't turn around when she heard his bare feet pad across the rug over to where she stood. "You have a nice room, considering the view of the stables."

A chair creaked behind her. "They wanted to put me upstairs with everyone else, but I told the bishop I wanted to be down here with the boys."

"And girls. You do have a few girls on your team, too."

Stanton chuckled. "Yeah, but boys and girls sounds like I'm running a parish school for children."

Allegra smiled, but barely. She was afraid to turn around. Afraid to speak. Afraid to do anything that would make her face too many new realities for her.

"Spend the night. Take the bed, and I'll take the chair. It's comfortable enough."

She turned around to face him, not bothering to hide the surprise in her voice. "Why? I mean, no. You can't sleep in the chair."

He raised an eyebrow. "Where would you like me to sleep then?"

A hungry voice inside her whispered the best way to stop being afraid was to distract herself. What better way than with the captain of her guard? Stanton pushed himself up from his chair and stood very close. He didn't touch her. He simply stared down at her. Raw need filled his eyes, and she did not care in the slightest that hers reflected the same.

He touched her face. Just a gentle trail of the back of his finger along her cheek. Her heart pounded in her chest and a jolt of aching want filled her.

"I'll sleep in the chair," she managed to force out.

Stanton's shoulders relaxed, though she couldn't tell if it was in relief or disappointment. "I'll take the chair. You have a lot of work to do in the morning and I won't have you distracted."

"I am the Contessa of Marsina. I shall do as I please," she said.

"I am the Duke of Barrington and I outrank you. Now, take the bed, Your Ladyship."

Allegra smiled up at him and nodded. Being here with him made her less afraid. Besides, no one would dare march through the entire barracks wing just to attack her here. There were no mysterious symbols on the walls here. Just Stanton Rainier looking at her like she was the most beautiful woman in the world.

Stanton picked up the heavy arm chair and began dragging it across the room.

"Where are you going?"

"There are enough obstacles ahead of you. Having people distracted by you staying here is an unnecessary one."

"I don't care if people think I slept with you," Allegra said. "I don't care what anything thinks of me." Provided they didn't think she was an elementalist, she meant it.

"Neither do I." Stanton sighed and put the chair down. He leaned against it and said, "Allegra, right now, we both have very important jobs."

"I understand," she said with a small smile. "It would have been nice, though. Throwing caution and reputation to the wind."

Stanton chuckled. "I'll be right outside the door. Call if you need anything."

"I will. And Stanton? Thank you. For everything."

He opened the door and dragged the big, worn chair outside. He said, "When this is all over, we should talk about whatever this is."

Allegra's heart flip-flopped. "I'd like that. Good night. Stanton."

"Good night. Allegra."

CHAPTER TWENTY-FIVE

WITH EXAGGERATED FANFARE, the great Queen Portia arrived. She was a tiny thing, and spoke with an even tinier voice. General Bonacieux was a constant presence at her side, which drove everyone's patience to the edge.

Stanton braced himself against his small window and looked out on the bustle of the abbey's back entrance. There wasn't enough room for all of the carriages in the stable, so the sturdy ones with covered boxes were expertly lined up in a row further off from the abbey. He assumed the open carriages were moved to the strong awning that stretched out on that side of the abbey that served to protect the windows and stonework from the occasional rock slide that happened on the rear of the building.

Things had been complicated since the night Allegra came to him. He pressed his hands against the window frame and focused on controlling his breath. They both agreed in their own ways that they had duties to preform that were more important than anything else. And yet, by saying that, they'd both acknowledged that there was something going on between them.

Why hadn't she tried to talk him into it, if that was why she'd come to him? It wouldn't take much persuading on her part. Sultry eyes, heavy breathing, a soft moan as flesh touched flesh, ripe nipples under his calloused hands, wet folds of skin around his mouth...

Stanton pressed his face into his hand. He needed a stiff drink. So he walked over to the little table in the corner of his study and poured himself a tall glass of brandy from the crystal decanter. He'd won the golden liquid two months ago from one of the visiting diplomats. She'd won it in turn from Father Michael. The Almighty giveth and He taketh away. Blessed be the name of expensive brandy on a chilly spring morning.

Lex poked his head into the room. "Got a moment?"

He motioned for Lex to enter. "Drink?"

Lex shook his head. "The wine from dinner isn't sitting well."

"That's the cheese. It's tasted off for months now."

"Sir, it's not the cheese."

"It's the cheese, I'm telling you."

Stanton took a long pull of his brandy, delighting in the warm path it cut down his throat and into his stomach. "So what's up?"

Lex hedged around the question before blurting, "Is there anything going on between you and the Contessa?"

Stanton lifted an eyebrow.

"I know it's none of my business."

"No, it's not."

Lex fidgeted, and Stanton made no effort to ease his discomfort. "All I'm saying, sir, is that I'm in charge of her personal security. So if you and her are…involved now, I need to know only so that I can adjust…my…erm…Look, sir, what's going on?"

"There's nothing going on, Lex." Stanton drained his glass.

"I'm going to regret this, but why the fuck not?"

Stanton barked out a laugh. "Lex, if I knew the answer to that question, don't you think I'd already be involved?"

"It's not because you think she's an elemental or anything, right?"

"What? No. It's nothing…do you think she's one?"

Lex waved his hand. "I couldn't care less if she was one or not. I just wanted to make sure that wasn't what was holding you up from making your move."

Stanton stared at Lex in shocked silence.

"Why are you staring at me like that? Sir, you know that I don't care about mages and all that. I know plenty and I will never turn them in."

Stanton stared at Lex. "You've never turned them in."

"That is the fundamental difference between you and I. You gave your oath to the Cathedral. I gave mine to the Almighty. I know the Lord Almighty doesn't care what asshole cardinals think, and only what is in my heart."

"Lex, this isn't about…"

"This is about accepting people the way they were born, sir. This is about trusting your friends." Lex stepped forward. "And the Contessa is my friend. I'm just looking out for her."

Stanton crossed his arms. "By putting it into my head that she's an elemental? How is that going to help?"

"Stanton, I've known you a long time."

"Oh, no." Lex only ever used his first name when things were bad.

"She's terrified someone, one day, will accuse her of being an elemental to her friends."

"She told you this, did she?"

Lex licked his lips. "Something like that. She's afraid if someone accused her, you might betray her. That is why she keeps pushing you away." Lex quirked a grin. "Sir."

"Are you saying you think she thinks I think she's an elemental?"

Lex rolled his eyes. "All I know is this: she is scared of all of us. She might look at you…" Lex snorted, "Like she's going to pounce and rip your clothes off, but she's also scared of you. You are a powerful man. You could ruin her if you wanted to. Anyway, sorry, sir. It's been on my mind for a while now."

Stanton sighed heavily and walked over to the decanter and poured himself another brandy. He drained it in a long, burning pull. "All right, Lex. You're worried about Allegra's enemies. Fine. I've had some horrible daydreams about Bonacieux's men dragging her out of the abbey in the middle of the night. We have the night shift rotation now, and we have guards near the servant entrances. Let's double the guard detail up on the cliffside. Enough snow's melted that we can risk sending more men up there. You know what? Find Cram and drag his elemental ass in here. Let's get some of his people helping."

"Sir?" Lex blinked in surprise.

"Well, if Cram and his people get to sit around eating the good cheese while we're stuck with the off stuff, then he can help put them to work."

"I...sir?"

Stanton smiled at his second-in-command. "What do you want from me, Lex?"

"I'm not even sure anymore, sir."

Dodd burst into the room. He looked around frantically, caught Stanton's eyes, and said, "We have a problem."

"WHAT DO YOU mean?" Allegra demanded. Dodd, Stanton, and Martin were standing across from her desk. Martin's uniform was dirty, and he stank.

"Your Ladyship, we were patrolling the southern fields, past the village. We have been keeping an eye on the camps there," Martin said for the third time.

"Yes, yes, but what do you mean about the General?"

Stanton licked his lips and said, "The agreement is one hundred men total. Everyone brought their own support, of course, and you've repeatedly stated support staff didn't count towards their numbers."

"That's correct. There aren't enough bakers and blacksmiths to meet everyone's needs in Borro."

"But...the General's supports are massive."

"Perhaps they have more hangers-on."

"No, Contessa," Stanton said. "I believe that the general is hiding his troops under the guise of support."

"But that would be in direct violation of the talks agreement," Allegra said. "I thought his troops were camped to the west of town?"

"They are," Martin said. "But these are camped further south."

Allegra frowned. "Should I confront him about it?"

Stanton shrugged. "If you do, you might be forcing his hand or angering him. But if you do nothing..."

"I'm announcing myself as weak and everyone else will bring forces, too. Then, someone will doing something stupid and we'll have a full scale battle on our front steps."

"Pretty much," Stanton said.

"Kat, what do you think?"

The Grand Duchess spoke from beyond the fabric privacy screens. She'd arrived an hour ago for the ball. And she was hiding from Father Michael's *and* Pero's bad moods in Allegra's private dining parlor. "The General needs to be put into his place. He is a well-known misogynist and, if that wasn't a good enough reason to despise the little upstart, he has been disruptive to these talks. You can't control how many of his men are beyond the county limits, but you can certainly push him over the border."

"Cartossa's border is only a half a day away from where he's set up, Your Grace," Martin said.

Stanton turned to Martin and said, "I want all the guards put on alert. Spread out through the basements, stables, and every nook and cranny through the abbey. Ask Father Michael and Viscount Reeves for help. Don't be obvious about it, but I want the entire abbey searched. Get Cram to help, too. If the General is planning something, I want to know."

"Yes, Captain."

Allegra tapped her fingers on her desk. "If we force them to move, they'll be beyond our control. Also, what's to stop them from disbanding and setting up smaller pockets all around the area, and even near opposing camps? I'm sure the General would be only too glad to authorize the occasional supply raid upon his enemies."

"True enough," Stanton said. "Your Grace?"

"I am here merely to offer my own personal opinion for Cousin Allegra to disagree with at every turn."

Allegra winked at Stanton. "I will speak with the Queen about this, I think."

"HER EXCELLENCY ALLEGRA, Contessa of Marsina," the butler announced when the footmen opened the double doors. Allegra inclined her head at the butler and strode into the room.

The Queen was perched on a heavily-embroidered chair. She was a short woman, so her feet dangled like a child's. She was a child, too, in so many ways. She was sixteen and a queen, but she was still only sixteen. Plenty of excellent mistakes were made at that age, only most people's mistakes didn't affect the fate of nations.

"Your Majesty," Allegra said, curtsying very low. She had worn her second best dress for this visit. Her skirts billowed out around her and she stretched out her hands to rest against the cornflower blue fabric. "Thank you for granting me this meeting on such short notice."

"Please rise," the queen said. Her voice still had a youthful pitch to it. "What can I do for you, Your Excellency?"

"Might we speak alone?"

Portia nodded to the footmen at the door. They stepped outside, the door latching behind them. Allegra stood and squared her shoulders. She folded her hands together in front of her, just as she'd been taught as a girl. She hated those lessons then, and she hated them now. But her tutor had been right way back then: people in power love their ceremony, so give it to them to extract favors later.

"Your Majesty, I have received a concerning report from one of my scouts. It appears a large force flying your banner are camped south of Borro in violation of my terms."

"You are incorrect. Our agreed-upon force of soldiers is camped west of the village."

"I'm talking about the second encampment, Your Majesty."

The Queen blanched. "I'm...I'm not...I mean, I don't know what you are speaking about."

Allegra narrowed her eyes and said very calmly, "Your Majesty, those troops are yours."

"They are not," she insisted.

Without the General here to feed her the appropriate lines, the Queen resembled a child lying about stealing cake from the larder rather than a fierce leader. Allegra did not wish to make an enemy of this woman. Likewise, she couldn't let her get away with blatantly disregarding the rules.

"I see. Thank you for clarifying. I shall send my people to arrest them, then."

"W-what?" Portia stammered. "You can't do that."

"Your Majesty, these vagrants are pretending to be under your aegis. They have been responsible for no fewer than eleven raids on other encampments. They must be dealt with."

"But…but…"

Allegra stepped forward and glared at the Queen. "Your Majesty, you are young, and we can all forgive a significant amount of foolishness because of that. However, this isn't a game. This is real life, and the peace of all of our nations hangs in the balance."

"How dare you!" Portia roared. She jumped down from her chair and glared up at Allegra, who was at least two hand lengths taller. "I am Queen Portia!"

"Then act like it!" Allegra snarled.

The Queen flopped back on her chair and said, in a sullen voice, "You're bluffing. You have a couple dozen guards and that's it. How are you going to arrest all of my men?"

Allegra bowed and said, "Thank you, Your Majesty, for admitting that you have broken the peace treaty. I shall inform the other delegates."

"Wait…what? I didn't. Wait! You can't!"

Allegra said, "Your Majesty, I am no Queen, but these peace talks are mine, sanctioned by the Cathedral. You are here on my invitation and not the other way around. I have already informed the other delegates about these aggressors and they are already forming a joint guard to deal with the situation. But since they are *your* men, then they were here on your authority. So, I'm sure the others will be very pleased to hear of that."

"What do you want me to do?"

Allegra approached her and said, "General Bonacieux no longer attends any leadership meetings. If you wish to have an advisor with you, ask Grand Duchess Katherine for assistance and guidance. She's your aunt."

"Twice removed," the queen said. "And she hates me."

"The Grand Duchess hates everyone," Allegra said. "She will still help you."

"What else do you want?"

"Get those men back across the border to Cartossa. They cease all raids and pillaging along the way."

"The General won't let you get away with this."

"My dear Queen, I outrank the General."

And, with that, Allegra marched out of Queen Portia's drawing room, head held high. And no one saw how much her hands trembled as she did.

STANTON WAS DISCUSSING the security arrangements for the ball with Beatrix and Dodd when General Bonacieux flung open his door. "You get that woman of yours under control, Rainier!"

"You must be confusing me with someone else," Stanton said. He'd already gotten the blow-by-blow of the exchange from Allegra, so he was prepared for this confrontation. That's why Lex and Martin were currently having a day-long meeting in Allegra's office and why the Grand Duchess and Cram had relocated there for an extended supper.

"You know exactly what I mean!" the General bellowed. "Out! The rest of you, out!"

"Stay," Stanton ordered Beatrix, who'd turned to go. Dodd, knowing better, hadn't even flinched to move away. "General, I don't know what you're talking about, but you are wasting my time. So either get to the point or go harass someone else. I'm sure there's a mage left in the village you haven't screamed at yet."

Bonacieux slammed his hand down so hard on Stanton's desk that the letters all jumped. "You will address this, Rainier. That contessa of yours is undermining my authority."

"You seem to be under the mistaken impression that the Arbiter works for me. She does not. I am in her employ, and not the other way around."

"You are the Duke of Barrington. Act like it, man!"

Stanton pushed himself up from his desk. He didn't make it any more aggressive than it needed to be. "General Bonacieux, you have broken the rules of the peace talks. If it were my choice, I would have expelled you and written the Holy Father to demand you be censored for this insult. Now, if you wish me to speak to the Contessa, I would be very happy to give her my opinion. Otherwise, please leave."

"I should have known you were a mage lover."

Stanton stared at him blankly, refusing to take the bait. The General stormed out of the room, slamming doors and shouting as he did.

"Dodd?"

He was already moving. "I'll take the servant stairs. Should be able to warn the others before he gets through."

THE NIGHTMARE WE KNOW

WALTER CLOSED HIS eyes as they wrapped the noose around the boy's neck. Little Ferret, as they all called him, wasn't old enough yet to know if he was going to become a mage. His dead parents were both elementals, which was why Little Ferret was one of them. They'd all assumed he'd turn out like them.

Dammit, he shouldn't have stolen that loaf of bread.

Little Ferret sobbed and sniffled. The elemental mages stood in a block with Walter. Oh, some of them hadn't identified themselves as such, but they wouldn't be standing next to him if they weren't. He was their leader, for better or worse. Ferret was one of their own.

If Walter lashed out, that noose would be around his neck. He'd open a crater in the town square before he'd let them tighten it. If they knocked him out so he couldn't, all of these men and women would go to war. Not even Allegra's pretty words could stop that.

But Little Ferret was one of his. He brought the little mongoose here in hopes he'd be safe for a few months.

The ground tremored underneath Walter and it snapped him back into the present. He grabbed control of his elemental power before he opened up the earth and accidentally killed himself.

"What are we going to do?" whispered a man he didn't know who stood next to him. "We can't let them kill him. He's one of ours."

The priest was reading a homily, on and on about the forgiving nature of the Almighty. All the while the hooded executioner prepared to murder a hungry little boy.

"I can't without hurting Ferret," Walter said quietly.

The man nodded. "All right. Everyone, get ready."

Walter's skin burned from the spike of blue-hot flame that shot from the man's hands. One cut through the noose's rope and continued to sail through the air. The other hit, not the executioner, not the priest, but the magistrate who'd sentenced a little boy to the rope.

"Run!" Walter ordered and the man broke through the crowd, guards hot upon his heels. Strong arms clamped down on Walter. "Boys, I recommend you take your hands off me or else this war is starting right here, right this minute."

CHAPTER TWENTY-SIX

THANKFULLY, THE MILITIA had managed to keep the fighting during Little Ferret's execution to a minimum. So when Allegra's horse galloped into the main marketplace, there was only curling smoke from recently-extinguished fires. She'd not known the little boy was to be hanged today. She'd not even known, for certain, that he would even meet the noose. She'd been promised the boy would receive leniency.

"Back!" Stanton shouted. "Everyone! Back!"

Flanked by Consorts and militia alike, Allegra pulled into the midst of the brewing fight. That didn't stop her heart from pounding or her desire to sink behind Rainier or the others. But this was her job now, and she would rather fester in the abyss than let some regressive farmers dictate the law to her. She had already been on her way when runners met her to say that Walter was about to be arrested. If she didn't get the situation under control now, all of her hard work was about to go up in actual flames.

She pointed at the Cartossian soldier who held Walter. "Let him go. Now."

The soldier did as she ordered and Walter shook off the manhandling. He approached the Consorts' flank of protection. His face was grim and he didn't sass off the soldier.

Allegra turned to the men and women gathered together in a clump of food splatters. She assumed those were the mages. "We need to be calm."

Allegra dismounted her horse amongst the jeers. Stanton glared at her and motioned for her to get back upon her horse. He'd told her specifically before they came that she was not to get off her horse no matter what. However, she was not going to get the crowd's attention by pacing back and forth around them.

She stepped upon the wooden hangman's platform. A shiver went through her knowing what it was for. The singed rope still dangled from the upper brace. "I stand before you as the Arbiter of the Cathedral's law and will," she said.

She noticed that it was strangers who jeered at her. Allegra might not have known the names of all of the villagers and refugees, but she knew their faces. She knew none of these hard-faced men. The runner had also said the market was full of strangers he didn't recognize, who'd been stirring up trouble all day.

"Go home to your families and your fields. We have all worked too hard, suffered too much to throw it all away today. Let calm prevail."

"Freak!" Someone threw a rotting potato and it splattered over the back of Dodd's green jacket.

Dodd yanked his horse around to glare at the crowd.

"These mages are not here to harm you. They merely want to live and exist just as you do," Allegra urged. "These villagers are also not here to harm you. They have invited you into their homes and lives. If they had rejected you, all of you who came this winter would have starved by now. They are not your enemy."

"Mage lover!"

"I speak for the Holy Father himself. Your behavior is illegal and against the Almighty's word. The Holy Father has sent me here to stop this outrageous behavior."

"Give us the mages!"

"There is no good that can come from this. This action today could even start a war. None of you want to see your sons and daughters fight and die in a war."

"Freak!"

"You must yield. They are peaceable, kind, gentle people and they are your neighbors."

"Send them to the mines!"

"Do your job!"

"Mage lover!"

"Mage lover!"

Allegra was shouting over the crowd now, a pointless attempt to get their attention. They were not going to go home. The rumors were true, then. Bonacieux's men had been stirring up the crowd. Between that and the stench of market day cheap gin, the crowd was ready for a fight.

A bottle sailed through the air at her. She flinched and closed her eyes. A gust of wind hit her and she slumped against one of the wooden posts for support. The bottle sailed end over end harmlessly to smash on the side of the hangman's podium.

She gulped. Someone had used elemental magic freely, here in the open, to protect her.

Five men wearing the red and white uniforms of Queen Portia's personal guard jumped a woman clad in tattered cloth. She screamed from beneath them.

"Please! I beg you. Do not do this." Allegra's voice strained from the shout, but it did no use. Too many had been wanting this day.

Mages and villagers alike jumped the guards. Clubs, axes, and magic flew.

"I beg you! Stop!" Allegra screamed. She jumped from the podium as Stanton and his men beat back the crowd with their clubs. She'd told them not to use lethal force, but there were still too many cries of pain and too many faces a sheet of blood.

Some of the crowd shouted angrily at her. Others shouted angry defenses of her. She shouted she was going nowhere. She would not yield to a mob. Stanton pulled his horse over to her and threatened to bash anyone who came too close to her. Still, she was so intent on arguing with the crowd that she didn't see the man with the bow until Stanton pushed her out of the way.

The arrow grazed Allegra's arm and she screamed, a high-pitched, agonized sound. Allegra fell to her knees at the sight of the blood welling through her white dress sleeve. The crowd fell into a stunned silence. The world fogged as Allegra blinked away the tears that welled in her eyes.

The Consorts and the guards protecting Allegra rushed into the crowd with their clubs, savagely beating anyone who wasn't running away. Allegra had ordered swords and bows only as a complete last resort, and the men had followed her order. However, as she watched a man fall to the mud face-first, his head a mass of blood, she knew all too well that many would die today.

A pitchfork grazed both Rahna's leg and her horse. The animal bucked, throwing Rahna into the mud. She landed with a scream of "Fuck! Fuck! Fuck!" and hit the ground with a thud, and more swearing.

Walter scrambled to Allegra's side. He shoved his arms under her armpits and began to haul her to her feet. "Ally! Ally!"

"I'm…fine…" Allegra's voice was slow, but she was gaining her focus again.

"Are you all right?" Walter shouted over the screaming and cursing of the courtyard.

Bonacieux's men, plus the strangers, had launched their own assault and were violently attacking known mages now. Walter shouted at Stanton, jabbing a finger in the direction of the mages, and Stanton dug his heels into his horse's flank and rushed over to assist. Dodd and Lex joined him.

Two villagers dragged Rahna out of the stampede, all the while she screamed and left a trail of blood on the muddy ground.

Then, seven women and three men stepped out of the small parish temple. They walked in silent, confident unison. A pained whimper escaped Walter. "Oh, no. Allegra, move! Get up! Rainier! Get out of here! Now!"

Walter heaved Allegra to her feet and stumbled away. When Allegra saw the flame ignite in the lead woman's hand, Allegra's senses came rushing back.

"No!" Allegra shouted at the mages, but they only gave her grim looks. "Please, no. Don't do this! No!"

Walter screamed for Stanton. Stanton pulled his horse to them and Walter helped pull her onto his horse. She winced and cried out from the pain in her arm, but she sat in front of Stanton. With one arm around her and one on the reins, he was weaponless now, but he followed the mages' advice as they shouted to get Allegra out of the way.

"Move! Get back!" Stanton shouted. Most of the villagers knew well enough to run and the market was mostly deserted.

"Please, no," Allegra said, openly weeping now and not because of the piercing pain in her arm.

Lex shouted and swore as he pulled a bleeding and shrieking Rahna up on his horse.

A blast of fire hit the wheelbarrow special gin, no doubt laced with too many chemicals and not enough grain. The flames were hot against her face.

"Oh no," Stanton whispered. "Oh, no."

Allegra watched helplessly as her own kind cut the strings on their humanity. She watched as they burned the houses. She watched as craters formed in the earth, swallowing fleeing men. She watched as buildings collapsed, crushing people to death.

But she wasn't helpless as she watched. No, she could have walked out there and struck while their backs were turned on her. She could have cut down those elementals and they would never have seen it coming.

It was Walter, and not her, that stood between the Consorts and the rushing wave of Bonacieux's terrified men. It was Walter that opened up hole upon hole, trying to slow everyone down without killing them. It was Walter that protected the fleeing villagers and refugees alike. It was Walter who pulled down buildings to throw rubble in between the elementals and Bonacieux's men. It was Walter who collapsed face-first into the mud from exhaustion.

She didn't do any of that. She watched. Safely behind a wall of armored, both material and magical, soldiers, and hid like a coward. For she was a coward. These were the true heroes. Even if they died, they would be heroes. Even if they lived, they were still heroes for they must know she would have them arrested and turned over to Portia's men. If they were lucky, they would be sent to the mines and not tortured to see how elementals worked.

This could have been her fate if she'd went with Walter Cram all those years ago. Her child would have been eight? Nine? Running alongside her, watching her burn a village to the ground.

Would she have chosen that path if she knew she'd still end up here, watching her kind destroy everything she'd worked so hard to prevent?

Sitting there upon the horse in the fog and steam and fire, as the earth shattered around them and the skies attacked them, Allegra was not so vain as to think she alone caused this. She was merely one piece, but a piece nonetheless.

So she watched. Watched and did nothing as the guilty and the innocent were burned, crushed, and ripped apart. This massacre would send ripples through the world. Their opponents would use this as a tool to crack down even harder. Advocates would argue one doesn't throw out all of the winter pears just because a few went bad. And, besides, had they always been bad or was the farmer wife's shoddy care to blame?

It didn't matter. None of it mattered now. She would have to retreat into the abbey, and soon. She would need to double her guard. She knew Stanton well enough to know he was already running the numbers and assignments, even as he was surveying the horrors in front of them.

Stanton's fingers brushed hers, and she allowed it. He didn't cup her hand or touch her any further than that. Just the gentle pressure of the back of his hand against hers, letting her know that he was there to protect her. That he understood. That he cared.

She was happy someone cared about her right now, for she feared she would never care again.

CHAPTER TWENTY-SEVEN

THE AFTERMATH HAD been hard for everyone. Thankfully, it rained later that fateful day and the fires didn't spread too badly. Even with that grace, however, it was still too much damage. There had been several smaller uprisings over the days that followed, though none lasted beyond dusk. People had lost their homes and shops. Of course they were angry.

The fighting spread throughout the region, though. The entire nation erupted into riots and protests, with elemental mages coming out of the woodwork to openly display their unique abilities – and everyone suffered as a consequence. Of course, they'd all heard of the great Walter Cram who stood before the Cathedral's very guards and protected innocents with his magic. He'd nearly died, the rumors said, and yet he did not yield to terror. He used his magic for good.

Of course, Walter had Allegra's protection. So the more the world clamped down on magic, the more people resisted, and not just mages. Why shouldn't the innocent peasants be protected from the searches and the exploitation, too?

Some blamed Allegra, while others blamed the Consorts. Still others blamed mages, and elementalists, and Bonacieux's men. Most blamed the magistrate and Little Ferret. The little snot nosed brat shouldn't have stolen the bread, and the bastard of a magistrate should have taken his upbringing into consideration.

Under Stanton's orders, two of Walter's people eventually found Little Ferret, who'd wisely run as soon as he'd been freed from the noose. Walter's people, escorted by two Consorts, got him to the Cathedral. Carrying letters with the Arbiter's seal identifying him as *Rafe Tal: Orphan*, Little Ferret was hired by the Consorts still stationed at the Cathedral as their all-around errands fellow.

And what was the great Arbiter of Justice doing about all of this? Why, she was throwing a party. The world was on the brink of full-scale conflict, and her assistant was planning the orchestra arrangements for a ball. Because that's what the aristocracy wanted. Not laws, not firm measures. A party.

Allegra poured herself her fourth glass of wine that afternoon. Her arm itched like crazy. It has only been a superficial cut. It simply bled messily and had shocked her. Rahna's injury was a little more serious, but between her magical gear on her uniform to the wound being a graze and not a puncture, so she, too, was healing nicely.

Nineteen people had died in Borro that day. Nineteen souls upon her head.

She'd stopped talking to everyone the last several days beyond the necessities. She had isolated herself during her private time. She threw herself into her work, frantically writing at all hours of the day and night, issuing missives and decrees. Everything and anything to try to stem the brewing conflict.

Still, it came as no surprise when he finally knocked on her door. "It's Stanton."

Not looking up from her leather-bound ledger, she asked, "Has everyone agreed to assist with security during the ball?"

Stanton nodded. "Everyone except Bonacieux, of course, but the Grand Duchess plans to speak with her niece."

"Thank you. That'll be all."

After a pause, Stanton said, "Allegra, are you well?"

"No," she said simply. She considered not giving any further reply, but she put her pencil down. She mustered her energy to give him a tight smile. "I cannot sleep, and every time I think of…of the event, I feel as though my heart is trying to rip itself from my chest. Cowardly, I know."

"It isn't," he said. "I have seen and done many things…"

"I can't. Stanton, I know you are trying to help, but...I can't. Not right now."

"Of course," he said. "I've missed our breakfasts."

"I don't have much of an appetite."

"Not even for pound cake?"

A ghost of a smile twitched on her mouth. "Not even."

CHAPTER TWENTY-EIGHT

STANTON SAT AT his desk writing the last of the letters he needed to deal with before he could sleep for the night. The attack at the market square had changed much. Three times, Allegra's life had been in danger now. All three times he had been standing there, helpless. Intellectually he knew there was only so much he could do, but his heart berated him for having exposed her to such risks.

Of course, his heart didn't understand that the Contessa had a mind of her own. And her mind said she would not shirk her responsibilities. He wished she would.

Footsteps interrupted his dark thoughts. He looked up to see Dodd and Lex poking their heads around his office doorway.

"Captain, what are you still doing up?" Dodd asked.

"Hey, Captain," Lex said, smiling. He was tugging on his ridiculous hat, the one with the massive ostrich feather in it.

"Just finishing up some work. What trouble are the two of you up to?"

"Bah," Dodd said. "We're all heading down to the dining hall to play cards."

Lex tapped his jacket and was rewarded with the jingle of coins. "Father Michael's sister is going to join us. I hear she's a bit of a card shark."

"She's more than a bit. And don't fall for Father Michael's pious demeanor again or you're going to lose that hat of yours. I've seen him and his sister wipe out an entire table of cardinals in under an hour playing two partner draw."

"Mother Aloni said the same thing," Lex said with a grin. "But I'm prepared."

"I have no qualms taking a priest and his sister down," Dodd said smugly.

"Well, good luck, kids. Stay out of trouble and don't cause any fights."

Dodd scoffed. "You're worse than my dad."

"He and your mother write to me often to ensure I'm looking after you," Stanton said sweetly. He wasn't even lying. Dodd's mother wrote more than Stanton's own mother.

Nadira walked in and curtsied. "Letter for you, Captain."

Dodd accepted the letter and handed it over to Stanton, who opened it. "I was hoping to get some sleep tonight, but if letters keep coming at all hours, perhaps you'll find me passed out on my desk in the morning."

"Wouldn't be the first time!" Lex said cheerily. "Well, if you change your mind, Captain, we'll be in the servant's dining hall where the real action happens."

"Don't bet your uniform. That's an order," Stanton said sternly.

Both muttered how unfair this was. Stanton ignored them and turned to his letter.

Captain, I'm in need of quiet conversation and an excellent bottle of brandy. I have the brandy, and could use the other. I keep a secret area in the northern attic. Simply go to the linen storage room near my rooms. Pull out the ceiling ladder. I can be found upstairs behind the tapestry of Tasmin.

If you wish to join me, please bring a blanket and a toasting iron. The servants removed mine.

A

He looked up at Nadira and said, "Thank you. Does she require a reply?"

"No, sir."

About twenty minutes later, Stanton balanced a candle, a blanket, and a toasting iron as he climbed up the steps to the upper attic. It was silent up there, except for his own heavy footsteps and breathing as he pulled the ladder back up. He latched it into place and looked about. There was a soft glow coming from over the tall bookshelves. He spotted the tapestry and pulled aside the edge, careful to keep his candle well clear. The tapestry wasn't attached to a wall. Instead, he noticed a metal bar was balanced on top of the bookshelves.

He stepped through the space and was greeted with the sight of a warm, crackling fire. Allegra was seated quietly on the sofa. She turned to look at him and, in the firelight, her silhouette was breathtaking, like from a dream or a vision from the Almighty. He held the candle up to his face and smiled.

"One blanket and one toasting iron, as ordered," he said.

Allegra turned back to her fire. "Good. I was afraid I'd have to drink this bottle of brandy myself."

"Best you not do that," Stanton said. "I believe you are expecting guests in the morning."

She sighed. "I'm always expecting guests."

He placed his items on the floor. He blew out the candle and put it by the fireplace. Then he took up a position on the worn sofa. He didn't sit directly next to her, but didn't choose the side chair, either. Tonight, well, he didn't know what to expect, but he knew Allegra well enough to know she would want him close.

Or, maybe it was just his own wants he was listening to.

"I didn't know this existed," he said. He looked around at the little room she'd arranged with the storage items. There was a rug on the floor and the worn sofa they sat on, large enough for someone to comfortably sleep on – even someone his size. The fireplace was old, but clean, and there was plenty of wood. There was a little table next to Allegra with a decanter of a golden liquid, and two crystal goblets. One was still empty. "This is quite the little getaway."

"Nadira helped me make it months ago," she said. She poured him a drink and he accepted it.

"Do you come here often?"

"All of the bloody time."

"How do you get in here, without anyone seeing?"

"There's a servant entrance in my prayer closet. I came in through that door over there." She pointed to what appeared to be a shelf of books.

"You've been sneaking around the abbey for months now, haven't you?"

She gave him a ghost of a smile. "Not as much as you'd think, actually. There's no way into the servant entrances without going past guards and other servants, and, well, everyone's a little protective over strangers in the corridors these days."

"Do you…come here alone?"

She eyed him. "Yes."

"Why am I here today?"

"Because, for once in my life, I simply wish to be me. No rank, no position, no magic. Just me," she gulped. "And I realized that I wanted to share that with someone. Just for one night."

If it were any other woman, Stanton would think she meant sex. However, Allegra had been very careful about intimacy.

"I'd be honored to share this time with you."

Allegra quietly sipped her brandy as Stanton took the bread she'd procured from the kitchen. The scullery maid had kindly cut the bread and found her some butter and a spreading knife. Then, packed it all into a small basket along with some additional supplies. The poor girl had packed enough for a party, but perhaps she'd assumed Allegra was hosting one.

She didn't speak, and Stanton filled the silence with amusing stories about the times Dodd and Lex had drunkenly made toast in the barracks and caught Lex's boot on fire. Allegra loved Stanton's stories, though she noticed he told very few of his own. She wondered if he was modest, or if he couldn't find the humor in his life. Or maybe, like her he had no true friends.

Part of her had hoped he wouldn't come. She needed the company, but she also worried that he could not provide the safety she needed. All she wanted was to curl into a ball and cry in his strong, comforting arms.

"This is very tricky," Stanton said. "I'm not used to cooking for more than just myself."

"Provided it isn't burnt black, I'll eat it."

"Don't distract me. I'm concentrating."

Allegra smiled at him, even if he had his back turned to her. It was one of the rare moments Stanton was out of uniform. His jacket was gone, as was his sword and belt. This was the first time she'd ever seen him about the abbey without it, and he looked naked somehow. More vulnerable. Of course, there was a rather large ax mounted on the wall, so if would-be assassins came after her in this secret place no one knew about, Stanton could defend her.

Stanton's long-sleeved tunic was embroidered about the neck with green ivy. His gray wool trousers she'd seen before, whenever his usual uniform was in the wash.

"So who knows about this place?"

Allegra tucked her legs up under her simple shift and dressing gown, and leaned against the sofa's armrest. "No one knows about it, except for Nadira and one of the chambermaids. She's never told anyone, that I know of. She makes sure there is wood and cleans the fireplace for me. Everyone else seems to think this is just another storage closet for old things that no one ever looks at anymore."

"But...why?" he asked, pulling the golden, buttered bread from the iron. "Hot! Hot! Hot! Hand me your plate."

She passed both to him and he began to organize toast, a slice of cake, and some preserves on each. Allegra drew in a breath, and then took a sip of her brandy. It burned going down, but it was numbing the harsher edges. "Here, there are no servants attending me. No guards. No priests. No sisters. There are no expectations on me here. I can be whoever and whatever I want. Here, I'm simply Allegra and no one else. I'm not even a mage here."

Stanton let out a sigh and said, "Then shall I just be Stanton? Just another man sitting in front of a fire after a hard few days." He glanced at her. "A lucky man. Allegra?"

"Hmm?"

"How are you?"

There was a lot of weight to the question. Not nearly as simple as fine or horrible, depressed or elated. She didn't even know what she was feeling.

"Would you believe me if I said fine?"

He handed her back the plate. "Probably not."

He joined her on the sofa and began to eat silently, letting her lead the conversation. He didn't push. He never did. That was one of the reasons she loved him.

Allegra took a sharp breath at that stray thought. It was Walter's doing to put that damn thought in her head, but there it was and there was no point denying it to herself. Stanton didn't even need to know, and she could admire him from up close, and yet, so far away.

"I'm having trouble sleeping. I keep seeing their faces every time I close my eyes." Allegra looked away from the fire. "I have nightmares."

"Understandable," he said. "Soldiers all experience the same thing."

"I'm not a soldier."

"No, your job is immeasurably worse for you hold everyone's lives in your hands. I do not envy you. My job is difficult enough, and I only have to keep my eyes on you at all times."

"I can't be that hard to look at, Captain."

A warm, low chuckle escaped his throat. "You are very easy to look at, Your Ladyship."

Allegra smiled. She knew it was sad, but she tried to force as much mirth into it as she could. "Always the gentlemen. I suppose we will let you keep your title one more day."

When her smile faltered, he touched her arm, very gently. "I'm so sorry you had to do what you did. If there was a way to take that pain from you, I would have gladly done it."

"I believe you," she said honestly. "But...Stanton, did I have to do it? Did I have to hand over people like Little Ferret and the others? Was there a loophole for mercy?" She shut her eyes against the tears. "My actions condemned innocent men and women to their deaths. And, in doing so, I condemned even more to their deaths when others took justice into their own hands."

"Do you remember when we first met? You asked about the village that had been attacked by the assassins."

"I remember. You didn't want to talk about it."

"I never want to talk about anything that happened those few days. I...I still have nightmares. I see the faces of my friends dead on the ground. I see the dead villagers I couldn't save. I relive being attacked." He sighed. "It's not as bad as it used to be. The edges have blurred now and I have a lot of distance from it."

"I'm so sorry."

"I'm not telling you for sympathy. I'm telling you because I understand. You cannot make any rash decisions right now because you are still coping with the shock and grief of what happened. But, while those faces might never completely go away, you'll be able to bear them in time. You'll have other dreams, and eventually you'll have some pleasant ones."

"I can hardly compare you being in battle with me sitting in a room playing judge, jury, and executor."

"The causes aren't the same, but the results are similar."

"I'm not sure I believe that, but thank you all the same."

They ate their toast and sipped their brandy. Little conversation passed between them, yet Allegra enjoyed the company. Stanton stoked the fire a couple of times and stacked it well to keep the area nice and cozy.

The brandy was doing its trick and her pain turned fuzzy. Stanton asked her a question about her estate. She asked him a question about his. More silence. She offered more brandy. He accepted. Silence.

"Stanton, have you ever been with a..." The words tumbled out of Allegra and it was too late when she caught herself. She grimaced and looked away. "Forgive me. I seem to have lost my manners in this brandy."

"Have I been with a woman?" He looked at her and smiled. "Is that what you were asking?"

"The intimacy of the moment overtook my good judgment. Again, I apologize."

"I think we are good enough friends that we can ask each other those types of questions. And, yes, I have been with a woman before. Not many, but a few. Though, it has been a very long while."

"A handsome, rich, heroic figure like you? Why ever not?"

"No one had caught my eye," Stanton said. He stared up at her and Allegra held her breath. If Stanton had been a mage, or even a sympathizer, she would have stripped herself bare for him by now. In fact, even knowing his opinions, she still wanted to pull her shift over her head and let him see her silhouetted in the firelight.

Would he find her attractive? Would the smooth curve of her hips catch his eye? Would he want to run his hands along her small, settled breasts? Would he kiss her? Love her?

"I'm not like Dodd. I need...I need more than a nice pair of breasts to entice me into someone's bed."

"I doubt Dodd needs a bed," Allegra said, her lips quirking into a smile. "A firm wall would surely do."

"Why did you want to know?"

"I have assumed you'd been with a woman. I had meant to ask if you'd ever been with a mage before."

Stanton began breathing, only his breaths were ragged. "Once."

Allegra closed her eyes. She couldn't tell if that was the answer she wanted or not. Was there even a right answer at this point? All she wanted was...

She sighed. "Was she special to you?"

"She was my first love," he said, very gently. "I adored her. We had lost touch with each other for a number of years, but eventually our paths crossed again at the Cathedral. We are now frequent writers."

"Oh," Allegra said, crestfallen. She had not considered he might be actual friends with any mages, intimate enough for him to ask questions of. She could never hide her situation from him. She had been foolish to even think she could.

Stanton misunderstood her disappointment because he said, "She is married now to the Marquis of Ramsgate."

"I've never met him," Allegra said absently.

"I met him once. He seems a good sort of man," he said. "So, I'm very unattached, in case that was your question."

Allegra looked up at him. "It wasn't."

"No?"

"Well..." She gulped. "I assumed as much, as you, um, never speak of any charming young ladies."

"I'm too old for young ladies," he said quietly. "Charming women, however, still catch my eye on occasion."

"I am sure there are several charming women here for the negotiations."

He touched her cheek with the back of his hand. "I've only noticed one, but she said she wasn't interested."

Allegra closed her eyes so that she didn't have to look into his intense gaze. She wanted more than anything to give in right now, to tug on his trouser buttons, to pull down his suspenders, to rip at the buckle. It had also been way too long since she'd been interested in someone, and months of being in love with the captain of her guard had done nothing to quell the needs of both her heart and her body.

Could she risk giving in? She could lose everything. No man was worth her life, not even one she'd fallen in love with. At least, that had always been her stance. Never be with a man who wasn't a mage. Never be with someone she couldn't inherently trust.

Did she not trust the man tasked with her safety? How could she trust him with her life, when she didn't trust him with her body?

"I believe it's your turn," Stanton said. "Have you ever been with a man, mage or not?"

Could she lie? Could she pretend to know nothing and be scared? No, she couldn't. There was a maturity in her passion that even she recognized. Shyness and nervousness were very different from lack of experience. She knew exactly what they were doing right now.

She knew the dance steps very well, as did Stanton. She leaned into his hand and said in a whisper, "I've only ever been with mages. They are the only men I've ever trusted."

The sound that escaped him was pure anguish. "Why?"

"A regular man who beds a mage has only to worry about his ego. A mage has to worry about her very life if she angers him. I could not risk a man threatening to call me an elemental."

"You and Cram?

She gave him a sad smile. "Yes."

He pulled his hand away and said, "Ah."

"No, Stanton, it isn't like that, the way everyone assumes. He despises me. Or, at least he used to. Our departure was very difficult. We have yet to find our way back to the friendship we once had, and I doubt we ever will."

"For that, I am sorry. It must have been hard for you."

"I regret what happened between us, but...Walter hated me by the end. His parting words were that he wished me to suffer the same pain I'd caused him. But, as angry as he was, I never feared or imagined that he'd call me an elemental. None of us would do that to our worst enemies."

"That sounds isolating."

"But safe."

Stanton pulled himself closer to her. He slipped a hand over hers as they rested on her thigh. His fingers brushed her legs and her breath hitched in her throat. "You would be safe with me. I give you my word of honor as a gentlemen. I would never call you that or endanger your life by using that word."

She wanted to believe him. She could kiss him right now, and forget everything. Wasn't that why she invited him here? Why *had* she invited him here?

Because she loved him and her defenses were gone. There was nothing left in her that held the energy to fight. She was vulnerable. She knew it. He knew it, she was certain, which was why he hadn't pulled her on top of him and ceased this endless prattle.

He touched her face and said, "Promise to give me a chance to prove you can trust me."

"What if I were an..." Her voice trailed off. She was too dangerously close to telling him.

"My dear Allegra, you aren't one, so there is no reason to worry. And there is no reason to believe I would debase myself and hurt you so horribly as to accuse you, and send you to your end." He leaned forward and whispered in her ear, "You must know me better than that by now."

She closed her eyes, but the tears still escaped. She let them fall, and remained as silent as possible. The hurt was too great.

"Besides," he whispered into her ear, "I thought you weren't a mage tonight."

And that was all she needed him to say.

STANTON STRUGGLED TO keep his need in check with Allegra's uncertainty. He wanted to push her up against the wall and tear her dress off her. He wanted to pull her torn bodice down to her waist.

He wanted to run his tongue along her flesh until she moaned and cried out underneath him. But no matter how much his own body wanted to control the situation, his compassion and his love for her overruled his desires.

He gingerly placed both hands on her jaw, to cup her face. Just a soft pressure. He couldn't imagine what this woman had seen to make her so afraid. There was firsthand knowledge, firsthand pain that had scarred her. He saw it in her eyes. He dared not ask, not yet. All of these months and he was still struggling to gain her trust. What had been done to her?

She wanted to trust him. Of that he was certain. He could also see the lust in her eyes. There was a string tied to both of their hearts and it tugged whenever they were out of sight of the other. That string would never been satisfied until she was atop him.

He ran his bristly cheek along the smoothness of hers and her fingers tightened. Still, she did not make any move to encourage him further, so he waited. He could wait for her. For her, he could wait the rest of his life.

"Besides, I thought you weren't a mage tonight."

Her expression changed abruptly. She cocked her head as if working through what life as a normal would mean for her, here in this moment between them.

Allegra stood, pulling herself away from Stanton's embrace. She slipped her long robe from her shoulders and it pooled on the floor. The chill in the air hit her flesh and her nipples hardened and pressed the thin linen of her shift. She pulled the thin fabric up over her head and dropped it to the floor shaking out her hair as she did it.

Almighty's mercy. She was beautiful.

ALLEGRA GULPED DOWN the fear in her throat and walked over to the unmoving Stanton. She knelt down on him and slipped her hands into the cushions behind his head. If she faltered in her control, the sofa would hide the evidence. With the firelight flickering and the cushions as protection, this would be her only chance.

She pushed aside the screaming voice of common sense about this being the absolute worst idea of her life and listened to the voice that said how much she wanted to exist without purpose or pressure. So she reached down and unbuckled the belt about his waist. Stanton's eyes were wide and he was breathing roughly. He wasn't even touching her.

"Do…do…you want this?" she asked. "I…I will stop if…"

Whatever control Stanton had left in him collapsed. He wrapped his strong arms around her, calloused hands on soft skin. He kissed her, tongues lashing and exploring. He broke off to run kisses along her jawline, her ear lobe, and trace a trail to her collarbone.

He fumbled with the flap on his trousers and Allegra tugged and pulled the fabric, all the while meeting his kisses with increased need. One of the wooden buttons came undone, flying in an arc before clattering to the floor. Allegra didn't care. They'd worry about buttons later.

With her help, he guided himself inside her. Allegra gasped. She gripped the sofa back hard, for fear she would lose her mind. When she'd regained control from her lust, Allegra leaned back, closed her eyes, and let her hips take over for a while. She didn't look at Stanton as he ran his hands along her breasts or along the small of her back. She just held on to the back of that damned sofa for all of dear life.

Stanton's breath was coming faster, as was hers. She didn't slow her pace. She didn't know how much she could hold on to any of this. Her mind, her magic, her lust. She just wanted to feel so badly; she wanted to feel.

So much of her life was devoid of feeling. It hurt so much with Walter because she had let herself feel. It was the first time she'd really given over everything and he had hurt her so badly. And she knew Stanton could destroy her. Not just her reputation or her estate, but utterly destroy her. He could be the one to arrest her and put her on a cart. She could be in the position to have to immolate herself to avoid the mines. She could become the killer she never in a million years believed she ever could be.

Stanton could hurt her that much.

And yet she moved her hips anyway.

His own grip on her faltered; he stirred to move her. She gripped the sofa back harder and said, "No. Stay like this."

"I'd like to...help you catch up to me."

"Stay like this," she repeated, not letting go her grip.

"All right," he said and reached forward to take each nipple in turn into his mouth.

She pulled herself closer, her ear against his. "This is only for tonight," she whispered. "I can't....just tonight, okay?"

"Just tonight," he whispered back.

There was resignation, more than disappointment, in his voice. He wanted this to be every night, but they both knew it could never be. She could never let the cardinals know she was with Stanton. They would use him against her. One day, they might use her against him. No, she had to keep it...She had to...

Tears stung her eyes and she closed them shut. Why the fuck couldn't she be normal like a normal person doing normal things? Why couldn't she be there, in this moment, with the man she loved and not have tears running down her cheeks?

She needed this to stop, but she needed it to keep going. She needed to finish what she'd started. So she moved her hips and matched Stanton's growing need. Her hands trembled from the strain, but she held on to that sofa's back and wasn't letting go. It helped her focus her magic and keep it under wraps. It meant she couldn't completely relax and enjoy herself, but she was never under any illusions she would get to enjoy the finish line.

So she focused on Stanton and knowing that she could put a smile on his face. Tears trickled down her cheeks, and she struggled to disguise her gasping sobs as gasping need as best as possible. She couldn't even tell them apart at this stage. It all hurt so much. Everything ached. She wanted him so fucking bad why dear Lord why couldn't she be fucking happy for once in her abyss-damned life?

"Ally, Ally love," Stanton whispered. He pulled her back, and pushed her hair out of her face. "Oh, love. Did I hurt you?"

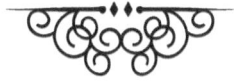

ALLEGRA'S EYES WERE wide and glistening from the tears that swelled in them. Some dropped off her eyelashes as she blinked. They followed a line that showed she'd been crying for a while now. Had he pushed her too hard? Had he hurt her?

"Ally, my love, what is the matter?"

She didn't answer. She just gulped and gagged against her sobs, trying to keep them under wraps. She was shivering now, the warmth of their exertions no longer a shield.

He brushed his lips against her wet cheek. "Who hurt you to make you so afraid?"

She broke into weeping sobs.

"My love."

That made her weep harder and she collapsed against him. "I can't…I'm sorry. I wanted to so bad, but I can't… I'm so sorry."

"You don't need to apologize. Ally, Ally. You should have told me before."

"I can't. Oh Lord, I can't."

"Whatever you need to cry out, do it. I'm here. I will never go anywhere. As long as you want me, I shall be right here, by your side."

"I can't promise…"

"I don't need any promises. I am offering. All you need. Whenever you need."

"It hurts so much," she whispered.

Stanton's heart broke. What had been done to her? Had she been violated or abused in some horrible way? Had she seen a friend hurt? What had happened to this strong, formidable woman to make her cower in the face of affection?

Was it really just the mage thing? Did she honestly believe her life was threatened as much as she always said it was? Had her family been unkind toward her because of it? Her father had taken her to those mines.

He didn't want to even consider the position he'd be placed into if she were an elemental, so he pushed it far from his mind. If she was one, Francois would have surely know and he would not have appointed her to her current position. He didn't believe Francois would turn her in, illegal though it would be, but he couldn't see the Holy Father putting her into such a prominent role. It would stress her out and anyone would slip up in that situation.

Still holding on to her, he picked her up and he struggled to his feet. He placed her down on the cold floor and found her shift. He pulled it gently over her head and let it settle over her body. She slipped her arms inside the garment and he picked up the coat. He helped her into it and then he arranged the pillows on the sofa.

Armed with a blanket, he lay back down first before beckoning her to him. "Come."

She obeyed, and with a small private delight he thought this was probably the first order she'd actually ever obeyed.

"Here, snuggle into me. I'll protect you. You rest now."

She sobbed harder, and he let her. Eventually, her sobs tapered off and, moments later soft breathing replaced her cries. She had cried herself to sleep in his arms.

He shifted his weight, careful not to wake her. He shoved a pillow under his neck and drifted off to sleep, the woman he loved nestled safely in his arms.

CHAPTER TWENTY-NINE

"WHERE THE FUCK is she?" Dodd demanded.

"Keep your voice down." Lex smiled at a group of passing servants entering the elite wing rooms with firewood before leaning back to whisper at Dodd. "Did you check her old cottage?"

Dodd nodded. "First place I looked. And, well, the Captain's bedroom."

"Is he in there?"

Dodd shook his head.

"Shit. She must be with him."

"Wouldn't he tell us?" Dodd asked.

"Would he tell us he went off to fuck the head of the legal arm of the Cathedral? Probably not, Dodd."

"I would," Dodd said. "Nothing to be ashamed of."

Lex sucked in a breath. "Dodd, not everyone wants to display their trysts for the world."

Dodd rolled his eyes. "Did you try the stables?"

"Martin's out there now. And I sent Rahna and Nathan into town to check. Jasmine and Andrews are gone up the mountain path to see if they are there riding again. How could no one see her leave? Did she jump out of the window?"

Nadira came out of the Contessa's suite with a basket of laundry. She noticed them whispering and approached. "Her Ladyship is in the attics."

"The what?"

Nadira pointed upwards. "There is a nook, back behind all of the paintings, that has three chimneys near a window. She finds it quite cozy. She's probably there." She glanced at Lex and said, in a quieter voice, "Especially if she wanted to...discuss something with Captain Rainier in private. The walls frequently have ears here."

"Where is the entrance?"

Nadira pointed to the linen closet and said, "Pull the ceiling string. The hatch stairs will fold down."

Dodd followed, but Lex put out a hand. "Let me."

Dodd gave Lex an odd look, but nodded his consent.

Lex accepted the candle from Nadira and climbed the narrow stairs. They left the stairs folded down, as it provided a little additional light. Dodd left his candle on one of the steps and closed the closet door. Again, everything to keep the Contessa's private life as private as possible.

Lex quietly crept around, whispering Rainier's name. Lex eventually found them, where Nadira said. There was an old couch pressed up near one of the chimneys. The Contessa was wrapped in a dressing gown and covered in a blanket. Likewise, other than Rainier's shirt being unbuttoned at the neck, he was dressed. He was even still in his boots.

Rainier was asleep on the couch, with the Contessa laying across him. Her legs were tucked up under her skirts, while only one of Rainier's legs were on the couch. The other dangled off the side, resting on the floor.

Lex wasn't certain what to do, and hesitated. Maybe leave and come back, shouting out their names? Shake them both awake? Drop something on the floor and hurry away? Which would cause the least amount of embarrassment?

Lex drew in a breath and decided to creep up to Rainier. They shook his shoulder until he stirred. Lex whispered his name until he opened his eyes with a jolt.

"Lex! What...what are you doing here?" Rainier lifted his head and looked down at the still-sleeping Contessa. "Oh. I dozed off. What time is it?"

"The Contessa missed morning tea. We've been searching for two hours."

"I'm sorry," Rainier whispered back. He shook Allegra and she moaned in protest. "Ally, wake up."

Ally?

She groaned again before blinking her eyes open. She squinted against the candle light and said, "Lex? What...oh!" She bolted upright. "I didn't mean to fall asleep."

"Contessa, I'm sorry for waking you, but you were missed at tea."

The Contessa gasped. "The Bishop!"

Lex nodded. "Cram said you were suffering a severe headache last night and that was most likely why you hadn't sent word. You were sleeping it off."

"Thank you," the Contessa said. "I'll go see him immediately. Is he still in his rooms?"

Lex nodded. "The Bishop? Yeah, last I saw he was still in there. He and Cram were...bonding. Do you want me to let the Bishop know?" Lex asked. Then, clarifying, "I mean, that you're just sick or late?"

The Contessa shook her head. "I'll be right there."

"Yeah, I'll leave you be. Sorry to...interrupt."

"THAT WAS AWKWARD," Stanton said.

"I suppose they are all talking about us now."

"I'm sure they were talking about us before."

Allegra smiled. "That is less comforting than I'd hoped."

Stanton put an arm around her and said, "We know what happened, and what didn't. That's all that matters."

"Stanton, I am sorry..."

He pulled her close and said, "None of that. I am not a child. I can wait, even if it's for something that might never come."

"I feel...lighter."

"You were holding back a lot of tears," Stanton said. He pushed a stray hair out of her eyes. "My room is closer. Get yourself tidied up and go meet the Bishop before he murders Cram."

Allegra grinned. "Don't encourage me to go slow."

They looked into each other's eyes and, for a brief moment, Allegra considered kissing him. But instead she smiled, nodded, and walked out of her attic hideaway.

And she really did feel so much lighter.

LEX STOOD IN Rainier's office and lied. They were growing accustomed to it, though the prick of guilt never did completely fade. Still, Lex felt it was the lesser of the evils. The Contessa's protection was Lex's primary duty, so by the Almighty's grace and Lex's hand, she would be protected.

"No new concerns?" Rainier asked stiffly.

"About this morning," Lex began.

Rainier looked up sharply. There were granite bricks softer than his clenched jaw. "This morning is none of your business."

"I hate to disagree, but it is. You see, from how I look at this, the Contessa is my responsibility. And I need to protect her, even from her friends."

Rainier put his quill down and leaned back in his chair. "You think I wish to hurt her?"

"I believe you might not be given much of a choice, sir."

Rainier stretched his arms out. "Enlighten me, Lex. What am I going to do to hurt her?"

Lex knew the Contessa was an elemental. They had little proof, admittedly, but in their heart, Lex *knew*. It would destroy Rainier if he had to arrest her. It would kill Lex, as duty would force them to stand in between the Contessa and Rainier's sword. Lex knew they were good, but Rainier was on an entirely different level. If they came to real blows, Lex would die.

But duty was duty. More than that, though, the Contessa was a good woman. She was trying to change things. Lex could respect that.

"Sir, I worry that…what if one of her enemies accuses her of being an elemental? By law, you'd have to arrest her."

"No one would dare," Rainier said. "Lex, seriously? That's what is bothering you? You're afraid I'm going to drag her out of here? I thought you had a better opinion of me."

"It's not about opinion, sir. It's about your job." Lex licked their lips. "And mine."

Rainier narrowed his eyes. "Are you threatening me?"

Lex shook their head. "The opposite, in fact. If word of last night gets out."

"It won't."

"But if it does, I worry about the consequences."

Rainier sighed. "Lex, you're a good soldier. More than that, I know your heart is in the right place. So let me say this. It seems like there is something between Allegra and myself, but there is not. We are in a delicate situation here, and there is no place for personal indulgences. Last night was a very rare exception. We ate, we talked, and we slept. There is nothing else."

Lex knew Rainier was lying, but they also knew there was something in Rainier's eyes that hurt him. Something clearly happened between them last night, but it wasn't going to happen again, if he was any judge of the disappointment in the Captain's eyes.

"All right, sir. I'm sorry to pry."

Rainier didn't reply. He merely dismissed Lex with a quick nod and went back to his paperwork. Lex stepped outside, closing the door behind them. Dodd was leaning against the opposite wall.

"Well?"

Lex looked back at the door. "He says there's nothing between them and not to worry so much."

"He's right about that last one. Seriously, Lex. You gotta relax." Dodd glanced at the closed door. "We'll keep her safe."

"Thanks," Lex said.

And the two friends walked off in search of gammon pie and pear pudding. Though Lex couldn't get the image of a chained Contessa dragged screaming through the corridors out of their mind.

"Dodd, can I trust you?"

"That's a dumbass question." He eyed Lex. "What's this about?"

"Walk with me to the stables. There are things I need to tell you."

CHAPTER THIRTY

ALLEGRA WAS A vision. She wore a dark vermilion gown, a daring choice for an unmarried noble woman on the wrong side of thirty. Whispers filled the room as Allegra strode confidently into the room. The dress was cut tight across the top of her breasts, with a translucent vermilion organza covering her arms and shoulders. The gauzy fabric was gathered at the neck in a thick, pearl choker.

Her dress was the least voluminous of anyone's in the ballroom, adding to the authority and confidence she exuded. She did not need massive panniers and farthingales to make her important; her title was all she needed.

Her corset was tightened beyond anything he'd ever seen her wear previously. Her shoulders were back, and her chin high. Her dark hair was piled on her head, all tight curls. Pearls hung from her ears. Pearls adorned her fingers, her wrists, and even her dress.

"I'm speechless," Dodd whispered. "The Contessa's pretty and all, don't get me wrong, but wow."

"She has everyone to impress, and has decided to be the most impressive." Lex laughed. "Well played, Contessa."

"All right, let's be on the watch for anything suspicious," Stanton said, still not peeling his eyes away from Allegra. She'd not yet looked in his direction. Instead, she was speaking to Queen Portia.

"Yes, Captain," Lex said. "Everyone's in position. All entrances and exits are guarded. I've deployed six men to patrol the perimeter. That doesn't count the Holy Father's people, and all of the guards for the various dignities. If anyone makes a move, we'll be ready for them. You should dance with her."

Stanton looked down at Lex and scowled. "I should do my job."

Lex let out a long-suffering sigh. "Love is dead. Come on, Dodd. Let's go see if the food is poisoned. I'm starving."

Stanton wore his dress uniform, which was basically the same as his every day uniform, only cleaner and less faded. Tonight, he wore all of his honors. Normally, he wore then sheepishly, but tonight he wore them proudly for hope that his reputation might fend off any dispute. He'd use any tactic at his disposal to keep them all safe.

LEX LEANED AGAINST the long table spread with various kinds of cold meats, pies, and cakes and sighed inwardly. At least, they thought it was an inward sound.

"What are you huffing about now?" Dodd demanded, stuffing half a slice of pound cake into his mouth. "Lord Almighty, they must have used all the sugar left in the abbey in this. This is so good. Want some?"

"Too sweet for me," Lex said, and they pulled out a chunk of meat out of the beef pie to pop in their mouth. "Pie's good. I'm worried, Dodd."

"You're always worried, Lex. The way I see it, the Captain and the Contessa are old enough to make their own mistakes, right? Isn't that what you're always saying about me?"

"I'm always saying you need to learn how to eat. Look at you! You're a mess." Lex brushed cake crumbs off the front of Dodd's dark green jacket. They sighed some more. "It would kill him if he has to arrest her."

"More to the point, it would kill her."

Lex tried to smile, but their heart wasn't in it. "What are we even doing here? A ball after what happened in town. Will people look back on this night and think those stupid people danced the night the world burned?"

"That's it," Dodd said. He took Lex's plate and put it down. He frog-marched Lex toward the corner table. "We're getting some wine into you."

"Contessa, I'm still not convinced these peace talks will get us anywhere, but this is the best ball I've been to in *years*," said Her Serene Highness, Princess Annabella of Markham and sister to the King of Amadore. "You have simply outdone yourself, my dear."

"I'm so pleased to hear you say that, Your Highness," Allegra cooed. She held a crystal champagne glass in her hand, though she'd not drank more than a sip. "I felt that we all could use an opportunity to mingle in a different environment. Also, I believe the peace talks are already getting us somewhere. Look around you, Your Highness." Allegra motioned with her hands. "I see mages talking with viscounts. I see slave owners speaking to freemen. I see obscure Contessas speaking to leaders of prestigious city-states."

The Princess laughed. "Indeed, my dear. I thought His Holiness had slipped into dementia when I received your letter of invitation, but I see that I misjudged you." She fanned herself. "And you are right, of course. As long as people are talking, they feel they are being heard."

Allegra motioned with her glass. "And no one feels more validated than when they are heard."

"My dear Contessa, when all of this nonsense is over, you must come visit me!"

Allegra produced her well-practiced, fake smile. This nonsense, as the princess called it, wasn't likely to be over for some time. This wasn't a spat between siblings.

Could these people not feel the hot breath of war upon their necks? Didn't they see the devastation in Borro when they passed through the village? Were all of the tents and makeshift houses suddenly invisible? Was the world so blind? Had she ever been this blind?

"I hope that opportunity will be soon, Your Highness." Allegra continued to smile. "In the interim, might I ask you for a small favor this evening?"

"Anything, my darling! I'm having too much fun to say otherwise."

Allegra leaned forward and, in a hushed whisper, said, "Might you give Queen Portia a hint that Bonacieux needs to seek early retirement?"

Princess Annabella snapped her fan shut. "That brute of a man had the nerve to interject himself into our tête-à-tête yesterday and demanded to know what I wanted with the Queen. Demanded! Of *me*! What was she thinking to bring that man here? Grand Duchess Katherine and I are already scheming, my dear Contessa. You have no worries on that score."

"Good. He insists on being in every negotiation with the Queen."

"My dear, let me give you a piece of advice. If he attempts to control you at any moment, you must be firm, decisive, and you must act quickly. Men like him never accept a woman's authority and appeasement will not work on him. I do not trust that man."

"Then my own suspicions have some company this evening." Allegra raised her glass to the Princess and said, "Your Highness."

Princess Annabella gave a slight bow of her head. "Your Excellency."

"Contessa, a moment of your time?"

Allegra smiled at Grand Duchess Katherine. "Always for you, dear cousin."

"Come now, our mothers are not here. We can speak plainly." The Duchess looked around. "Accompany me to the dessert table? I have a desire for nothing but sweets tonight."

Allegra motioned with her hand. "Lead the way."

When they were closer to the music and less likely to be overheard, the Duchess said, "I plan to ask Captain Rainier to lead the dancing with you later. I hope you don't object."

"Stanton has been practicing, or so I gather from Lex and Dodd. Rahna, one of the Consorts, has been teaching him."

"Stanton, is it? Not Captain Rainier? Not His Grace?" The Duchess smiled. "Has someone been mixing her business and her pleasure?"

Allegra didn't fall for the bait. She gave her cousin a bored expression and said, "Why isn't the duke here?"

She rolled her eyes. "His lover didn't wish to travel. They both feel these talks will end faster than the travel to get here will take."

"Cynical," Allegra said. She took another sip of champagne.

"I'm impressed by what you've done here, Allegra."

"All I've done is throw a party. Any fool can do that."

"This is not a party," the Duchess chided. "This is peace. Representatives from all of the great powers across Serna are here and for one purpose: to stop fighting. You did this in less than a year. I am very proud of you."

"Save your pride for when I have all of these great powers agree on anything."

"Enjoy your triumph, Allegra. There will be few in the days ahead. Now, if you will excuse me, I believe it's time to begin the dancing."

ALLEGRA STOOD ON the balcony and soaked in the cool evening air. The ballroom had become an oppressive press of bodies and people, and the private terrace was a balm to her frayed nerves. A moment later, Allegra heard footsteps and turned to see Lex approaching.

"Hello, Lieutenant," Allegra said. "Here to check on me?"

"It was more of an excuse to get away from the heat," Lex said. "But I'm fine with pretending it was for your safety and well-being."

Allegra snorted. "May I ask you a question, Lex?"

"Of course."

"What has it been like you for?" At Lex's quizzical expression, Allegra clarified. "Looking differently than you feel."

"Ah." Lex shrugged. "I don't think...I mean, it doesn't bother me the way it did when I was younger. I have a good life now."

"That's made a difference?"

Lex snorted. "Being accepted by people for who am I? Not needing to hide anything? Yeah, that makes life a lot easier to enjoy."

Allegra smiled, though it was a sad, almost bitter expression. "I've never felt that way in my life."

Lex frowned. "Contessa…"

Allegra raised a hand. "It's fine. I received a letter from your mother this morning. She said to keep an eye on you for her."

Lex chuckled. "I feel sorry for her some days. She wanted a frilly daughter so bad. I must have been quite a disappointment to her."

"I don't think that."

"Oh, you mistake my meaning. I don't regret anything, only the parts where my mother can't have it all, too. I wish they had been able to have other children, not just me. It would have made many, many things easier, and not just the very obvious."

"She seems very accepting of you. She's even proud to know you're working with me."

Lex leaned his elbows against the railing. "I'm glad. You know, it was that damned corset that got us talking again. Mom had such a horrible time with all of it. Dad took it better than I thought he would, but Mom…she was devastated. She had always had this plan for my life and it wasn't what I wanted."

"What changed?"

"She came to visit me at the Cathedral. I'd made an off-hand comment at dinner about how chafed I was from my corset and how it dug so badly into my hips. Well! That sent her into a fit. She insisted on bringing her maid in to measure me. So, you have to picture this. I'm in Captain Rainier's office, bring measured by my mother's maid, all the while they are arguing over how much my tits could be tied up before I couldn't breathe anymore. Rainier kept knocking on the door because he needed his office, and my mother kept scolding him."

Allegra chuckled. "But they did it."

"They did it, all right. Now, Mom and I write. She asks me about training or jobs I do, and I tell her what fashions people are wearing and what the latest court gossip is. It's funny because neither of us care about those topics, but we know the other does, so…I don't know. Dodd says this is how most parental relationships are."

"My father took me for a tour of a mage prison and explained how all of the women in it were evil and belonged there."

"Ah. Well, I think I got the better deal out of it."

"Was it all worth it? In the end, I mean."

Lex looked at her like she was a simpleton. "Look at my life. I have a job I love, loads of supportive friends. Really, I have a great life." Lex looked down at himself. "I'm lucky, too, that my body more or less matches what I want it to be like. I wish my courses didn't happen, though."

Allegra smiled. "That probably isn't unique to you."

"Probably not. Why are you asking about this?"

"Living authentically sounds glorious and liberating," Allegra whispered. Her thoughts turned dark and she said, "As opposed to being what they all expect of you. Living a genteel life full of petty nothings all the while screaming on the inside. Is it even possible to live in the open after a lifetime of being someone else?"

"Contessa, what do you mean?"

Allegra shook her head. "It's not important. I'm going to go enjoy a waltz. It's probably going to be my last."

"I'm sure you have many dancing years left in you, Contessa."

"Would you kindly tell Stanton to come up to my room after the dance? Give me fifteen minutes or so."

"Of course," Lex said, confused. "You could tell him yourself."

"I could, but he doesn't listen." Allegra smiled at Lex and said, "It's time I follow your lead, Lex, but first let me have this dance."

STANTON WATCHED ALLEGRA float into the ballroom. He tried not to stare. He failed. She was radiant. She spoke to the orchestra and they ended the music. She picked a glass of wine and spoke to the crowd.

"I am honored to be in this room today with all of you. This is a momentous achievement. Indeed, when I set out on this path, there were more days than not where I was convinced we could never achieve this. And look at us tonight! All of us eating and dancing together."

Stanton watched the reaction of the crowd. She knew how most of them felt about her. They wanted her to fail. They had done everything they could to make her fail. But she hadn't, and now they were all forced into this room with the likes of Walter Cram to save face. It made him smile.

"The coming days will be difficult and fraught with challenges. We will be tempted to second guess, which will only be natural. We will look back on tonight and ask, perhaps, was it all in vain? Did we make mistakes? Were we led astray?"

Stanton paused at this. He didn't understand what she was saying. Why would she imply that?

"But I tell you in all honesty that this was the right path. The founders of our faith gave their lives to fight demons in the other world. Their sacrifice to go through the portal meant we could live in safety on this side. Without their sacrifice, we would not have this moment. So instead of fighting amongst ourselves, let us honor the Guardians and show their courage in the face of our current adversity."

Allegra talked about religion and demons, which Stanton found strange. She'd been talking more about it every day lately, and had asked many questions. She'd also developed interesting views, as opposed to her complete dismissal of all religious things. Had she found a renewal of her faith, or was she merely looking for a new path to get the nobility to justify freeing the mages?

"I promise I will let all of you sleep tomorrow until at least supper," Allegra said, and the crowd laughed. "And I made the servants swear not to kick any of you out until the sun rises. So let us raise our glasses and salute peace."

Stanton smiled and said, "Peace" when the others clinked glasses. He noticed General Bonacieux didn't say it, nor did he vary his posture in the slightest. He was not here for peace that was for sure. If anything, he was here to agitate.

Allegra approached him and smiled. Her eyes were puffy and the whites of her eyes streaked with red. She gave him a weary smile and said, "I came to ask if you'd like to dance a waltz with me before I retire for the evening."

"It's only ten o'clock!" Stanton exclaimed.

"I'm exhausted."

"What about your guests?"

"I plan to spread the word I have a headache and put the Grand Duchess in charge. But, honestly, they probably won't even notice I'm gone."

He bowed to her and took her offered hand. He led her to the dance floor and the swirling crowd made room. She held his hand out the way she'd been taught and had the other on his shoulder. Together, they danced the careful steps as the orchestra played a slower country song.

"It's too bad Dodd and Lex had to work," he said.

"Why?"

"Didn't you know? They are cello players."

That brought a genuine smile to her face. "Indeed?"

"I've heard them play. They do duels sometimes, where they're given a song to play and they compete against each other. Other times, they play accompanying each other. They can even play a couple of pieces on one cello."

"I'm sorry I'll never get to hear that."

"Oh, once all this business settles down, I'll get them to play. Just for you."

She didn't say anything. A tear trickled down her face.

"What is the matter?"

"I'm simply tired."

"Do you wish to stop dancing?"

"No," she said.

Stanton pulled her closer. Not enough to make the old ladies gossip about their impending marriage, but closer than his old dance teacher would have approved.

"I liked your speech."

"Really?"

"It was more religious and reflective than you usually give, but I liked it all the same."

"I'm feeling more religious and reflective these last few months."

"What's changed?"

She was quiet for long enough that Stanton thought he'd have to prod her for an answer. But she finally said, "Everything."

"I'd accuse you of having a crisis of faith, but you've always said you had none."

"Perhaps it is my lack of faith that is having the crisis."

"Is there anything I can do?"

Her voice trembled when she said, "Never leave me."

Stanton stopped dancing. "Allegra…"

Tears trickled down her cheeks. In the candlelit room, he was sure no one would notice unless they were staring. Even still, he picked up dancing once more so that they didn't draw attention. He didn't care now about the gossips and pulled her close, the way newlyweds and young lovers danced together.

"I would never leave you."

She smiled up at him and in a broken voice said, "I believe you mean that."

"Allegra, what is wrong? Tell me. I will help if I can."

"There is nothing the matter. This is honestly the best moment of my life."

It hurt him because, deep down, he knew it was true.

LEX WAITED FOR Rainier to raid the buffet table before approaching him. "Captain, the Contessa asked me to pass along a message. She wishes for you to visit her in her drawing room."

"Did she say why?"

Lex shook his head. "No. She told me this before she danced with you."

"There's something odd going on here, isn't there? It's not me, right?"

"Nothing been the same since that man showed up," Lex said, thrusting his chin in Walter Cram's direction. "I think there's a lot of history there."

"I'm sure there is."

"I heard them fighting, the night I brought him to the abbey. I stayed outside her room, just in case. I heard her tell him if he ever touched her again, she'd scream for help and make sure he was dragged off to the mines."

"Why didn't you tell me?"

"She never had to scream," Lex said. "I didn't want to be gossiping about her personal life." Lex frowned. "That was before I knew...well..."

Stanton snorted. "It's not like that."

"It should be."

Stanton didn't say anything.

"Sir, what she said to me. Something about screaming on the inside. The way she said it. That's a woman living a lie and cracking from the pressure."

Stanton didn't want to admit it, but he knew what Lex said was true. He'd been feeling the same in the pit of his guts, where his sense and instinct lay. But he'd pushed it down as best as he could. He didn't want to believe Allegra was lying and, more importantly, he didn't want to think about what the lie could be.

"I think she might be an..."

"Don't say the word," Stanton ordered. His tone was harsh and unyielding. He glared down at Lex and said, "Don't say anything."

ALLEGRA TORE HER dress, but she didn't have the strength to call for Nadira or another maid. So she wrangled herself out of it, and hoped the seams were repairable. Then again, she'd never wear the dress again, but perhaps it would fetch Nadira a good price in the city next time she went. That assumed, of course, they didn't arrest Nadira, but Allegra hoped Stanton would shield her servants from the authorities as best as possible.

Of course, Stanton was the authorities.

Allegra was now wrapped in a simple wool dress with a linen petticoat and linen shift. She wore her most comfortable corset; hopefully, she wouldn't be paraded naked through the streets of Borro.

Allegra finished writing the note with instructions for her belongings. She placed it on the mantle and wrote CAPTAIN

RAINIER on it. Hopefully, he'd see it before the confiscation of her belongings began.

Stanton knocked on her door. "Allegra? It's me."

Allegra squared her shoulders and brushed her sweaty palms against her dress. "Come in."

She was standing in the middle of her drawing room. The candles were all lit, but her fire had died down to embers.

"Thank you for coming."

"Thank you for asking for me."

He shut the door behind him and approached her. She didn't move, didn't flinch. She barely breathed. Everything was about to change. Her entire life was about to end.

"Lex said it was important."

"It is. Do you remember when I told you about Basina?"

"Yes."

"I didn't tell you all of it. During my tour, all I heard about was how witches were lustful sluts who had sex with demons. They were there because of their base desires. I was twelve years old. I didn't even know what a slut was. I didn't have the context of what they were discussing, other than I knew it was wrong to be a mage. I was wrong."

"Allegra…"

"No, let me finish while I still can. Eventually, I was found out and sent to school. When I was fifteen, an older boy I liked kissed a girl in front of me. It was to tease me. I walked as far as I could away from the school and, in a fit of rage, I caught myself on fire."

Stanton's eyes grew wide.

Allegra held out the palm of her hand and a flicker of flame danced in her palm. "You see, I wasn't just a mage. I was an elemental. I had no idea how to control it. And the emotions of a fifteen-year-old girl were too much for my untrained magic to handle."

"Oh, Allegra." He was staring at her hand.

"An instructor saw and threw me into the pond. I'd burned my hair and my dress, but I was thankfully fine. I lost my eyebrows, too, and was teased for a long time about that. The instructor lied and said I was playing with fire and had caught my dress on fire. I was put into a special class for girls interested in nature, to keep me out of trouble. It was a front, I discovered. All of those girls were elementals, just like me."

Allegra tossed the ball of fire into the fireplace. The dry wood she'd put there earlier sparked to life and the room was filled with the instant flash of light and heat. "Beyond those girls – some of whom are downstairs in the ballroom – there are four people who know about me. Rupert, Walter Cram, Father Michael...and now you. Nadira doesn't even know."

"Why...why are you telling me this?"

"I never believed in demons. I believed the only ones that existed were the ones who imprisoned mages for no other reasons than their own sadistic fears. I know now there are demons, real ones. But..." Allegra pressed her lips together. "I think...I think those demons wouldn't need to come here if we weren't all scratching to get away from the demons our laws have created. And I can't do this anymore. I'm tired, Stanton. I'm so tired."

"Allegra."

Tears trickled down her cheeks. "I have been fighting whoever it is that's been summoning demons into the abbey for months now. Months of my life I've been fighting the very thing I've been saying doesn't exist. I'm tired. Just...make this end for me."

"This will ruin your life."

"I can't do it anymore. I *can't*. So shackle me, drag me out of here. I will not fight you tonight. If you take me, I'll go. But don't be there tomorrow, because I will fight come dawn. I will not arrive at one of those colonies. Dead or alive, no matter the cost, I will not be subjected to that life." She raised her chin. "But I will no longer hide."

"But why now? Why tell me?"

"I can't lie to you anymore."

"Why not?"

"Do I really need to say the words?"

"No. I suppose not."

Stanton stared at her, the shock evident on his face. She had blindsided him. She'd done such a good job hiding and she couldn't do it anymore. It was over. The farce had ended. She was cracking from the pressure.

"Just...just say the truth."

Stanton took one step away from the door. Just one single step. He closed his eyes and said in a gentle voice, "Your secret shall ever be safe with me."

Allegra stared at him in disbelief. "I...I don't understand. Why ever not?"

Stanton took another step and took her face into his hands. He was breathing heavily now, and his voice was rough. "Would you like me to show you why I won't?"

And Allegra, Contessa of Marsina, mage, elemental, Arbiter for the Holy Cathedral let go. She grabbed him by the back of the neck and pulled him towards her. His mouth was hot on her. Her heart pounded in her chest.

Stanton was pulling off his jacket, struggling not to disrupt the kiss. Allegra tugged off her overcoat and it pooled around her and the desk. Several letters and papers fluttered to the floor. She didn't care in the slightest.

She pushed Stanton away just long enough to tug his crisp linen shirt over his head, taking care to run her hands along the rippled muscles of his chest and shoulders. She had thought about this on too many cold nights over the winter, when all she wanted was to feel his nakedness under her.

He tugged at the pins in her bodice until the fabric ripped and pins went flying. He tugged until seams ripped. Allegra managed to yank her arms out of the smock's sleeves. Stanton pulled the dress down over her hips. He was kinder with her petticoat, but only because it had an obvious way to unlace down the front.

He moaned at the sight of her breasts pushed upward in the modest corset she wore. He flipped her around and began unlacing the garment. Allegra placed her hands against the desk and stared at her papers. All of her work. Neatly arranged in piles. It would take her hours to resort everything.

When he pulled her corset down over her hips, not bothering to completely unlace it, Allegra brushed her arm across her desk. Papers, ink pens, and a bottle of wine went flying. She could deal with it all later. She turned back to face him and scooted up the desk.

She was breathing as heavily as he was. Stanton sunk himself in her and she moaned. She pulled herself tighter to him. Eventually, her shift came off and Stanton managed to stop long enough to tug his tall dress boats off, allowing his trousers to fall to the floor.

STANTON WAS GROWING too close to the brink. He gave Allegra one final kiss before withdrawing. His body protested, but he resisted sinking himself into her wet flesh once more. He left a trail of kisses down the length of her body and ignored how one of her hands had the faintest glow. Yes, he loved her, but right now, he wanted her to quiver under the lash of his tongue. Her moans quickened. She grabbed his hair as she moaned, "Yes. More. *More.*"

He obliged.

And he slipped his hand over her glowing hand.

ALLEGRA FELT THE heat rise in her hand, and in other places, and it was difficult to release in one place while holding back elsewhere. But Stanton wrapped his fingers around hers and pulled her hands up over her head, pinning them to the desk. He didn't care that they would have been warm to the touch. He climbed up her once more and only pulled one hand away long enough to guide himself in.

They hadn't spoken, for which she was glad. She simply wanted to feel him inside her. To push aside everything for one moment and...

She gripped his fingers when she cried out. A handful more thrusts and Stanton grunted before collapsing on her, panting.

"That was...unexpected," Allegra said sheepishly.

Stanton laughed. "I'm as surprised as you are. You don't regret it, do you?"

"No," she whispered. "I'll get my clothes on. You have a job to do."

"What do you mean?"

"You can't let me continue. I know that. So thank you for letting my last day of freedom be with you."

Tears trickled down her face, but she smiled through them. She would let him arrest her and, once handed off, she would burn herself alive. That would be a better fate than what was in store for her.

He stopped her. "I gave you my word. I will not turn you in."

She touched his cheek. "You gave the Cathedral your word when you took your oath."

"And I gave you my oath just now. In my eyes, that is worth more than any ceremony to men. Allegra, I am in love with you. Tell me you know that."

"I know." She closed her eyes.

"Then, believe me when I say nothing will change." He smirked. "Except hoping to sneak into your bedchamber on occasion."

She laughed. She had endured months of loneliness next to this man she had fallen in love with, and she could have told him all along. He would have understood.

She cracked open her study door. The drawing room was empty of servants and footmen, thankfully. They were all still downstairs dealing with the ball. She grabbed Stanton by the arm and tugged him to follow.

"Let me grab my clothes first," he said, stumbling after her.

"You don't need them," she said and led him to her bedchamber. Where, as it happened, he didn't need his clothes after all.

CHAPTER THIRTY-ONE

LEX PACED THE corridor of the Contessa's rooms under the guise of providing security and discretion for a secret meeting taking place. Lex fiddled with the sword that dangled at their hip. It slid easily from its sheath.

Lex gulped, but raised their chin and continue the pace of impatience. If Rainier brought her out against her will, Lex would defend her. That was their job. They were assigned to that very task: the personal defense of Her Excellency, Allegra, Contessa of Marsina. To allow her to be dragged from her own residence in irons…

Lex gulped again. Captain Rainier was more than just a man. He was a hero. *Lex's* hero. They did not want to fight him, but Lex also knew they would pull out that sword and stand in his path if the Contessa was arrested.

There was the rub of it all: Lex would defend the Contessa to their dying breath because they'd given an oath. Somewhere along the way, that oath became cemented in friendship. Lex admired the Contessa's strength in the midst of this entire shitstorm of impossibilities.

And they felt a little responsible if the Contessa confessed her secret to Rainier. Her words last night to Lex cut so deep.

I'm going to go enjoy a waltz. It's probably going to be my last.

Lex should have done something right there and then. They should have grabbed the Contessa by her petticoats and dragged her off to a closet, locking her there until she came to her damned senses! What was she thinking! She was the most powerful woman in all of Serna right now, even more powerful than Queen Portia. She would do more harm than good by coming out and...

Lex drew in a deep, steadying breath.

"Damn it all to the abyss."

"It dawned on ya, huh?"

Lex whipped their head around to see Dodd leaning against the opened door. He was still in his uniform, sword also at his side. His bottom two buttons were undone, the way Dodd's jacket always ended up when he was expecting a fight.

"What do you mean?"

Dodd stepped inside, closing the double doors behind him. He didn't move closer. He held on to the door handles. "Us asking her not to tell Rainier she's an elemental is like when your mother..."

Lex drew in a deep breath and looked away. "Dammit, Dodd. You're not helping. He's going to arrest her. She's going to be killed, you know it." Lex gritted their teeth. "All I had to deal with was disappointing my mother! She is...she is trying to lead us away from a damned war. We need her."

"I know, Lex."

"And I can't...I can't let him. I can't let her. I made a promise."

"I know, Lex. That's why I'm here."

An overwhelming feeling of...Lex didn't know what the word was for it, other than it was overwhelming. Lex wanted to slap, punch, kiss, hug...

Instead, Lex smiled and said, "Thank you."

Dodd made a face. "Aw, you'd just get yourself hurt if I wasn't here."

"I hope..." Lex frowned and looked back at the door to the Contessa's private apartment. "I hope she didn't tell him."

"Yeah. Me, too."

ALLEGRA OPENED HER eyes and experienced a moment of disorientation of wondering who was in bed next to her. Her heart pounded when she looked over at Stanton's naked form, partially obscured by the heavy quilts she favored. He was so handsome. The portrait in the Cathedral's hall of heroes did not do him justice. It didn't capture the gold undertones of his skin, nor did it capture the way his deliciously full lips seemed to always be in a state of a half-formed smirk, even now when he was fast asleep.

It had been wonderful. He'd been a gentle and kind lover. She was glad for the memories that would hold her for what was about to come.

Carefully, Allegra slipped out of bed and began the business of dressing herself. Some of her underclothing had made it to the bedchamber, and she struggled into the special riding corset for which Lex's mother had so graciously provided the instructions. Allegra laced up the sides over her shift, her hands shaking the entire time.

She pulled the wool petticoat over her head, likewise lacing up the neck and tugging the shoulder straps into place. Tears trickled down her cheeks, but she continued her work. She would get the tears out of the way now so that he wouldn't see them when he was forced to betray her.

Allegra understood the rules. His words last night were sweet and loving, and she believed Stanton meant every single one of them. But it is easy to confess one's love and devotion by candlelight, and it is much more difficult to live with those consequences by the sun's glaring dawn light.

She leaned on the memories of his love and his touch, and pushed aside the anger and blame that wanted to well up. She wanted to hate him for what he was about to do when he opened his eyes. She would not allow herself to do so. He would turn his back on her, but she would not.

"Why are you up?" Stanton murmured from the bed.

Allegra gulped audibly, pushing down the lump in her throat. When she was certain there would be no quiver in her voice, she spun around. A flickering smile twitched on her lips, but she likewise forced them into submission. She gave him a bright smile that she knew didn't touch her eyes. "I'm getting dressed."

"You don't need to work this morning. Come back to bed," Stanton urged.

Allegra lifted her chin and stood so tall her old dance and decorum teacher would have been proud. "I felt it would be easier for you if I prepared myself."

Stanton frowned for a moment before realization crossed his face. Pain flickered in those beautiful eyes. "You think I'm going to arrest you. After what happened?"

"I understand that..." Allegra's voice quavered and she closed her eyes to gain control over her composure. When she was certain she was in command of her emotions, she continued. "You have a duty to the laws of the land. I respect that, and I know you will do that duty, even if it means arresting the woman you profess to love."

"Profess? Profess? Is that what you think happened? You think I lied to trick my way into your bed? Is that what you think of me?"

The salt of her tears stung her cracked and bruised lips. "What do you want me to say?"

"That you love me. That this wasn't a game." Stanton pulled the blankets to cover his lower body and stood up. "I want you to trust me."

"I don't understand," Allegra said between small sobs. "You've made it so clear. Elementals are dangerous. They need to be shackled. It's your duty —"

Stanton took three long strides to stand in front of her. One hand firmly held his quilt in place and the other touched her face. "Protecting you is my duty. Handing you over to vultures is not protection."

"I love you, Stanton." The words hitched in her throat. "It has been a long time since I've loved anyone, but I love...love...I love you."

He let go of the quilt and wrapped her in his strong embrace. Allegra drew in deep breaths, trying to control the sobs that sat on the surface of her feelings. "You are simply too exhausted to see what is plain in front of you. I believe a restorative is in order."

"I don't need drugs," Allegra said angrily. "I simply wish to not feel this oppression weighing me down. I want to feel normal."

"Allow me to take some of your burden. You can trust me with it."

Allegra didn't hear anything he said through her sobs of relief.

STANTON STARED DOWN at the note he'd left upon his pillow.

My dearest love,

Lex and Dodd are pacing in the corridor so I must face my own music. I shall call upon you as soon as duty allows.

Nadira wishes me to tell you that several individuals drank far too much of Father Michael's good brandy last night and have all canceled their appointments with you today. You should have seen her grin when she discovered me half-dressed in your chambers.

Until tonight,

S

He'd written three versions of the note before he settled upon this one. He was never one for love letters, not even when he was young. The language of courtship never came easily to him, and now years and experience had tempered the youthful vigor that could throw out good sense for bad poetry.

He looked down on her sleeping form. She was naked again, wrapped in the heavy quilts. He stoked the fire for her; the servants had been barred from the room by the locked doors. How confused Nadira was when he'd stepped out of her bedchamber. Then, that smug smirk on her face after she'd passed along the schedule change and walked away.

He could trust Nadira to keep the secret of their affair. Though, if what Lex said was true, most of the abbey had been expecting this months ago. Well, he was anything if predictable.

Stanton tugged his jacket one last time and opened the double doors that led into the corridor where he knew Lex and Dodd were waiting for him. When he stepped out, he did not expect the swords at their hips, nor the grim expressions on their faces.

They already knew. Of course they did. They'd tried to warn him, Lex especially. He had been too stubborn to listen. He didn't want to face the possibility of having to choose. Of course, once faced with it, it turned out not to be a difficult choice at all.

It was more than him just loving her. Serna *needed* her.

"Good morning," Stanton said in a matter-of-fact tone. "I wasn't expecting either of you here so early."

"How is the Contessa?" There was an edge in Lex's voice that Stanton rarely heard focused at anyone.

"Asleep." At their visible relief, he walked passed them. He did stop at the doors to say, "It was your duty to keep her secret safe. As it is mine. And Dodd? Do your buttons back up. Someone will think you were here to fight me."

He threw open the doors and walked back to his own bedchamber. There might have been a lightness in his step, but there was no one awake yet to notice.

CHAPTER THIRTY-TWO

AND SO IT was the next two weeks. A blur of meetings and compromises that merely stalled the coming war, and nights spent in Stanton's arms. Allegra knew she was smiling more these days; even Father Michael had commented on it.

"My dear child, how your face lights up these days. Are you sleeping well again?"

She'd smile and say something about how the ball had given her hope for the coming months. It was a lie. She knew it. He knew. But it was comfortable. Reports coming from all over were unbearably grim. The rebellions, once isolated pockets of resistance, were across all of Serna. There was no stopping the momentum now. All she could do was mitigate the harshness around the edges. Even with her great reach, she could not stop all of the waves from crashing against the rock.

She wasn't even sure anymore if she wanted to stop the rebellions. She was sleeping again, mostly due to Stanton tugging her away from her papers and coaxing her into bed. And while she didn't always go straight to sleep, she did eventually sleep. With sleep came clarity. All this time, Allegra had been trying to stop the war. There was no stopping what was coming. In fact, her every move had accelerated conflict.

Stanton wouldn't let her judge herself too harshly. He even accepted the demon marks in stride and offered discreet assistance to Walter. Walter, for his part, asked Allegra in private if she'd hit

Stanton over the head; he couldn't see any other way that someone like Captain Rainier would ever lend assistance to him.

It was all so good and so perfect, so when Lex and Walter came crashing into her office that early morning, she should have known it had all been *too* perfect.

The last time Allegra had been in the richly-appointed Garden Suites, the wall before her had been covered with a bright yellow paper, giving the room an open, inviting air of youthfulness. Now, that paper was blackened and burnt as a portal stretched across the same wall. A massive, grotesque hand reached out from the abyss beyond. This was nothing like the small bat-like creatures Allegra had been fighting with Walter. There was no way any of them could stop this beast if it came through to this side.

"Tell me what is happening this instant!" Queen Portia shrieked. She was still wrapped in her dressing gown and her hair was tied in a tail at the base of her neck.

"Your Majesty," Allegra said, her voice hushed as the beast's growl shook the floor. "Please tell me the truth. Are you a mage?"

"Don't be—"

Walter slapped Portia across the face. He pointed at the dark tendril that resembled a grasping finger. "Don't lie to me!"

"Walter!"

"Dude, man, that's the queen!" Lex said.

Tears trickled down Portia's face, past the red imprint of Walter's hand. "I didn't do this. You have to believe me."

"I believe you," Allegra said and gave Walter a hard glare.

"Please, I'm begging you. Don't tell anyone I'm an elemental. They'll kill me," Portia whispered. "They *will* kill me."

"They will," Walter mumbled. "Shit."

Allegra turned to face the portal and stretched out her hand. She channeled the magic, just as Walter had taught her and how she'd be practicing against all of those tiny little bastards over the past few months. She pushed it at the demon and it reacted violently. It thrashed and bellowed.

"Guys? Um, can't you do this a bit quieter?" Lex asked. For someone who'd just been exposed to the existence of demons, he was holding up pretty well in Allegra's opinion.

"The Arbiter is an elemental, too?" Portia said through her sobs.

Allegra sighed. "Yes, so now we both have secrets to keep. Now listen and do as Walter says and we'll all get out of here in one piece."

Walter ignored Lex. He physically moved the queen. "Stand here. What kind of magic do you have?"

"Water," Portia said. "I can't make it just appear, though."

"Lex, hand me that basin of wash water. All right, Your Majesty? I'm going to give you a crash course on how to do this, okay? I need you to stop crying because Allegra has about ten minutes in her before she passes out. Okay?"

Sweat dripped off Allegra's forehead, stinging her eyes. More sweat pooled at the small of her back, making her skin itch underneath the oppressive layers of fabric. She ignored all of it and focused all of her magic at the growing portal. Walter had taught her to tap into the underlying will of magic, and not just the obvious fire. He'd said it was the *will* that she could use more than just fire. Unfortunately, she wasn't nearly as practiced as Walter and she thought his ten minute estimate was overly generous.

Allegra tried again whispering the words Walter had always said: b*ack to the abyss with thee, foul reflection of mine sins.* They did little to assist her magic. She had not believed the tales, not even when she was a child. So she had little belief to pull from now. The stakes were so high, though, that she kept saying them over and over. If she still didn't believe in the stories, at least she believed in demons now.

"You are not welcome here!" Allegra shouted at the beast and pushed harder. Fire streamed from her outstretched hand and directly at the creature's digit. It screamed, a distant, echoing sound. Wind howled out of the portal, tugging Allegra's hair from its fashionably neat bun.

Somewhere in the haze of concentration, Lex had left and returned with seven more mages in tow. Some Allegra recognized as servants or valets. Some she didn't recognize. Walter gave them a stern nod and they all turned their will against the beast and the howls shook the floor once more.

Allegra's concentration flagged. She collapsed down to one knee as Queen Portia stood next to her and stretched out two very frail hands toward the ever-growing portal.

"Help her!" Both of Walter's hands were focusing energy at the portal.

Lex put a supportive arm around Allegra. Her eyes were heavy and she was afraid she'd vomit if she opened her mouth to speak.

Another backlash of energy shook the room.

"Dammit, Cram!" Lex said. "The entire abbey is going to hear what's going on!"

"I can't make the demon be quiet!" Walter shouted back. He glanced down at Allegra and said, "Allegra! Let go. We got it."

The heat dissipated from Allegra's hand. She collapsed to the cold floor, the smooth wood a welcome relief against her flushed skin.

A supportive hand squeezed her shoulder. Allegra blinked the daze from her eyes and saw Lex's grim expression looking down at her. He smiled briefly at her; a strained expression. Then Lex stood and moved further away from the group and drew his sword.

Walter and the other mages focused on the portal, each saying their own words of magic and power. Walter continued to repeat the incantation from the Holy Writ. The others did a mixture of Walter's incantation or their other phrases. Queen Portia merely wept, pausing only to swear whenever she lost control of the spell and had to begin again.

The demon roared in defiance as Walter pushed against an edge of the portal. The portal began to shrink on that side, pushing the demon's arm back against the horn-like appendage that jutted from its snout. One of the others cried out and a gust of wind blew the demon's arm into his horn, impaling him.

The demon roared again, only this time in rage and pain. Allegra staggered to her knees, but fell over. She was still too weak.

"Allegra! Stay down!" Walter shouted.

She obeyed.

THE OUTER DOOR flung open and heavy steps pounded across the drawing room. Lex raised their sword into a defensive position and waited for whatever or whoever was about to storm into the room. Lex had wanted to get more help to protect the mages in case whatever that thing was came through, but Lex also didn't want to leave them here alone. There were enough people in the abbey who'd foolishly kill all of those mages without a second thought. They'd already had to leave them alone once to get a chambermaid to grab a few servants Cram said to fetch. Who, as it happens, all turned out to be elementals.

Lex heard a thump and glanced over their shoulder. Another mage had collapsed unconscious to the floor. Lex gulped and gripped their sword tighter.

The inner door swung open and General Bonacieux stormed into the room. "Where is the…" The General gasped when he saw the demon portal. "What…what is this?"

Lex held their ground. "General, you must leave now. For your own safety."

"Lex!" Cram snarled. "Get him out of here!"

"Is that…a demon? Are they summoning a demon?" the General shouted. "Why are you summoning a demon in the Queen's bedchamber?"

Bonacieux went for his sword, but Lex pointed their own sword at him. "We are attempting to contain the situation. Leave us to our work."

"This is what you called contained? The Arbiter is on the floor almost unconscious. There is some kind of…creature being summoned in the midst of this holy building and…" he stopped. "Your Majesty?"

Queen Portia turned to face Bonacieux, tears trickling down her face. In a very weak, exhausted voice, she said, "I'm so sorry."

"You are one of *them*?"

Portia nodded grimly, but didn't pull her hand away from the pit. Tendrils of water rippled around her hand, and a small spray pushed against one edge of the portal, hissing and spitting whenever fire splashed upon it. The demon screamed when a cloud of steam hit its left flank.

"Why didn't you tell me?"

"I was too afraid."

"You should have told me," Bonacieux said in a small, defeated voice. "You should have told me, child."

Portia wept. "I'm sorry, sir. I couldn't tell you."

The General nodded sadly. "Indeed, I understand."

Lex lowered their blade, but kept a firm grip all the same. Lex did not trust Bonacieux. "General, we need to let them work or the abbey will be overrun with demons."

Portia fell to her knees, the spray of water finally exhausted. She scooped up another palm of water from her basin and tried again, but the water harmlessly seeped through her fingers.

"What is happening?"

Lex blew out a breath. "I don't understand all of the technicalities, but someone has been placing spells throughout the abbey in an attempt to draw out demons. The Contessa had given Mr. Cram here permission to destroy the spells. However, they had no idea their actions were in fact drawing the attention of larger, stronger demons. We believe this one has come through by following the...destruction. Queen Portia, being an elemental, caused the final rift."

The General grunted. "So the Queen caused this?"

"It was an accident," Lex said. "In fact, it might have been a trap. Whoever was originally casting these portals open and summoning the demons is to blame."

"I see," the General said. He looked down at the Queen and said, "This changes everything."

Lex stared at him. The general was not behaving the way Lex had expected. The General hated mages – all mages – and the penalty for being an elemental in his land was death. They didn't even ship them off to the mines anymore; they were immediately killed. The Contessa had been negotiating to end the death penalty, and the General had been the loudest objector.

The General stepped over to where Queen Portia knelt and rested a hand on her shoulder.

Lex tensed and said, "Step away from the Queen."

The General ignored Lex and said, "Your Majesty, I will do my duty."

"Thank you, General," the Queen said in a relieved voice.

And then Bonacieux plunged a long, steel needle through the back of her neck and clear out through the other side. Then, he kicked the center of the queen's back and pushed her through the portal.

Lex shouted and attacked the General, but he was prepared. He dodged three lunges before pulling out his own blade and blocking Lex's fourth attack. Bonacieux used his strength and size to his advantage and kicked Lex in the shins. Lex stumbled, but kept their feet.

Lex clipped Bonacieux's bicep and he shouted out in pain. Lex managed another strike and slashed a long, but shallow, line across Bonacieux's thigh. But Lex paid for it by opening their flank up to the General's thrust. The sword cut through Lex's side, a stinging sensation that burned as the pain registered.

"Lex!" Cram screamed. "Shit!"

The demon grabbed one of the mages with his talon and dragged him into the portal. Walter shouted incantations from scripture and pushed against the demon, never quite turning all of his attention away from Lex, however.

"I shall tell the world how you killed Queen Portia," the General shouted, kicking Allegra in the guts.

"Get away from her." Lex dragged themselves over to Allegra, even as blood oozed from their side. The healing buttons and special embroidery in Lex's jacket helped slow the bleeding. Still, they'd need a bandage and some herbs, and a proper physician to look at it and soon. But, for now, the last of the healing stones did their work.

Allegra held up her hand and a weak blast of flame shot from her hand. It was anemic though, and the General stepped aside from the attack.

"Save your strength, foul creature. You will need it before I'm done with you."

Then the General limped out of the room, a trail of blood dripping behind him. None of the mages could risk pulling their attention from the demon portal, and Lex and Allegra were too hurt to help. So Lex watched him go, hatred filling inside them. He'd killed Queen Portia.

DODD HAD BEEN sitting in his dugout for most of the morning. He examined the countryside with his spyglass. He was well-positioned here, with the treeline to his back and crouched as he was in the large hole caused by a fallen tree. He was wearing mostly brown and black clothing, but he gathered about him broken tree branches to help conceal him further. He operated under the sensible plan that if he had a spyglass, the enemy probably did, too.

All of the Consorts, and most of the Cathedral guards took turns up on the cliff side in case of an attack. Borro Abbey was situated in such a way that an attack would be difficult, not to mention foolish. The abbey was perched on a cliff, partially carved from living rock. The only proper road was a switchback that snaked its way up the fertile fields that worked their way up the small mountain. Then, finally, his perch.

However, it was the abbey itself that caught Dodd's eye and he focused his spyglass there. The windows for the royal suites blackened nearly an hour before. In the last ten minutes, servants and guests alike rushed from the abbey. Most were carrying luggage. Bags tossed into carriages. Horses hitched and galloping away as fast as they could.

He eyed the windows along the corridor. Were those flames in the windows? His question was answered by a burning form exploding through one of the windows and falling to their death below on the brick courtyard.

Dodd's heart pounded in agonized realization when he saw men in Cartossian uniforms torching the cottages. They were under attack. It was Bonacieux's men doing this!

Dodd carefully eased himself out of the pit and crawled along the tree line. It was a longer route to get back to the abbey this way, but he'd be less likely to get caught.

An arrow embedded itself in a tree ten feet in front of him. Dodd dove for cover and smacked his elbow against a stump. His arm went immediately and painfully numb. He pushed past the pain and scrambled to his feet. Another arrow struck, further away this time. There was no point being cautious now.

The church bells chimed. Dodd crashed through the trees, blowing his whistle. He hoped that one of the lower posts would hear the call and help the abbey. Right now, Dodd had to stay ahead of the arrows that were pinging off the trees too close to him.

Why would Bonacieux attack the abbey? And, why would he attack it with just the handful of soldiers directly nearby? Why didn't he call for help from his people in town? This made no sense.

Dodd held on to a wooden railing for dear life as he skidded down the main trail's steps and out of the archers' line of sight. Eventually, the barrage stopped; the archers had turned their attention elsewhere.

Dodd dropped to the ground and risked looking through his spyglass. Rahna, Kingsley, and Martin were in the courtyard fighting the soldiers. He could see guards—local militia, Cathedral guards, personal guards, Consorts—protecting the leaders and important guests as they escaped outside through the various servant entrances.

The windows of the royal suites' corridor blew out in one massive explosion. A roar, like Dodd had never heard before, broke the air. He stared helplessly as a giant talon punched its way through part of the abbey's wall.

Dodd's jaw dropped as he stared dumbfounded at the...*demon?* Was he really seeing a demon?

"That son of a bitch is huge," Dodd whispered. "God Almighty, is this real?"

He saw several bodies hurl themselves out of what he knew was Queen Portia's window. All but one bounced off the staggered awnings that were designed to help protect against rock slides. The one poor chap did bounce off the awning, all right. And impaled himself on the demon's claw.

Hysterical sobs interrupted him and Dodd jumped to his feet. He dropped the spyglass in the grass and brandished his sword. He whirled and was met with the terrified faces of twenty children.

"What the fuck are you doing up here?" Dodd demanded.

There seemed to be three women in charge. The eldest was about his age, give or take a few years, and wore a stern, matronly gown. While her dress neckline only covered to her collarbone, the stiff linen wrap criss-crossed her chest to hide any skin. She glared at him through her narrow, hooded eyes. "Kindly watch your tone around the children, sir."

Dodd didn't have time for the niceties of society. "There's trouble. Get these children out of here!"

The children varied in age from being carried to almost old enough to begin school or an apprenticeship. Several gasped and whimpered, while others excitedly talked about swords.

"Children!" the head mistresses said, clapping her hands together. The hubbub died down. She turned to Dodd and said, "Where do you suggest we go? General Bonacieux has lost his mind. He's caught fire to the abbey and is attacking any guard who is trying to stop him. He's killed several mages already! The Arbiter is nowhere to be found, we can't find the children's parents, and the abbey is going up in flames!"

Dodd glanced behind him, back at the burning abbey. He could clearly smell the smoke now. Soon, he'd be back in sight and a target again unless he was careful. Dragging along a group of kids was going to make it even harder.

"I am Miss Shu Tay. I'm Lady Devereux's governess. We grabbed all of the children from the nursery on the second floor and climbed down the vines." She motioned at the two women with her. "These are Sisters Linda and Jasmine. They only just arrived at the Cathedral. They came to help."

Dodd considered the situation. He couldn't put out a fire by himself. Nor could he protect twenty-odd children from a band of trained soldiers all by himself. If Rainier was here, he'd say for Dodd to get the children out. Rainier would never want a group of children caught in the crossfire of anything.

"Okay, let's take the horse trail. It goes around the bend of the abbey. With luck, we'll come out the other side and can make our way down and not meet any trouble. Then we can figure something out from there."

Miss Tay's eyes widened. "Would they harm children?"

Dodd picked up his spyglass. "General Bonacieux has done much worse."

"MOVE!" STANTON SHOUTED as he pushed terrified guests out through the abbey's front door. "Get out of here before the roof comes down! Move! I don't care if you're naked! Move!"

He caught sight of Rahna helping a half-naked Father Michael across the foyer, expertly dodging the flames. One side of her face was a mask of blood. One of Bonacieux's men attacked them, and Stanton rushed him.

"Rahna! Go!" he shouted, parrying a blow from a sword.

The man was no match for Stanton and fell. Stanton had no time to look about him, for part of the ceiling collapsed. He staggered back; the foyer was divided lengthwise by a wall of flame. If they didn't get out in the next few minutes, they were never leaving this place.

"Beatrix! Tell everyone to regroup at Orsini!"

Dammit, where was Allegra? He'd seen Nadira and Serafina escape, but neither had seen Allegra. Dodd was missing, too. As was Queen Portia and Cram.

Stanton sheathed his sword and grimly began a zigzagging path out of the inferno.

"Captain!"

Stanton rushed to Lex, who dragged himself down the railing, carefully avoiding the flickering flames. His legs gave out before Stanton could reach him and he tumbled down burning stairs, his roll helping to extinguish the flames on his uniform as quickly as they were igniting.

Stanton thanked the Almighty that Lex was a tiny fellow and draped him over one shoulder. Then Stanton rushed with the last of the servants and Consorts out of the burning building as a chandelier crashed to the stairwell.

"Bonacieux killed Queen Portia," Lex said. He spat out a mouthful of blood. Most of it dripped down the front of Stanton's jacket. "Fucker stabbed me in the guts. Contessa said not to wait for her. She's going to try to make it to Orsini."

Stanton coughed and gagged on the black smoke. He rushed out of the abbey and ducked as several stones exploded. Projectile masonry scattered the courtyard. "She made it out?"

"Cram said they'd all jump out the windows and hope they hit the awning right. I came to get you, but the building was already on fire by the time I hit the stairwell."

"They can't jump from that distance and expect to live," Stanton said. "Where's Bonacieux? All I've seen is his men."

Lex weakly shook his head. "No idea, Captain. Have you seen Dodd?"

"No, sorry. He was supposed to be up in the hills, though. He might have already gotten out."

Lex made no reply.

"All right, Lex. Let's get you to the carriages. Let's get out of here before Bonacieux starts killing fleeing people."

ALLEGRA'S THIGHS BURNED almost as much as her smoked-filled lungs did. She was covered in bruises and she was sure she'd sprained both her ankles in the fall. Babies wailed and children whimpered, but they didn't stop until they were far enough into the trees that they couldn't be spotted from the main walking trails that crisscrossed around the abbey.

When they finally stopped, Dodd pulled out his leather-wrapped spyglass and surveyed the area. He nodded, satisfied. "I can't see a thing from here with all this smoke. Chances are, they can't see us."

"Wearing that dress isn't going to help, though," Walter complained.

Allegra frowned down at her dress. Peach quilted satin with a vibrant rose print. "I would have worn something more appropriate if I'd known I'd be running through the trees." She gasped and panted for air, her lungs burning from the exercise and choking clouds of smoke. She stretched out her fingers, which ached from grasping the edges of her gown while they ran. Her ankles were killing her and she was sure one of them was already swelling. "There's still the three tiny demons out there we didn't get, plus that large bastard is still going to get through. How long can they live in our world?"

Walter shrugged. "I don't know."

"Contessa, we need to get you out of here," Dodd said firmly. "Let Cram deal with it."

Allegra looked back at the burning corpse of the abbey. Soon, there would be mounts looking for survivors in the hills, and she suspected many of them would be Bonacieux's men. They had to put as much distance between them as possible.

But she glanced at the scared priests and children with her. If she didn't stop the demons, she would be condemning these people to death. The demons would circle back. She was certain. They were predators. If what Walter said was even slightly accurate, they didn't belong to this realm and existence. They would attack and murder without conscience.

"If we lose you, we lose all chance at peace," Dodd urged.

"He's right," Walter said. "We need to get you to Orsini. Tell Francois what happened with Bonacieux. We all saw him murder Queen Portia. We can get military help from everyone once they know what happened."

"I'm an elemental!" Allegra said in a hushed tone, so that the children couldn't hear. "When Bonacieux tells everyone..."

"Me and Lex will say Bonacieux is lying!" Walter shouted. He glanced at the frightened children and said, much calmer, "We'll lie for you. He killed the Queen. No one will give a shit what he says once word gets out."

"But...we need to stop those demons first," Allegra blurted out. The words felt right once they were said, however, and she more firmly said, "I have to help stop them."

"I'll help," Walter said. He wasn't panting nearly as hard as she was, but then his life these days was *on the run*.

Dodd glanced at the women and children. He lowered his voice. "We're dragging all these kids with us. We'll never make it."

One of the priests stepped forward. "We will part ways with you here. The General's soldiers will not attack religious women and their charges. No offense, Your Excellency, but I suspect having mages with us will not be a protection in the wake of..."

Allegra held up a hand to stop the priest. "I'm not offended in the least. I agree, in fact. Having Walter with us also makes it more dangerous."

"Thanks, Your Excellency. Most appreciated," Walter said deadpan.

Allegra flashed him what she hoped was a sardonic grin, but feared was laced with too much worry and exhaustion. "I can't believe he killed the Queen."

"He'd mad," Dodd said. "He must be mad."

Allegra shook her head. "No, he just thinks he's right."

Walter blew out a breath. "Lord, that's even worse."

Dodd nodded, seemingly coming to a decision. "All right, Your Ladyship. My orders were to protect you. I've not been given new orders, so I'll do as you say. You want to chase demons, well, I'll chase them with you."

Allegra smiled at him, and then looked over at the priest. "Take the children along this trail right to just under the tree line. Keep going until you hit the boulder field. Trust me, you'll know it when you come to it. Head down the mountain once you reach it. Eventually, you'll come across a wide trail. That's where the abbey's wood is hauled in." She glanced at the smoldering clouds above. "Well, where it used to get the wood. If you take that trail, you'll either meet up with other merchants, or you'll eventually land yourself in Jennings. You'll be able to get help there."

Allegra looked at the children. Some weren't in long-sleeved dresses. "Help me out of my skirts. You can use it as a blanket."

"What will you wear?" one of the women asked.

"I'll be moving a lot faster than the children. I can't be wearing this."

With the help of the two women, Allegra got out of her satin skirt. She also pulled off her hip panniers and handed them over. "Pillows for the wee ones." Then she pulled her heavy underskirt and petticoat back on, tying both tightly around her waist. She smoothed out her ornate and decorative jacket.

Dodd glanced over her. "It looks like you stole half an outfit."

Allegra forced a smile. "It'll be easier to run in this. Walter?"

"Two of the demons went that way." Walter pointed.

"That's pretty much where Bonacieux's men are," Dodd said.

"I think we should circle back, meet up with some people I know, and then go after that straggler. I say let the army look after the other two," Walter said.

"Is there a way for non-elementals to kill a demon?" At Walter's shrug, she said, "So, what? We're going to let the demons tear them apart?"

"Yes."

Allegra noticed Dodd's annoyed expression, but decided not to argue the point. "Let's discuss about the ethics of that later. For now, let's find some help."

"First, let me deal with the beast inside the abbey," Walter said. "Dodd? I'm going to need you to hold me up when I fall."

"Why are you planning to fall?" Dodd asked.

"Because I have to try to crush that portal without bringing the entire mountain down, and I'm exhausted. I expect I'm going to collapse."

As Walter prepared himself for another taxing spell, Dodd glanced at Allegra and said, "I hope Lex made it out."

Allegra looked down at the black curtain of smoke where her home burned. "I hope a lot of people did."

STANTON KNEW HE'D waited past what would be considered the last possible moment. He'd seen Martin shoving several princes and viscounts into a stage coach when it was clear the abbey was lost. Lex, Martin, and a few of the Consorts escaped and were no doubt headed to Orsini.

No sign of Dodd or Cram. Neither of many of the servants, the militia, or many of the children. He hoped Dodd had seen what was coming and removed anyone staying in the northwest cottages out of harm's way. Perhaps Dodd would also be on his way to Orsini.

Stanton looked at the smoldering abbey in the distance. The earth shook all the way to where he stood. Stanton closed his eyes.

He knew where Allegra was, and his heart sank with that realization. Cram always did seem the type to go down in a blaze of glory. Damn, he hoped Cram hadn't taken Allegra down into the pit with him.

"She might have made it out, Captain," Rahna said. Even she couldn't hid the grim undertones of her words.

He didn't answer. He didn't turn his gaze away as the black smoke painted the sky. He'd held out as best as he could, while the Consorts and the servants got as many of the innocents out of harm's way as possible. They still had a long fight ahead of them. Even if they were able to retreat unmolested, war was declared upon the Cathedral itself. The rule of warfare and of law itself was broken by this action.

Stanton took a deep breath. So this was how the outbreak of war felt. It was as soul crushing as he'd imagined it would be.

He looked down from his horse at Rahna and ignored the tears that welled up in her eyes. "Have the Consorts spread the soldiers and militia out. Some with each coach. We also need soldiers around the flanks. Tell everyone we're going to try for Orsini. If we can get ahead of the General's soldiers tonight, we should be able to make it. Then we can consult the Holy Father."

"Yes, Captain."

Stanton looked at the burning abbey. Later, he'd have time to mourn. Not until all of these people were safe.

"Let's move, people," Stanton ordered to those who'd gathered near him.

He prayed that Allegra and the others made it out somehow.

THE END…FOR NOW

Allegra, Stanton, and all of the Consorts will be back in
The Nightmares We Know.

Did you enjoy this book? Please consider leaving a short review
to help other readers know if they might enjoy this book, too.

Want to know when the next book comes out? Sign up for my
new release email at **kristadball.com/new-release-sign-up/**

ABOUT THE AUTHOR

KRISTA D. BALL WAS born and raised in Deer Lake, Newfoundland, where she learned how to use a chainsaw, chop wood,and make raspberry jam. After obtaining a B.A. in British History from Mount Allison University, Krista moved to Edmonton, AB where she currently lives.

Somehow, she's picked up an engineer, two kids, six cats, and two very understanding corgis off ebay. Her credit card has been since taken away.

Like any good writer, Krista has had an eclectic array of jobs throughout her life, including strawberry picker, pub bathroom cleaner, oil spill cleaner upper and soupkitchen coordinator. These days, when Krista isn't software testing, she writes in her messy office.

ALSO BY KRISTA D. BALL

The Dark Abyss of Our Sins Series
The Demons We See
The Nightmare We Know
The Sins We Seek (*forthcoming*)

Spirit Caller Series
Spirits Rising
Dark Whispers
Knight Shift
Mystery Night
Dead Living
Blood Family

Collaborator
Traitor
Fugitive
Rebel

Ladies Occult Society
A Magical Inheritance
A Ghostly Reqest
In the Society of Women (*forthcoming*)

Tales of Tranquility Series
Blaze
Grief
Interlude (short story collection)
Fury
Schemes
Liberate
Ambush

Nonfiction
What Kings Ate and Wizards Drank
Hustlers, Harlots, and Heroes
Appropriately Aggressive

As Dinah Lewis
First Impressions
Love in the Spotlight